PRIMAL Unleashed

JACK SILKSTONE

PRIMAL Unleashed previously published by Amazon Publishing.

Published by Jack Silkstone

www.primalunleashed.com

ISBN-13: 978-1533168450
ISBN-10: 1533168458

PRIMAL Books are dedicated to those who have fought for a just cause.

PROLOGUE

SOUTHERN AFGHANISTAN, 1989

The first mortar bombs dropped from the night sky directly inside the Russian platoon's defensive perimeter. The whistle of incoming projectiles sent men scurrying for cover, their survival instincts sharpened by three long years fighting the mujahideen. Captain Alexis Krijenko was sprinting for the nearest weapons pit when the barrage exploded, slamming him into the ground.

He shook his head to clear the shock. Strong hands grabbed his equipment harness, dragging him to the safety of a crudely constructed foxhole. A second barrage exploded, showering Krijenko with dirt as shrapnel sliced through the air inches above his skull. Crouching in the bottom of the pit, he faced Dostiger, the man who'd saved him. The Ukrainian laughed, his scarred and pitted face split into a psychotic grin.

"About time the Mooj found us, Captain!" Dostiger bellowed as more explosions filled the air with smoke and debris. "I thought they'd never come." The Spetsnaz platoon had waited all day but their adversaries were patient, holding off their attack until the sun had set behind the jagged mountaintops.

Krijenko's tired eyes met the manic stare of the Ukrainian. "They'll be on us within the hour, you crazy bastard."

"The Mooj want whatever's in that godforsaken hole, Captain," Dostiger yelled, gesturing toward the shaft carved into the heart of the mountain.

"No, comrade, they want our heads," he countered.

Dostiger's eyes grew even wider and his ugly grin more sadistic. "Fuck them! Let the filthy Muslims try. I'll send them to meet their prophet." He patted his Dragunov sniper rifle; the notches on its scarred wooden stock were too numerous to count and Krijenko knew that before long many more would join them.

***

Twelve hours earlier the Russian Spetsnaz platoon had been relocated from their usual hunting grounds in Helmand Province. They'd been driven east to Kandahar Airfield, a staging base for the withdrawal from Afghanistan. After ten years of brutal conflict, a ragtag army of mujahideen had defeated the mighty Russian war machine. Finally the men of the bloodied 40th Army could return home.

The sun sat low in the sky as Krijenko's men waited in the shell of a battle-scarred building, watching their comrades depart in a continuous stream of massive Antonov transport aircraft. They looked on blankly as the long lines of soldiers edged toward the departure point. Meanwhile Dostiger dozed, slumped against his equipment.

Eyes bloodshot and skin gray from exhaustion, Krijenko managed a haggard smile as a line of regular troops ran forward eagerly, waved on board by a young, fresh-faced officer armed with a clipboard.

Finally it was their turn. Krijenko surged forward with his men. They almost reached the line when the clipboard-wielding officer stopped them.

He couldn't believe it. It was their turn to depart, but his war-weary Spetsnaz platoon was being waved to another holding area. His soldiers stared angrily as another group took their place. No warning, no explanation; the young officer simply handed him a set of orders and waved his clipboard toward a pair of waiting Mi-17 transport helicopters. They wouldn't be going home.

Demoralized they hauled their equipment across to the helicopters and began stowing their heavy-weapons and boxes of ammunition. They were interrupted by a helmet-clad loadmaster.

"Personal weapons only," he yelled into Krijenko's ear over the increasing scream of the helicopter's twin turbines. "High-altitude flight, comrade. Leave anything you can. If we're too heavy, then…" He gestured with his gloved hand, chopping at his neck.

Krijenko scowled as his men discarded their heavy weapons, piling the grenade launchers, machine guns, and mortars on the tarmac. These weapons had given the Spetsnaz a distinct advantage over the mujahideen.

Once the platoon was on board, the two helicopters took off, circling Kandahar before heading north. Krijenko noted the absence of the attack helicopter escort that usually accompanied all air movement in Afghanistan. An ominous sign that this was no regular mission. Krijenko kept his concerns to himself as they gained altitude. His men were veterans and he had earned their trust. They would follow him on any mission, no matter how bone-tired and no matter what the odds. He watched them, one by one, dip their heads as the thud of the rotors and vibration of the aircraft lulled them to sleep. Battle-hardened, they had long ago learned to rest whenever the opportunity arose.

Dostiger peered with anticipation through the plastic bubble window, the sun-faded dome morphing the barren rocky ridges and green valleys below into an alien environment. For three years this mountainous terrain had been his home; a harsh and unforgiving place that had claimed the lives of thousands of invaders. It was a land of warriors: Mongol, Persian, British, and now Russian blood had soaked this soil. For the Ukrainian it had become a hunting ground. At last count he had sent one hundred and seventy mujahideen to meet their maker, and now whatever god was watching over him had given him the opportunity to make it an even two hundred.

Dostiger smiled sadistically as he looked back at the platoon dozing in the belly of the helicopter. They wanted to go home, but not him. Something in the depths of his soul told him that this was where he was supposed to be. In these rugged mountains he would find his destiny.

A change in the pitch of the rotors woke the rest of the

platoon. The scream of the turbines rose, the helicopter approaching ceiling height.

The loadmaster held up two fingers to indicate two minutes out. All signs of sleep gone, the men checked weapons, tightened equipment, and prepared for potential combat. Their eyes were alert, bodies tensed and ready.

Krijenko's steely gaze locked onto the window. The rocky crags looked close enough to touch but nothing seemed familiar about this area. His men would not have the advantage of knowing the ground. Nor would they have the reassurance of heavy weapons and air support. He looked back and met Dostiger's stare. The mad Ukrainian smiled.

The helicopter shuddered as it clawed its way upward to a flat clearing on the side of a barren mountain. With a final lurch it cleared the razor edge and descended onto a roughly constructed landing zone. The clamshell rear doors swung open as it hit the ground and the loadmaster frantically waved them clear. The men fanned out, weapons ready, eyes scanning for any possible threat. They found cover behind boulders and in folds of the earth, encircling the aircraft as its rotors idled.

Krijenko stepped off onto the windswept mountain, crouched, and rapidly assessed the terrain. The landing zone was large, easily accommodating the two helicopters. It was dominated on three sides by jagged ridgelines and rocky outcrops, while at the lower end a rudimentary road snaked away to the south. Parallel to the road, large boulders and deep gullies would allow any enemy a protected approach. Krijenko spat into the dust as he stared at the terrain; experience told him he lacked the manpower to defend this ground.

He gave a nod to let his team leaders know they had positioned their men well, before his eyes were drawn to an open pair of giant blast doors set into the mountainside. The entrance leered at him like a gaping mouth. Around the doors a small team of army engineers was rigging explosive charges. They were preparing to seal the tunnel.

An officer walked around the idling aircraft to Krijenko. Everything about the man screamed military intelligence, from his swagger to the long leather jacket that flapped in the wind, snapping against his black boots. Krijenko rose and stood to meet him face-to-face.

"Captain," the intelligence major said curtly. "Captain, you will hold this position until the engineers are ready to seal the shaft."

A question formed on Krijenko's lips, but the superior officer cut him short.

"No questions. The mission is simple. Keep the Muslim rabble away until our men seal the shaft." He gestured to the engineers, still busy at work. "This facility must not fall into the hands of the mujahideen. God help you if you fail."

Without waiting for a reply the man turned on his heel and joined a line of civilians as they scurried out the tunnel into the waiting helicopters. Krijenko noted the fear etched on their pasty white faces. These were noncombatants, men who were supposed to be kept far from the reaches of the enemy.

As the scientists hurried into the rear of the helicopters, the intelligence officer paused in a side door and looked back over his shoulder at the Spetsnaz platoon. Krijenko thought he saw the slightest trace of pity, then the hatch slammed shut and he was gone.

The doors on both helicopters closed and Krijenko turned back to where the engineers were busy moving explosives into the shaft. Brown wooden boxes were stacked ten high. Enough explosives to bring down a mountain.

The scream of turbines snapped his attention back to the helicopters beating their blades as they lifted off. Stones, flung like shrapnel, pelted the soldiers as the rotor wash tore across the landing zone. The thumping cadence of the choppers faded into the wide expanse of the Afghan sky. The mountain fell silent. Krijenko, his platoon, and a team of army engineers were alone.

***

The Soviet High Command had not expected the

mujahideen to advance so quickly. Driven by a ruthless commander, they had surged south with a determined focus, moving heavy weapons on the backs of mules and horses. Familiar with the terrain, their scouts located Krijenko's platoon without being spotted. Mortars and heavy machine guns had been carried up the steep ridgelines in silence, crews siting the weapons with deadly efficiency. As the sun fell below the horizon and darkness set in, they attacked.

The Spetsnaz soldiers defended their positions desperately throughout the night. Mortar and rocket fire was unrelenting, the flashing explosions cutting down five of Krijenko's best men. Stripped of weapons and ammunition, their bodies lay face down to the rear of the fighting positions, blood soaking into the hard earth. Three furious assaults from separate sides had been repulsed and as dawn approached, the platoon was exhausted and low on ammunition.

Krijenko shrugged off the sense of futility as he crouched in a hastily dug weapons pit scraped from the rocky ground by bare hands and bayonets. His two remaining team leaders and the commander of the engineer detachment were huddled next to him. Their tired eyes nervously scanned the perimeter, vigilant for the next enemy attack.

The young engineer faced Krijenko and spoke rapidly. "Comrade, my men have prepared all the explosives and we're ready to seal the shaft."

Dostiger, the Ukrainian team leader, leaned in toward him, his rank breath revolting the engineer. "What the hell is in there?" He gestured toward the shaft, barely visible in the early-morning twilight.

"I don't know. They didn't tell us," the engineer stammered. "My, my orders were simple; bury it so it can't be found." The young man refused to look at Dostiger's pockmarked face; the ugly Ukrainian terrified him. "It's something they don't want the Mooj to have. I don't know."

Dostiger stared at the open shaft and his brow furrowed. "We should check it out, Captain. It could be worth something."

Krijenko shook his head. "My orders are to seal it, Dostiger, and seal it I will." He looked back at the engineer. "Go. Do it!"

The young man hurried back to the opening where his two remaining sappers were laying the final lengths of slow-burn fuse. He was eager to finish the job before the sun rose over the horizon and exposed his men to the mujahideen positioned along the dominant ridgelines. Already the sky was glowing with the approaching dawn.

As the engineers lit the fuse, mortar rounds pounded the landing zone in a fearsome barrage. The lethal bombs slayed another four Spetsnaz soldiers, their bodies shredded by the shrapnel that lashed their fighting positions.

As the engineers sprinted from the shaft across the open ground of the landing zone, a DSHK heavy machine gun opened up from one of the surrounding ridgelines. 12.7mm high-velocity rounds riddled their bodies, hydrostatic shock destroying flesh and shattering bones, ripping the men to pieces. They were dead before they hit the ground.

The Afghan skirmishers advanced, flitting from cover to cover as their fire-support positions suppressed the Spetsnaz platoon. Krijenko, manning a dead soldier's machine gun, worked feverishly to hold off the mujahideen, but one by one his men fell silent as they succumbed to the relentless onslaught. He watched a grenade detonate in Dostiger's position. The mad Ukrainian was thrown clear, one leg torn and bloodied.

The barrel of the machine gun glowed red as Krijenko pumped the trigger, sending short bursts lancing into the advancing fighters. The last belt of ammunition disappeared in a final burst and the gun fell silent, the bolt slamming forward on an empty chamber. Krijenko reached into his chest harness and drew a pistol, leveling it at the Afghan warrior running at him. His first round entered the man's head below the cheek and blew out the back of his skull. There was no second bullet.

Krijenko never saw the fighter who shot him in the neck. The projectile ripped through the spine, killing him instantly. The pistol fell from his hand and he collapsed. As the first drops of the Russian officer's blood soaked into the ground, the earth erupted, throwing his body into the air. The explosives detonated along fault lines, causing thousands of tons of rock to collapse into the shaft. A blast wave of dust and rubble blew out from the mountainside, sweeping the forward line of mujahideen fighters from their feet. The engineers had done their job well.

As the dust settled on the bloodied bodies of the slain Spetsnaz, the Afghan warriors regrouped; their heavy-weapons teams filtering down from the high ground to join the assaulting force. They moved out of the shadows and began searching the Russian defensive positions, stripping the corpses of valuables. A tall figure strode through the scavengers, his white robes unmarked by the dust and smoke of the battlefield.

The man's dark eyes stared intently at the wall of rock that denied him his goal. Frustration momentarily passed over his hard features and he turned away, distracted by the moans of a bloodied and broken body that lay at his feet. One of the Afghan fighters drew a wicked-looking blade and raised it back in a sweeping arc, ready to dispatch the casualty.

"Wait," the white-robed leader demanded. He knelt down next to the wounded man, his Russian halting but clear. "What was hidden here?"

Dostiger smiled and chuckled. "You and I, we will never know." The Ukrainian was delirious from loss of blood and the morphine injection he'd stabbed into his thigh.

The Afghan grunted stiffly and leaned closer. "You will die here, Russian."

Dostiger's grin widened and blood dribbled from his lips, staining his fatigues. He laughed manically. "We all die, comrade. How many of your fighters will I join in hell?"

The mujahideen commander stared at Dostiger's face before he rose and turned to the fighter next to him. "Find a stretcher. The fearless one comes with us."

CHAPTER 1

WESTERN HIGHLANDS, SIERRA LEONE, 2000

A white UN Land Rover and a battered Bedford truck slowly wound their way along a narrow dirt road in the western highlands of Sierra Leone. The vehicles pushed on through the overgrown vines and saplings, the African jungle's attempts to reclaim the track. The earthy smell of rotting leaves filled the air and sprawling trees blocked the sunlight, spawning growths of moss and fungi.

An Australian officer, Lieutenant Aden Bishop, rode in the front of the Land Rover next to the driver, a young Sierra Leone soldier. Behind him, Colonel Kapur reclined in the backseat. Although the Indian UN officer was technically in command, he was content to let Bishop take charge. Their mission was to inspect the Kilimi refugee camp, a routine undertaking that the colonel would not normally participate in. He had only volunteered for the short-notice tasking to impress the UN military commander. Usually he preferred to remain in Sierra Leone's capital, Freetown, relaxing in the air-conditioning of the UN headquarters.

Trailing the four-wheel drive, the Bedford truck transported ten Indian UN soldiers perched on its hard wooden benches. Well-armed and enthusiastic, the peacekeepers had excellent discipline, which made up for their limited training. Clad in their heavy khaki uniforms and light-blue berets, they silently endured the stifling heat of the canvas-topped truck, the ancient suspension amplifying every bump.

The diesel engines of the convoy bellowed as the drivers pushed them hard, climbing the slippery track toward Kilimi. Native birds were startled from the trees and larger animals crashed through the heavy undergrowth to escape the noisy intruders. Every few miles the two vehicles passed small villages unmarked on the map.

Bishop squinted as the morning sun streamed through gaps in the thick jungle canopy, raising the humidity to oppressive levels. He removed his UN beret to wipe his brow, and checked the map. The young Australian officer struggled to navigate in the dense jungle; the huge trees that punched up through the shadowy undergrowth filled the sky with a wall of greenery, blocking out the view and making it impossible to identify any useful landmarks.

As they drove past yet another isolated village, Bishop's driver pointed out a cluster of ramshackle huts. "Sir, my grandfather was born there." Chickens scratched in the mud around one of the rusted corrugated-iron walls. Looking across at the lieutenant the driver smiled. "I know this area well, sir. I won't get you lost."

"I'm not worried about that, Erasto," Bishop said as he looked up from the map. "I'm more worried about how far the militias are from the camp." His brow furrowed as his thoughts turned to another refugee camp at Songo. A rogue RUF militia had attacked it only two weeks earlier and a UN patrol had watched helplessly as the refugees were hacked to pieces. The peacekeepers' orders forbade them to fire except in self-defence.

After the incident Bishop had been sent to Songo to provide a detailed report. Over a hundred refugees had been maimed or slaughtered; the smell of the rotting corpses was still fresh in his mind.

The young driver continued, "Well, usually many RUF in this area but now most have gone."

"Most?"

"Yes, sir. Some are still here but not many. Most have gone back to their villages. Only some criminals remain, but they will be afraid of us."

Bishop was skeptical. He knew the drug-fueled militias were not easily deterred. To make matters worse the team was babysitting a ranking UN officer, a tempting target for kidnapping.

Colonel Kapur leaned forward to tap Bishop on the shoulder. "You can tell the young private not to worry; a section of Indian infantry is more than enough to deal with a handful of criminals."

Bishop clenched his jaw and kept his eyes fixed on the road ahead. The sheer arrogance of the colonel disgusted him; the man wouldn't directly address the private who was their full-time driver. It was below his status to talk to an enlisted soldier, and a native one at that.

Kapur continued, "This is your first real mission, is it not, Lieutenant?"

"Yes, sir, that's correct," Bishop responded curtly.

"Well, I've served with the UN a number of times. I have also led missions against the rebels in Kashmir. Considering your inexperience you are lucky that I chose to accompany this mission."

"Very lucky, sir."

The colonel took it as a compliment, sat back, and began studying his own map.

What a cock, thought Bishop. This man clearly has more experience drinking coffee than commanding soldiers. The overweight colonel even had the audacity to wear his dress uniform in the field. The buttons on the sweat-stained shirt strained against his protruding belly. With all his ribbons and braid he looked more like a bandmaster than a soldier.

Despite the presence of the pompous colonel, Bishop was enjoying his first deployment. He appreciated the multinational aspects of working with the UN, and as a junior officer he was gaining valuable experience operating in a high-threat environment.

The dangers that lurked in the surrounding terrain weren't obvious as the convoy made their way through the thick green vegetation of Kilimi National Park. As they passed through villages, young men and women spilled out of their huts, happily waving at the passing soldiers. It was only their handless limbs and scarred bodies that hinted at the inhumane crimes that had occurred here and the threat still posed by the roaming militias.

The UN has failed these people, reflected Bishop.

A young boy grinned at him, waving vigorously as the Land Rover crawled past. Leaning against a crude crutch, the boy's right leg was missing from the knee down. The soldier in Bishop wanted to hunt down and tear out the throats of the animals who had perpetrated the act, but the UN rules of engagement forbade him. In the back of his mind he doubted his ability to follow this directive. What kind of man could stand by and watch these RUF bastards hack the limbs from children, he rationalized.

Bishop checked his map again. They had almost reached the refugee camp and had encountered no sign of recent militia activity. Was it possible the RUF fighters were actually abiding by the guidelines laid down in the cease-fire? Bishop remained wary. Many of the RUF were no more than criminals and a refugee camp was easy pickings for heavily armed thugs.

The road narrowed even further. They inched forward over a simple log bridge and continued up into the highlands. Thick red clay caked the tires, and the drivers struggled to keep from sliding off the crude path and down the steep embankment into the green abyss below.

Bishop looked up as the Land Rover slowed. Spotting something ahead, the driver dropped down a gear. In the distance two armed men were standing in front of a battered white pickup parked across the track. A third was manning a heavy machine gun mounted on the truck.

"Looks like trouble, sir." The young driver sounded worried.

"It's OK, Erasto. It's probably just some of the local militia," Bishop reassured the nervous youth. "Pull over and we'll sort this out." The UN officer was only a few years older than his driver, but his confidence and training gave him a leadership presence that belied his age.

They slowed to a halt. Bishop opened the Land Rover's battered door and stepped down. His boots sank into the mud. A cloud of mosquitoes swarmed up from septic puddles of water. He swatted them casually, the mud and insects barely registering. His mind focused on the potential threat posed by the armed men.

The sound of squelching boots behind him drew his attention and he turned to face the Indian section commander.

"Doesn't look good, sir," said Corporal Mirza Mansoor.

"I hear you, Mirza," Bishop replied quietly, his hand instinctively moving to the holster on his hip.

"A very dangerous position, sir," Mirza said, matter-of-factly. The Indian's hard Asiatic features displayed no emotion.

"Yeah, we're wedged in pretty tight. If they arc up with that machine gun, we're cactus," Bishop muttered. Beads of perspiration ran down his face.

"Do you think they are RUF?"

"Maybe, maybe not. Could be locals."

"Well, sir, whoever they are, they don't look friendly."

"They're certainly not a reception party, that's for sure," Bishop agreed.

"What do you want us to do?"

From the backseat of the Land Rover, Colonel Kapur interrupted, speaking through the open window. "Corporal, the RUF wouldn't dare come into the exclusion zone during the cease-fire. These men here must be locals and there are only three of them. We will simply approach and discuss our access to the Kilimi camp."

Bishop glanced down at the senior officer and nodded. "The colonel is probably right."

Mirza raised an eyebrow.

Bishop continued. "Odds are they're just trying to make a few dollars by charging the refugees passage. We should be able to bribe our way through the checkpoint."

Mirza pointed up the road at the vehicle. "Do you want me to take some of the men up there and find out what they want?"

Kapur made to speak but Bishop interrupted him. "No, the colonel and I will go talk to them."

"OK, sir, we will be ready."

"Good. Tell your men to stay with the vehicles but be prepared to follow us up. The last thing we want to do is provoke a bunch of trigger-happy militia." He pointed out their current location on the map. "If they won't let us through, the camp is only on the other side of this crest. We can always double back and approach along one of these tracks with a recon party." Bishop had worked with Mirza for barely a month but already he trusted the Indian corporal. Everything about the smaller man inspired confidence, from his well-pressed uniform and immaculately cleaned rifle to his steady, almost icy demeanor. Even the thin mustache was fitting in an old-school way; he was a born soldier and Bishop had no doubt the blood of India's fiercest warriors ran strong in his veins.

"Understood, sir." Mirza gave a nod and headed back to his men. The other nine soldiers had already dismounted and were dispersed in the dense foliage either side of the track.

Bishop opened the rear door of the Land Rover and Kapur reluctantly pried his rotund body from the seat. A twitch appeared at the corner of the senior officer's eye as he stepped into the mud. "It might be better for me to stay with the vehicle," he said. "We don't want to appear overly intimidating to these men."

No chance of that, thought Bishop, you look like the Indian version of Elton John. "Should be OK, sir. They'll probably respect an officer of your rank."

"Yes, good point, lieutenant," Kapur replied unconvincingly, adjusting the beret perched on his bald, perspiring head.

They walked steadily uphill toward the checkpoint, two figures in stark contrast. The corpulent colonel in dress uniform waddled behind Bishop's athletic frame clad in distinctive Australian combat fatigues.

As they drew closer, Bishop saw the gunmen were only teenagers. They all wore grubby, torn jeans, and sported the usual talismans and charms to ward off bullets. He smiled grimly as he noticed one of them wearing a bright-red life jacket over his bare torso; some of the Africans had strange ideas regarding protective equipment.

The tallest of the boys was leaning against the hood of the vehicle, a cigarette hanging limply from his mouth. He waited until the approaching UN officers were only a few steps away, then jerked upright, hefted a G3 assault rifle, and gestured to his comrades. The shorter boy, who was casually cradling an AK-47, stepped forward and slowly raised his hand. The third swiveled the heavy machine gun toward them from the back of the rusted pickup.

Bishop stopped only a few paces away. He was close enough to notice their eyes were glazed, and slid his hand to the grip of the Browning 9mm nestled against his hip. It was the norm for UN officers to carry only handguns, but faced with three heavily armed gunmen, Bishop wished he'd insisted on being issued a rifle. He carefully positioned himself a few paces back from the Colonel, slightly out of the immediate firing line, aware that drugs and alcohol could result in unpredictable behavior.

A sideways glance at the battered Toyota pickup caused Bishop's stomach to lurch. Jammed onto the spike of a snapped side mirror was a severed human head. Flies crawled into the open eyes and a black bloated tongue protruded between decaying lips. The putrid smell assaulted the young lieutenant's senses and he struggled to keep his composure, the taste of bile filling his mouth.

All three gunmen stared intently at the gold braid decorating Colonel Kapur's uniform, like children intrigued by the costume of a clown. The tall youth with the cigarette stepped forward confidently, pointing at Kapur.

"You some kinda big boss man?" He reeked of alcohol and unwashed sweat. "My name is General Terminator!" The young African stabbed a thumb into his bare chest, then swept his arms wide. "An dis here area is under control of dah West Side Boys!"

The hairs on Bishop's neck rose. He realized the checkpoint could only mean one thing; the rest of the gang was already in the refugee camp. It was going to be the Songo massacre all over again.

The youths were members of one of the most feared RUF groups in Sierra Leone, a gang that raped pregnant women and sliced open their bellies to gamble on the sex of the unborn child.

Kapur froze, unable to respond, much to the amusement of the West Side Boys. "Who is da big boss now, man? Run back to your mama before the Terminator kill you all!" the gunman screamed. He was completely unintimidated, his ego fueled by the UN officer's fear and a cocktail of alcohol and drugs.

Bishop stepped closer to the colonel. "We just need to get to the camp," he stated, keeping his fists clenched to stop his hands from shaking.

The leader of the trio spat at him. "Fuck off, you white Yankee fuck. You not going anywhere."

Before Bishop could respond, Kapur grasped his arm, pulling him away. "We need to go now, lieutenant."

Bishop lowered his voice, "Sir, I am going to offer them a bribe. It might change their minds."

"No, Lieutenant Bishop. You will–"

Sharp, rapid cracks of gunfire in the distance cut him off and his eyes grew wide. More bursts of automatic fire were accompanied by screams and shouts.

The West Side Boys started whooping, jumping up and down, and punching their weapons in the direction of the refugee camp. They laughed, making crude gestures at the colonel. "Don't be afraid, big boss. We will save some of da young girls for you."

Rage and shame boiled up in Bishop as he imagined the RUF gang storming through the camp, raping women and mutilating men. Images of the aftermath of the Songo massacre flashed through his mind.

Stepping behind the petrified colonel to block the boys' view, he disengaged his pistol holster's thumb-brake. Grabbing Kapur roughly by the front of his shirt, he pulled him close enough to smell the rancid stench of the man's sweat.

"I'll shoot you myself if you try to stop me. Now give me the cash," Bishop snarled. The colonel looked stunned. Hand shaking, he pulled a thick yellow envelope from his pocket and passed it to the Australian.

Bishop caught the eye of Mirza, who was cautiously walking up the muddy track. He gave the Indian a sly hand signal and turned to face the crazed gunmen. They were laughing with each other, excited at the prospect of joining the action.

Bishop's confidence drained away as he assessed the situation. Deep in his gut he knew it was too risky to try to negotiate with 'General Terminator'; the mix of drugs and alcohol in the youth's bloodstream would make him irrational and impulsive. Clammy with sweat, he wiped his right hand on his pants. His chest tightened, constricting his breathing.

Swallowing nervously, he forced himself to address the young gunman. "Please, General Terminator, what is happening? Who is firing?" Bishop meekly moved closer, his left hand waving the wad of US currency to draw his attention. "Can we pay you to get through to the camp?"

"I told you to fuck off, Yankee. Take your fucking money and go home before I cut off your hands as well!" Terminator cackled like a jackal, turning back to grin at his two comrades. "Short sleeves or long sleeves?" He laughed at the joke, enjoying the attention of being the big man.

Bishop realized in a panic that he'd misjudged the situation. Armed with only a pistol he was faced off against three RUF fighters with automatic weapons.

Terminator's expression abruptly became serious and he swung his rifle toward Bishop. Cocking it, his voice took on a savage tone. "Go home, Yankee pig, or General Terminator will blow your head off and fuck you right up!"

Bishop tensed as the G3 pointed directly at him. In his mind he could see the bullet leaving the barrel and burying itself in his stomach. The youth looked back toward his companions, and Bishop snapped. He leaped forward, pushing the barrel of the rifle away from his body, and in one smooth action drew his pistol from its holster. The Browning barked twice in quick succession, the 9mm rounds smashing into Terminator's sternum, ripping through his heart, blowing its remains out through the back of his rib cage. The teenager toppled back into the mud, a look of shock on his face. A choking sound came from his throat as his shattered lungs filled with blood.

Bishop had never shot anyone before, but the severity of the act didn't have time to register. Without thinking he adopted a two-handed grip and adjusted his aim to target the second youth who was bringing his rifle up. The fore sight and rear sight aligned on the gunman's head. Bishop fired rapidly. Two rounds went wide but the third penetrated the teen's skull, spraying his brain across the side of the battered Toyota pickup, streaks of blood and gray matter blending with the rust.

The blast of Mirza's AK-47 snapped Bishop out of his instinctive shooting as the third gunman was blown over the tailgate of the Toyota, his red life jacket shredded by the bullets. The Indian moved forward deliberately, his AK-47 tight against his shoulder, alert to the possibility of additional fighters.

"Are they all dead, sir?" Mirza asked as he pushed past the pickup to scan the jungle ahead.

"Yeah, you did well, corporal," Bishop replied, trying to sound confident. "There were only three of them."

He holstered his pistol and knelt next to the corpse of Terminator, hands shaking as he checked the G3 rifle and stripped ammunition from the body. Bishop avoided looking at the lifeless face. This kid should be in school, he thought. What the fuck was he doing out here? What was he doing with a gang of animals like the West Side Boys? Did I have to shoot him? He shook his head and buried the thoughts; now was not the time for questions. He was now committed to saving the refugees even if it meant more killing.

Bishop was aware he was blatantly breaching his rules of engagement. The UN mandate hammered through this brain, again and again, the inhumane futility of it. In the distance a woman screamed. A long, shrill scream. Fuck this! he thought and hurried back to the UN vehicles with Terminator's rifle and ammunition.

CHAPTER 2

KILIMI REFUGEE CAMP

Colonel Kapur stood in shock as Bishop sorted his equipment on the hood of the Land Rover. Checking his map, he identified a concealed route into the refugee camp and stuffed the document into his thigh pocket. He swiftly stripped the battered G3 assault rifle he'd taken from Terminator's corpse, checking its serviceability. As he methodically inspected the components, Mirza and two of the other soldiers approached.

Bishop scrutinized the rifle as he spoke, "You know what I have to do."

"Yes, sir," Mirza murmured, glancing over at the colonel, then back to Bishop.

"I can't ask you to come."

"Three of us will go with you. The others will stay here and look after the colonel and the driver."

"Be ready to move in two minutes."

Bishop reassembled the rifle, satisfied that it would work reliably. He slammed home a magazine and cocked it, placing the other four magazines into the pockets of his shirt and pants. This is the first and last time I go outside the wire without body armor and a rifle, he told himself. Hastily, he tied a short length of cord around the stock of the weapon, allowing it to hang from his shoulder. Finally, he changed the magazine in his pistol and reholstered it. Ready for action, he glanced at the colonel and tossed the thick wad of bribe money to him.

"Stay here, sir. If we don't come back within the hour, leave for Freetown."

Kapur nodded, horrified at the calm demeanor of the young man who had just slain two teenage gunmen. It was clear what Aden was going to do next.

Bishop gathered Mirza and the two other soldiers in front of the Bedford truck. "OK, men, we don't have much time." Gunshots still echoed intermittently from the direction of the camp, and ominously, the screaming had stopped. "We're going to the camp and we'll do whatever we must to protect the refugees. Do you understand?"

"Yes, sir," they replied in unison.

Bishop looked the group over and continued. "I appreciate you all backing me up." When this was over, Bishop knew that Colonel Kapur would most likely punish them.

"Sir, we wouldn't let you go on your own."

Bishop gave Mirza a nod, then pulled out his map. "Alright, we're going to move down this track through the jungle, avoiding the main road. Stay with me, I'll lead. Understood?"

"Yes, sir."

"Alright, job's on, let's roll."

Bishop, weapon held ready, moved swiftly along the steep track, sliding through the dark soil and rotting leaf litter. The three other men kept pace, patrolling silently behind him.

At the bottom of the slope they splashed through a shallow creek before coming to the edge of the jungle. As they reached the thick bushes bordering the camp, they crouched, watching for movement. The first ramshackle wooden huts and white triangular UNHCR tents looked deserted. Behind them, row after row of similar dilapidated shelters stretched for over five hundred yards, bounded on one side by the jungle and on the other by a dirty brown waterway littered with rubbish and plastic containers. In the distance Bishop could make out the hazy green mountains of Guinea, a safe haven for the antigovernment militias.

More screaming echoed through the empty camp. He signaled the men to move in. "Listen up. I'm on point; you cover the flanks and the rear." He used his finger to draw their positions in the dirt. In diamond formation they could deal with a threat from any direction.

"I want the bastards dead: no prisoners, no wounded— dead!" Bishop's hushed voice was sharp with anger and the

Indian soldiers all nodded nervously. "Alright, men, let's do this."

The small team pushed out from the foliage, cautiously moving across the bare ground to the camp. The fetid stench of human refuse and rotting garbage hit them as they reached the first line of patchwork tents. Carefully stepping over piles of rubbish, they kept their rifles ready, eyes continually scanning.

As they penetrated deeper into the camp, the conditions worsened. Bishop noticed bullet holes in a sheet of corrugated iron used to patch a hut; the blood splattered across it looked fresh. The distant screams and yelling grew louder as they advanced. A women's terrified shrieks were punctuated by gunshots.

Bishop signaled a halt. He crept forward, looking for a vantage point to observe the center of the camp. As he stepped across a narrow drainage ditch, the soft dirt gave way, dumping his boot in raw sewage splashing it up his leg. He swore as he clambered out of the mess and into an abandoned hut. Crouching, he peered between two sheets of rusted iron.

Not more than thirty yards from him, ten RUF fighters had herded a nearly a hundred refugees into the clearing. Huddled on their knees in the mud, the men, women, and children looked like terrified animals waiting to be slaughtered. Some wept silently. Others clutched each other with skinny arms, eyes wide with fear.

Scattered about the group were mutilated bodies. Drenched with blood and missing limbs, the corpses were a savage warning against resistance. To the side was a bloodied pile of amputated arms and legs.

Unaware of the demise of their sentries, the gunmen screamed with lung-bursting ferocity, fired their weapons into the air, and lashed out at the prisoners. Bishop watched as two young gang members dragged a screaming woman into a blue UN medical aid tent. "Bastards," he muttered through gritted teeth.

Two more RUF trained their weapons on the wide-eyed

refugees while the others gathered around a huge man wielding a machete. My god, Bishop thought. He's a bloody giant. The RUF commander moved like a predator. His scars marked him as a veteran killer; old gunshot wounds disfigured his bare muscled torso and a vicious scar twisted around his throat. His clothes reflected his status, the closest to any form of military uniform worn by the gang. Camouflage pants were tucked into a shiny pair of black jungle boots and a tangle of talismans dangled from his neck. The ensemble was topped by a dirty blue UN beret.

The RUF fighters gathered around their leader, cheering as he waved the bloodstained machete above his head. He grabbed a young boy and pinned him face down in the mud. He rammed his boot into the child's back so his arms splayed out on either side.

Bishop was transfixed on the grisly scene. He knew exactly what was about to happen but couldn't move. Fear paralyzed him.

The commander's biceps bulged and he swung the blade like a broadsword. The machete sliced through the skinny arm with a sickening crunch of bone, burying itself in the thick red mud. The boy's blood-curdling scream came to an abrupt halt as he fainted.

Retrieving the severed arm, the big man held it high for the terrified refugees to see. Spittle sprayed from his mouth as he raged, "You spineless bastards, we fight for your freedom and you force us to do this!" He flung the arm into the growing pile of limbs, a thick cloud of flies lifting from the congealed, bloodied flesh as it landed with a wet thud.

Bishop collapsed to his knees. Vomit sprayed from his mouth, his body wracked with dry heaves and eyes filled with tears. He didn't notice Mirza enter the hut; it took a firm grip on his arm to snap him out of shock.

"Sir, sir, are you OK?" Mirza whispered.

Shame gave way to fury as he wiped his mouth.

"I'm fine." Bishop wiped the tears from his eyes and looked up. His teeth clenched. "Are the men ready?"

Mirza nodded confidently and led him out of the derelict hut where his men waited.

Bishop exhaled. "Let's do this."

They advanced into the clearing with Bishop in the lead. His rifle barked savagely as he concentrated fire on the startled group of RUF. High-velocity bullets tore into the bodies of the gunmen, rending flesh and shattering bone. The three Indian AK-47s roared, laying down automatic fire in support of Bishop's single shots.

The leader dove to the ground at the first sign of the troops, evading the deadly hail of bullets that ripped through his followers. Frantically he crawled behind the closest line of shelters.

Catching a glimpse of the fleeing boss, Bishop charged forward, his weapon blazing until the breech locked open on an empty magazine. He dropped the smoking rifle, the sling around his shoulder caught it as he drew his pistol, cutting down another gunman in a volley of bullets. The RUF fighter collapsed backward as Bishop emptied the entire magazine into his chest.

The dying man's ugly features contorted in pain. A frothy mixture of blood and mucus dribbled from his lips.

Bishop slammed a fresh magazine into his Browning, and with a loud slap, released the slide, chambering a round. He casually raised the pistol and shot the man cleanly through the forehead.

Eight of the gang members lay mortally wounded or dead as a result of the fusillade of fire laid down by the UN peacekeepers. Two of them were riddled with bullets, their pants around their ankles. They would never rape another woman.

The RUF commander had fled with one of his men into the depths of the camp. Bishop gave chase, striding away from the twitching corpse. As he picked up the pace he holstered his pistol and changed the magazine on his rifle.

"Wait for us!" Mirza yelled.

Bishop sprinted through the empty camp, ears ringing from

the gunfight. "Where is that son of a bitch?" he muttered. Running between the threadbare tents, he caught a glimpse of movement ahead. Instinctively he dropped, skidding through a pile of trash. A volley of bullets cracked through the air above him. Rolling sideways, he pumped the trigger of his rifle, the rounds smashing into the firer's position, spraying it with splinters of wood.

The shooter exposed his body for a split second as he sought cover. It was enough time for Bishop to snap off a single aimed shot instantly dropping the gunman. The corpse continued forward under its own momentum, slamming through the flimsy wall of a hut.

Bishop edged forward, his sights focused on the crumpled wall. Movement flashed to the left. He whipped round.

The massive RUF commander bore down on him screaming and swinging a machete. Bishop blocked the blade with his rifle. The force jarred the weapon from his hands and snapped the improvised sling. He lashed out with a fist but the blow bounced off the man's face, the impact jarring his wrist.

In one smooth motion the African reversed his strike, punching the handle of the machete into Bishop's gut, driving the air from his lungs and catapulting him onto his back.

The machete flashed down again and buried itself into the thick red clay. Bishop rolled and snatched the Browning from its holster. The muscular African moved faster. He kicked the pistol away and pounced, swinging the machete down. Bishop caught a wrist with both hands. The veins in the commander's forearm bulged as his brute force and weight pushed the blade down.

Bishop felt a strong hand grasp his throat, closing the airway in a death grip. His hands faltered as he struggled for air and the machete touched skin. The burn of fatigue sapped the strength from his muscles.

The African spoke in guttural tones, his voice laced with animal hatred, "I'm going to chop off your hands, you little bastard. Then I'm going to carve out your heart and eat it."

Darkness clouded Bishop's brain. He faintly registered the

sickening crunch of a rifle's buttstock connecting with the side of his assailant's head. The pressure on his throat released and the machete-wielding hand was ripped away. He struggled to his feet, gasping to clear his head and regain full consciousness.

"Sir, are you OK?" Mirza asked.

Bishop couldn't hear anything; his mind had blocked out everything but the task at hand. He staggered to recover his pistol from the mud and turned to face the big African who sat dazed on his knees. Blood trickled from the man's mouth and side of his head.

Picking up the machete, he felt the weight in his hand. He inspected the pocked edge of the blade and images of severed arms flashed in his mind. Raising his pistol, he aimed at the man's forehead.

The RUF commander managed a sickly smile. "You're too fucking weak to kill with steel, like a real man."

Bishop holstered the Browning. Rage fueled his muscles. He raised the machete high with both hands and drove it down, his body almost pitching forward with the force. The blade smashed through the man's forehead, cleaving it apart like a block of wood under an axe. Blood and brain matter sprayed up Bishop's arms. The man's eyes rolled back, one either side of the rusted blade wedged in his face.

He released his grip, and with a guttural moan the dead body fell backward, the machete protruding from his head, limp arms splayed out on the ground. For a few seconds he watched the corpse spasm before shock hit him hard like a punch to the gut. Fuck! That could have been me, he thought.

Mirza grasped his arm, dragging him to his senses. The Indian lectured, "Sir, you can't always rely on yourself. A single straw is useless, but together, many straws make a broom."

What? Broom? His thoughts muddled, Bishop rubbed at his throat, leaning wearily on the corporal. "Is that the same straw that broke the camel's back, Mirza?" he croaked. "What are you, a fucking philosopher now?" His words sounded ungrateful but the expression on his face told a different story. "Thanks, mate."

"You're more than welcome, sir. You will be happy to know we have secured the camp," Mirza said, "and I have moved the vehicles down."

"Did you get the rest of those bastards?"

"We killed ten of them; any others must have fled. We won't see them again, at least for today."

Bishop nodded and with the aid of Mirza's shoulder, staggered back to the center of the camp.

The remainder of the UN peacekeepers had already moved up to assist the traumatized refugees as they tended to their injured and dead. The convoy was now parked in the camp's central square and the soldiers were distributing what limited supplies they had.

Wails of grief rent the air as relatives filtered back from the jungle and located family members: dead, maimed, or unconscious. Bishop surveyed the scattered bodies, slain gunmen lying among the slaughtered refugees.

Propping himself up against a sheet of sun-warmed, corrugated iron, he stared blankly at the armless body of the boy. One of the Indians was attempting to find the child's pulse. The soldier shook his head; it was futile. The ground around the boy's body was soaked with blood. The Indian's combat trousers stained crimson at the knees where he knelt by the boy.

Bishop stared at his trembling hands; they too were covered in blood. Tears welled in his eyes as thoughts of blame assaulted him. Did his indecisiveness cost that child his life? Could he have saved the boy with one well-aimed shot? He noticed some of the refugees watching him and forced his head to clear. Struggling to his feet, he stumbled to the medic, who was working intently on a young girl.

"Is there anything I can do?"

The medic looked up, face gaunt and pale. "Yes, thank you, sir. This one needs a splint."

"Is it just her arm?"

"Yes, sir, her arm is badly broken and she is going into shock."

"OK, I'll help this one. You take care of the others." Bishop knelt next to the girl. Forgetting his own fatigue, he carefully tucked a reflective space blanket around the tiny body.

As the young officer worked on splinting the arm, Colonel Kapur strolled over and watched. Growing impatient, the senior officer tapped Bishop on the shoulder.

"Lieutenant! I've contacted UN HQ and we have been ordered to return to base immediately. You need to explain yourself to the force commander!"

Bishop's fists clenched and he stood slowly. Anger flared, then subsided as he looked down at the frail body wrapped in the silver space blanket.

"If you don't mind, sir, I would like to make sure we provide all the assistance we can," he said wearily.

The colonel nodded, content that at least a portion of authority was back in his hands. He was happy to entertain Bishop's philanthropic ways in exchange for a little civility. When they returned to Freetown, the trigger-happy lieutenant would be put in his place.

***

FREETOWN

The UN mission force commander was a busy man. The Indian four-star general was doing his utmost to maintain a precarious cease-fire with a peacekeeping force comprised almost entirely of developing-world soldiers. Most of them were simply there to collect the UN dollar and wave their national flags. Very few actually wanted to enforce the cease-fire with the RUF; they left that to the poorly equipped forces of the Sierra Leone government.

Sitting in his makeshift office, the general methodically sorted through the pile of reports on his battered desk. The room had been part of an old primary school; the national education system had collapsed years ago. An ancient air conditioner rattled on the wall, leaking water and uselessly blowing hot air. The room's original furnishings had been looted and replaced with a street market mismatch of items. It wasn't the usual work environment for the senior officer but that was irrelevant. He had far more pressing issues.

Reaching across the desk for the 'Incident Reports' folder, the general contemplated Colonel Kapur's account of the Kilimi incident. He had to admit the actions of the young lieutenant were bold, even though they broke half a dozen of the UN-mandated rules of engagement. The colonel's comments were damning. Bishop was described as insubordinate, reckless, and trigger-happy, attributes highly unsuitable for the role of a UN peacekeeper.

The general's thoughts were interrupted by the entry of his US liaison officer, a CIA paramilitary operative that he knew only as Vance. The towering African American barreled through the door like it was attached to a Western saloon. The door crashed behind him. "General Singh, what the hell are you gonna do about this Kilimi cluster?"

The general sighed. "I haven't decided yet. Part of me wants to promote the young man and place him in charge of an entire battalion of infantry. A combat leader like him could pull the RUF into line within a week."

A broad smile split Vance's huge bald head. "Damn straight. As far as balls go, that kid's packing a pair the size of cannonballs," he bellowed as he lowered himself into the only other chair in the room. The tiny school chair groaned and threatened to splinter under his weight.

The general nodded as Vance continued, "Somehow I don't think that pansy-ass head of mission would approve. Word on the street is he wants to make an example of the lieutenant."

"A pity," replied the general. "We could use more men like him, but the RUF are screaming murder. Lieutenant Bishop killed one of their most respected commanders."

"Horseshit! The evil bastard was a rapist, a murderer, and a criminal. Even by RUF standards he was fucked up. I've tried to have him killed three times. Hell, most of the RUF were terrified of him."

The general rolled his eyes. He didn't want to know about the black ops that Vance was conducting. While he respected the CIA man, his methods were more than a little disconcerting.

"Vance, the issue here is not the actions of the RUF, it's what to do with the lieutenant. The head of mission wants to charge him with war crimes."

"What the hell? That's bullshit."

"Yes, but—"

Vance interrupted. "If Bishop hadn't intervened, those butchers would have slaughtered the whole damn village."

"You and I know this, but the head of mission wants to show the RUF we're serious about maintaining the cease-fire. I've never seen him so furious." The general's face displayed a look of concern. "He's worried that if the media gets hold of this, it could jeopardize everything. He has to hold someone accountable and that someone is probably going to be Lieutenant Bishop."

Vance slammed his hand down on the arm of the flimsy chair. "Bishop did what any soldier should have. If anything, we should have that gutless colonel's head in a noose."

The general was moved by Vance's words. He was a straight shooter, one of the few people who seemed to understand the reality of the situation in Sierra Leone. For a moment he thought Vance may have been right. With men like Bishop leading his forces, maybe, just maybe, they could make a difference.

He shook his head. As long as the UN hamstrung his soldiers and continued to seek a peaceful resolution, what could he really achieve? The decision was made. Bishop would be sent home. They would let the Australian Army discipline him.

***

The sun was low on the horizon. Bishop sat on his pack, waiting on the tarmac to board the C-130 transport aircraft.

Although it was late in the day, Lungi Airport was still hectic, the contractors working in the sweltering heat to unload the line of aircraft. The UN mission was expanding, and the tiny airport operated at maximum capacity as a continuous stream of food and humanitarian supplies were delivered.

Bishop paid no attention to the activity; he was racked with anxiety and guilt. The slaughter of the RUF gunmen had made him uneasy, but the actions were justified. It was the vision of their leader hacking off the boy's arm that played over and over in his head. He tried to suppress the images hammering in his brain and forced his thoughts back to the UN headquarters, where the force commander had told him he was being sent home. The Indian general had been severe. Bishop had stayed silent.

Vance had stopped him as he left the general's office. "Hey, LT," the big man had called out. "You did a damn fine thing out there. A lot of people are alive because of you."

Bishop had no idea who the African American was, but he looked like Special Forces. "Tell that to the dead refugees at Kilimi," he had countered.

"Don't be so hard on yourself. That whole camp would have been slaughtered if you hadn't stepped up."

"They still might be." Bishop eyeballed him. "What's to stop those West Side animals from rolling back in now and murdering the lot? A couple of old men armed with AKs?" Bishop shook his head. "The UN has hung them out to dry."

"I know you're angry, buddy, but a lot of people are trying their hardest to make this work."

"Yeah, well, trying isn't fucking doing and it sure as hell isn't saving lives! Until the UN takes off the gloves and cracks down hard, this… this is all for nothing."

"That's why we need more men like you. Men who are willing to put their balls on the line and make a difference." Vance crushed Bishop's hand and pumped his arm in a handshake.

"You ever need a job, LT, look me up." A business card appeared and the CIA agent slipped it into the startled

Australian's shirt pocket. "We can always use more men like you."

Vance's words had embarrassed him. Bishop usually didn't have time for Americans, but this one was different.

A whine of hydraulics interrupted Bishop's thoughts as the ramp of his aircraft lowered. He stood up, waiting as a forklift off-loaded a pallet of cargo. Once the ramp was clear he swung his pack over his shoulder and walked toward the idling aircraft.

"Sir!" The voice was clear over the droning turboprops. Bishop stopped and turned. Mirza jogged up and grasped him by the shoulder. "Sir, I heard what happened and I want you to know I think it's bullshit."

A smile lit up Bishop's sullen jaw. The corporal had adopted a few Bishop-isms. "No need for the 'sir' anymore, Mirza. It's just Aden. What punishment did you cop?"

"I was charged and lost rank." He shrugged. "Now I am a private, but at least I can stay and finish the mission."

"I'm sorry, Mirza."

"It doesn't matter. You reminded us of why we became soldiers." Mirza's stern look split into a wide grin. "Maybe one day we will fight together again—side by side."

"That would be an honor, my friend, that would be an honor."

They shook hands, then Bishop turned toward the aircraft and walked up the ramp. As it closed, he took one last look at the man who had saved his life. Part of him wanted to stay, serve with men like Mirza, and try to make a difference, but he knew that ultimately the UN mission was hopeless. He resigned himself to being sent home.

CHAPTER 3

CLUB KYIV, KIEV, UKRAINE, 2004

"No, I will not sell you just one missile," Dostiger said as he slammed his fist down on his desk. "Your superiors ordered an entire shipment. Not one, a shipment!"

The Iranian agent's eyes darted around the room as he avoided the crazed Ukrainian's gaze. The opulence of the arms dealer's office unnerved him. Located in Kiev's most exclusive nightclub, it emphasized the power and influence of the man he'd angered.

He swallowed, his mouth suddenly dry. "Things have changed. The Americans have sold Israel the latest countermeasures, and our sources tell us they're fitting them to all their aircraft, military and civilian—"

Spittle left the Ukrainian's mouth as he cut in. "I'm not selling cheap Chinese junk! These missiles are state-of-the-art. They will tear the Israeli jets from the sky no matter what toys the Jews bolt to them."

"You tell us this, but how can we—"

"Because I would not sell them otherwise. Because I do not sell empty promises. I sell weapons that kill!"

Dostiger took a deep breath, stood, and poured a whiskey from the decanter on his desk. Limping, he turned and walked to the one-way glass that separated his office from the nightclub below. He watched the writhing mass of bodies on the dance floor and sipped his scotch.

"How many weapons have I sold you?"

"But—"

"And have they not worked as I promised?"

"Yes, of course. You always deliver."

He turned back to face the Iranian. "No! The Revolutionary Guards come to me because no one else can deliver!"

The Iranian flushed. "Let us buy just one. We will do tests, and if we are happy, then we will buy more."

The Ukrainian smiled, a twisted grimace of a smile. "And let you copy the technology?" There was a guttural laugh as Dostiger limped back to his desk.

"We would never—"

"No? Because that's exactly what I would do." Dostiger sat down. "But then I would also want a demonstration." His lips stretched into a grin.

"What… what do you mean by 'a demonstration'?"

"The Revolutionary Guards want to shoot down Israeli planes, yes?"

"No, not the Guards. Hezbollah!" the visitor replied.

"Hezbollah, Guards," he shrugged. "What matters is business and Iran will not part with money unless results are guaranteed. Yes?"

"That is correct," the Iranian said sitting up in his chair.

"So! I will demonstrate the weapon."

"What sort of demonstration?"

"A display of the missile's capability against an Israeli aircraft." Dostiger's face was impassive but his voice was cold. "A passenger aircraft. If the demonstration is successful, then Iran will purchase ALL of the missiles."

"You would attack an unarmed Israeli passenger jet to ensure the sale?"

"Correct!" Dostiger's eyes glinted.

"What about reprisals? What about the Americans or Israel? Surely they will hunt even you down?"

The Ukrainian laughed. His pitted and scarred face reminiscent of a macabre gargoyle. "What are the Jews going to do? They will blame Hezbollah, use it as an excuse to occupy more Lebanese soil, and I will make even more money selling rockets to your comrades."

"You're not worried they'll come for you?"

Another laugh. "The Americans will not touch me! The CIA wants the latest Russian technology as much as everyone else. One jet and a handful of Jews are… inconsequential."

"Maybe to the Americans, but Mossad—"

"Mossad? Israeli intelligence are toothless fools; outside of the Middle East they are nothing. Look around, comrade, I own the Ukraine. Here I am a king. Do you think I should fear Mossad when I am surrounded by the best security money can buy?"

The Iranian could only nod. Dostiger's headquarters was indeed a fortress. Heavily armed guards manned all the entrances and CCTV cameras watched every space.

"My men will conduct the attack, and I will continue my business as I always have."

"This will need approval from the head of the Guards," the Iranian said.

"The decision they need to make is whether or not they want to continue doing business with me. Tell them to watch the skies over Israel. I will show them what my missiles can do."

The Iranian smiled for the first time and stood up. He held his hand out. "You are a cunning man, Dostiger."

"Not at all." Dostiger shook the Iranian's hand. "I am simply a businessman."

***

BARCELONA, SPAIN

The dingy internet café was hardly the most enticing location in the picturesque city of Barcelona: half a dozen obsolete PCs, cheap plastic chairs, cracked linoleum, and the stale stench of cigarettes. It wasn't the place to be enjoying a holiday but Bishop didn't notice. While other tourists explored the history and culture of the coastal city, he scrolled through the latest news from the world's conflict zones.

He noted the ongoing violence in Iraq with disgust. The headlines were all the same: bombings, kidnappings, beheadings, and increasing casualties. More soldiers dying, more innocent civilians slaughtered, and all for what? Oil. No one seemed to care that thousands of people die every day in other conflicts throughout the world. Shaking his head, he closed the web page and logged into his email.

There were two new messages. Bishop's mood improved instantly as he opened one from his father. His parents had arrived safely in Tel Aviv and were visiting friends. In a week they would meet him in Spain, his mother's birthplace.

The second email was from Mirza Mansoor. Ever since the incident in Sierra Leone four years ago, they had remained in contact, exchanging emails. It had turned out that Mirza was a veteran special forces operator. The reason the Indian had been in Sierra Leone in charge of a regular infantry section was not something he'd been willing to divulge. However, Bishop knew that Mirza had gone back to an elite unit, despite being apparently demoted by Colonel Kapur. The Australian's career, on the other hand, had been sidelined. His otherwise perfect record marked with a single count of insubordination.

Bishop opened the email:

I hope you are making the most of your holiday, my friend. Make sure you are taking the time to relax and enjoy life outside the army.

I have started a new job with a contractor based out of India, good money but a little boring. Thanks again for the job reference. Hope you visit sometime soon.

Mirza

He typed a quick response and hit Send. Gathering his belongings, he paused at the counter to settle the account.

"Ah, are you Mr. Bishop?" asked the pimple-faced youth behind the till.

Bishop looked over his shoulder, quickly scanning the other users in the room. None of them looked familiar or particularly threatening. He turned back to the attendant. "I might be. What do you want?"

"A man left this for you." He handed over a crisp white envelope.

Bishop opened it and pulled out a business card.

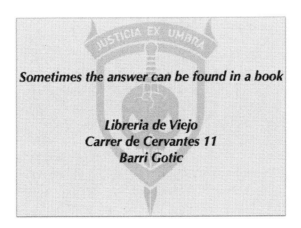

Sometimes the answer can be found in a book

Libreria de Viejo
Carrer de Cervantes 11
Barri Gotic

He looked around the room again and out the window to the street.

"Who gave you this?" he asked.

"An older man: big black American."

"When?"

"Umm, hour ago, maybe more. He said to give it to Mr. Bishop, with the brown jacket."

Fuck, thought Bishop. Is this a scam? How the hell does he know my name? He looked back at the card. It resembled a military patch, the sort of thing Special Forces sometimes wore. 'Sometimes the answer can be found in a book'? It felt like a puzzle, a clue to some sort of treasure hunt.

He took the card back to an internet terminal and punched the address into Google Maps. It was close, only a few blocks away. He rocked back in the chair, trying to make sense of it all. He knew there was no way he could turn his back on this. He threw a few coins on the counter and left the café.

Walking out onto the busy footpath, he joined the throngs of tourists, occasionally glancing back over his shoulder, searching for a tail. Nothing, no one seemed to be paying even the slightest attention to him.

Hauling a battered *Lonely Planet* guide from his leather satchel, he thumbed through the pages. He briefly read the description of Barri Gòtic, the Gothic quarter of old Barcelona. The route seemed simple enough, a pleasant walk through the ancient streets.

Although Bishop had been staying in Barcelona for almost a week, he hadn't made any effort to explore the city. So far he'd either been thrashing himself with a vigorous exercise regime, drinking in dimly-lit bars, or surfing the internet. Maybe it was time to stop dwelling on things he couldn't change and make the most of his holidays. At least the cryptic card had given him something to break the self-destructive pattern he'd fallen into.

Strolling through Barcelona, Bishop began to see the city in a new light. The sheer magnificence of the architecture enthralled him, the ancient buildings steeped in over two thousand years of history. He wandered absentmindedly, forgetting his mission, drawn away from the traffic-lined roads into the quiet cobblestone streets.

When he finally remembered to check his map, he had been walking for nearly thirty minutes. He looked around to gain his bearings. The streets were old and narrow, hemmed in by ancient sandstone walls. By pure luck it looked as if he had stumbled into the Barri Gòtic. He checked the brass plaques that announced the names of the streets, searching for his destination. Bingo! Carrer de Cervantes, the street he was searching for.

The ancient alley narrowed, the old buildings closing in on both sides. Stones underfoot were worn smooth and he could almost hear the cries of medieval street merchants hawking their wares. He paused at a small doorway cut into a sandstone wall. An ancient sign that hung from rusted chains proclaimed LIBRERÍA DE VIEJO.

A brass bell jingled as he pushed open the sturdy door. He inhaled the musky smell of gently aging books. A weather-beaten man perched behind an antique cash register beckoned him in, smiling.

Bishop gave the old man a once-over, scanning the rest of the shop for any potential threat. The narrow room was packed from ceiling to floor with leather-bound books and manuscripts. Several rolled parchments gathered dust on the highest shelves, evidence that the annals of this establishment had graced Barcelona for more than a few decades.

"He said you would come."

The voice startled Bishop and he turned back to the man. "Excuse me?"

"Your friend, he said you would come." The old man had left his stool and was hobbling toward Bishop, a book tucked under one arm.

"I'm sorry. What do you mean?"

The shopkeeper laughed. "He said that a lost soldier would come. You have the presence of a soldier, but you wander like a man with no path."

"I used to be a soldier but that's another story. Tell me about this man. What did he look like?"

"Like you. Once a soldier, always a soldier."

Bishop's eyes narrowed and he handed over the card from the internet café. "Have you seen this before?"

The old man adjusted his glasses and studied the card intently. "This writing, it is Latin." He ran a finger along the script that crested the shield embossed on the card. "*Justicia ex umbra*. It means 'Justice from the shadows.'" The shopkeeper handed the card back. "I have never seen a card like this, but those words, I have seen those words before."

"*Justicia ex umbra*?" Bishop queried. "Where?"

The old man handed Bishop the book he was holding. "In the book your friend sent you to find."

Bishop took the battered text and studied the cover. A single word was embossed in the wrinkled leather: *Susurro*.

"Your friend is wise. Books do have a way of finding those they will help the most. This one has been translated into English, maybe it can help you." The shopkeeper turned and hobbled back to his stool.

Bishop stepped up to the counter. "Sometimes the answers we're looking for can't be found in a book."

The old man frowned as he sat, his features disappearing

into a landscape of crevices. He spoke quietly, "There is always someone who has walked the path before you, my friend. In books they leave their lessons for those who are wise enough to find them."

Bishop considered the comment. The old bugger has a point, he thought as he opened the yellowed pages of the book and scanned a page. How many soldiers have doubted their cause over the years? How many have found themselves at a crossroads? He closed the book and placed it on the counter. "Are you sure you don't know anything more about this so-called friend of mine? Or this card?"

The old man stared back blankly and shook his head. "But you can have the book; it is already paid for."

"Thanks." With a sigh, Bishop stuffed it in his satchel and pushed open the door, returning to the cobbled streets of ancient Barcelona.

Lounging in bed that evening and aiming to read a couple of chapters before hitting the bars, he became so engrossed that when he finally put the book down, the faint glow of dawn could be seen from his hotel window.

The book was the history of a secret society known as El Susurro: the whisper. It existed outside the law, a private army using clandestine methods to protect the people of Valencia from the horrors of the Spanish Inquisition. Bringing justice from the shadows.

The concept resonated with Bishop. Now there's a worthy cause, he thought. Fighting for the weak! Bringing a modicum of justice to the world!

For the next few days Bishop continued to explore Barcelona. The book never left his mind, nor the means by which it had entered his life. Despite his training, he never identified a tail, nor felt like he was being watched. Slowly the suspicion began to ebb.

A week later the book was a distant memory as Bishop traveled by high-speed rail to meet his parents in Valencia. The train sped swiftly across the Spanish countryside and he relaxed, gazing out the carriage window. Suspicion and unease were chased away by memories of childhood vacations and old family friends. Finally he'd left behind the worries of the world and was enjoying his holiday.

CHAPTER 4

EL AL FLIGHT LY395

Mark and Estela Bishop boarded the El Al Airlines flight eagerly. After a pleasant few days visiting old friends, they were flying from Israel to Spain to spend a week with Aden. One short week; not nearly long enough. It had been six months since they'd last seen their son.

Despite the years of separation imposed by military service, the bond between the Bishops and their only child was strong. They tried to talk to Aden at least once a week, no matter in what far-flung country he was stationed.

Estela hated the photos of him with guns and riding in tanks; Aden was her little boy, her adorable, mop-haired angel who'd clung to her on his first day of school.

Mark always remembered him as the young officer in his ceremonial uniform. Nothing had made Bishop senior more proud than the day he watched his son graduate from military college.

The couple still traveled regularly, despite retirement. Years of working as journalists had gifted them with friends to visit all around the world. As the 737 took off, they relaxed, used to the cramped economy seats. They laughed as they scrolled through photos on their camera, Estela's head resting on Mark's shoulder.

In the cockpit the pilots bantered with the flight engineer as they monitored the autopilot guiding the aircraft toward its thirty-five-thousand-feet cruising height. The skies over the Mediterranean were clear; it was going to be a pleasant flight.

As the jet reached ten thousand feet, the tranquil silence of the cockpit was shattered by a blaring alarm. Red lights flashed across the flight controls and the pilots stared at each other in disbelief. The plane's missile warning system had detected a launch!

Far below the aircraft, a predator had initiated its hunt. Like the nose of a wolf, a thermal seeker sniffed out its quarry. The missile leaped into the sky, accelerating to three times the speed of its lumbering prey.

The aircraft's automated system reacted instantly, forcing the aircraft into a tight turn and throwing flares from a dispenser in its tail. Burning at over a thousand degrees, the flares hung under parachutes in an attempt to confuse the heat-seeking warhead.

The hunter couldn't be fooled; a sophisticated computer identified the flares and discarded them as targets, locking back onto the thermal signature of the engines.

It took five seconds for the shoulder-launched missile to cover the distance from the firing tube to the aircraft. It detonated in the jet's right engine sending fragments slicing through the 737's thin aluminum skin. White-hot shrapnel shredded hydraulic cables, fuel lines, and flight surfaces.

The unmistakable sound of the high-explosive detonation jolted Mark Bishop in his seat. Estela's head smashed into his shoulder as the plane banked violently. Oxygen masks jettisoned from the ceiling. He glanced out the window and knew it wasn't turbulence. A jagged piece of the wing was missing, the engine ripped from its mounting.

"Everybody remain calm and stay in your seats," transmitted a voice over the speakers. "We are experiencing some unexpected technical difficulties that have forced us to take emergency maneuvers. Cabin crew prepare for an emergency landing."

The plane pitched forward, causing screams and panic. A baby shrieked. White-faced flight attendants clung to the headrests and tried to reassure passengers. Vibrations shook overhead lockers open and baggage lurched out of the compartments, crashing into people as the plane flipped through a series of evasive maneuvers.

"Crash position! Crash position! Brace! Brace!"

Heads whipped down, 132 passengers bracing themselves in prayer, some silent, some not; all far too late.

Mark whispered into Estela's ear. Her fingers dug into his hand, eyes clenched tight.

The aircraft plummeted.

Across the aisle someone retched.

Mark held his wife tight. "I love you—"

The 737 didn't have a chance. Eight minutes after taking off from Ben Gurion International Airport, flight LY395 hit the ground and exploded.

In the largest single terrorist attack in the history of Israel, 132 people were killed. The nation wept in shock, and Aden Bishop lost both the people he loved most.

***

VALENCIA, SPAIN

On the outskirts of Valencia, thunderous gray clouds loomed over the township of Montemayor. The storm had rolled in off the ocean and blocked out the late-afternoon sun. Torrential rain was lashing the countryside.

A small crowd had gathered at a desolate hilltop cemetery, a single olive tree offering negligible protection from the wind as it howled between ancient gray headstones.

The funeral of Mark and Estela Bishop continued despite the inclement weather. It was a modest but solemn ceremony. Five generations of Estela's family had been buried here and the short service was steeped in tradition.

The local Catholic priest's cassock whipped back in the wind as rain dripped from his headdress, but he pushed on valiantly. The wind tore at the printed eulogies in the hands of the congregation. A few ripped away and gusted above the heads of mourners before colliding with the branches of the olive tree.

Aden stood apart from his distant relatives and parents' friends. He watched, silent, cold, and isolated. Inside, however, there was a raging maelstrom of anger, loss, and fear. The freezing rain did little to temper him.

The icy wind brought whispered comments as mourners turned to leave the stark setting.

"Is that Aden?"

"Yes, the soldier… poor boy…"

Mourners conveyed their condolences to Mark and Estela's only son. He barely acknowledged them. Their faces were hazy childhood memories.

"So emotionless…"

"He was always such a quiet boy…"

"I heard he was court-martialed for war crimes…"

As Bishop stood silently by the muddied grave, he looked around, hoping to find a familiar face among the dwindling group. He realized he didn't actually know any of these people and for a moment regretted not telling his close friends of the loss.

He stood before his parents' final resting place long after the funeral concluded. He watched on as laborers threw the last shovelfuls of mud on the grave, and the light gradually disappeared from the sky. Drenched by the unrelenting rain he stood steadfast, his only company the cold granite angels guarding the tombs of Valencia's dead. Guilt racked his thoughts and rage numbed his mind.

Shivering, Bishop finally tore his eyes from the headstone engraved with his parents' names. His hair was soaked flat and streaming rivulets of water ran down into his raincoat. He needed to feel: the cold, the rain, the wind, anything. His body and his mind, all of it was numb. He turned stiffly, walking back through the downpour toward the wrought-iron gates.

As he approached the entrance he noticed a large black car parked outside. Beside it stood a tall figure in a long dark overcoat holding an umbrella.

A booming American voice cut through, "I'm sorry for your loss, LT."

He shielded his eyes from the rain, squinting to identify the man. The voice was familiar, but he couldn't make out his features. "Who… who is it?"

"Come on, buddy, it hasn't been that long." The man

stepped forward, raising the big umbrella to cover them both, while his other hand grasped Bishop's shoulder.

"Sierra Leone, 2000, you saved a lot of lives, remember?"

"Vance, holy shit!" Bishop whispered.

"That's right, buddy, the one and only."

"You came all the way out here?" He stared up at the imposing African American. "How did you find me?"

"I've been keeping tabs on you for a while, LT."

For a split second Bishop's grief was replaced with a spark of interest. "Me? Why would you be keeping tabs on me? And I'm not LT, I'm not a soldier anymore."

Vance raised his eyebrows.

Then it clicked. "It was you, wasn't it? The card, the bookstore, *Susurro*!"

Vance laughed deeply, gripping Bishop's shoulder with his huge hand. "You got it, buddy. You might not be a soldier anymore, but you'll always be a warrior. Now how's about we jump in this fine automobile of mine and get out of this goddamn rain." Vance gestured toward the black sedan. "And I'll tell you a little more about that book."

Bishop's body was riddled with pain; hours of immobility in the driving wind and freezing rain had taken their toll. He was so exhausted he could barely move and just stared at Vance blankly.

The years had not been kind to the American. His face was weathered, the dark skin drooping slightly under his neck and eyes. The man bore a passing resemblance to the actor Laurence Fishburne in the movie *The Matrix*. Are you playing the same game? Bishop thought. Do you want me to take the blue pill?

"Is this where you give me the pitch?" Bishop's voice was so flat it was barely human. "Is this where you sell the CIA to me? Give me the whole 'You can avenge your parents' spiel, is that it?"

"No—"

"I just put my parents in the ground and you're using it as an opportunity to try and recruit me into the fucking CIA."

Tears welled in Bishop's eyes. "I just left one political puppet show, Vance, and I'm not joining another, ever."

Stepping out from under the umbrella, he continued his bleak walk down the hill.

"BISHOP! BISHOP!" Vance yelled after him.

He lifted the collar of his jacket against the torrential rain and continued. Behind him he could hear the American's heavy footfalls.

"BISHOP! This isn't about your parents. This is about you!"

Vance slapped a vast hand on Bishop's shoulder and stepped around to face him. The big man abandoned the umbrella and ignored the rain as it dripped off his bald head and down his collar.

"I've been watching you, Bishop. Since you left the Army, I wanted you to read that book. To understand before I asked you to join." His tone softened. "Look, I'm sorry about your parents, but this is bigger than them. It's bigger than you and me. It's about bringing a little justice into the world."

Bishop turned away, staring silently into the darkness.

"Listen, I don't work for the CIA anymore."

The Australian's eyes were glazed.

"Bishop."

"I'm not interested in contracting." The rain had finally penetrated every layer of Bishop's clothing from his head to his toes. Thin streams of rain ran off his eyebrows and down his nose. He shivered.

"I don't work for any contractors, Bishop, or any government, for that matter. I work for an organization hell-bent on bringing justice to the world, and we dance to our own tune." Vance reached into his pocket and pulled out a business card. He extended it to Bishop. Rain dripped off the card. Bishop just stared, so Vance held the card up. It read:

PRIORITY MOVEMENTS AIRLIFT

"Never heard of them," Bishop said.

Vance smiled, held him steady, and stuffed the card into his pocket. "We don't exactly advertise what we do. A lot of very powerful people wouldn't be particularly happy with what we get up to. Now let's get you out of the rain."

Vance motioned to the car and it crept up, stopping beside them. He hauled open one of the passenger doors and guided the exhausted Australian into the dry interior.

Once they were both seated in the back, the car glided forward. Vance pulled out a hip flask and sloshed a few inches of scotch into a steel tumbler. Bishop looked down at the liquor. Vance pushed it into his hands and with a shrug he threw it down his throat. He handed the cup back and looked the older man in the face.

"So what is it you actually do now, Vance?"

"Like I said, we bring a little justice to the world."

Bishop wiped the rain from his face. "Like *The A-Team*?"

Vance laughed. "Yeah, bud, something like that."

The car gathered speed.

CHAPTER 5

KHOD VALLEY, AFGHANISTAN, 2012

Physically, Ishmael Khalid was not an impressive man. He was of average height with narrow shoulders and hawklike features. What he lacked in physical presence, he made up for in sheer intensity. Like a bird of prey, his stare was unyielding, cold, and distant. Thin lips and a hooked nose emphasized the likeness.

The Afghan was a warrior and commander; his entire adult life had revolved around war. As a teenager his first blood had been Russian, and after his father was killed by the Spetsnaz, Khalid had inherited leadership of his village. With that death came responsibility for a hundred warriors, vast lands, and loyalty to the warlord, Khan.

It was service to Khan that had brought him back to the Khod Valley, not ten miles from the site of his father's death. His orders were to take twenty of his best men and ambush anyone attempting to push north up the valley.

The ground Khalid had chosen was well sited: an open piece of terrain in the valley floor running into a bottleneck, with both sides dominated by steep, barren slopes. Vehicles driving along the narrow track that followed the canyon floor would be forced to bunch together, maximizing the effectiveness of his men's advanced weaponry.

Khalid smiled as he pictured the carnage the ambush would bring. With the weapons supplied by Khan's arms dealer, his men would make short work of anyone trying to interfere with the activities further up the valley on the mountain.

The warriors Khalid commanded were not like the ragtag Taliban who fought the Americans. They were Khan's own personal army. Trained by Chechen mercenaries and equipped with state-of-the-art weaponry, they were funded by the warlord's opium fields. Although they called themselves

Taliban, they had long ago abandoned traditional robes for combat fatigues, boots, and chest harnesses. They all wore the distinctive black head-scarves of Khan's army.

From his camouflaged command pit high up on the rugged cliff face, Khalid felt the excitement of imminent combat. His forward sentry had reported a US patrol moving directly toward them. He watched the entrance to the valley through the high-powered scope of his Accuracy International sniper rifle. Khan preferred to avoid direct combat, relying on mines and improvised bombs to inflict casualties, and this would be the first time his men had fought head-to-head with the US Army.

The distant rumble of diesel engines echoed up the valley as the American formation crept into view. Khalid instinctively leaned forward. It was a standard light-armored Stryker patrol. He counted five vehicles: three gun cars, two personnel carriers. The lead vehicle moved slightly off the track to avoid any mines on the road, stopping regularly to scan the terrain. Khalid was familiar with Strykers; information on the eight-wheeled light armored vehicles was easy to find on the internet.

He permitted himself a wry grin as he watched the American soldiers employ the same basic tactics that the Russians had used. Avoiding tracks where possible, they halted to the rear of rocky features, using the terrain for protection. "Different enemy, different tanks, but always they think the same way," he gibed, turning to the man crouching next to him. "See the first three vehicles? The ones with the turrets?"

"Yes, Khalid."

"Those three must be destroyed first. They are far more deadly than the others."

The younger fighter nodded in agreement as Khalid keyed his field telephone and passed on his instructions to his trusted lieutenants hidden in their camouflaged bunkers.

"Omar, you target the second vehicle. Zakir, you target the third. On my command, my brothers."

The Afghan commander waited for the two teams to acknowledge his message before looking back through the scope of his rifle. All the vehicles were now inside the kill zone, with the lead Stryker creeping through the rough terrain. He looked over at the man next to him and smiled. It was the exact path he had predicted they'd take.

Khalid grasped a firing device in his gloved hand. Flicking off the safety bail, the initiation system armed as the first vehicle edged into position; almost directly on top of where the first set of antitank mines had been placed.

"Allah give victory to the holy warriors, *allahu akbar*," Khalid whispered, then depressed the firing switch. Three antitank mines detonated under the rear wheels of the Stryker, thirty kilograms of explosives slamming upward through the hull in a thunderous explosion that reverberated throughout the valley. The crew was killed instantly. The vehicle flipped on its side, fuel and plastics burning fiercely. The intense heat and force of the explosion set off the ammunition and the Stryker was ripped apart with a flash.

As the blast claimed the lead vehicle, Khalid's men fired their Spike antitank weapons at the next two Strykers. With a roar the Israeli-built missiles leaped from hidden bunkers, their sensors locking onto the targets below. They streaked downward, the shape-charged warheads exploding a short distance before impact, spitting molten jets of metal through the thin armor on top of each turret. It took only seconds for the vehicles to ignite, simultaneously suffocating and engulfing the crew in flames.

With the three lead vehicles destroyed, the two personnel carriers to the rear of the formation had run out of options. The crew commanders dropped their ramps. Infantry swarmed out into a defensive screen.

Khalid ordered his men to engage and armed the other mines he'd sown. As his thumb pressed the trigger, the five antitank mines detonated in a single massive explosion directly below one of the remaining personnel carriers. The blast obscured the vehicle in dust, adding to the smoke already streaming from the other burning wrecks.

The last personnel carrier attempted a rapid reverse, using

the smoke to hide from Khalid's weapons. It looked as if it might escape, until another missile streaked from the hillside. Its fate was the same as the others, a twisted, burning funeral pyre.

With all five of the American vehicles destroyed, Khalid focused on the surviving infantrymen. His mortar team dropped rounds on them, the hot steel of sophisticated airburst shells shredding bodies as they desperately sought cover. Khalid used his sniper rifle to methodically pick off the wounded men. One by one, the high-velocity armor-piercing rounds punched through the soldiers' body armor.

In minutes the ambush was over; five armored vehicles left burning on the battlefield with thirty men dead or dying. The stench of burning metal, fuel, and flesh fouled the air.

***

North of the ambush, at the mountain that dominated the valley, Pavlo Yanukovych watched the enslaved locals. From the tunnel entrance at the barren cliff face, the workers extracted wheelbarrow loads of rubble, depositing the rocks onto rapidly growing heaps. The heavy thump of jackhammers emanated from the shaft's opening, pneumatic tools smashing through the slabs of rock that denied Khan and his men their goal.

While the workers wore traditional robes and headdress, the former Russian combat engineer had an assault vest over his shirt, and faded khaki pants. His combat boots were battered and a G36 assault rifle hung from his shoulder. Everything was covered in a fine layer of dust.

The sounds of the distant ambush brought a concerned look to Yanuk's face and he turned to find Khan staring at him. Yanuk didn't fear many men; as a combat veteran and the henchman of an arms dealer, he was used to dealing with dangerous criminals, but Khan unnerved him.

"So, Russian, it seems the Americans have arrived. We may not have as much time as we anticipated. We must speed up the excavation!" Khan's English was almost perfect. It was the only common language between the two men.

Yanuk replied haphazardly, "Ah, it will risky, but we can make short to five days." He turned away from Khan, embarrassed at his poor English.

"If the Americans reach us before we complete our task, you, my friend, will be the first to suffer. Let me assure you of that."

Yanuk stared into the distance, biting his tongue. An expert in both chemical weapons and military engineering, the Russian's experience was critical to the mission, something the Afghan leader didn't seem to comprehend.

The tension was cut by the high-pitched ring of Khan's satellite phone. The warlord pulled the bulky device from his robes. He paused to ensure the call was secure before lifting it to his ear.

"Khan, it's Khalid," the voice came through.

"What has happened, my son?" The two men conversed in Pashto.

"We ambushed the Americans moving up the valley: five armored vehicles destroyed and thirty men killed."

"Very good! Did you take casualties?"

"We had no losses, but we used more ammunition than anticipated."

"Good work. Did any of the infidels escape?"

"No. We took care of them all. The jammer should have stopped them contacting their headquarters."

"Good, good. The Russian says it will take no more than five days for us to finish the excavation. Do you have enough ammunition to stop another probe?" Khan asked.

"Yes, but they will be more cautious next time. We expect the bombers to eventually come."

"Move to the new position and make sure that you take the necessary precautions. Plans are in place to keep the American aircraft busy elsewhere."

"Of course, Khan, we will move immediately. We will have the missiles ready, just in case. I will report in once we are ready."

The phone beeped again, indicating the call was terminated. Khan looked at the timing, thirty-five seconds. He believed it would take at least a minute of conversation for the Americans to crack the commercial encryption system. He put the phone away and turned to Yanuk.

"My men have been successful. You will have your five days, Russian." Khan turned his back on him and walked down the slope to his camp, dialing on his phone.

"Yes?" an unfamiliar voice answered.

"It's Khan. Tell Dostiger that everything is proceeding on schedule."

There was a pause as the message was relayed to the arms dealer. For security reasons, Dostiger rarely spoke on the phone, preferring to leave the handset with one of his bodyguards.

"Are you there?" the voice asked.

"Yes."

"Dostiger wants to talk to you."

There was a pause as the phone changed hands.

"How are you, Khan?"

"I am well. It is good to hear your voice, my son."

"Yes. I have been busy with our Iranian friends. How is our project progressing?"

"We have had minor setbacks but nothing that cannot be resolved."

"Minor setbacks?"

"My men dealt with an American patrol."

"Americans? Already?"

"This is not an issue, Dostiger; the arrangements I made with the Taliban remain in place. The Americans will not come in force, and if they do, it will be too late."

"So the digging is on schedule?"

"Yes, we will finish here as planned. Do not doubt me, my son. It is Allah's will that has brought us here and it is Allah's will that we succeed."

"Yes, Allah's will. Of course."

"You may not be a believer, Dostiger, but you are still guided by Allah's hand. With your help I will drive the Americans from our lands, as I did the Russians before them."

Dostiger laughed. "Khan, with my weapons you cannot fail. And once we give our brothers in Iran what they want, then Afghanistan will be yours."

CHAPTER 6

TEHRAN, IRAN

Mohammad Rostam was not a man who made jokes or laughed at others' attempts at humor. His office in the Iranian Ministry of Intelligence and Security reflected this demeanor. The furniture was utilitarian and devoid of personal items. The desk was usually Spartan, but today Rostam was sorting through a pile of reports, his brow furrowed into a deep crease as he furiously thumbed through them.

He continued to turn pages as he picked up the phone. "This is the director of Special Projects. Have Agent Ebadi come to my office immediately." Without waiting for a reply he hung up, his eyes never leaving the open document.

Rostam was still reading when a soft knock heralded the presence of Afsaneh Ebadi.

"Enter!"

She swung the heavy door open, elegantly striding into his office.

"Good afternoon, sir."

Rostam's eyes lingered over her. Everything about Saneh was sensual. Long raven hair framed her high cheekbones and almond-shaped eyes. Her hourglass figure was evident despite the tailored business suit.

He appreciated her beauty, however, unlike his colleagues, did not lust after her. For him, her looks were simply an asset, another tool in his substantial pool of resources.

"Agent Ebadi, your area of operations is Eastern Europe, isn't it?"

"Yes, sir."

"What do you know about Dostiger's current activities?"

"Dostiger, the arms dealer?"

"Yes."

"Sir, I haven't seen any recent reporting but it would be safe to assume he is still expanding his business."

"I don't want assumptions, Agent Ebadi. Tell me what you actually know."

"He has extensive access into both the former Soviet arms market and the wider European markets. Generally he only deals with sensitive high-end military technology, providing sophisticated weapons to the highest bidder."

"Who's he been dealing with?"

"We've linked him to various Islamic terrorist organizations and also to some governments, including North Korea, Pakistan, and China. As you're aware, we have also employed his services."

"What about the Guards? Has Dostiger been linked to them?"

Saneh paused, thinking. The Iranian Revolutionary Guards were a rival of MOIS and it was well known that Rostam hated them. They had become a formidable military force with far too much influence over the government. In the eyes of many Iranians the Guardians of the Revolution had become Iran's greatest threat.

"Sir, I believe the Guards have used Dostiger's services on at least one occasion. In 2004 they delivered a shipment of advanced surface-to-air missiles to Hezbollah."

"2004? Didn't Hezbollah shoot down an Israeli passenger jet in 2004?"

"Yes, sir, but my sources suggested it wasn't Hezbollah. They believed a third party facilitated the attack prior to Hezbollah receiving the shipment."

"And you think that third party was Dostiger?"

"Yes, sir, that's correct. The attack was a presale demonstration."

"Ruthless bastard!" Rostam smiled. "Have the Guards used him since?"

"Not that we are aware of, most of their weapons procurement has been small arms and explosives sourced through low-level traders and delivered direct to their client organizations. As you know, sensitive weapons procurement is primarily a MOIS responsibility."

"And our most recent dealings with him?"

"It would have to be last year when my team brokered a deal for the purchase of Israeli Spike missiles for reverse engineering."

Rostam's eyes narrowed, his voice low and questioning, "You said before we didn't have any recent reporting of his activities. If we have been dealing with Dostiger as recently as last year, how is it we haven't kept a close eye on him?"

"We do have a source in Kiev who has low-level access into Dostiger's organization, but reporting is minimal. Dostiger has very strict operational security and there have been no opportunities to penetrate any of his more sensitive ventures."

"So you are telling me that we know nothing about his recent activities?"

"Frankly, sir, Dostiger has not been a priority on the MOIS Eastern European collection plan. He poses little threat to us and we consider him more of an asset than a liability."

"Well, Agent Ebadi, Dostiger has just become a priority target. The Guards have contracted him to source a WMD for them." Rostam slid a file across the desk and gestured to the seat in front of him. "Sit down."

Saneh lowered herself into the chair, crossed her legs, and opened the file in her lap. She scanned the pages with interest. The report provided the bare details of Dostiger's contract with the Guards to procure a weapon of mass destruction. The exact location and nature of the WMD was missing but the overall information was assessed as reliable. Saneh realized the information could only have come from within the highest ranks of the Guards' leadership.

"Well, Ebadi, you're the Dostiger expert. Is he capable of delivering a WMD?"

Saneh matched his gaze and handed back the report. "Sir, when we first started dealing with Dostiger he was unable to source any significant WMD capability for us. However, that was over three years ago and now there are new factors at play." She gathered her thoughts before continuing. "The former Soviet states have come under increased economic pressure. He's also continued to develop new client and procurement contacts."

"So it's possible then. What type of weapon do you think he could deliver?"

"With this limited information, it's hard to say. Whatever it is, it would probably originate from Russia, and it's more likely to be chemical or biological than nuclear. The Russians claim to have a tight hold on their WMDs, but with the right contacts and the right price, you could probably get one out. It all depends on how much money the Guards are offering Dostiger."

"Funding isn't an issue here. If Dostiger has access you can be sure the Guards will meet his price."

Saneh looked concerned. "If the Guards get their hands on a WMD, it will give them the capability to influence not only our government, but other nations as well. This would seriously affect our national interests."

"You are absolutely correct, Agent Ebadi." Rostam's voice took on a harder tone. "We both know the Guards want nothing less than complete control over the military and eventually the government. Such a weapon would give them the influence to stage a coup or even start a war!"

He leaned forward, fixing her with an intense stare. "We cannot sit idly by while Dostiger procures the tools that could allow the Guards to plunge the entire region into war. The Americans need little excuse to destroy us as it is."

She nodded. "And the Israelis won't risk the Guards being able to provide a WMD to any of their terrorist pets."

"Exactly, we must maintain the status quo and allow our legitimate government time to develop our own weapons gradually and with diplomacy."

"Then what do we need to do to stop Dostiger? Is there any other information on how he is getting this weapon?"

Rostam tapped the report on his desk. "Currently this is it. I have already initiated a covert investigation into his dealings with the Guards, but we're limited in how far we can go with them. We cannot afford a confrontation while they remain influential within the Supreme Council."

"Do you want me to commence planning an operation in the Ukraine?"

"That is exactly what I want you to do." Rostam didn't usually trust women to lead field operations. From his perspective they had their uses, but only under the direction of capable men. However, he had no 'capable' men available. A recent Israeli counterintelligence operation had robbed him of two of his best operatives, so Saneh would have to do. "You are now seconded to Special Projects and will report directly to me. You are to be in Kiev within the next forty-eight hours and initiate a collection operation against Dostiger."

"This is a priority mission?"

He nodded. "I'm overseeing this personally. My strike team is on standby and we will intervene as soon as you have the intelligence we need. I cannot overstate the importance of this operation. The Guards must be stopped. Do you have any questions?"

"Just one more, sir. Is it likely that any other agencies are dealing with this situation?"

"I doubt it, but if they are, I am sure you can put your charms to good use."

"Yes, sir." She gave a slight grimace.

"That's all. Contact me once you arrive in Kiev." Rostam turned his eyes back to the reports on his desk. As she rose and turned to leave, he raised his head. "And Agent Ebadi. I'm sure I don't need to tell you how useful a WMD would be to MOIS, do I?"

***

The Tandis shopping mall in central Tehran was an ideal location for a covert meeting. Bustling crowds and numerous exit routes aided counter-surveillance measures while the thick concrete walls of the building blocked the signals of most electronic surveillance equipment.

Ivan had planned his meeting meticulously. He had already conducted a reconnaissance of the venue, his security team was in place, and now he just needed to wait. Browsing the shelves of a bookstore, dressed in a cheap nondescript suit, he appeared to be another middle-aged worker shopping during his lunch break. The store attendant barely noticed him as he glanced at his phone and strolled out into the white-tiled mall. The text message from his security team was brief:

Client is in location. Clean.

Ivan had rehearsed the route. A short stroll through the crowds took him to the discreet location he had selected earlier, a local Persian restaurant popular for business meetings.

"*Salaam*." The well-dressed maître d' greeted him with a broad smile on his face and a flourish of his hand.

"Good afternoon. The booking is for two. The name is Amin," Ivan replied in English.

The headwaiter was taken aback for a moment by the crisp British accent. He continued in English. "Of course, sir, your friend is waiting."

The rough-hewn wooden tables were packed with businessmen consuming traditional cuisine, drinking strong tea, and smoking cigars. A light haze had spread across the room; the rich aromas of the food and the earthy smells of the cigars created a comforting atmosphere.

Ivan's Iranian contact was sitting in a booth near the rear exit. Two cushioned benches were built into the alcove, divided by a simple table. Dim lighting and ornate wooden barriers provided an element of privacy.

"Ah, Ivan, I hardly recognized you with your hair," the man exclaimed as he shook the Russian's hand vigorously.

Ivan self-consciously touched his wig as he sat down. "Ah well, don't tell anyone I'm balding." He cupped his hand to his mouth. "It's a secret." Although his appearance differed, his relaxed smile put the Iranian at ease.

"So, my friend, what is this information you are so eager to share with me?" Ivan asked as he leaned forward, pouring dark tea for both of them.

"You must understand. This is very sensitive, very important."

"You know I am always generous. If the information is as significant as you say it is, then the reward will match."

The Iranian lowered his voice. "We have information indicating the Guards are attempting to source a weapon of mass destruction."

Ivan stopped pouring the tea, the cup left half-full.

The Iranian continued. "Reliable information, of course."

He put the pot down and smiled. "How?"

"They are talking to an arms dealer based in the Ukraine, a man known as Dostiger. This is everything we have on him." The man slid a memory stick across the table.

He listened intently as the Iranian explained the details. He took no notes, relying on the stick and his memory.

The meeting finished quickly. Within an hour Ivan was in the backseat of a car headed for Tehran International Airport. He summarized the meeting into a few short paragraphs and typed the message into his phone. Then he attached the contents of the memory stick, compressed the file, and embedded it into a document. Within thirty seconds the file had passed through no less than fifteen separate email accounts before it arrived in an innocuous-looking account monitored by staff in the PRIMAL Headquarters.

CHAPTER 7

SYDNEY, AUSTRALIA

Aden Bishop sat in a café alongside the Elizabeth Bay Marina, watching the sailing boats return from a day out on the blue waters of Sydney Harbor. He smiled as he watched a couple laughing and walking along the wooden decking of the wharf, their young daughter racing ahead, trying valiantly to catch a seagull. He was envious for a moment. Sometimes he wished he could lead a similarly idyllic life. Since that fateful day eight years ago when he'd accepted an invitation from Vance, he'd been exposed to the dark underbelly of the world. There was no going back.

He rolled the ice cubes in his gin and tonic and downed the drink. "Another Bombay and tonic, thanks, mate," he said to a passing waiter with a smile.

"Straight away, Mr. Bishop."

He grimaced at the formality. As a regular at the café, he knew all the staff, yet they still insisted on calling him Mr. Bishop. Like most of the people in Sydney who knew him, the staff simply thought of Bishop as a business executive, the kind that was successful enough to forgo a suit and tie, comfortable in a polo shirt and jeans.

To the casual observer Bishop was nothing special, an average-looking man with a crooked nose, short dark hair, and a strong jaw. Yet subtle differences set him apart from the soft corporate types. Piercing eyes, dark brown to the point of being black, showed an alertness absent among those enduring the daily grind of office work. His casual clothing hid the solid build of an athlete, a conditioned warrior. Not many noticed these subtleties, and even fewer guessed at who the real Aden Bishop was, or the shadowy world he inhabited.

Today was an opportunity for Bishop to reveal this world to an old friend, something he eagerly anticipated. He was checking the emails on his phone when a familiar voice startled him.

"Hello, Aden."

He looked up into the smiling face of Mirza Mansoor.

"Mirza, it's bloody good to see you." Bishop jumped to his feet and grasped the lightly built Indian's hand. "Been far, far too long. I haven't seen you in over a year."

"Closer to two, I think."

"You might be right. The last couple have sped past, that's for sure." Bishop directed Mirza to the other chair as he spoke. "And you, look at you. Haven't changed a bit." Bishop may have developed a few gray hairs and a few more wrinkles, but Mirza still looked the same as he had in Sierra Leone. His fledgling mustache had grown into a neatly trimmed beard but his hard Asiatic features showed no signs of age. Bishop had always thought he looked like a modern reincarnation of a Mongol warrior. There had to be Genghis Khan's blood somewhere in his lineage.

"We all grow older as surely as we grow wiser, my friend," Mirza said as he sat down.

"Well, I don't know about wiser," Bishop replied with a grin, as the waiter delivered his next gin and tonic. Mirza ordered an iced tea.

"So, Mirza, what do you think of Sydney?" Bishop asked, gesturing out toward the harbor, where the sun's rays had begun dropping behind the white sails of the Opera House.

"I've never seen anything like it. So beautiful. Thank you for bringing me here."

"Not a drama at all. Means a lot to me that you could make it. Although I do have an admission to make," Bishop said, pausing to sip from his glass. "I may have brought you to Sydney under false pretenses."

Mirza turned to him with a look of shock on his face. "Do you mean tomorrow is not your birthday?"

Bishop snorted into his drink. Wiping the gin from his face, he laughed. "No, Mirza, my birthday is in December. Remember we visited the temples in Cambodia on my thirtieth?"

Mirza frowned. "I believe you are right, so why did you say it was your birthday?"

"Because if I didn't have a good excuse, you wouldn't have cut short your job in Papua New Guinea. You're far too loyal to your employer. You've barely had a day off and you've never turned down a job. You're the most steadfast man I know."

The Indian dropped his head and studied the tablecloth.

"Mirza, I invited you here because I have a proposition."

Mirza looked up as the waiter placed his drink on the table. He thanked the man and took a sip from the glass. "What sort of proposition?"

"I want you to come and work with me."

"In logistics? I don't think I'm cut out for that sort of work. I'm a soldier, Aden, not an officer."

"A soldier who guards oil pipelines. Come on, Mirza, is that what you really want to be doing? Let's face it, you're a glorified security guard."

Mirza's hard features darkened. "I have a good job, Aden. A good job that lets me support my mother. Some of us have responsibilities; not all of us can run around the world chasing pretty girls and driving fast cars."

Mirza was back studying the tablecloth, his ears and face red with shame. For a man who had served his country as a warrior, to be called a mere security guard was a slap in the face.

"Mirza, I'm sorry. That's not what I meant."

The former soldier looked up, his eyes shining. "That's the problem with you, Aden, you never think."

He contemplated the words for a moment before the awkward silence was broken by the shrill ringtone of Bishop's phone. "Excuse me, I have to take this."

Mirza nodded and Bishop headed over to the railing on the side of the wharf. He answered the call, the screen of the phone indicating the line was secure.

"Bishop, it's Vance. Sorry to call during your break but we have a situation developing."

"What's up?"

"Getting a lot of reporting that something big is going down in the 'Ghan with the Iranian Guards. It's a little sketchy at the moment but I think they're trying to get their hands on a WMD."

"In Afghanistan?"

"Yep, the Khod Valley, to be precise."

"The Iranian Revolutionary Guards Corps are trying to recover a weapon of mass destruction in Afghanistan? Are you taking the piss, Vance?"

"Look, Bish, I ain't gonna go over the details now. Bottom line is we need you back ASAP. I'm recalling the whole team."

"Yeah, OK, but what about Mirza?"

"Mirza? Damn. I forgot about that. I guess that's up to you, buddy. If you think he's ready, we'll use him. We're gonna need all hands on deck for this one."

"And transport?"

"The Gulfstream will be at Sydney Airport in a little under an hour."

"I'll be there."

"OK, see you soon." Vance terminated the call.

Bishop looked back across to where Mirza was still sitting watching the boats on the harbor. He pocketed the phone and walked back.

"Walk with me, Mirza, I want to talk to you about something," he said, taking his jacket from the back of the chair. He left some money on the table and they walked down the wharf.

"Aden, are you alright? The phone call wasn't bad news, was it?"

"Huh? No, not at all. I just have a lot on my mind."

"You still haven't told me why I am here."

"Mirza, are you happy with what you are doing?"

"Like I said, it allows me to take care of my mother."

"What if money wasn't an issue? Would you still do what you do?"

Mirza stopped and turned to face Bishop. "The truth? No, I

wouldn't. There is no honor in it. I joined the army to be a warrior. To protect women and children, not pipelines and politicians."

"I thought as much." Bishop looked him in the eye. "Mirza, I want you to come and work with me."

"Doing what? Shipping cargo around the world?"

Bishop laughed. "Mirza, I don't ship cargo."

"But you said you work for Lascar Logistics?" Mirza looked confused. He'd always thought Bishop worked for Lascar, an air-freight company based in the UAE.

Bishop started walking again, heading into the adjacent park, distancing them from the tourists on the wharf.

"Mirza, I work for an arm of Lascar Logistics known as Priority Movements Airlift, or, as we call ourselves, PRIMAL."

"So you do express delivery?"

"We conduct clandestine operations across the globe targeting those who exist outside the reach of justice."

Mirza stopped walking and stared at Bishop for a moment. "I'm sorry." He shook his head in disbelief. "You said targeting those who exist outside the reach of justice?"

"Yes."

"Like who?"

"Criminals, warlords, terrorists, drug dealers, corrupt politicians, businessmen, the list is long, Mirza. It's a full-time job."

Mirza's eyebrows furrowed but his eyes gleamed. "What? Who? I don't understand. Are you some sort of government agency? Who do you work for?"

"PRIMAL works by our own rules, Mirza. We find injustice and we correct it. It's that simple." Bishop grasped his friend by the shoulder. "Remember Sierra Leone? It's the same but without the red tape and political bureaucracies. This is where the honor is, Mirza, bringing a little justice to the world."

"Who funds your operations?"

"Let's just say that PRIMAL has a very wealthy benefactor. The question is, are you interested in joining us?"

They were standing at the end of the park where the open

grassy area met a road. Bishop extended his arm and a cab darted out of the humming traffic and pulled in against the curb. As Bishop opened the door, he turned back to face Mirza.

"There's a Lascar jet waiting at the airport. No doubt you have hundreds of questions, but this isn't the place." He gestured toward the waiting cab. "We'll grab our bags on the way. I'll explain more on the plane. You in?"

CHAPTER 8

LASCAR ISLAND, SOUTHWEST PACIFIC

Any teenage gamer would have stood slack-jawed in awe had they found themselves in the PRIMAL operations room. 'The Bunker,' as it was known, was crammed with computer workstations linked to high-definition screens covering the bare rock walls of the underground room. The monitors displayed everything from satellite imagery to helmet camera feeds and real-time news footage. They were PRIMAL HQ's situational awareness, the eyes into the world that allowed the Bunker's staff to direct covert activities globally.

Everyone was busy at their terminals when Vance barreled into the room.

"Heads up, team. Orders Group in two hours," the voice of the operations director boomed.

Chen Chua, PRIMAL's chief of intelligence, rose from his seat. "The intel brief is good to go. We just have one new piece of information since your last update."

"Outstanding. Give me the lowdown," Vance said as he settled into his huge padded chair in the center of the room.

The slightly built Chinese American raised a remote control and one of the wall screens displayed a digital map. "OK, we just completed a trace on one of the numbers communicating between Afghan and Ukraine. The handset was originally purchased by a Ukrainian firm, Antonov."

Vance swiveled his chair to face the screen, which had zoomed in on satellite imagery of an airfield. "You talking about Antonov, the Ruskies who make transport jets?"

"Close. They're Ukrainian, not Russian. The imagery you see is of Antonov's headquarters and testing facility just outside of Kiev. It seems Dostiger is using someone there as a front man. Similar to how PRIMAL uses Lascar Logistics as cover."

"Got it. So how did we trace the handset?"

"Our usual contact checked some databases," Chua responded curtly. His agent within the US National Security Agency was one of his most sensitive sources. The NSA wasn't aware that someone was accessing its intelligence or its satellites, and Chua wanted to keep it that way.

Vance nodded. "Alright. Continue."

Chua sat back down at his terminal. The desk was littered with energy drink cans and he quickly drank from one before continuing. "We've identified Dostiger's front man at Antonov. It should provide us a solid lead." He pressed the remote again and the screen switched to a biographical data slide with a link analysis diagram. "Bishop's intelligence pack has already been updated. Additionally, I've had our agent, Ivan, move to the Ukraine to provide covert support. Everything is in place for Bishop's team to go in."

"Solid work, bud," Vance said, noting the dark circles under the intelligence chief's eyes. "Is there anything else? What about the 'Ghan?"

"Negative. Until we get Ice on the ground we're not likely to get any new information."

"I'm thinking we partner Mirza with Ice. From what Bishop tells me, he's all over the Afghan piece."

"He's also fluent in Pashto."

"OK, lock it in. What about the Dostiger file? You haven't sent it to Bishop yet, have you?" Vance asked.

"No. I figured it would be better for us to brief him personally."

"Good call, when he finds out about Dostiger, he's gonna lose his shit."

***

The Gulfstream jet's wheels screeched as it touched down on the small tropical island. A cloud of birds took flight, startled by the roar of reverse thrust that echoed off the basalt cliffs. Like the battlements of an ancient castle, huge slabs of gray rock jutted out of the lush jungle that covered the slopes of a now extinct volcano.

Mirza had his face pressed to the window, eyes wide. "PRIMAL is based here? It's beautiful!" he exclaimed, looking out at the clear blue waters of the Pacific rolling in on a pristine white beach.

Bishop laughed. "Yeah, we're pretty lucky. Our little piece of paradise."

They taxied past a line of shabby transportable buildings and Mirza looked on curiously. Apart from the buildings, aviation fuel tanks, and a large metal hangar built against the cliffs, the island seemed empty.

"So is this place your actual headquarters, Aden?"

"Yep."

"It is very small." To an outsider the modest airfield appeared to be an old refueling depot for aircraft hauling freight across the Pacific Ocean.

"Wait till you see the facility."

The sleek business jet turned off the end of the runway and rolled into the World War II–era metal hangar that butted up against vertical cliffs. As the aircraft came to a halt, Bishop jumped to his feet, grasping his backpack.

"Welcome to Lascar Island, our home away from home," he said.

As they stepped off the aircraft into the hangar, the oppressive humidity hit them. Mirza was glad Bishop had given him time to change into shorts and a T-shirt.

Two electric golf carts waited for them on the concrete floor of the hangar, along with one of the most intimidating men Mirza had ever seen. He stood well over six feet five, with broad shoulders, massive arms, and a trim waist. Mirza was a big fan of eighties action movies, and he thought this man looked exactly like Dolph Lundgren in his prime: the same square features, even the short-cropped blond hair and cold blue eyes. He could've stepped straight out of a Marine Corps recruiting poster.

"Mirza, stop gawking and get over here and meet Ice."

The Indian suddenly realized he had stopped walking.

Trotting forward, he extended his hand to the behemoth.

Ice grasped his hand firmly, a broad grin splitting his chiseled features. "Mirza, bro, it's awesome to finally meet you. You wouldn't believe how much this crazy bastard talks about you. Welcome to the team."

"Thanks, Ice," Mirza said. The American accent surprised him. He almost expected something a little more Eastern Bloc.

"No worries at all. Any friend of Bish is a friend of mine, and considering you saved his life, you go straight to the top of the pile."

Mirza blushed and looked back at Bishop.

"Cut it out, you big dolt. You're embarrassing him," Bishop said as he climbed into one of the golf carts. "Mirza, I've got to report in, but Ice will show you around the facility and get you squared away before orders. Ice, we still on for sixteen hundred?"

"Yeah, buddy, no change."

"OK, you kids have fun," Bishop said as he drove off.

Ice picked up Mirza's bags and dropped them into his cart. "Got the warning order an hour ago. Looks like you and I will be banging into Afghan. You good to go on free-fall?"

"I have over fifty jumps."

"You'll be fine; when we get some downtime I'll run you through the basics again."

"I would appreciate that."

"Don't be overwhelmed, bro, just take it all in your stride," Ice continued as they jumped into his cart. "Things tend to go down pretty damn quick when you're on team. Have to be flexible and ready to roll."

They pulled away from the business jet and followed Bishop's cart as it motored toward the granite cliffs at the back of the hangar. As they drew closer, a split appeared in the middle of the massive wall. Hydraulics whined and two false-stone doors slid apart, allowing the two carts to pass through.

Ice turned to Mirza as they passed through the gap. "Welcome to the house of PRIMAL."

CHAPTER 9

PRIMAL HEADQUARTERS

Mirza sat in the cart, his eyes bugged out like golf balls as they drove into another, even larger, aircraft hangar.

"A hangar inside a hangar?" he whispered. Ahead was a vast cavern carved deep into the solid rock of the volcano. It easily contained the two large transport aircraft that were parked inside among an assortment of equipment and supplies.

"Pretty impressive, hey? Best thing is, it stays cool all year round," Ice said as he drove across the polished concrete floor.

Mirza suddenly realized the temperature had dropped significantly; even under the brilliant lights on the roof, the cavern was still cool and dry.

"The Japs built part of it during World War Two," Ice explained. "Abandoned it at the end of the war. Then we found it a couple of years ago, dug it out, and moved in."

"You couldn't ask for a better hideout."

"We're the only ones that know it's here."

"You're surely joking. No one outside of PRIMAL knows that this exists?"

"Correct. Well, they know the island is a refueling and maintenance facility for Lascar Logistics, they just don't know what else goes on here."

"But what about communications traffic? Surely the Americans would pick it up with their satellites."

"I'm not a geek, but from what I understand, it's all routed off the island. The guys will brief you on what you need to know."

Mirza whistled. "This must have cost a king's ransom. Who pays for it all?"

"Let's just say our little brotherhood has a very wealthy benefactor."

Ice swerved the little cart toward an imposing four-engine

aircraft that Mirza recognized immediately as an Ilyushin-76 heavy lift transporter. The Russian-built jet was a common sight at airfields all over the world, easily identified by its hulking silhouette and bulbous nose. With its high wings it always reminded Mirza of a vulture. They drove under one of the wings and pulled up at the rear ramp.

"Hey, Mitch," Ice yelled as he led Mirza into the aircraft's hold. "Get your ass out here. There's someone you have to meet."

A bearded face appeared over the top of a cargo pallet.

"What's up, chaps?" a distinctly British voice asked.

"Just showing the new kid around the block."

"Hang on a tick then." Mitch scrambled over and jumped down, landing next to Mirza. He wiped his hands on his flight suit and shook Mirza's hand.

"Welcome aboard. Name's Mitch."

Ice explained, "Mitch is PRIMAL's resident tech head. If you break it or you want it souped up, then Mitch is your man."

From the neck up, the Brit looked like a geek; his ears stuck out from a shaved scalp and he sported a goofy grin that made his scraggly beard seem a little comical. However, Mirza noticed that, like Ice, he appeared very fit. It was evident that the PRIMAL team took their physical conditioning seriously.

"Yeah, that is kind of true," Mitch said. "I take care of all the team's toys, although it does seem I spend most of my time fixing kit that this oaf breaks."

Ice laughed. "Screw you, bro. You spend all your time messing around with your precious airplane."

"How many times has your ass been on the wire, champ, and I've saved it with the Pain Train, eh? More than once, so pay some respect to the big girl. She's got feelings too." Mitch patted the aircraft's aluminum skin like it was a living creature.

"The Pain Train?" Mirza asked.

"Yeah," Ice responded. "PRIMAL's specialist airborne platform. Looks like a run-of-the-mill air transporter, but Mitch has decked this baby out to do just about anything. She can jam radar, track aircraft, deliver bombs, drop supplies, and even launch drones. She's an all-singing, all-dancing Special Operations support aircraft, state-of-the-art!"

"All that from one platform? That's superb!" Mirza said as he inspected the aircraft.

"Well, if you like that, my good man, then you're going to love this." Mitch reached into the pocket of his flight suit and pulled out a device. "This is a little piece of technology I custom-built myself. I call it iPRIMAL."

"iPRIMAL?" Mirza said, staring at what looked like a large smartphone.

"Well, actually it's your combat interface, but iPRIMAL makes it sound sexier." Mitch handed Mirza the device. "That little bad boy lets you harness all the power of PRIMAL when you're not at home. It can access any information that we can feed over a satellite connection."

Mirza turned it over in his hand. It was a little larger than his iPhone. He prodded the screen with a finger and it activated, displaying a variety of menu options.

"Ice'll teach you how to use it. He's a total nerd."

Ice laughed. "Yeah, I'd make a great instructor. It took me weeks to figure out all the functions. Damn thing's built for little midget hands."

"You got it in the end, mate," Mitch said.

"So this is for me?" Mirza asked.

Mitch flashed a smile. "Of course. You're part of the team now, squire. Right, sorry to be rude, Mirza, but I've a ton of work to do to get this old girl ready, so I'm going to have to leave you chaps to it."

Mirza held up the iPRIMAL. "Thanks again."

Mitch was already deep in the cargo hold. "Don't mention it."

Ice and Mirza climbed back into the cart and headed toward a set of doors at the rear of the cavern.

"So what's your background, Mirza? Bishop said something about the Special Frontier Force?"

"Yes, five years. I was in Special Group." Special Group

was an even more elite part of the Indian SFF, specializing in intelligence gathering and counterterrorism operations. "What about you?"

"Me? Ten years in the Marines, five more with the CIA."

"Have you been working with PRIMAL for long?" Mirza asked, trying to calculate Ice's age. He guessed the big man was a little older than Bishop, probably around thirty-five.

"You could say that. Back in the company days I used to work with Vance."

"Vance?"

"Yeah, you'll meet the boss soon enough. By the way, I heard about what happened with you and Bish in Sierra Leone. Bold move, very bold move."

"I had to follow Aden's lead."

"He's one crazy cat, that's for sure. But you didn't have to follow him." Ice turned his head to look Mirza in the eye. "Glad you did though, because between me and you, that's what got you into PRIMAL." Ice stopped the golf cart in front of a pair of doors imbedded in the rock. He jumped out, activated a security panel, and the doors slid open, revealing a freight elevator the size of a double-car garage. It easily accommodated the cart.

"So you've seen the hangar, now we'll take you down into the facility." Ice activated another panel and the elevator jolted slightly, beginning its descent. "We've got three levels. First is accommodation, mess, gym, and all the comfort stuff. The second is where we're heading, training facilities, armory, workshops, etcetera, and the third is the Bunker."

The elevator jolted to a halt. "We have to be in the Bunker in a little over an hour, so we're going to take this opportunity to get you kitted out."

The doors opened to a well-lit corridor carved into rock. It forked off in two directions and Ice pointed down the left-hand side. "I'll show you later, but down there we've got the kill house and the shooting range." He turned the cart right and they continued.

"You have a kill house?" Mirza's eyebrows raised.

"Sure, but that's not the best bit."

They drove into a massive cave that clearly served as a warehouse. One side of the space housed all manner of vehicles: Jet Skis, four-wheel drives, motorcycles, and even a couple of mini-subs. On the other side, shelves were stacked with gear, including racks of weapons ranging from compact pistols to automatic grenade launchers. Any piece of equipment anyone could possibly want for special operations or covert activities was held in the one facility.

Mirza felt like a kid in a toy store and he looked at Ice with a huge grin on his face. He laughed as he left the cart and walked over for a closer look at the mini-subs.

Ice yelled after him, "I call it 'Warmart.' Now let's get you kitted out before we head up to the Bunker for orders."

CHAPTER 10

THE BUNKER

"Welcome to the Bunker. This is where it all happens," Ice said as Mirza followed him through the sliding door.

"So it seems," whispered the Indian. The rest of PRIMAL headquarters seemed like a ghost town in comparison. The operations room was packed with an eclectic audience seated along the walls beneath huge LCD screens. Key staff were busy among the central computer terminals. Mirza guessed that most were former US military; the room looked like a futuristic version of a US Army command post he had once visited, except in place of the uniforms were a variety of outfits, from Mitch's flight suit to Ice's Hawaiian shirt.

Mirza noticed Bishop sitting in the corner and gave him a wide grin. Bishop caught his eye and gave him a thumbs-up.

Ice directed the new PRIMAL operative to a seat along the rough-cut wall. As Mirza sat, his eyes were drawn to a heavily-built, bald-headed African American who was talking to a smaller Asian.

"That's Vance, the director. He's in charge of operations," Ice whispered. "The little guy is Chua, our chief of intelligence. They run the show."

Everyone went quiet and stopped what they were doing as Vance moved to the front of the room. He stood impassive in front of the central LCD screen, crossed his muscular arms, and locked eyes with Mirza.

"Before we begin I want to welcome the newest member of our team. Jump up, Mirza." Vance's deep voice filled the entire room.

Mirza stood abashed as all eyes turned to him.

"Mirza, my name's Vance, and I'm in charge of this ragtag bunch of pirates. Sorry we haven't had time for formal introductions. There is a situation developing that requires a bit of high speed and low drag, if you know what I mean."

"Sir, I am at your service," Mirza said. If he was intimidated, it didn't show.

"And we appreciate having you on the team. Make yourself comfortable and we'll get this ball game started," Vance said as he headed back to his seat. "Chua, please outline the intel picture."

PRIMAL's chief of intelligence was far more animated than Vance, moving around the room as he spoke. "You may have already heard about the Taliban uprising occurring in southern Afghanistan," Chua started. He pressed his remote and the central screen displayed a map overlaid with broad red arrows. "For two days now insurgents have commenced large-scale offensive operations in both Helmand and Kandahar."

He used the laser pointer in the remote to indicate on the map as he briefed. "Coalition reporting assesses that the offensive in Helmand involves over two thousand insurgents. British and US forces are currently restricted to their bases and have sustained a high number of casualties. Insurgent forces now occupy a number of minor towns in the area."

There were some hushed voices from the back of the audience and Chua looked up from his notes, over to where Bishop sat whispering to one of the other operatives. "Aden, did you have something to add?"

Bishop leaned back in his chair and spoke up. "Chen, don't get me wrong. This is all sorts of messed up, but what does it have to do with us? The Yanks have more than enough assets in-country to target the insurgents. Surely PRIMAL has more worthy causes to fight without getting involved? What about our upcoming Congo operation or —"

Vance's deep voice interrupted. "There's more to it, Bish. Listen." The director swiveled around in his chair and shot him a stern look.

Chua continued, "I've assessed that this Taliban offensive is supported by a third party and was orchestrated to draw attention away from a specific, more concerning operation. This is based on multiple reliable sources. Firstly, a satellite phone call was intercepted from the Khod Valley in Oruzgan Province."

Chua pressed a button on the remote and the voice cut was displayed on the screen behind him. He gave everyone a minute to look at it.

TRANSMISSION COMMENCED

Original Language: Pashto.

PERS 1: Khan, it's Khalid.

PERS 2: What happened?

PERS 1: We ambushed American forces moving up the valley, report five armored vehicles destroyed.

PERS 2: Very good. Did you take any casualties?

PERS 1: We have had no losses, although we............ *static*............

PERS 2: Good work, brother. Dostiger will be pleased. Did any of the infidels escape?

PERS 1: No, we took care of them all, the jammer stopped them contacting............ *static*............

PERS 2: Good, good, the engineer says it will take no more than five days for us to finish the excavation. Do you............ *static*............

TRANSMISSION BROKEN

Ice's brow furrowed. "Is this telling us that a bunch of Talibs wiped out a whole goddamn Stryker patrol?"

"Related coalition reporting indicates the patrol is missing," Chua replied. "I assess it's been destroyed. Obviously these are not your usual run-of-the-mill Taliban. They're not hiding in the hills shooting off rockets willy-nilly and blowing themselves up with IEDs."

"So what are they doing?" Ice asked. "Sounds like some sort of recovery op."

Chua nodded. "That's exactly what they're doing. A Taliban unit led by someone called Khan is defending this excavation site in Oruzgan. The wider offensive is orchestrated to slow the coalition response and buy time to complete the excavation."

The Chinese American looked down at his notes before continuing, "So what are they excavating and why? Well, further communications analysis has indicated that these Taliban are working for an arms dealer in the Ukraine known as Dostiger. Additionally, one of our agents in Iran has revealed that the Revolutionary Guards have contracted Dostiger to acquire a WMD for them."

Chua took a sip from a can of energy drink before continuing. "We assess that this Dostiger is using the Taliban to recover some sort of WMD the Soviet Army left behind in Afghanistan, possibly buried inside one of the many caves or tunnel complexes. Historical CIA reporting reveals that the Russians were conducting experimental weapons testing on the Afghan population in the eighties. My assessment is that the remains of a biological or chemical weapons-testing facility still exist in the vicinity of the Khod Valley."

Mirza slowly raised his hand. "Ah, sir, apologies for interrupting, but I was wondering why the Guards need a WMD. Doesn't Iran have its own weapons program? From what I've seen in the news, it's nearing completion." A few other PRIMAL operators nodded.

"I am glad you asked, Mirza. Although the Revolutionary Guards were initially created to protect the regime, they have become so powerful that Iran's leadership no longer trusts them. The Iranian government has isolated the Guards from WMD development. They are concerned that with a WMD the Guards could rally enough support to launch a coup." The intelligence officer paused to look back at Mirza. "Does that answer your question?"

"Yes, sir. Thank you."

"OK, so the Guards are running unsanctioned operations to acquire this weapon. Our source reveals that the Iranian intelligence organization, MOIS, is currently aware of what the Guards are doing and has initiated an investigation. MOIS doesn't seem to know about the Afghan link, but they are going after the arms dealer, Dostiger, and have deployed a team to the Ukraine."

The corner of Chua's mouth turned up in a slight smirk as he caught Bishop's eye. "Oh, and Aden, the MOIS team leader is reported to be a very attractive young woman by the name of Afsaneh; probably not your type, though. My reports indicate she speaks half a dozen languages and holds a Masters in English. Not exactly catwalk material, if you know what I mean." Chua smiled at Bishop and everyone in the room laughed.

Bishop looked embarrassed. He didn't think anyone but Ice knew about the model he had briefly entertained in Spain a couple of months back. "Yeah. Thanks, Chen, that's very interesting, but tell us more about this arms dealer. How long has he been working with the Guards?" Bishop sat forward in his chair, eyes burning intensely. It was no secret that he was obsessed with the Iranian Revolutionary Guards and their links to terrorists ever since the attack on Flight LY395 that claimed the lives of his parents.

"We've just received a comprehensive file on Dostiger. You'll get it after these orders," Chua answered.

Bishop wondered why he hadn't been given the file yet. He slouched back in his chair. "What about our coverage in Kiev?" He knew from an earlier warning order that he was being tasked with the Ukraine job.

"At this stage it's very limited." Chua's tone was serious again. "The Forward Integrated Support Team that you'll be working with has minimal knowledge of the area. One of the FIST members was born in the Ukraine but hasn't lived there since he was a boy."

"And our own HUMINT? Does Ivan have any of his old connections?" Bishop asked.

"Our network doesn't extend to the Ukraine. I've tasked Ivan to start recruiting sources in but initially you'll be starting from scratch. In the intelligence pack you'll be given, we've identified Dostiger's front man who works for Antonov. It should provide a starting point."

Chua checked his notebook before concluding, "OK, that's all the intelligence we have. Any updates will be provided directly to the field. Are there any further questions?" Chua looked around the room before returning to his seat.

"Thank you, Chua," Vance said as he moved to the front. "Team, from the intelligence chief's brief I'm sure you understand that the shit is rolling downhill at a rapid rate."

He nodded at Bishop before continuing. "I appreciate that we don't usually do ops in the 'Ghan but if we don't step in, the Guards could have a WMD within four days. With everyone else bogged down fighting the Talibs down south, there ain't gonna be anyone else to stop them. As for Dostiger in the Ukraine, we've leaked this to both the Israelis and the US, but their cluster-fuck bureaucratic systems mean that by the time they decide to act, it'll be all over.

"Bottom line is we have to mount an operation in both Ukraine and Afghanistan. We can't risk the Guards supplying a bunch of jihad-preaching fuckers like Hezbollah with a WMD. They get their hands on this shit and it's war in the Middle East."

Vance looked over the room. Satisfied that he had everyone's complete attention, he crossed his arms and continued. "Alright, team, these are the initial orders for the op. Our mission is to target Dostiger's operations in order to deny the Iranian Revolutionary Guards access to a WMD."

Vance directed his intense gaze at Ice then Mirza. "Our main effort will be the insertion of a recon team into the 'Ghan. Task: To locate the Taliban WMD extraction team and use offensive fires from the Pain Train to destroy them before they can recover the weapon. Ice, I need you and Mirza on the ground ASAP. You'll be fully supported by the Pain Train for both surveillance and fire support. Locate the site and Mitch'll smash it. I'll give you confirmatory orders once you're in the air."

Ice looked across at Mitch sitting opposite him and gave the bearded tech guru a slight nod.

Vance continued, "Remember, Ice, you need to stay out of the shit. These aren't the same Taliban we fought in 2001. They're gunned up, well trained, and spoiling for a fight. There are thirty dead Americans who can vouch for that."

"Acknowledged, boss. We'll be in and out like ghosts. The Talibs won't even know we're there," Ice said.

"Bish, you'll take the lead on the Ukraine side of the op. Yeah, Ice is the main effort, but we still need to cover all our bases. We can't count on MOIS to deal with this Dostiger asshole, so you'll fly to Kiev, RV with the FIST, and commence a surveillance operation. Ivan will provide covert support if you need it and we'll position another aircraft in Kiev."

Bishop nodded. "So if anything goes wrong in the 'Ghan, I'll be in place to interdict the WMD, yeah?"

"Bingo."

Bishop looked across the room to Ice and Mirza. "Mirza, if old man Ice is slowing you down, don't stress, I'll take care of things from my end," he said with a wink.

"Remember, Bish," Vance growled, "this is a covert op. No blowing shit up or jazzing up the local law enforcement. If Dostiger realizes we're onto him, he'll just get the fuck out of Dodge. Keep this clean, not like that shitshow in the Philippines."

The recent Philippines operation that Vance was alluding to had started as a simple case of surveillance, followed by a precise assassination. Instead, Bishop and his team had taken it upon themselves to sink a people-smuggler's ship, initiating a gunfight with the criminal's guards and the local authorities.

"OK, OK, I get it."

"This is strictly low-profile, Bish. Chua has worked up your cover. We'll discuss it with you immediately after these orders." Vance cast his gaze over the room before concluding. "OK, y'all, that ends the initial orders for the op. Anyone got any final questions?"

The room was silent.

"Team, we're making this job the highest priority. All other operations have been placed on the back burner. The Bunker will now commence twenty-four-hour ops in support of both teams. Chua will update you as the situation develops and I'll deliver additional orders on the fly. In the meantime, you all know your duties. Let's get to it!"

CHAPTER 11

THE BUNKER

The Bunker launched into a flurry of activity. The staff hit their terminals, scanning for information. Others clustered around the wall-mounted monitors, discussing the finer details of the plan. The cavern echoed with staccato keyboard taps and intense discussions. It was business as usual at PRIMAL HQ.

Chua caught Bishop's eye and nodded to a briefing room. Vance followed. They gathered around a table.

"This should be everything." Chua slid two large envelopes to Bishop. "Passports, credit cards, and enough hard currency to buy your way out of trouble."

Bishop swept the envelopes from the table and slid them into his thigh pocket. "Thanks, mate."

"I take it you've already had a look at the initial intelligence package I sent to your phone?" Chua asked.

"Yeah. The new FIST looks good to go." Chua's package included photos and biographical details for the members of Bishop's new Forward Integrated Support Team. Where possible PRIMAL used these contracted teams to do the dirty work. Usually led by an operative like Bishop, these expendable mercenaries were the best money could buy. It was a way of ensuring a minimal number of people were exposed to the covert organization. Only the PRIMAL operatives ever knew who they really worked for.

Chua nodded in agreement. "Ivan always recruits the best."

"Yeah, he's certainly got an eye for it," Bishop said. "Alright, so tell me more about this Dostiger character. His file was pretty light."

Vance leaned forward. "Two things I want to cover first. Firstly, Afsaneh Ebadi. This bitch is one badass intelligence officer. She's compromised more agents than the Rainbow Warrior. She's got brains and she's got some killer assets that she ain't afraid to—"

Bishop interrupted, "Look, I get it, Vance. I've read her bio and while I'd just love to sit here and discuss my track record with women, I do have a plane to catch."

Vance paused for a moment, then his voice took on a deeper tone. "You sit, and you listen, Bish. There is too much at stake here for mistakes. You fucked the Philippines mission up royally and you—"

Bishop cut in. "I got the job done!"

The PRIMAL commander spoke slowly, "Taking out one people-smuggling piece of shit was supposed to be easy. It was supposed to be real discreet. The amount of blowback we had to deal with had the potential to compromise all of PRIMAL's operations. SOCPAC's investigation into the incident is still open and they're still wondering who the hell is running black ops on their turf."

Bishop said nothing and Vance continued, "If PRIMAL is going to be able to continue its operations under the nose of the CIA, JSOC, and every other spook agency around, then we need to stay the fuck out of the news. Do you understand me?"

"Yes."

"Listen, buddy, I know you're under the pump. We all need a decent break. I just need to know that you can do this job right."

"I hear you, boss. I'll do my best."

Vance nodded at Chua. "OK, tell him."

Chua pressed some buttons on his phone before speaking. "Aden, I'm transmitting you the Dostiger file. Our man in Iran milked this out of a source this morning."

Bishop said nothing.

Chua continued, "According to the Iranians, Dostiger was responsible for supplying the missile that downed Flight 395."

Bishop stared at him.

"Bish?" Vance exchanged glances with Chua.

"I thought the Israelis followed up all the leads?"

"As far as they were concerned, they did. They bombed a number of Hezbollah facilities and assassinated the commander they thought responsible. Latest reporting suggests it wasn't Hezbollah that orchestrated the attack."

"So who the fuck did?"

"According to this, it was Dostiger."

Bishop was stunned. It had been over eight years since his parents were killed in the attack on the Israeli airliner, and this news opened up old wounds. The retaliation by the Israeli Air Force had inflicted significant damage on Hezbollah, and Bishop had consoled himself with the likelihood that the men responsible for his parents' death had been brought to justice.

Chua continued, "MOIS are under the impression that Dostiger's men carried out the attack as a test, a precursor to delivering the missiles to the Revolutionary Guards."

Bishop's fists were clenched. The color drained from his face. He breathed out, forcing an element of calm into his voice. "So Dostiger supplied and fired the missile as a test? A bloody test?" He jumped to his feet. "It would seem that we have some unresolved business with this arms dealer."

"Indeed," Vance said. "Look, Bish, you'll have your chance with Dostiger, but for now this operation must be dealt with delicately. Can you handle that?"

He nodded, eyes hard, knuckles white as he grasped the back of a chair. "Absolutely."

Vance stood up. "Good, now get your ass to Kiev."

***

THE PAIN TRAIN, SOUTHWEST PACIFIC

Ice had long ago come to the conclusion that traveling by military transport was for suckers. Cargo aircraft made for terrible airliners. The constant drone of the engines, lack of heating, hard aluminum seats, and absence of in-flight services made for a dull and uncomfortable transit. He hoped Bishop was enjoying the Gulfstream jet.

The Pain Train was one of the most sophisticated special

operations support platforms in the world but it still failed dismally in the provision of creature comforts. Despite having an impressive internal cargo space, only a small section at the front of the aircraft was free for Ice and Mirza to prepare their gear. The remainder was filled to capacity with munitions pods and surveillance drones. These remote-control UAVs could be launched out of the cargo hold when they were required.

As the big Ilyushin winged away from Lascar Island, Ice and Mirza sat silently wedged in the fold-down seating under a red fluorescent glow. They both wore similar clothing: cargo pants and soft-shell jackets in a desert-camouflage pattern. Once they reached the ground they would don Afghan robes over their chest rigs.

The Pain Train leveled out at cruising altitude and Ice slipped on his comms headset, gesturing for Mirza to do the same.

"How you doing, bro?"

"Good. Just trying to familiarize myself with iPRIMAL." Mirza had strapped the device to his forearm and was inspecting it closely. The new recruit's head was still spinning from the last twenty-four hours. Being whisked from Sydney to Lascar Island was enough of a shock, but being sent on a last-minute mission was totally unexpected.

"Once we get on the ground you'll get it quick enough. It all makes sense when you have live feeds," Ice said as he pulled a laptop out of a kit bag and opened it.

Mirza nodded, but was still determined to learn how to use the iPRIMAL before they parachuted in. He was acutely aware of how well trained the PRIMAL team was. Yes, he had over six years' combat experience in a premier special operations unit and had also jumped freefall into five live missions, but that didn't alleviate the feeling that he was a bit of a random cog, not quite meshed in with the rest.

Ice continued, "I'll patch into the Bunker now. Vance wants to talk through the mission." He activated the laptop and established a video conference.

Vance's face appeared on the screen, his voice through their headsets. "How you guys doing up there?"

Ice replied, "All good. My ass is numb from these damn seats, but we're good."

"Suck it up, big man. I don't hear Mirza bitching." PRIMAL's commander gave them a wink before sliding back into a serious demeanor.

"Gentlemen, I hate to say it, but we're going in half-cocked on this one." Vance's face disappeared off the screen, replaced by a satellite map of the Khod Valley in southern Afghanistan. "Once we locate the ambushed Stryker patrol, we're gonna drop the two of you in behind this ridgeline." A marker appeared on the screen identifying the position. "We're looking at a covert approach on the Russian facility, before the hostiles evac the package." A red circle appeared on the likely position of the target. "Once you have eyes on, you'll call in the Pain Train and waste the tangos. That's it, nice and simple." Vance's face reappeared on the screen. "Any questions?"

Mirza spoke first. "Sir, what sort of backup do we have if this turns into a gunfight?"

"The priority is to remain covert but if the shit hits the fan, the Pain Train will provide close air support. We'll have full coverage from the drones so you shouldn't get caught with your pants down."

Ice followed on, "What about the extraction plan? How are we getting out?"

"Contracted chopper out of Kandahar. Backup is the Skyhook."

"So what happens if one of us is injured?" Mirza asked softly.

"You stabilize the casualty and we'll get the closest medevac in," Vance stated. "The US Air Force CASEVAC unit at Kandahar Airfield can have a chopper in the area within 90 minutes. Use your cover call sign and we'll worry about the rest after they evac you."

Mirza looked confused. "Cover call sign? Won't the US air controllers pick up the Pain Train and question the call sign? You're not going to be able to fly around NATO-controlled airspace without being detected."

"We're registered as a CIA contractor. No one's going to ask questions. It also means we can dial up US casualty evac. It's worked well in the past."

"Still, we don't have our own dedicated CASEVAC or extraction plan? This all sounds a little ad hoc, sir."

"Don't I know it, Mirza. Look, I'm not real happy about this, but it's the best we can do on short notice."

Ice nodded. "No problems, with the Pain Train providing support, we'll be OK."

"That's right. Mitch will be your guardian angel, boys. If there's anything else you need, just holler."

Mirza lifted his iPRIMAL up to face the laptop camera. "All hooked up, sir."

"OK, team, kick some ass and stay safe."

The link to the Bunker closed and Ice pulled up a digital map of the area. Mirza pointed to the contour lines. "The terrain is steep. It might be wise to leave our armor behind."

"I agree. I'm going to run with just my vest and a day pack with extra water and ammo. We're going in a little light but we'll move fast. The quicker we find the target, the better."

"Any preference on weapons?" Mirza asked, unzipping a weapon bag. He ran his hand over a .50 caliber sniper rifle.

"That's Dorothy." Ice grinned. "Probably be a bit heavy for this mission. I'll run with my four-seventeen; you want to roll with a sniper rifle?" Ice favored the Heckler and Koch assault rifle. It had a faster rate of fire than a sniper rifle and good range.

"I'll take the suppressed SVU." The Russian-designed sniper rifle had been a favorite of the Indian during his time in the SFF.

They worked methodically preparing their gear, checking weapons, ammunition, and other vital equipment. Ice waved Mirza over as he pulled a nylon bag from the overhead netting. "You used a Skyhook before, Mirza?" he asked as he unclipped the sack's compression straps.

"A what?"

Ice unzipped the bag and began pulling out the contents, laying them out on the aircraft floor. "Skyhook is an old favorite of Vance's; he put it to good use down in Latin America. Naturally he brought it with him when he started PRIMAL."

"Vance started PRIMAL?"

"Pretty much. Got tired of doing the CIA's dirty work."

"You were there in the beginning?"

Ice looked up from the nylon harness he was laying out. "I was."

"If you don't mind me asking, Ice, why did you leave the CIA and join PRIMAL?"

"I got sick of the politics, Mirza. Got tired of having fat cats decide which bad guys got away scot-free and which ones took a bullet. One man's terrorist was another man's oil broker. We had a unique opportunity to start PRIMAL and we took it. Simple as that."

"Bishop mentioned a wealthy benefactor."

"Yeah, someone had to pony up the cash; this isn't a cheap business we're in."

Mirza watched silently as Ice laid out the final pieces of equipment.

"People do this for their own reasons, bro. I guess I'm trying to make good on the bad guys I had to let go." He finished with the contents of the bag. "We've got twelve hours till we're over the target area. Could be an additional half hour before we get an exact fix on the drop zone. Once I take you through this, I'll catch some z's, and you should probably do the same."

Ten minutes later the Skyhook was packed away, and Mirza watched his new partner relax back into the web seating and almost instantly doze off. There was no way Mirza could sleep; he was both nervous and excited. The extraction equipment Ice had shown him was insane, to say the least. The thought of having to use it was enough to make him nervous. Yet Ice had explained it to him as calmly as a mother teaching a child to tie his laces. At least now he understood why they called him Ice.

The former Marine's veins must have run cold with it; nothing fazed him.

CHAPTER 12

THE PAIN TRAIN, SOUTHERN AFGHANISTAN

While Ice and Mirza dozed, Mitch Ferry was busy in his control center at the front of the aircraft. Just behind the cockpit, he sat in a high-backed swivel chair, busy operating the computer terminals that controlled the aircraft's sensors and weapons, as well as the deployable drones, or UAVs.

Three large LCD touch screens were affixed to the walls of the compact alcove. The central screen displayed the aircraft's position on a digital terrain map, while on the other two Mitch was running diagnostic tests on the aircraft's targeting pod and weapons. His favorite Prodigy track blasted through the cordless communications headset as he nodded his head to the bass, fingers flashing between his keyboard and the touch screens. The music faded out as the pilot opened a channel on the intercom.

"Mitch, we're ten minutes out from the UAV launch position."

"Acknowledged. I'm powering up the systems now."

"We'll drop back to one hundred and fifty knots for the launch. Can you run the UAV till we circle round to drop the team?"

"No problems at all." Mitch tapped a screen, bringing up the latest weather data. "Looks like we have a little over two hours until first light. We need to get the lads in under darkness."

"Acknowledged. We'll be well within that time frame."

"Excellent." Mitch switched radio channels to the cargo hold.

"Look lively, bucko. You awake?" Mitch raised the Pain Train's loadmaster in the hold of the aircraft.

"Just woke up, buddy. What's happening?" a voice

answered.

"Are you ready to launch the bird in ten?"

"Yeah, she's good to go."

"Tip-top, I'm coming back to brief the lads now."

"Ready when you are."

Mitch slid down a short ladder behind his workstation and opened the door that separated the flight deck from the cargo hold. He saw that Ice and Mirza were fully kitted, wearing their helmets with night vision goggles flipped up. Mirza looked up from his iPRIMAL but Ice still looked fast asleep, slouched back on his parachute.

Mitch reached out to shake Ice's shoulder and the big man spoke as his eyes snapped open. "We good to go?"

"About to launch the UAV, chocks away within the hour."

"Roger, can we check comms in the next fifteen?"

"Soon as I get back to my station, I'll bring you both online, yeah."

Mirza gave him a thumbs-up and Ice replied, "OK."

Mitch turned then paused. "Oh, and Ice."

"Yeah, bro."

"Let's fuck these clowns up."

"Fuckin' A, man. Fuckin' A."

***

"I'm looking for a graveyard," Mitch muttered as the Pain Train reached the UAV release point. Thirty dead Americans and their destroyed vehicles lay scattered somewhere below.

The Brit had used the aircraft's targeting pod to scan around the last reported location of the ambushed patrol, but as expected, from thirty thousand feet the resolution was grainy. He would have to rely on the lower-flying drone to locate the ambush site and a suitable drop zone for Mirza and Ice.

Mitch felt the aircraft shudder as the pilot throttled back and the loadmaster lowered the Pain Train's ramp. Three of the compact delta-wing Sentry UAVs were lined up in the cargo hold.

"Drone chute out. UAV is away!" the loadmaster reported as the little aircraft disappeared into the night.

Mitch felt the Pain Train accelerate back to cruising speed. Within seconds a flashing symbol popped up on the master control screen as the drone went live. He tasked it to fly over the target area, maintaining a four-kilometer standoff to avoid detection.

On one of the other screens he brought up the gray-scale image of the terrain being beamed from the UAV's sensors. It looked like a moonscape as the UAV's camera panned over the rocky mountains. Using the joystick, Mitch zoomed onto a thin winding river and spotted the thermal blooms from a small village perched on its banks.

"Early risers, eh, already cooking breakfast," he said to himself.

He moved the sensor along a track as it followed the river. Ten minutes ran into twenty and he still hadn't found what he was searching for. He glanced up at the timer ticking down on the top of the screen. As the image passed over a narrow point between two ridgelines, he spotted the remains of the American patrol; five burnt-out vehicles.

He zoomed out, searching for a suitable drop zone. On the near side of the western ridgeline was a flat, open area halfway up the feature. He touched it on the screen, marking it with a waypoint, and sent the coordinates to Ice.

In the cargo hold Ice looked down at the iPRIMAL strapped to his forearm as it flashed. "Game time," he said.

Using his fingers he panned out from the digitized map and noted both the position of the destroyed patrol and the DZ Mitch had selected. It was a suitable choice: fairly flat. He hated hard landings.

"You happy with it, chaps?" Mitch inquired over the radio.

"Looks good," Ice responded.

"Tip-top, five minutes out. Coming in upwind; you'll have a two-knot tail chaser. First light is in approximately thirty minutes."

"Roger, can you light up the DZ?"

"As soon as you jump, the UAV will laze." Through their night vision goggles Mirza and Ice would be able to see the infrared laser pointing out of the sky like the finger of God, marking the drop zone.

The two operatives struggled to their feet, adjusted their harnesses, and tightened up their helmets. The loadmaster switched off the lights in the hold, activating a dull red glow. The packs and weapons strapped to their fronts caused them to move like pregnant women as they waddled to the rear of the aircraft, past the pallets of Viper Strike munitions and the two remaining UAVs. The loadmaster was waiting near the ramp, at the side door purpose-built for parachutists.

"Two minutes," Mitch announced over the radio and the loadmaster held up two fingers.

"One ready," Mirza said, nodding to the man.

"Two ready," Ice responded behind him.

"One minute," Mitch transmitted as the loadmaster slid the door up. Wind ripped into the hold, tugging at their equipment and clothing. Mirza felt the surge of adrenaline as he glanced out the door into empty space below. Despite the rushing wind, all he could hear was his pulse pounding in his ears.

"GO! GO! GO!" Mitch's voice bellowed over Mirza's headset. Training overcame his apprehension and he stepped forward out of the doorway. The blast of air and noise buffeted him as he was ripped clear of the aircraft, then there was only the rush of the wind as the Pain Train disappeared and he plummeted through the pitch-black night toward the earth.

He reached for the parachute release handle and wrenched it free. The chute was ripped upward, snatching him from his free fall like a giant hand grabbing the harness. He flicked down his night vision goggles and activated them. They revealed a greyscale landscape with no light sources other than the night's stars. He spun the parachute in a tight arc, searching for the laser.

"Mirza, you OK?" Ice's voice sounded in his headset as he spotted the finger of brilliant light and used the chute's toggles to turn toward it.

"I'm OK."

They were now under their canopies, deep in hostile territory, and gliding rapidly down toward the drop zone.

The almost alien voice of Mitch broke in over their radios with a burst of static. "Gents, the Pain Train is off-station in five. We'll be back in four hours once we refuel. I'm handing over the UAV control to the Bunker."

"Get back as soon as you can, Pain Train. I feel like my balls are swinging in the wind without my guardian angel," Ice responded.

"Wilco. Good hunting, lads. Pain Train out!"

***

Far below the Pain Train, high above the mountains above the Khod Valley, a makeshift camp was beginning to stir. As the first fingers of light spread across the camouflaged tents, the thumps of a starting generator resonated off the surrounding cliffs. It ran ragged for a few seconds before settling into a rhythmic pattern. A moment later the noise was joined by the chatter of a hydraulic drill emanating from a shaft burrowed into the mountainside.

Within minutes the first wheelbarrow loads of rubble appeared from the tunnel, grubby Afghan men shuffling under the weight of the rock. They looked weary, having been forced to toil at the task for nearly four days. Several had been killed the previous day when some poorly placed shoring collapsed.

The punishment was severe. The two dazed workers who were recovered alive from the rubble had been beaten to death, their faces smashed in by one of the Taliban wielding a shovel. The remaining Afghans worked desperately, in fear of the ruthless gunmen watching over them.

Yanuk sat on a pile of rocks watching the workers intently, a cigarette dangling from the corner of his mouth. The operation was supposed to be complete in forty-eight hours and they were falling behind schedule. A number of mishaps had slowed their progress: the shoring collapse, generator breakdowns, and even a landslide brought on by blasting.

"Bloody hajis are sabotaging me," the engineer swore. Although Khan's men had made an example of the two responsible for the tunnel collapse, he was still suspicious of the rest. He stubbed out the cigarette on a rock and crouched down to warm his hands on the compact gas burner that was struggling to heat his coffee. How it could be this cold in the morning and still be one hundred degrees by midday was beyond him.

Yanuk looked up from the stove to see that Khan and an entourage of fighters had climbed up from their camp to inspect the progress. The ten Taliban warriors all wore similar attire: plain robes with wrapped black headdress. A couple of them stood out with modern digital-camouflage body armor, recently scavenged from the ambushed Americans. Yanuk thought they looked ridiculous with the distinctive camouflage vests worn on top of their more traditional garb.

Not once had the Afghan warlord invited him down to the tents they had erected below the work site. Khan and his men had established a comfortable camp complete with carpets and servants. At night Yanuk watched them through his night vision goggles. While he slept in the open and ate from tins, these peasants were living it up like they were on some sort of camping trip; feasting on roasted goat and taking turns to sodomize one of their young servants.

The Russian engineer downed the last of his coffee and rose, slinging his assault rifle over his shoulder. He took a deep breath and walked over to where Khan was watching the slave labor.

"They are working too slowly, Yanuk." Khan's perfect English irritated him.

"We will make the deadline."

"Perhaps, but we have a problem."

"There is no problem. We make the deadline." Yanuk clenched his fists by his side. He wanted nothing more than to slip his fighting knife from his forearm and bury it in the arrogant warlord's throat.

"The problem is not here, my friend."

Yanuk frowned.

"There are some vehicles approaching from the south," Khan said, gesturing down the ridgeline toward the valley.

"What? Who? How do you know?"

"My comrades." Khan gestured to the Taliban behind him. "They have informed me that men they think are American Special Forces are approaching the valley."

"Your men must stop them. I cannot go faster!"

Khan pointed to the Taliban and said, "My friends are bringing more of their men to ensure we are safe. But now you understand why we must work quicker."

"If your men help, we could dig faster—"

"No!" Khan fixed him with a cold stare. "My warriors do not dig. They will defend us. Make the Hazaran dogs work harder."

Yanuk didn't trust himself to reply as Khan turned away, his entourage following him as he strode back to his camp. As far as he was concerned, the Taliban were nothing but peasants with guns. He angrily tossed his lukewarm coffee into the dust and turned back to the dig site.

CHAPTER 13

KIEV, UKRAINE

Bishop stepped out onto the business jet's stairs and the icy-cold air hit him, turning his breath into fog. He continued down the steps onto the tarmac, where a heavy-set man was leaning against the door of a black BMW.

"Welcome to Kiev, Mr. Fischer," the man said with a thick Russian accent.

Bishop sized him up: barrel-chest; large round, shaved head; jeans and a leather jacket. The Russian perfectly matched the photo of Aleks in the intelligence pack Chua had uploaded onto his phone. Bishop had already read his file and knew every aspect of Aleks' former career in Russian intelligence.

"You can call me Aden." He offered the big man his gloved hand.

The Russian took it with an iron grip, shaking it with vigor. "My name is Aleks, Aleks Andreyev."

"Pleasure to meet you, Aleks." Bishop opened the rear door of the car, throwing in his leather bag. He slid into the front and opened the glove compartment.

"Your pistol is there with the phone you requested," Aleks explained as he turned the ignition.

Bishop checked the compact Beretta handgun before returning it to the glove compartment and pocketing the phone. "Thanks, Aleks, I take it the rest of the hardware is all in order?"

"*Da, da*, you'll see it soon. We go to the house now," Aleks responded with a grin as he guided the luxury car toward the security checkpoint at Zhuliany Airport. He flashed a Ministry of Internal Affairs pass at the bored guards, who waved him through. As usual, bribes and forgeries ensured easy passage through customs and border security.

Aleks accelerated out of the gate onto the highway heading

toward the center of Kiev.

"How far to the house?" Bishop asked.

"It is in Podil Raion, not far, on the West Bank."

"Is the rest of the team assembled?"

"*Da*, all of them are there."

"Excellent. I take it there were no problems getting everything we need?"

"*Nyet*, it was all delivered. The men are very pleased with the equipment. It is good to work with a company that is willing to spend money."

"A bit different from the FSB, yes?" Bishop said referring to the Russian security service.

"*Da*. Cheap bastards bought shit. We make them look amateur," Aleks responded with a chuckle.

"Good, good. I'll brief the whole team on what's going on when we get there." Bishop looked out of the dark tinted windows, watching the light morning traffic and the passing scenery. The buildings that lined the streets were a blend of historic architecture intermingled with the cold, efficient construction of the Communist era. Towering gray concrete apartment blocks rose out of lower-level terraces and cathedrals like the hulking battlements of a castle.

Perfect for surveillance, thought Bishop.

As the BMW entered the business district, he noticed an increase in modern high-rise office blocks. Since the breakup of the Soviet Union, Kiev had embraced the wealth that came with a free market, and massive glass-fronted towers stretched up to the sky, neon signs proclaiming the presence of capitalist banks.

"First time in Kiev, boss?" Aleks asked as he calmly weaved the BMW through the traffic.

"Yeah, how'd you guess?"

"You look out the window like child at the zoo." Aleks chuckled.

"That obvious, hey! All part of my cover, *da*." Bishop laughed in return.

A few minutes passed in silence until they entered a rundown neighborhood and Aleks spoke, "Nearly there."

He was driving the BMW down a wide road with rusted tramlines running along the center. In the distance Bishop could make out where the road met the Dnieper River, and he noted the row of yellow construction barriers blocking access to the half-completed iron girder bridge.

For a moment he was lost in his thoughts. *He's in this city; the bastard who killed my parents is in this city and I am going to kill him.*

"Boss, you don't like my driving?" Aleks said interrupting his thoughts.

"What?" He realized his knuckles were white from clenching his fists. "No, not at all, mate, just a little tense."

"*Da*, we all feel like this, but it will be OK." The Russian gunned the BMW, overtook a rattling Communist-era tram, and swung the car into a narrow cobblestoned side street.

Run-down houses butted up against both sides of the road, blocking the rays of the morning sun. Bishop could sense the desperation of poverty among the old buildings.

Perfect part of the city for dodgy characters like us, he thought. The car nosed into the driveway of an old three-story town house wedged in a row of equally drab buildings. Aleks reached into the center console and activated a remote control. As the garage roller door slowly rose, one of the faded curtains on the second level moved slightly and Bishop caught a glimpse of someone watching them.

"Here we are, comrade," Aleks announced, parking the BMW next to a white Mercedes van, the roller door closing behind them.

"Very quaint," Bishop said.

"*Da*, I'll take you upstairs and introduce you to the others." Aleks led Bishop up a short staircase into the kitchen.

As they moved through the room, Bishop noticed it was in drastic need of renovation. The cracked linoleum and missing tiles were complemented by a musty smell reminiscent of a retirement home. *At least it's warm,* he thought.

They continued up another flight of stairs into the main

living area. Like the kitchen, the decor left a lot to be desired. Peeling wallpaper, a stained cloth couch, and an antiquated television were a stark contrast to the state-of-the-art equipment setup among the cheap furniture. A number of sturdy black plastic cases lay open on the moth-eaten carpet displaying cutting-edge weapons and communications equipment. A couple of late-model laptops sat on a table with a mass of cables running from them.

Two men looked up from the laptops as Bishop entered. A third stood at the window with a submachine gun held ready.

Aleks broke the silence. "Gentlemen, allow me to introduce our team leader, Mr. Fischer."

Bishop looked around at the four men. They stared back with guarded eyes. Although he'd not met them before, he recognized them from their files. This was a new team and they had not yet worked together, so his introduction would have to break the ice.

"Sorry about the accommodation, gentlemen. It seems we're on a tight budget." The four contractors looked around at the millions of dollars' worth of equipment with bemused smiles. Each had received a substantial sum of money for this job and the promise of a bonus upon completion, so obviously funding was not an obstacle for the organization that Mr. Fischer represented. Although none of them knew exactly who that was, they assumed it was the British government. Bishop's accent wasn't typically British but the man who recruited the team had implied that he was an agent for the Secret Intelligence Service.

"Gentlemen, I've gone over all your files, and needless to say, I'm pretty damn impressed by the caliber of the team." He paused, looking each of them in the eye. "You've been selected because you all come with a unique set of skills." He nodded at the bald-headed Russian who had picked him up from the airport. "Aleks is a weapons man and our driver." He gestured to the handsome Czech poised at the window with his submachine gun. "Miklos is our sniper and surveillance operator." He nodded to the short, swarthy Russian sitting behind the laptops. "Pavel is our technical surveillance man, and lastly," he indicated the blond man sitting on one of the equipment cases, "our covert entry guru, Wilhelm."

"Kurtz," the youthful-looking German corrected.

"I'm sorry?"

"Nobody calls me Wilhelm; they call me Kurtz," the German said.

Aleks laughed and Kurtz glared at him.

The Russian composed himself. "I'm sorry, it's just your name is so funny."

Bishop looked at them both. "You lost me. How is it funny?"

The lanky German cut in. "Because it means short; *kurtz* is German for short."

Bishop smiled. "It's a good nickname. Kurtz. I like it."

"Much better than Wilhelm," added Aleks. "I like it too."

Kurtz shrugged and Bishop looked around at the team. They seemed relaxed together. On the flight from Lascar Island Bishop had studied each man's background in detail. He'd noted that all of them were extensively trained in covert operations and close-quarter battle.

"Well, less about you Kurtz, and a little more about me. OK?"

The team laughed again.

"As Aleks has mentioned, my cover name for this op is Timothy Fischer. My real name's Aden. My background and employer are irrelevant. What is relevant is the importance of this mission."

Pavel spoke first, his accent a softer version of Aleks' guttural Russian. "So, Aden, what *is* the job?"

"If you hand me one of those laptops, I'll tell you." Bishop took the laptop and inserted a USB key from his pocket. He opened the briefing package that Chua had given him.

It took him half an hour to brief the men and another half-hour to answer their questions and talk through the details. Although they were mercenaries, these men had been carefully selected for their willingness to fight for a cause. Bishop knew that by telling them exactly what they were dealing with, he was ensuring their absolute dedication. The only information he omitted was the personal aspect to the mission. The men didn't need to know about his parents.

"OK, bottom line, we need to find out everything about Dostiger. Where he lives and works, who he spends time with: his entire pattern of life. We're starting from scratch and the first lead we're going to follow is his link to Antonov."

Nodding at Aleks, Bishop continued, "Tomorrow I'm going to meet with an Antonov representative, Dmitri Krenkov, at their head office. Aleks will drive me in the BMW. The rest of you will need to be ready to start surveillance as soon as Dmitri makes a call to Dostiger."

"Is your organization going to monitor his cell phone?" asked Pavel, the technical specialist.

"Yes, they've already locked down half a dozen phones in the vicinity of the Antonov administration building. Odds are that one of them is his. Once we meet I should be able to get his exact number," Bishop responded.

"What if he uses a landline to call Dostiger?" Pavel questioned.

"We're still trying to work around that one. We think he's more likely to use his cell phone. Dostiger is probably suspect of landlines."

"Could we disconnect all landline communications to the area?" Pavel asked. "Just to make sure."

"Isn't that a bit obvious? Might make them suspicious."

Pavel laughed loudly. "Clearly you haven't worked in the former Soviet Union before, Mr. Fischer. Nothing here is reliable: electricity, telephone, even water. No, they will suspect nothing. It's normal."

"Alright." Bishop smiled wryly. "Let's make it happen." Nodding to Kurtz, he continued. "OK, once we have Dostiger's headquarters pinpointed, we'll break in and get everything we can on him."

"*Ja*, no problems, boss," Kurtz said, patting the black case he was sitting on. "I have everything I need here. I could break into the Bank of England and no one would be the wiser."

Bishop didn't doubt his claim; the former German counter-terrorism officer's file was impressive. The only blemish was the circumstances leading to his early retirement. It was alleged he had beaten a rapist to death but he had never been formally charged.

"Do we take weapons?" asked Miklos, the lithe, Czech sniper. "Your friend provided some pretty serious hardware." He pointed at the weapons laid out on the floor.

"Yeah, we roll heavy from here on in. Dostiger's a nasty piece of work and I want to be ready for anything he throws at us." He paused for any final questions before concluding, "Alright, tomorrow is going to be a big day, gentlemen, and we've got a lot to do. Take the opportunity to prep your kit and get some rest. I'm going to confirm my appointment with Mr. Krenkov and tomorrow morning we'll run over the final details of the mission."

CHAPTER 14

KIEV/GOSTOMEL

The BMW was making short work of the distance between Kiev and Gostomel, the home of Antonov's huge aviation factory and testing facility. Aleks had deftly maneuvered the sedan through the capital's heavy morning traffic before unleashing the powerful engine on the forest-lined highway.

As they tore through the countryside, Bishop mentally prepared himself for the task ahead. Dmitri needed to believe he was a purchasing agent for Gulf Air Logistics, an aviation company Chua had organized to use as a cover. If he couldn't convince Dmitri, the meeting with Dostiger would never happen.

The PRIMAL operative wore a tailored navy blue suit with a crisp white shirt and silk tie. He had combed his usually unruly brown hair to one side and donned a pair of black-framed glasses.

Almost Clark Kent, he thought. Still, one does have to look the part.

As they approached Gostomel, Bishop dialed the Bunker and waited for the secure connection. "Chua, you there?"

"Got you loud and clear." The satellite link was good despite the thousands of miles between Lascar Island and Ukraine.

"Ten minutes out. Is our asset in place?"

"Confirmed. We are good to go," Chua said.

"Awesome. You need anything else from me?"

"Yes, well, Krenkov's number might save some time."

Bishop laughed. "OK, I'll see what I can do."

"Good luck, Aden, I'll be listening." Chua ended the call.

He turned to Aleks. "We're good to go. Have you heard from Pavel?" Aleks was monitoring the team's radio communications.

"They're in place at the telephone junction point. He'll disconnect the lines once you're in."

"Everything's ready then."

Aleks grinned and said, "As you say, our geese are in a row."

Bishop snorted. "It's ducks."

Aleks looked confused.

"It's ducks in a row."

The big Russian still looked confused and Bishop couldn't help but smile. "Never mind. Let's do this."

***

Dmitri Krenkov was everything Bishop expected. Well mannered and slick, he was ever the professional salesman. At first glance he seemed charming; well dressed in a single-breasted suit, with an open smile and friendly demeanor. However on close inspection the suit didn't sit quite right on the man's thin frame and the smell of aftershave was a little too strong.

Dmitri's eagerness to please made Bishop wary. No, I don't trust this bastard at all, he thought. I'll be fucked if I'd buy a pair of shoes from him, let alone multimillion-dollar airframes.

"Ahh, Mr. Fischer, welcome to Antonov." Dmitri met Bishop in the main building's foyer, grasping his hand as if the two of them were long-lost friends.

"Mr. Krenkov, it's a pleasure to meet you." The ever-so-slight Australian twang had transformed into an English accent. He carefully extracted his hand from the salesman's grasp.

"Please, call me Dmitri. It is very good to meet you too. Can I offer you some refreshments or would you like to move straight out and see the aircraft?" Dmitri asked, guiding him in through the foyer.

"I'm fine for now, thank you. I'm actually looking forward to seeing the jet. I've heard so much about it." Bishop pushed his glasses back up his nose with one hand, clutching his slim briefcase with the other.

"Of course, of course, come this way."

Bishop was led through a short corridor that he knew, from his study of aerial photos, led to one of the gigantic aircraft hangars. The company's website proudly boasted that this was one of two 'heated hangars' that allowed maintenance operations to continue all year round.

They pushed through a pair of heavy doors into the wide expanse of the facility. Even his study of the aerial imagery hadn't prepared him for the vast space inside. It was at least three times the size of PRIMAL's facility on Lascar Island.

"Very impressive, yes?" Dmitri asked.

"Absolutely. It's huge."

"Inside we can service any aircraft, even the Mriya, which is the largest aircraft in the world." The Ukrainian puffed his chest out with pride. "It was built here as well."

Bishop could visualize the entire PRIMAL fleet fitting inside with room to spare. Today, however, the hangar was almost empty; only a single AN-72 was parked in the far corner. He was familiar with the peculiar-looking aircraft. The Lascar Logistics fleet operated a number of them and PRIMAL had one in its inventory.

Unlike most commercial jets, the AN-72's engines perched on top of its wings, giving the impression it had a massive set of ears. Those 'ears' created a phenomenon whereby the exhaust gases of the engines blew over the top of the wing, creating lift. This additional lift had earned PRIMAL's variant of the aircraft the nickname 'Jumper'.

Dmitri continued talking as they walked across the bare concrete toward the aircraft. "The AN-72 is one of our most successful designs. We have sold them all over the world. Its unique short takeoff and landing capability has made it especially popular with freight companies working in developing nations. Although the original aircraft was designed in the 1970s, we have continued to make improvements."

For a full twenty minutes Bishop listened to Dmitri's pitch while the salesman led him around the aircraft pointing out its features. He was particularly interested in the advanced cockpit.

With the assistance of a French aerospace company, Antonov had completely upgraded the control systems of what was essentially an outdated aircraft.

"So what do you think?" Dmitri asked as they stood in front of the nose of the jet.

"It's even more remarkable than I was led to believe." Bishop did not have to feign enthusiasm; he really was impressed by the upgrades that Antonov had made.

"You mentioned on the phone that your company may be interested in purchasing a number of aircraft. How many do you think they might want?" Dmitri asked eagerly.

"It will be dependent on price, but I've been authorized to purchase up to four aircraft."

"I'm sure that we can arrange a very good price for your company, Mr. Fischer. Will you be requiring any logistical support?"

"Of course. We expect a five-year servicing contract included in the overall quote."

"Very good, sir. I will get my people working on a deal right away." The Ukrainian reached into his pocket and gave Bishop a business card. "This has my personal number. If there is anything you need while you are here in Kiev, you need only ask."

"There is one thing you may be able to help me with." Bishop reached into his wallet and handed his own card over.

The salesman took the card and inspected it. He frowned as he turned it over.

Bishop explained, "A more discerning client, with very deep pockets, has asked that I inquire about the availability of this particular asset." On the back of Tim Fischer's business card, in pencil, was written one word: Krokodile. It was the nickname for the formidable Mi-24 attack helicopter. "My client wants four platforms, ammunition, fuel, and servicing."

Dmitri spun the card in his fingers, looking at Bishop inquisitively. "So who is this wealthy client, Mr. Fischer?"

"I take it you know someone who can provide?" Bishop matched the Ukrainian's stare.

"I'm not sure I do, Mr. Fischer. Antonov does not deal in such merchandise. Perhaps you are mistaken about your inquiry?"

"Perhaps, perhaps not. My number is on the card if you hear of anyone who can help me."

"I will see if there is anything I can do, Mr. Fischer, but I am not making any promises. If that is all, I can escort you back now."

A slightly more reserved Dmitri walked Bishop back out of the building. They shook hands once more and Bishop walked over to where Aleks was waiting in the BMW.

"How did it go, boss?" The Russian's guttural accent was a contrast to the greasy tones of the salesman. He was glad to be back in the company of his driver.

"I think I might have blown it," he replied, punching Dmitri's number from the business card into his phone. Chua would now have complete access to Dmitri's handset through the Bunker.

"*Nyet*, it will be fine. He thinks you have money, he will call."

"I guess we'll find out very soon."

Aleks accelerated the car back onto the Gostomel highway. They sat in silence until a few miles out of Kiev Bishop's phone rang.

"Are we on?" he asked, answering the call.

"The mission was a success." Chua sounded excited. "Dmitri just finished a call to an unknown he calls 'boss'. I am ninety percent sure it is our man Dostiger. My Ukrainian is a little sketchy but he mentioned 'Krokodile' a few times, and the name Fischer."

"That's our man. Did you get a fix?"

"Yes, just pulling up the imagery now." Bishop could hear Chua typing at his terminal. "Got him. Hmmm, very nice. He lives in Pechersk on the Dnieper River."

"Good work. How does it look for surveillance?"

"Lots of high-rises close by. I'll send you a full target pack within the hour. I'm going to see if there are any apartments for rent in the immediate area."

"Nice one," Bishop said.

"Sending you the address now."

"Thanks, mate. Aden out."

He checked his watch, noting it was getting late on the island. Bishop knew the intelligence chief would have been working around the clock. His team covertly monitored many of the world's most sophisticated communications intercept systems, a lot of work for a small team of analysts. More often than not, it was Chua who worked the longest hours to make sure the teams on the ground had the best support available.

"So?" Aleks interrupted his thoughts.

"What?" Bishop looked at him. "Shit. Sorry, mate. Job's on. We have his location and now we have his primary phone."

"*Da*, is good. I told you not to be so hard on yourself, boss. We'll get this Dostiger, no problems." The big Russian smiled infectiously.

That's the easy part done, Bishop thought. Now we just have to break into the house of the most dangerous man in the Ukraine and thwart his plans to supply a psychotic warmonger. I'd much prefer to park a car bomb in his lounge and blow the shit out of him.

***

PETRIVKA, KIEV

On the other side of Kiev, a different team was also collecting intelligence on Dostiger. Parked by the side of the road, Afsaneh Ebadi sat in the back of a cheap hire car rubbing her hands. Despite the sun outside and her fur-lined jacket, the sedan's heater was struggling to keep her warm.

"Turn the heat up a little, please," she said to the MOIS agent sitting in the driver's seat.

"Yes, ma'am," he replied, turning the knob, his eyes never leaving the street ahead. The car's engine was running, ready to pick up Saneh's source.

They didn't have to wait long before the voice of her third man was broadcasted over the radio. "Alpha, this is Alpha One."

Saneh pressed the transmit button of the compact radio on her hip. "Go ahead."

"Target is entering the pickup zone. He's clean."

"Acknowledged. We're making the pickup now," she replied.

The driver pulled away from the curb and drove a block before turning down a side street.

"There he is," she said, pointing at a hunched-over figure with a hood pulled low, shuffling along the sidewalk.

They pulled in against the curb and Saneh leaned over and opened the door.

"Get in."

The source slid in next to her. He was a monster of a man, one of Dostiger's security guards, and barely fit into the back of the compact sedan.

"How are you, Anton?" She asked as they pulled away.

The Ukrainian source pushed his hood back and scratched his shaved head. "I'm good now that I've seen your pretty face." He spoke English with a thick Slavic accent.

"Not as pretty as yours is handsome," she said with a smile.

His face was far from attractive, dominated by a chunky, pockmarked nose, but his lecherous grin showed he appreciated the compliment.

"So what have you got for me, Anton?"

He fished into his jacket and pulled out a pen and notebook. "I have the address," he said, carefully writing in the notebook. He ripped out the sheet of paper and handed it over. "You must not forget, Dostiger's house has the best security in the whole of the Ukraine. You won't get in without an army."

"Thank you," Saneh said as she pocketed the paper. "Now, what else have you got?"

"Ah, ah, I couldn't really find the answers you're looking for," he said with a stutter.

"That's OK, just tell me what you know."

"Well, he's doing something big; always away these days."

"Yes?"

"Been going to Odessa. He's got a place there…"

"A place?"

"Yeah. I've never been, but it must be important. Everyone's afraid to talk about it."

"Afraid?"

"Yes," he said softly.

"What kind of place is it?"

Anton looked away, staring at the passing traffic as they drove through Kiev's quiet back streets. "I don't know. Ah, it is hard for me to ask these questions. If Dostiger finds out, he won't just kill me. He'll fucking torture me."

"Come on, Anton, he's not going to torture you."

"Yes, yes, he will! He's got a special room for it at the club. I'm serious. If he finds out, then I'm fucked."

"I understand, but if you hear anything more, you'll be sure to let me know, won't you?"

"I'll try," the big Ukrainian muttered.

She pulled out a wad of cash, throwing it onto his lap.

His eyes lit up as he pocketed the money. "Yes, thank you, thank you. I'll try my best."

She tapped her driver on the shoulder before turning back to the source. "I've included a bonus in that payment. You've done well, Anton. You're a good man, better than Dostiger realizes. If you were Iranian I'd recruit you in an instant."

"Ah, thanks." The man's rough face turned bright red.

"Now we won't meet again for a while, but you have my number. As soon as you know anything more about Odessa, be sure to give me a call."

"OK, thanks," he replied as the sedan pulled up to the curb. With a nod, he opened the car door and stepped out into the cold.

CHAPTER 15

KHOD VALLEY

Ice had no doubt that when man finally set foot on Mars, it would look a lot like the mountains of Afghanistan. He and Mirza had been on the move for two hours and they had yet to see even the slightest sign of life. Not a blade of grass, not a lizard or a bug, nothing.

Ice was on point, resting next to a large boulder, his tan robes blending into the dirt and rocks. His pale-blue eyes continued to scan the terrain as his lungs heaved. He looked back at Mirza climbing the steep track. The hardy Indian didn't seem to be noticing the effects of the thin air.

Reaching into his assault vest, Ice pulled out a map and studied it intently. Despite having his iPRIMAL strapped to his arm, he still carried the paper version. Old habits died hard.

In the two hours since inserting, they'd only covered a kilometer of lateral distance. From the contour lines on the map, Ice estimated they had climbed at least a thousand feet in altitude. He checked back down the slope to the insertion zone where they had buried their parachutes and confirmed it against the GPS built into the iPRIMAL.

"How are we doing?" Mirza asked, crouching next to him.

"Not bad, bro. Some of us better than others." He laughed, still breathing heavily. "You must be used to this altitude?"

"Yes, it is like home." The thin mountain air reminded Mirza of his birthplace in the Kashmir valley.

Ice placed the map on the ground and used the point of his combat knife to show Mirza their position on the side of the ridgeline. "We're going to keep following it up here," he explained, pointing to the mountain peak. "I'd wager our Taliban buddies are over here somewhere." He gestured to another ridge that also sloped up toward the summit. "The Stryker patrol got ambushed down here." The knife point buried itself slightly in the map's plastic coating as Ice tapped the valley between the two ridges.

"So if we stay on this side they won't be able to see us," Mirza said.

"That's the plan. We can pop up to the top and have a bit of a sneaky peek but I agree we should travel just off the actual ridge." Ice began folding the map. "Once we get closer to the excavation site, we should have the Pain Train in support. God knows how many of the bastards are up there."

Mirza glanced up at the cloudless sky. "It would be nice to have air support back."

"Tell me about it." Ice glanced at his watch. "Three hours till they're on station."

They were interrupted by a pinging noise in their earpieces. Ice checked his iPRIMAL. Using his fingers to navigate through the menus on the touch screen, he accessed the live feed being transmitted from the UAV flying high above them. Although it was being controlled by an operator in the Bunker on Lascar Island, Ice was directing its actions through a simple chat app.

So far the small aircraft, nicknamed Sentinel, had located the ambush site but had not reported anything else of value. The pilot had transmitted a short message:

No targets found. Moving north.

Ice confirmed the move with a few taps on the screen. He looked across at Mirza, who was watching on his own system. "Thought we would have located something by now. Hope we're not chasing our tails up here."

Mirza nodded in agreement.

Another beep emitted from his earpiece, announcing an incoming call over the satellite radio built into the combat communicator. "Ice, this is Bunker, over."

Ice recognized Chua's voice and replied, "Ice here, go ahead."

"Be aware I'm picking up radio transmissions from a US

Special Forces call sign about two clicks to your south."

"Damn. The last thing we need is some Green Berets getting themselves into the shit," said Ice. "They could fuck the whole show. Go on."

"Call sign Texas 1-3 is just short of the ambush location. They keep trying to raise their headquarters so I'm guessing their comms are being jammed," Chua said.

"So how the hell are you getting them?"

"Same way I'm talking to you. We're using the satellite receiver on the Sentinel to boost the signal."

"Does that mean if we lose the UAV, we lose comms to you?" Ice asked.

"No. We can do the same thing with the Pain Train."

"OK, so what do we know about Texas 1-3?"

"Not much. I'm going to push Sentinel down to have a look. You OK with that?"

"No problem. They running any air cover?"

"Negative. All coalition air support is tied up down south." PRIMAL HQ was still monitoring the situation in southern Afghanistan, and the Taliban offensive had not yet subsided; if anything, it had gained in intensity.

"Roger. Give me a bell when you get something more."

"Affirm. Bunker out." Chua ended the transmission.

Ice turned to Mirza. "We got to move fast, bro. Those SF guys could be in a world of hurt."

***

Unfortunately for Texas 1-3, Ice and Mirza were not the only ones in the valley aware of their presence. Ishmael Khalid and one of his fighters had moved a mile down from their new ambush position to watch for the approaching Americans and their Afghan allies. Khan had told them they were coming but Khalid wanted to see for himself.

The two Taliban warriors lay behind a rocky outcrop, watching the dust cloud from the approaching vehicles. Khalid had his sniper rifle resting on its bipod and was peering through the high-powered scope. As the convoy neared the location where he had destroyed their comrades, Khalid rolled to one side, taking a satellite phone from his chest rig. Khan picked up on the second ring.

"Khan, it's Ishmael." He spoke in the hushed tones instinctive to soldiers in the field.

"Allah be with you, my son. Can you see them?" the warlord asked.

"Yes, your friends were right. They're definitely Americans. Three of their Humvees and another four trucks."

"How many men?"

"Maybe ten Americans and another fifty Afghans."

"Afghans?"

"Yes, Afghan Army."

"Traitors. Can you kill them all?"

"I can try, but once we've destroyed the Humvees, the traitors will flee," Khalid said.

"I will send more men if you need them."

"No, our positions are well prepared and any more fighters would give them away. I have enough men."

"Allah willing, Khalid, but I will keep the others in reserve. How long until the Americans reach you?"

"One hour, maybe two. I think they will be cautious once they reach the ambush site. Maybe they will push the traitors forward on foot."

"Have you seen any more of the spy plane?" Khan asked.

"No, but if it returns, we will destroy it."

"Only after you kill the Americans. If you shoot first, it could bring bombers."

"Understood. How much time do we need?"

"Twenty-four hours, then we can return to our own valley." Khan was not happy to be so far from his own base of power in the north.

"Good, good. I'm having fun but I miss my wives." Khalid reveled in combat but he too was ready to leave.

"Not long now, my son."

"I will call you once it is done. Allah's will."

"Allah's will," replied Khan, ending the conversation.

Khalid put the phone back in his vest and grasped the stock of the sniper rifle, tucking it back into his shoulder. Although the enemy approached in a cloud of dust, he could make out individual men moving forward cautiously. As he predicted, the Humvees had stopped short and the Afghans were pushing ahead on foot.

Khalid had seen enough and nudged the man next to him. "Stay here. I will return to the position."

"I move when the Americans reach the track?"

"Yes, it will not be long. Just make sure they don't see you. Allah be with you." The veteran warrior crawled back from the outcrop and rose. Cradling his rifle in his arms, he turned to walk back along the ridgeline. This far out from the Americans there was no need to crouch or dash from cover to cover. As he walked back to his fighting position, he glanced up at the sky, wondering if the American spy plane would return.

CHAPTER 16

KHOD VALLEY

Ice and Mirza had pushed hard to reach the top of the ridgeline in less than two hours. Their position on the mountainous spur now afforded them a view down into the valley to where they could see the American patrol approaching.

"Single target moving along the ridgeline," Mirza's voice came over the radio. They were lying about fifty yards apart, systematically searching the terrain on the opposite side of the valley through their high-powered optics.

"Where?"

"Directly across, below the prominent crest, moving north."

Ice crawled forward and scanned the terrain on the opposing slope through the scope of his assault rifle. The location was almost six hundred yards away and covered in rocks; he almost missed the target. There was no doubt the solitary figure was one of the men they were looking for. He was wearing chest webbing and carrying a sniper rifle.

"Seen," Ice whispered.

"You want to take him down?"

"Negative. Let's just watch and see where he's heading."

They didn't have to wait long. The target moved to what appeared to be a rugged stone outcrop, lifted the edge of a camouflage net and disappeared from view.

"Damn! We would never have spotted that," transmitted Ice.

Now that he knew what to look for, Ice scanned the surrounding area. He counted five similar outcrops that could be well-camouflaged fighting positions. "I count five," Mirza whispered over the radio.

"Same. More than enough to hit our SF friends hard."

"Ice, Texas 1-3 is on the move. They're going to be inside

the Taliban engagement area in no time."

He opened a channel to the Pain Train. "Pain Train, this is Ice. I need an ETA."

"We're thirty minutes out, old man, inbound as fast as we can," Mitch's crisp accent came through.

"Roger, sending targets now." He looked down at the screen on his forearm at the image beamed from the Sentinel UAV. Using his finger, he zoomed out to get a clear indication of the distance between his position, Texas 1-3, and the Taliban. Zooming the image back in on the concealed positions, he dropped five markers on them. Satisfied with the locations of his targets, he sent the data to the Pain Train. By his calculations, Texas 1-3 would reach the engagement area in about ten minutes, but as Mitch said the Pain Train wouldn't be on-station for another thirty.

The impending ambush could provide cover for Ice and Mirza to slip past the Taliban and infiltrate further up the valley. Alternatively, if Ice warned the Americans, they might just pull back, leaving him and the Pain Train to deal with the Taliban. He checked his watch; he literally had seconds to make a decision.

He selected the communications menu and contacted PRIMAL HQ. "Bunker, can you hear me?"

"Loud and clear," Chua replied.

"Can you patch me through to Texas 1-3?"

"Give me two minutes."

He peered through his scope at the SF convoy as it moved from the valley floor up the mountain pass.

***

Captain Kevin Daley, the commander of Texas 1-3, watched anxiously from his Humvee as it crept cautiously along the narrow track that wound its way up the mountain pass. His truck's doors had been removed, allowing him to sit sideways with his weapon covering the cliffs on the right-hand side.

In front of the vehicle two platoons of Afghans were

patrolling on foot. The fifty soldiers spread out on either side of the track, scanning the high ground for potential ambush and checking the track for IEDs. They had been working with the twelve-man Special Forces Operational Detachment for over six months and were all battle-hardened veterans.

"Water, Jimmy." Kev reached over his shoulder and his communications sergeant handed him a bottle.

Jimmy spat his chewing tobacco out of the Humvee and looked back out at the valley walls towering over them. "You think the fuckers who killed the Stryker boys are still hangin' round?" he drawled.

"Not sure, buddy. We'll be OK though."

"You sound scared, boss." The sergeant knew the captain well enough to give a bit of cheek.

"Fuck, no! I just think a bit of air support wouldn't go astray." Kev wasn't impressed that all aircraft were committed to the fighting in the south. "I'm not real happy having to deploy the Kandak forward like this, but it's the only way we're gonna stop these assholes getting the jump on us." 'Kandak' was the local term for a company of Afghan Army soldiers.

"Fuck, better them than us," Jimmy said.

The captain looked over his shoulder and fixed him with a dark stare.

"Shit, boss, I was kidding, but did you see those Strykers? Those guys died real bad." Jimmy used his gloved fingers to stuff a wad of tobacco under his lip. "We need some fucking Warthogs up top. Those bad boys'll blow the tits off the towelheads." The A-10 'Warthog' was a favorite; the devastating firepower of its 30mm Gatling gun could change the tide of a battle in seconds.

"Well, we don't have them, buddy, so we gotta—" Kev was interrupted by an unfamiliar voice coming through on the radio speaker.

"Texas 1-3, this is Nemesis 4, over," the voice transmitted over the secure military frequency.

As far as Kev was aware, there were no other friendly forces in the area. "Jimmy, who the hell is Nemesis?" Kev asked as he grabbed the radio handset, pressing it to his ear.

"No idea, boss."

Kev transmitted, "Nemesis 4, this is Texas 1-3. Who are you?"

"Texas 1-3, we are a friendly call sign. You are approaching an ambush on the eastern ridge. You need to halt immediately, over."

"Nemesis 4, this is Texas 1-3, what is—"

A huge explosion rocked the Humvee. The driver jumped on the brakes and they slammed to a halt, smashing the captain's helmet into the dash. Through the cracked windshield Kev watched the Afghan infantry scramble for cover as the eastern ridgeline opened up in a barrage of muzzle flashes. Plumes of dust and smoke enveloped his men as they sought refuge from the onslaught.

Kev rapidly assessed the situation. The muzzle flashes were appearing from what looked like a textbook defensive formation, and he immediately knew they'd hit a well-prepared ambush with heavy weapons sited for maximum effectiveness.

The .50-caliber heavy machine gun in the Humvee turret opened up with a steady thud, spraying rounds into the valley walls. The gunner screamed as he fired, "INCOMING! GET THE FUCK OUT!"

"GO! GO! GO!" screamed Jimmy as he dove out of the cabin headfirst, the driver hot on his heels.

Kev leaped from his seat, hitting the ground in a roll. A missile hit the stricken Humvee and detonated. Heat washed over him and time slowed as the vehicle exploded, throwing shrapnel, burning equipment, and the remains of the .50-cal gunner across the track. The blast snapped Kev's head forward, smashed the bridge of his helmet into a rock, and knocked him unconscious.

***

Ice was lying on his stomach watching Texas 1-3 through his rifle scope when the first missile launched and slammed into the hood of the Humvee. Almost instantaneously all five of the enemy positions on the opposite ridgeline erupted with a roar of machine gun, grenade, mortar, and rocket fire. The Afghan soldiers dropped to the ground as the formation was lashed by a maelstrom of shrapnel and lead.

Ice adjusted his rifle sight and scanned the enemy position for a target. "Free to engage," he said over the radio. He steadied his crosshairs on the nearest muzzle flash and fired five rapid shots, the rounds kicking up dust around the fortified position.

"Boss, they're too well dug in. I can't get a clean shot," Mirza transmitted.

"Watch for an opening. Try and suppress until the Pain Train comes on-station," Ice replied. "Pain Train, what's your ETA?"

Mitch came in over the radio. "Eight minutes out, chaps, targets loaded, ramp down. We're ready to drop." Ice double-checked the target coordinates on his iPRIMAL.

"Roger. Targets are ready to receive. Bring the Pain." As Ice finished speaking, a missile jumped from a position they hadn't spotted, the back-blast lifting the camouflage netting covering the firing position. The missile streaked across the valley, slamming into one of the Humvees. Ice brought his rifle to bear on the new position. He caught a glimpse of the missile tube but it was outside the range of his assault rifle. "MIRZA!"

"On it."

Ice saw a flash and the missile launcher fell from view as Mirza's shot struck its target. "Direct hit!" he said. Apart from that shot, Ice knew they weren't able to effectively suppress all the Taliban's heavy weapons. The other ambush positions continued to rain fire down on Texas 1-3, and if the Pain Train didn't arrive soon, the Afghan soldiers and SF mentors would be annihilated.

***

Texas 1-3's remaining Humvee was parked in a shallow

depression, the MK19 grenade launcher on top of it firing rapidly as the operator launched volley after volley of grenades into the ridgeline. The weapon was firing at maximum range, lobbing grenades into the general ambush area, but it wasn't close enough to be effective against the fortified positions.

Kev could vaguely register the distinctive sound of the 40mm rounds as he came to and his eyes flickered open to see Jimmy crouched over him, using a bottle to splash water on his face.

"What the fuck's going on, Jimmy?" Kev croaked as he came to his senses, adjusting his helmet. The thump of the grenades intermingled with explosions, rifle shots, and ricochets, creating an overwhelming cacophony of sound.

"Some bastard smoked us with a missile," Jimmy yelled. He had the radio on his back and Kev's second-in-command was next to him, leaning against the Humvee, the handset pressed into his head.

Kev scrambled to his knees and slid in beside them.

"Shit, Kev, I thought we lost you," the master sergeant yelled over the noise of the battle.

"What's the situation?"

"Alpha and Bravo platoon are both under heavy fire. We've taken a shit-ton of casualties, and the Kandak commander is trying to pull his men back. His radio operator's dead, so I am talking direct." The senior soldier handed the radio handset back to Jimmy. "I can't raise HQ and certainly can't raise any fucking air support."

"So what's the plan?" Kev asked.

"I'm trying to use the rest of the team to provide suppressing fire and get the Afghans to pull back. Problem is, the fucking enemy positions are fortified. They're using heavy-caliber weapons and outranging us." The veteran operator shook his head. "Boss, these aren't regular Taliban. I've never seen anything like it."

Kev knew they needed to come up with a solution or all his Afghan infantry would be wiped out. The obvious plan would be to flank the enemy up the ridgeline but this could take hours, and by that time both platoons of the Kandak would be KIA. The look on the master sergeant's weary face said it all. The situation was hopeless.

"Hey, boss!" Jimmy yelled, holding out the radio handset. "It's that Nemesis fucker again."

Kev grabbed the handset off Jimmy, holding it to his ear.

An ice-cold voice came through the handset, "Texas 1-3, this is Nemesis 4. Do you read me, over?"

Kev replied immediately, "This is Texas 1-3. I don't know who the hell you are but we need assistance ASAP!"

"Texas 1-3, tell your forward troops to keep their heads down. We have close air support on-station in five minutes. Hang in there, the Pain Train is inbound. Nemesis 4 out."

"What the hell?" yelled Kev. "Who the fuck is this Nemesis, Jimmy, and what the fuck is a Pain Train?"

CHAPTER 17

PECHERSK, KIEV

During the seventies and eighties, towering concrete apartment blocks had popped up all over Kiev. Even the most exclusive suburbs had not been spared from the scourge of Communist-era construction. The graceful architecture of the pre-Soviet years, elegant town houses, intricate churches, and historical monuments, was overshadowed by hulking gray blocks of high-density living.

In the suburb of Pechersk the extravagant dwellings of Kiev's elite stood side by side with the drab existence of the city's working class. Dostiger's estate was located in the most exclusive part of the old suburb, yet it still had a number of apartment blocks nearby. It was these tall buildings that Chen Chua was scrutinizing from Lascar Island over ten thousand miles away.

Using a customized version of Google Earth, Chua identified which buildings would provide the best surveillance position for Bishop and his team. A few minutes' browsing on a Ukrainian real-estate web page had identified a suitable apartment available for short-term lease, and within a few hours, Bishop's team had established a covert observation post on the top floor of a fifteen-story apartment building.

The serviced apartment was advertised as a luxury penthouse, but the reality was very different; it looked like the set of a bad eighties TV show. White leather couches and lime-green linoleum tiles may have been fashionable thirty years ago, but now they were about as stylish as disco. The place was a dump but Bishop didn't care. The apartment had the one redeeming feature the team needed: From the full-length balcony it offered a 270-degree panorama of downtown Kiev and perfect views of the Dostiger residence.

Discreetly positioned on the balcony were two compact,

remote-stabilized video cameras mounted on sturdy tripods. Thick black cables ran from the cameras into the apartment, plugging into a pair of laptops open on the dining table.

The FIST's technical surveillance operator, Pavel, was working intently at one of the laptops. The screen displayed two high-resolution video feeds. One was zoomed in on the guardhouse at the front of the residence. The second was recording a wider shot of the entire estate, from the guardhouse and high wrought-iron fence with its heavy gates all the way back to the black Range Rover parked at the entrance to the two-story mansion.

"How's the setup going?" Bishop asked as he sat in the chair next to the swarthy Russian.

"Almost done. Just finished hooking up the antennas." Pavel tapped a few commands into the second laptop and the screen came alive with dancing lines. "If someone turns on their phone in that house we'll have the number before they can say hello."

"What about landlines?"

"More difficult at short notice. I can patch them but it means I need to get into the junction box."

"I'm not real keen on that."

"I agree, we risk compromise."

"Yep, this'll have to do." Bishop watched the lines dancing on the screen for a second before looking back at the residence. "The place is certainly a fortress. Those walls have got to be at least a foot thick. And that fence, doesn't like visitors, does he?"

"In the briefing you said that Dostiger is very secretive, very…" Pavel struggled to find the right words.

"Security conscious?" Bishop offered.

"Yes, security conscious. Perhaps he keeps his information on paper, not on computer. Or maybe his computer is not connected to the internet."

"Which brings us back to the big problem."

"Yes, how do we get in there?" Pavel tapped the image of Dostiger's estate with the back of his pen.

"More importantly, how do we get in and out without Dostiger knowing?"

"You see these?" Pavel zoomed in on one of the trees. The high-resolution camera lost none of its clarity as the lens adjusted.

"Sneaky fucker," Bishop said. There on the screen was a small CCTV camera painted the exact color of the tree trunk. "How many more are there?"

"I have found six. I think maybe a few more. All of them are controlled by the guard at the gate."

"Did you show Kurtz?" If anyone could break into the house it was the young German. Before being contracted by PRIMAL he had spent a couple of years developing his covert entry techniques while conducting counterterrorism operations with GSG 9.

"*Da*, he is in the bedroom with the plans to the house. I think he has a few ideas."

"Good work!" Bishop gave the Russian a thump on the shoulder and walked across the living area to the master bedroom. As he entered, Kurtz looked up from a laptop.

"*Guten Tag.*"

"Hey, mate," Bishop said. "How's the planning going?"

"*Ja, gut.* I have a concept of how we're going to do it. The biggest issue is the guard. To get in and out undetected we need to hack the cameras. The only way we can do that is to get into the guardroom."

"Poses a problem. How're we going to crack it?"

"Take down the guard, hack the cameras, in and out in fifteen minutes."

"Sounds good. Just need to make sure Dostiger isn't at home when we go in."

"Well, he won't be home if he is meeting with Herr Fischer." The German winked.

Bishop laughed. "True. Let's hope Dmitri gets back to me soon."

"BOSS!" Pavel yelled from the other room. "I think we have a problem."

Bishop moved back into the living room, followed by Kurtz. They stood behind the Russian as he peered intently at one of the laptop screens.

"Boss, I don't think we're the only ones interested in Dostiger." He zoomed the camera in on a single man standing at the corner of the high wrought-iron fence. The man's face filled the entire screen. He may have passed for a local at first glance but under the scrutiny of the high-powered lens, his dark skin and close-cropped beard looked Middle Eastern. Pavel snapped a few stills and dropped them into a facial recognition program.

"I think that the Iranians might have a minder on Dostiger," the Russian observed as the results of the scan appeared on the screen.

No known matches. Biometric genealogy consistent with Central Asian region.

Likelihood of ethnicity: 75% Persian, 15% Farsiwan, 10% Tajik.

Damn, he has to be Iranian, thought Bishop. The only question is, MOIS or IRGC? He peered at the camera footage. "Stop. Did you see that?" He pointed at the side of the man's head. "Back it up a frame."

Pavel stepped back the recording, and as the man in the image turned his head slightly, they all saw the clear, coiled lead running under his collar from his ear.

Bishop poked his finger on the screen. "He's wearing a radio. The bastard's talking to someone. Can we trace the signal?"

Pavel's fingers were already dancing over the keyboard of the second laptop. "It's UHF. I've isolated the channel. He's talking to someone close by." Pavel split the computer screen and brought up a feed from the other remote camera. "White car, three blocks south from the target."

The camera zoomed in on the vehicle, a cheap Toyota sedan that looked like a hire car. Through the windshield

Bishop could make out the two occupants, a man next to a striking, dark-haired woman.

"Wow," exclaimed Kurtz as the image sharpened and the woman's face came into focus. "Very nice, Mr. Fischer, very nice."

Bishop recognized Afsaneh Ebadi from the intelligence pack Chua had given him. Her long, raven-black hair flowed out from under her fur hat and her exotic features were unmistakable. Not much chance that another strikingly beautiful Persian would be attempting to run covert surveillance on Dostiger.

"It's Iranian intelligence," said Bishop. "There was always a chance they'd get a sniff of this."

"Well, boss, if you don't mind me saying, they're going to give away the whole show if we don't do something," Kurtz said. "Dostiger's security would have to be blind to miss these amateurs."

"You're right." Bishop paused in thought. "Get Miklos. I want him on the roof in two minutes. MOIS needs to be taught a lesson in covert surveillance."

***

Saneh listened in as her handheld radio crackled. "Alpha, this is Alpha One. Nothing to report. No sign of the target."

"Acknowledged. Remain alert. We are still expecting our target to leave the location this afternoon," she replied. She was starting to doubt her source had provided the correct address. They had been watching this residence for over twelve hours with absolutely nothing to show for it. The three members of her team had been cycling through a standard routine. One was on close surveillance, one waited in the vehicle, and the other rested in a nearby hotel.

Saneh was supposed to be on rest in the hotel but had chosen to join the extraction vehicle for a shift, something she was regretting now that they were two hours into a six-hour rotation. She was struggling to stay awake despite three sugar-enhanced coffees. To make matters worse, her surveillance partner wasn't much of a talker. He remained completely alert and utterly disinterested in conversation.

Saneh's radio emitted a short burst of white noise then nothing. She keyed the handset. "Alpha One, Alpha One, do you read me?" There was no response, then the radio crackled and an unfamiliar voice transmitted.

"Your communications are being jammed, Agent Ebadi. Please remain in the vehicle." The crisp British accent emitting from the radio's speaker startled her. She looked across at her partner and raised the handset.

"Who is this?"

"My name is Tim Fischer and I'm in the service of the British government."

"Why are you contacting me, Mr. Fischer? I haven't done anything to warrant the attention of your government."

"Saneh, you are compromising a very sensitive operation."

"What are you talking about? What do you want from me?"

"We need to meet. I'm not willing to discuss this any further over open communications. Listen carefully. You are to cease your surveillance immediately. Can you see the new five-story office building a block behind your vehicle?"

She turned around in her seat. "Yes."

"In two hours, drive to the parking lot beneath that office building and we'll meet."

Saneh looked at her partner and he shook his head. Her voice took a more aggressive tone. "Wait just a second, Mr. Fischer. You have no idea what I'm doing here in Kiev. I suggest you mind your own business and stay out of mine."

The wing mirror next to Saneh exploded, a subsonic bullet tearing it from the side of the car. She jumped away from the noise, scrambling to recover her Makarov pistol from the car's center console.

"If I wanted you and your men dead, Saneh, you would be. It's in both our interests to meet. You have two hours."

She took a deep breath and raised the radio. "Fine, I'll be there."

"I look forward to it."

The radio gave a short burst of static before Bishop's voice was replaced by her team member. "Alpha, this is Alpha One. What is going on? You disappeared off air."

"Alpha One, we are aborting the surveillance. Break off and meet us at the hotel," Saneh ordered.

***

A lone figure stood inside the entrance to the underground parking lot, leaning casually against the wall. His heavy winter coat barely concealed the armor and weaponry he had strapped to his body.

"White Toyota turning into the parking lot now," Kurtz broadcast. The approaching car paused at the boom gate and he hit the button, raising it for Saneh and her team. "One female and two males," he added, looking into the vehicle as it passed.

"Acknowledged. I have them now," said Miklos from his hidden position.

The sedan drove down the ramp into the parking lot. The entire floor was empty except for a single BMW and a Mercedes van parked in the far corner. Located under a recently constructed office block, the lot was not yet in use. Plastic sheeting, bags of cement, and construction trash had been heaped in one corner. The polished concrete floor squealed under the wheels of the Toyota as it weaved between the columns of concrete, stopping two car lengths from where Bishop was standing.

The door facing away from him opened and a solidly-built man got out of the car, his eyes scanning the immediate surroundings. Bishop recognized him from outside Dostiger's residence and gave a friendly nod. The Iranian lowered his head back into the vehicle and the rear door on Bishop's side opened. Saneh slid out of the backseat.

Bishop was a little taken aback by how attractive she was; the grainy shots in her file barely did her justice. Even in her bulky jacket she was poised and elegant. She strode toward him with a determined look on her perfectly formed features. Anger flashed in her dark eyes and Bishop knew he had some ground to make up if he was to develop any level of rapport with her.

He extended his hand and greeted her warmly. "Saneh, it's a pleasure to meet you face-to-face."

"No, Mr. Fischer, the pleasure is all mine," she replied cordially, shaking his hand and looking him straight in the eye. She seemed completely unfazed by the fact that Bishop held all the cards.

"Please, call me Tim. There's no need for formality."

"It would seem there is no need for manners either." Saneh glanced pointedly at the shattered mirror on her car.

"I apologize for that, but I needed to make sure I had your attention."

"Well, now you have it, Mr. Fischer." She folded her arms under her ample chest. "So why don't you say what you need to say."

Bishop smiled. He couldn't help but like the straightforward attitude of the MOIS agent. "It would seem that when it comes to a certain Mr. Dostiger, we share similar goals. I wanted to meet with you so we could exchange contact details. I think there's an opportunity for us to help each other out."

"Are you suggesting that we work together?"

"In a roundabout way, yes."

"How?"

"Well, we may find that we have resources that can complement each other."

"Does that mean I can continue my surveillance operation on Dostiger?"

"Given our little demonstration, I think that is better left in the hands of my organization."

"Fine, I have other means at my disposal."

"I'm sure you do. Your reputation as a resourceful and capable agent precedes you." Bishop nodded and smiled ever so slightly.

Saneh was caught off balance by the compliment. "So, is

your organization willing to cooperate with mine?"

"I speak with the full support of my superiors. If you have any queries or information that would benefit us both, you can contact me on this number." Bishop passed her one of his Tim Fischer cards.

Saneh took a cell phone from her pocket and entered the number. The local phone that Bishop was using buzzed in his pocket. "That's my number, Mr. Fischer. I would appreciate it if you would reciprocate the agreement."

"I certainly will, and I hope to hear from you soon." He gave her a genuine smile as she turned away. As Bishop watched her walk back to the car, he was drawn to the way her hips moved in her tight-fitting jeans. Try and keep it professional, he reminded himself.

Once the Toyota had left the complex, he opened the door of the BMW and climbed in next to Aleks.

"That seemed to go well, boss." Aleks was grinning from ear to ear.

"What's that supposed to mean?"

"The woman, she likes you, *da*," Aleks said smiling.

"What? She hates me. I threatened her."

"A woman like that, she is not intimidated. She will be impressed."

***

Saneh sat quietly in the back of the Toyota as her team drove to their hotel. The meeting with the British agent had not gone as she had anticipated. She had expected a confrontation and yet it had been very cordial. The MI6 operative had almost been friendly. She pulled her second phone from her jacket and dialed Rostam's office.

He picked up after a single ring. "Yes."

"Sir, it's Saneh. We have a situation."

"Go ahead."

"It seems that the British Secret Service are onto Dostiger."

"How do you know? Explain," Rostam demanded gruffly.

"A British agent compromised our surveillance operation. Sir, before you say anything, it's not as bad as it sounds."

"How the hell can it not be bad?"

"I met with the agent. He's very well informed but it's doubtful that he has someone on the inside. He's fixated on watching Dostiger's residence, but I have information that it's a waste of time. My source says Dostiger's running all his operations from the nightclub."

"The one in Kiev?"

"Yes, sir, Club Kyiv. I think it might be worth my while to meet with Dostiger."

"Considering our other options are fast closing, you might be right." There was a pause as Rostam weighed up the options. "Tell me more about the compromise. You said you met with the British agent."

"Yes, sir. He was particularly insistent that we call off our surveillance. He also mentioned that our organizations should share information."

"Do you think that MI6 is aware of the Guards' ambitions to obtain a WMD?"

"Without a doubt, sir. Why else would they be here?"

"Perhaps they are cracking down on arms dealers. No, you are right. It's too much of a coincidence."

"Perhaps they are not actually MI6, sir."

"Israelis?"

"Who else would be watching Iranian affairs so closely?"

"Yes, very true. One thing we can be sure of is that, be they MI6 or Mossad, we can leverage off their strengths. They almost certainly have more assets focused on Dostiger than we do. It seems we can recover from your failing by playing on your one true strength."

Rostam couldn't see the effect his words had on Saneh, her free hand clenched into a fist, her knuckles white. "Yes, sir."

"If the opportunity arises, I want you to seduce this Fischer, whoever he is. Gain his trust. You can use the information about the nightclub if you need to."

"Then what, sir?"

"If this team recovers the weapon, we'll use our strike team to snatch it from them."

"Sir, if MI6 is successful, then isn't the mission complete? The Guards will have been denied their goal?"

"No. I want that weapon, Saneh. I don't expect you to comprehend this, but it is the key to MOIS finally taking the position it deserves. The Guards have had their day in the sun, now it is our turn."

"Yes, sir. I was planning to go to the nightclub. Do you want me to contact Dostiger directly?"

Rostam pondered the proposition. "Yes. Let him know we're back on the market for a weapon. It might give him the opportunity to look for a better deal than the contract with the Guards."

"What about MI6? Do you want me to let Dostiger know Fischer is onto him?"

"Do you listen at all, Saneh? Fischer's going to work for us. We need him to succeed, not fail."

"Yes, sir. Of course."

"Report to me at twenty-two hundred your time tomorrow. Oh, and Saneh…"

"Yes, sir?"

"Don't mess this up. There won't be a second chance." Rostam terminated the call.

Saneh folded her phone and slid it back into her pocket, slumping into the backseat of the Toyota. This mission wasn't going at all how she had planned it.

CHAPTER 18

KHOD VALLEY

Mirza and Ice were powerless to stop the Taliban from exacting a heavy toll on the soldiers trapped in the valley. They'd managed to claim a few kills but their precision fire was of limited effectiveness against the fortified enemy positions.

It had been over five minutes since the ambush initiated and the weight of fire had barely decreased. The Taliban were now focusing their mortars on isolated groups of Afghan Army soldiers, forcing them to move from cover, then mowing them down with machine guns. Over half lay dead or wounded and most of their commanders had been killed. Those still alive clung to the earth, seeking refuge from the death that lashed them from high on the valley wall.

Ice's rifle ran dry and he watched the carnage through his scope for a moment, willing the Afghans to fight back. He ejected the empty magazine from the assault rifle, replacing it with another twenty-round mag. Within seconds the weapon was nestled back against his shoulder and he fired five rounds at one of the machine gun pits on the other side of the valley, blowing chunks of rock off their defenses. The barrel of a machine gun was sticking out of a gap, firing steady bursts of lead down into the valley. Ice leveled his crosshairs on the weapon and squeezed off a single shot. Half a second later he saw a puff of dust as the round ricocheted off the rock.

He closed his eyes. Breathing out fully, he opened them, aligning the crosshairs on the target again. He waited for the camouflage netting that covered the Taliban position to sag as the wind lulled, then squeezed the trigger. The barrel of the machine gun flashed as his round impacted, silencing the gun.

"Ice, this is the Pain Train. We're two minutes out," Mitch's voice came in loud and clear over the radio.

"'Bout time, guys. Texas 1-3 is getting seriously fucked up

down here," Ice replied, his usual calm drawl replaced with a hint of urgency.

"Sorry, my good man, refueling at Kandahar was slow."

"Do you confirm all the targets?"

"Roger, plus I've tagged a couple of extras. I now have seven targets, five bombs each."

"Give me everything you've got.."

***

The Pain Train came in hard and fast. Mitch had already programmed the thirty-five Viper Strike munitions with their GPS coordinates. Each one would deposit five pounds of 'enhanced blast' explosives directly onto their designated targets. Compared to conventional bombs, 175 pounds of explosives was insignificant, but when every individual warhead was landing simultaneously and with precision, the effect would be devastating.

"We're thirty seconds out. You clear of the ramp?" Mitch asked the loadmaster over the intercom.

"Roger. Bombs are on the ramp. I'm all clear." The loadie had moved the Viper Strike weapons pod to the back of the ramp. When Mitch fired the bombs, a small charge would launch each one clear of the aircraft in a single wave of ordnance. Like hounds on the scent of a rabbit, they would home in relentlessly, their GPS smart chips guiding them to their targets.

Mitch watched the enemy position through the Pain Train's targeting pod, located under the aircraft's nose. On his screens he could see the release point rapidly approaching. "Twenty seconds out, standby," he said as the pilot made a few final adjustments to their approach.

"Ten seconds." Mitch armed the bombs with a click of his mouse. His finger hovered over the enter key: "Five, four, three, two, one, bombs away."

***

Captain Kev Daley didn't notice the tiny silhouette of the Ilyushin-76 aircraft high above him and hadn't heard anything more from the Nemesis call sign. His men had reported a sniper engaging the enemy and he knew someone friendly was still up there. Without that suppressing fire, he had no doubt that all his Afghans would be dead by now, massacred in the dusty corridor of death that stretched out in front of him.

Out of the twelve Green Berets in his detachment, Kev only had six still capable of fighting. One was dead, the remainder wounded or out there somewhere in the ambush zone. To make matters worse, he still couldn't raise his headquarters for any air support.

They had one last functioning Humvee. As it launched another volley of grenades, Kev raised his M4 carbine and steadied it on a rock, firing off a few rounds. Next to the heavy thump of the automatic grenade launcher, it sounded like a firecracker. The nearest enemy was over eight hundred yards away, and his rounds were barely able to make the distance. He felt totally helpless; his men were dying and there was nothing he could do. He ducked as machine gun fire bounced off the armored Humvee, the rounds ricocheting into the dust.

Kev had fought the Taliban numerous times during his three tours of Afghanistan but never had he come up against such a well-trained and equipped enemy. He shook his head at the situation. To his front he saw two of the Afghans dash across the open ground as the enemy machine gun fire lapsed. They sprinted toward the Humvee, desperately trying to escape the engagement area. Kev fired a few single shots from his carbine in an attempt to cover their movement. In response a machine gun opened up along the ridge, the distinctive sound of a PKM firing an automatic burst. Kev watched in horror as the two men were cut down, their bodies riddled with bullets.

With a scream of frustration, he leaped to his feet, scrambling to the top of the mound of sand and rocks that protected him from the enemy gunfire. Another burst of machine gun fire laced the dirt around the dead Afghans, the ricocheting rounds zipping past his head.

"FUCK YOU! C'MON, FIGHT ME, YOU BASTARDS," he screamed as he brought his rifle up to his shoulder, pumping round after round in the direction of the enemy. The gunner in the Humvee joined him, thumping away with his grenade launcher. Within seconds the rest of the team was standing side by side with Kev, screaming at the tops of their lungs, blazing away in fury. Their rounds impacted uselessly on the distant slope while the Taliban positions continued to fire. Suddenly, in a blinding flash, the enemy disappeared, a dozen plumes of dust forming a cloud that blocked out the hillside.

The men on the crest ceased firing, looking at each other in disbelief. A second later a thunderous shock wave ripped through them, dust and grit pelting their bodies, forcing them to turn and take cover. The noise was deafening, like a storm cloud had broken directly over them. As the wave of violence passed, it was replaced with an eerie silence.

Kev spat out a mouthful of dirt. He cautiously made his way back up to the top of the mound where the rest of his men were back on their feet.

"Goddamn! They're fucked, boss." Jimmy pointed up at the enemy positions. The hillside was covered in smoking craters.

"That's a truckload of bang," Kev muttered.

"Hey, check that out." Jimmy pointed skyward, almost directly above them. The dark outline of what looked like a military transport could be seen banking around hard. "I bet that's a Pain Train!"

"Looks like a Russian transporter to me," Kev said.

"Well, it did a good job on the towelheads," said Jimmy, stuffing another wad of chewing tobacco into his mouth.

"There's a missile!" One of the men pointed out a tiny dart shooting up from the top of the valley. They all recognized the distinctive spiral smoke trail. Every one of the battle-hardened soldiers held their breath. Was a Taliban missile about to destroy their savior? The lumbering transporter seemed oblivious to the threat until it banked, harder than any transporter should have been able, and plummeted directly toward them, spitting flares back from under its wings. The missile overshot the Russian plane, exploding into one of the decoys.

Still the aircraft plowed onward, a line of oily smoke trailing it. "Shit, it's going down," shouted Kev. It screamed overhead, throwing a wave of dust over the men. They shielded their eyes, bracing for it to slam into the earth. Just as it seemed the jet would crash into the valley floor, it gained altitude and thundered over a ridgeline, disappearing from sight.

The Green Berets cheered, pumping the air with their fists and backslapping. The enemy positions on the hill were silent, completely destroyed.

"Alright, mount up. Our boys are wounded out there," Kev ordered. The men scrambled to the remaining Humvee and Afghan pickups.

As the vehicles raced into the engagement area, Jimmy was busy on the radio.

Kev looked back from the front seat of the Humvee. "Jimmy, how's the comms?"

"Yeah, boss, HQ just came on net. They got two birds inbound for CASEVAC."

"You warned them of the missile threat?"

"Yep, they'll be coming in low and fast! Sixty minutes out."

An hour was a long time and Kev knew more of his men were probably going to die of their wounds before they were evacuated.

***

Back on the Pain Train, Mitch was running diagnostics on the aircraft. Shrapnel from the surface-to-air missile had damaged one of the four engines, reducing the aircraft's power and causing it to leak hydraulic fluid. The situation was critical. If they continued to lose hydraulic pressure, the controls would fail and they would crash. His fingers flashed over the keyboard as he attempted to isolate the problem.

"Come on, old girl, come on," he murmured to himself.

"Bingo." Mitch isolated the hydraulic leak, restoring full control to the pilots.

One problem solved, he moved to the next, breaking the news to Ice. "Ice, this is Pain Train. We have just taken evasive action from a missile attack."

"No shit! You just barreled past me fifty feet off the deck. By the way, you're trailing smoke."

"Yeah, we sustained damage, returning to Kandahar. I'll let you know when we'll be back on-station."

"Roger. Job well done. Target is neutralized."

"Always a pleasure, lads. Once again Pain Train delivers the goods, toot-toot," Mitch said with a grin.

"Saved my ass again."

"Buy me a beer when you get back. In the meantime, how about you zap those rocket jockeys before we come back to play? You get a fix on their position?"

Mitch knew they had been very lucky to evade the missile without suffering more serious damage. The aggressive flying of the PRIMAL aircrew had saved them but Mitch did not want to tempt fate again.

"Yeah, we saw where the missile launched. Shouldn't have any problems finding them," Ice said.

"Alright, good luck, chaps."

"Stay safe, Pain Train. Ice out."

***

The metallic taste of blood filled Khalid's mouth and his ears rang. Despite the pain, he smiled. He knew his body was battered, but he was alive. Somehow he had been thrown clear of his pit when the bombs had exploded around him. "They will pay dearly for that," he said to himself. "It is Allah's will that I live to fight another day." He knew it was not his destiny to die in battle. He would die an old man surrounded by his wives and the sons that would continue his legacy.

Khalid slowly pushed himself up from the ground and onto his feet. He surveying the damage from the strike. Each of his positions was a smoking hole in the ground. The charred bodies of his men looked like the battered corpse of a goat after it had been trampled under the feet of horses in a game of buzkashi.

Death was nothing new to Khalid. He had seen worse and lost better men. It was facing the wrath of Khan that worried him; he had failed his master. Now only a ragged bunch of regular Taliban stood between the Americans and Khan's extraction site.

Khalid turned to hobble up the hill, hoping his surface-to-air missile crew was still alive. As he stumbled forward, he felt a stab of pain in his back. He touched his sternum, feeling a bloodied exit hole in his chest rig. Without a sound he toppled forward and died under the afternoon Afghan sun, far away from his wives and sons.

***

Ice scanned the Taliban position through his scope. Their fortified bunkers had been reduced to mounds of scorched earth; he could barely make out the broken bodies covered in dust and debris. He held his scope on the twitching corpse of the final survivor. Ice was satisfied with Mirza's choice of a chest shot, letting the target know he was dead.

He glanced down at the feed coming from the UAV as it flew above the US soldiers; they looked pretty beat up. The three remaining vehicles had formed a tight circle in the engagement zone and men were dragging their wounded comrades into the makeshift casualty point. Ice used his iPRIMAL to activate the secure frequency the Americans were using.

"Texas 1-3, this is Nemesis 4, over," Ice broadcast.

"Nemesis 4, this is Texas 1-3. You guys rock." The voice of the radio operator sounded flat, despite his enthusiasm.

He smiled grimly. "Good work holding out, guys."

"Nemesis, you saved our butts, dude. We were up shit creek without you."

"Yeah. Sorry we took so long. Listen, Texas, is your boss there?"

"Roger, I'll put him on." There was a slight pause as the radio changed hands.

"Nemesis, this is Captain Kev Daley of call sign Texas 1-3. Thanks again for helping us out."

"It's cool, Kev. This is Ice, of call sign Nemesis 4. We're just sorry we couldn't get air support earlier."

"No hard feelings, Ice. Without you we'd still be waiting."

"Kev, how are you guys looking on the ground?"

"We're shot up pretty bad. Thirty dead and eleven wounded leaves me with twenty able-bodied men. Most of them have minor injuries."

"Understood. What's your plan now?"

"Well, this unit is combat ineffective. Choppers inbound to extract the wounded and recover our dead."

"Roger. Me and my partner will provide overwatch from here."

"Much obliged, Ice. Once CASEVAC is complete I'm going to take the rest of my men and we're going to get the hell out of this valley."

"You gonna drive out of here with just one Humvee and your two pickups?" Ice couldn't blame the man for wanting to extract.

"That's the plan. Someone else can deal with this shitfight. My priority is to get my men back to Kandahar and refit to fight. What about you?"

"We're heading up the mountain."

"What? Why? How many men you got up there? You said you and your partner?"

"Kev, my partner and I are trying to find a former Russian experimental weapons lab and stop a WMD getting into the hands of Iranian agents."

"Jesus Christ, Ice, who the hell are you working for? CIA?"

"Something like that. Just believe me when I say that the intelligence behind this is rock solid. Those were hardcore Taliban mercenaries we just wasted, not the usual ragtag bunch.

I'm pretty damn sure they were defending the facility."

"No shit. They knew exactly what they were doing."

"I need to get up there, find the facility, and blow it to hell."

This was exactly the kind of mission Kev thrived on. "Can you get more air support?"

"Yes, but we need to take out those SAMs before our bird gets back on-station." Ice hoped the Pain Train would be repaired by the time they neutralized the anti-air weapons. "Kev, look, I know this is a big ask, but I need you and your remaining men to hit the mountain with me. I've lost the element of surprise and there's only two of us."

There was a pause on the other end of the radio.

"How many of these bastards do you think are left?"

"We just destroyed their main security force. There's probably no more than a squad of guards and the SAM shooters."

"You'll cover my evac?"

"Of course."

"Fuck it, OK then. We'll get the wounded and dead out, then we'll find this facility of yours and kill the rest of these assholes."

CHAPTER 19

Kev and Jimmy helped the team medic load the last of the wounded into the two pickups before they jumped in the Humvee and escorted the battered vehicles back down the track. The master sergeant had already marked out a landing zone and two MH-47 helos were only fifteen minutes out.

They had only made it a few hundred yards before Jimmy handed his boss the radio handset.

Ice's voice came over the frequency. "Kev, we have a problem."

"Go ahead."

"I have visual on an estimated hundred-plus fighters massing behind the eastern ridge."

"How far out?"

"They're on the move, no more than fifteen minutes from your LZ. We can slow them down but you need to get the fuck out of here."

"Goddamn it, Ice, we're all getting out of here. The choppers can extract us all. We'll hold off the Taliban till you marry up."

"Negative. They're moving in platoon-size groups along the ridgeline. If you don't go now, you're fucked."

"Do you realize what you're saying?" Kev said.

"Go! We have this in hand. We'll bypass the Talibs and find their missiles. Once we've neutralized the air defense we can call in air support. No more of your men need die today."

Kev clenched his gloved fist. "Roger. We'll set up a defensive perimeter around the LZ and wait for the choppers."

"Affirmative. We now have eight more enemy KIA but we're going to have to slow our engagement and conserve ammo."

"Stay in contact. Texas, out."

Kev turned to Jimmy. "Let the choppers know it's going to be a hot LZ. Company-size Taliban element approaching from the northeast."

"Got it, boss."

Kev and his men formed a perimeter two hundred yards out from the extraction site. They lay in wait, weapons ready. Behind them wounded men moaned quietly, the team medic moving between them, desperately trying to keep them alive.

***

Khan's first wave of reinforcements approached cautiously. They moved in an extended line, silhouetted against the sky as they crossed the ridge, weapons held at the ready.

On the opposite ridge, Ice and Mirza watched from a depression along the rocky slope. They were all but invisible to the Taliban, drab robes blending in perfectly with the rocky terrain. Through their high-powered scopes the PRIMAL operatives could see the Afghans clearly as they descended toward Texas 1-3. Some carried AKs, others rocket launchers and machine guns. A few wore US Army digital camouflage armor over their robes, no doubt scavenged from the bodies of the dead American patrol.

"There's too many," Mirza whispered over the radio.

Ice checked the elevation on his rifle and took aim. "Need to cull their numbers a little." He exhaled slowly and squeezed the trigger. The weapon jumped against his shoulder and a Taliban fighter toppled over. "Tango down."

"They have to be in range of Texas 1-3 by now," Mirza said as he fired his own rifle.

As if waiting for the Indian's cue, the American Special Forces opened up, blasting the Taliban with a wall of lead. The line of advancing fighters dropped to the ground, hitting back with an equally heavy weight of fire. A second, then a third line of fighters followed up, pushing forward in pairs, firing as they closed in on the US and Afghan soldiers.

"These fuckers are insane," said Ice as he hit another target. "They just keep coming." As the enemy warriors fell to the combined fire of the snipers and the Green Berets, more rushed down the hill to replace them.

"This isn't normal," Mirza reported between his own shots. "They're disciplined."

Ice panned his scope down the slope to where Texas 1-3 was defending. The Green Berets and their Afghan Army partners were putting up a valiant fight, but one by one they fell as he looked on, the wave of Taliban surging forward relentlessly.

"You're right. Where the hell are those helos?"

"I don't know, but I'm getting low on ammo," Mirza replied as he fired again.

"Roger, make them count."

The Taliban surged forward as the remnants of Texas 1-3 peeled back to the extraction zone and their wounded men. Ice identified the team's radio operator crouched next to another American, the thin antenna giving him away. He watched as the commander fought side by side with his radio operator, laying down fire as they moved. They constantly changed their positions, going through a routine of firing, reloading, and moving.

"Texas 1-3, this is Nemesis. Any news on those choppers?" Ice broadcast over the American frequency.

"Negative, Nemesis. We've got no comms with aircraft."

Ice and Mirza had used most of their ammunition and still more fighters joined the battle. All along the perimeter, the weight of fire from the Special Forces and their Afghan allies began to wane. Ice could see the Taliban pushing forward harder, sprinting from cover to cover. He watched as the radio operator struggled with a jammed weapon.

"Mirza, cover them."

A pair of Taliban dashed forward to overrun the command team's precarious position and both snipers fired at once. It took half a second for their bullets to travel from barrel to target. Both Taliban dropped.

The forward line of fighters had come within fifty yards of Texas 1-3's outer perimeter when Ice heard the faint beat of rotor blades approaching from the south. All along the defensive line, Kev's men had their spirits lifted by their imminent rescue. It only seemed to make the Taliban more determined to advance.

As the first black twin-rotor chopper came into view, a fighter rose from the ground hefting an RPG launcher to his shoulder. Mirza spotted him moving from cover and shot him cleanly through the head. The dead man fell to the ground but managed to trigger his rocket, launching it sideways. It streaked across the valley and slammed into the mountain next to Ice's position, showering him in shards of stone and dirt.

"Ice, you OK?" asked Mirza.

"Yeah, I'm fine. Thank God the cavalry's here."

With a noise like tearing canvas, a six-barreled minigun opened up from above, spraying a lethal barrage of fire across the Taliban. They scrambled for cover as a downpour of glowing red tracer ripped up the ground and churned flesh to pulp. Ice looked up to see the MH-47 helicopter circling with both the side-door minigun and back-ramp machine gun blazing.

Behind Kev and his men, a second chopper was already on the deck and medics were rushing to load Texas 1-3's wounded. Its minigun was also firing bursts, shredding any enemy foolish enough to present themselves.

From their position high above the evacuation site, Ice and Mirza engaged the enemy with single precise shots. With the Taliban suppressed, the Green Berets rapidly withdrew to the landing zone.

An RPG hissed upward from behind a cluster of boulders, narrowly missing the circling chopper. A savage burst of minigun fire lashed out, shredding the rocketeer. With a roar the second bird lifted off, swapping places with the other helicopter as it landed to pick up the last few soldiers.

"FALL BACK!" screamed Kev, standing on the helicopter ramp to wave his men onto the helicopter. "FALL BACK!"

The men raced back in pairs, covering each other as they dashed to the helicopter. Jimmy was last; he continued firing to cover the few remaining Afghans who were struggling to carry their wounded comrades. He turned to sprint to the waiting helicopter as a volley of RPGs shot into the air. The second helicopter maneuvered wildly, evading the rockets but giving the Taliban seconds to engage the fleeing Americans. A burst of machine gun fire hit Jimmy, pitching him forward into the dirt.

Kev dashed straight for the wounded soldier, firing from the hip as he ran. He could almost see the grin on the warrior who had raised his weapon for the kill. Kev faintly registered the single shot that exploded through the man's head, negating the threat.

Grabbing the loop on the back of Jimmy's body armor, like a father scooping his child from the floor, he tossed the wounded soldier over his shoulder and sprinted the last twenty yards to the chopper.

He stumbled as a round slammed into his armor and he fell forward onto the ramp, Jimmy tumbling from his shoulders into the cabin. His men hauled him inside as the MH-47 leaped into the air with the scream of turbines and a whirlwind of dust. The machine gun on the back ramp spat rounds at the shrinking Taliban as the two helicopters raced away, hugging the valley floor. The aeromedics were already working on the wounded and one approached Kev as he lay fighting for breath on the cabin floor.

"You hit?" the medic screamed over the engines and downwash, a concerned look on his face.

Kev struggled to his feet. "Negative, I'm fine. Hit the armor. Look after Jimmy," he replied and the medic moved off as one of the loadmasters handed Kev a headset.

"Sir, are you Captain Daley?"

He nodded, slipping on the headset.

"Call sign Nemesis wants to talk to you."

"Nemesis-4, this is Texas 1-3." Kev shielded the microphone from the wind with his hand.

The calm voice responded immediately. "Good to hear your voice, Kev. I thought I saw you go down."

"Negative. You saved my bacon again. I owe you big time."

"It's me that owes you. We just mopped up the last couple

of Taliban. You guys massacred them."

"Happy to oblige, buddy. Listen, you stay frosty out there, OK, and if you get back to Kandahar, look me up."

"Will do, Kev. Take care. Thanks again."

"OK, Texas 1-3, out."

Kev slumped back into the webbing seats and looked around wearily. His men lay on stretchers or sprawled on the aircraft's seating. They were battered, worn, and tired, but at least some were still alive.

CHAPTER 20

Khan stood at the top of a craggy feature gazing down into the valley below. The dry winds tugged at his spotless white robes, causing his black headscarf to stream out behind him. He looked almost biblical, as if Moses stood upon the mountain ready to cast the Ten Commandments onto the rocks below. However, Khan did not look down from the mountain at his people breaking God's law; he looked down at the remnants of his army.

On the slopes of the mountain in front of him lay the charred corpses of Khalid and his men. Further along the valley floor, the broken bodies of the other Taliban lay scattered, shot to pieces by the Americans and their helicopters.

Khan's forces had been decimated. Now he only had a handful of his own men remaining and less than half of the local Taliban fighters. Under his calm exterior, anger seethed, rage burning through his veins like molten lava. He fought the urge to scream at the top of his lungs.

"Someone has orchestrated this. Somewhere there has been a betrayal." The Special Forces, the Russian transport aircraft, and the spy plane. It was all too much of a coincidence.

"Yanuk, come!" Khan yelled at the men who had accompanied him. The sullen Russian detached himself from the group, assault rifle cradled in his arms as he swaggered across to the warlord. "Yanuk, call your master. He needs to explain himself." The Russian didn't argue. He took the satellite phone from his pouch and dialed Dostiger's number. One of the bodyguards answered.

"Khan wants to speak to the boss. Put him on." He handed the phone across to the warlord.

"Dostiger, is that you?"

"Khan, what is happening?"

"I was hoping you could tell me." Khan's voice was like ice.

"What are you talking about, comrade?"

"My men are dead!"

"What?"

"The Americans came and brought their bombs."

"You told me those bastard Americans and their fucking planes were taken care of. Is the site still intact? Can you finish on time?" Dostiger said with urgency.

"If we are left undisturbed, we can still recover the weapon within twenty-four hours. If the Americans return, all will be lost."

"You promised me the Americans would be focused in the South. You promised me that you could deal with them!"

"Their aircraft was Russian. These were not just Americans." Khan's usual calm demeanor was cold, revealing his anger. "They came searching for us. The operation has been compromised. Someone has betrayed you."

"No one could have compromised us. We have taken enough precautions. You're paranoid."

"Be very careful, my son. I think the infidels are watching."

"Then we must move faster. Transport has already been arranged. Focus on getting the weapon and contact me when you are ready. Do you have enough men?"

"I will rely on the local Taliban but my remaining men will be ready with the missiles in case the Americans return."

"Use all of your men, Khan. Send for more if you can. Dig all night."

"If it is Allah's will, we cannot fail."

***

Mirza watched the group of Taliban through the scope of his sniper rifle. There had to be at least forty new fighters standing above the destroyed position, surveying the damage.

He settled his crosshairs on the one that seemed to be their leader. From nearly a mile away he could still make out the long flowing robes. He glanced at the rangefinder in the bottom of his scope; it read 1,400 yards. He could probably fluke the shot but there was no point. It would only reveal their position, triggering the Taliban to move into the mountains and hunt them. He lowered the weapon and slid backward into the cluster of boulders that Ice was using to hide.

Ice looked up from a map as Mirza slid in beside him.

Mirza spoke softly. "Still about forty of them down there. We sure could use the Pain Train right now."

"Still waiting on an update from Mitch." Ice checked the screen of his iPRIMAL. "Only an hour or so till darkness, then we'll move." He pushed the map toward Mirza and passed him a pencil. "Show me where you think that missile launched from."

He studied the map for a few seconds then made a mark on the side of the mountain. "Here, above this flat area."

"Hmmm. My guess would be that is where the extraction site is," Ice said.

"That would make sense; then the missiles are just above, in an elevated position that can protect the site."

"We'll get a chance to check it out tonight. How's your ammo and water?"

"Adequate, I still have another three magazines, grenades, and at least four liters of water."

"Good. I don't anticipate shooting from here on in, but better safe than sorry. Try to get some rest, buddy. We'll move after sunset."

Mirza nodded and sipped from one of his water bottles. He'd already made himself comfortable, lying against his pack.

Once Ice had stowed the map in his chest rig, he unwrapped an energy bar, snapped it in half and threw the other piece to Mirza. "So you got any family, buddy?"

Mirza chewed his half of the bar. "Yes, I have a mother in India."

"That all?"

"That's all. My father and brother were both killed when I was ten. I have looked after my mother ever since."

"Tough gig for a little fella, hey. I know what it's like; my old man walked out on us when I was eleven."

"But you had brothers and sisters?"

"Yeah, a younger sister. Mum was an alcoholic, so like you,

I had to run the family."

"Your sister, where is she now?" Mirza propped himself up against a rock.

"She's married now, to a lawyer. Good guy. She grew up alright, that one." Ice finished chewing on the bar and slid the wrapper back into a pouch. "She's a doctor; works in a children's hospital."

"You must be very proud."

"Yeah, she's a great kid. Better person than I'll ever be."

Mirza smiled as he imagined Ice as the man of the house at an early age, forced to grow up quickly and deal with responsibility beyond his years. The thought gave Mirza confidence. He began to doze off when his earpiece beeped.

Ice activated the call.

"How you tracking, lads?" It was Mitch.

"We're OK. How's the bird?"

"Not looking great. That rocket chewed the old girl up pretty bad. We sustained heavy damage to one of the engines and the hydraulic system."

"How long?"

"I've fixed most of the damage but we're waiting for a parts delivery. HQ's dispatched a jet this afternoon but it could be anywhere from six to twelve hours before we're airborne."

"So for the next twelve hours we need to stay out of trouble," Ice said. "Problem is if we wait that long we could lose our chance."

"Why is that? Chua said we probably have forty-eight hours till they can move it."

"That was before half of NATO joined the party. Nope, my guess is they will get it out a hell of a lot faster now. We'll have to run the gauntlet and take down their air defense tonight."

"I'm pretty sure I can get the Pain Train up early tomorrow morning."

"Alright. That gives us all night to take out the missiles."

"Just don't get in trouble, because I'm not going to be there to bail you out."

Ice laughed. "It's Mirza out here with me, not Bishop. We'll be fine."

"OK. Good luck, lads. We'll see you early in the morning." Mitch terminated the call.

The sun had started to dip behind the mountains bringing a frigid chill to the air. The two men prepared for the long night ahead. They changed into cold-weather gear, donning heavy polar-fleeces under their assault vests. From experience Mirza knew it would get icy cold this high up in the mountains. It was not going to be a pleasant night.

CHAPTER 21

THE BUNKER

Vance looked up at the main screen in his office waiting for the video link to establish with Bishop. He wearily glanced across at a smaller monitor displaying the various times zones around the world. It was 0300 hours here at the island and 1800 hours in Kiev. No wonder he felt like shit; he had been up for over twenty hours.

Sitting across from the director was Chen Chua. Vance marveled at the energy of the intelligence chief. Despite being on the go for close to five days and surviving on only a couple of hours' sleep, the skinny Chinese American looked fresh and alert.

"How the hell do you do it, Chua? If I drank that much Red Bull, I'd bounce off the walls for a couple of hours then crash like a Malaysian passenger jet."

Bishop's face flashed up on the screen, startling both of them. It was almost as if he were in the room. "Vance, Chua, how's it all going?"

Vance smiled, greeting Bishop in his deep voice. "How you doing, buddy? Good job on the Antonov gig this morning."

"No worries."

Vance picked up his pen. "So how's it all going? Give us a rundown on the last fourteen hours."

Bishop took Vance and Chua through a step-by-step report of what had happened. He began with his assessment of the team and finished with the surveillance of Dostiger's home and his meeting with Saneh.

"So what's your take on the Dostiger residence?" Chua asked. "Do you think you can get in and out without being compromised?"

"My man doesn't think it's going to be a problem. We just need to wait for the right moment."

"How's the security?"

"Yeah, Dostiger has it locked down pretty damn tight, but nothing we can't handle. When he leaves the house he usually takes most of his goons with him."

"So when are you going in?" Vance asked.

"Tonight. I just took a call from Dmitri Krenkov and he's arranged a meeting for me with Dostiger at his nightclub in town. Once he leaves the estate our boys will go to work."

Chua spoke up. "Aden, we have some information here that may jeopardize the meeting with Dostiger. MOIS has been in contact with him."

"When?"

"We picked it up three hours ago. The phone number linked to Dostiger was called by the number you provided for Agent Ebadi," Chua answered.

"Do we have a cut on the conversation?"

"Negative. Only a date, time, and general location."

Bishop sighed. Chua continued, "Both Vance and I think that this changes the situation significantly. It's possible that Saneh has sold you out to Dostiger. Remember, he's worked with MOIS before." Chua glanced at Vance before getting to the point. "We think it might be wise for you to cut the meeting away."

"Hang on a second. It's unlikely that Saneh sold us out. At the moment we're her only ally, and let's face it, she needs all the friends she can get."

"All the more reason for her to sell you out, Aden. She can earn serious kudos with Dostiger," Chua said.

"No. She wants to stop him from selling weapons to the IRGC, not line up a job as a go-go dancer in his club. She'll try to make him a better offer than the Guards. And she'll want to keep her links to us as a wild card, just in case she can't influence him. Plus she has to know we're tracking that phone. I think she wanted us to know she was contacting him."

"Possibly, but is it worth the risk?" Chua asked.

"Yeah, it is worth the fucking risk. That's the point. We don't know anything about this guy. At a minimum we need to get a close look at him."

"We could stick with our electronic and covert surveillance. Your team can still break in and we'll get photos eventually."

"No! We don't have enough time to stuff around on this one, Chua. This may be the only opportunity we have for a face-to-face."

"Look, Aden, I know you want this guy dead, we all do, but you can't make this personal yet. We need to focus on the mission."

Bishop glared through the screen at Chua, who kept talking. "There's too much at stake here and Dostiger's already going to be on edge. Not only has he received a call from MOIS, he also took one from a handset in Afghanistan." Chua had already sent Bishop a short update on Ice's battle in the Khod Valley.

"I'm not making this personal," Bishop replied coldly. "The fact is, right now we've got nothing suggesting that Dostiger has linked Tim Fischer with any of this. I've no doubt that Dostiger's run a background check, and the fact that he still wants to meet suggests he's taken the bait. Now if I don't go to the meeting, then he'll start getting suspicious and that'll pretty much shut us down."

Vance's booming voice interrupted the discussion. "OK, that's enough. At the end of the day it's your call, Bishop. You're the man on the ground. If you think it's a go, then that's your call."

"I think it's worth the risk. We need to get all we can on this guy. Things haven't gone well in the 'Ghan and you both know there's a good chance we'll have to make the snatch at this end. I, for one, would like to know who the hell I'm dealing with."

Chua didn't look happy but would back Bishop in any decision he made.

Vance nodded. "OK, but goddamn it, be careful. I don't want this going sideways."

Chua added, "Remember, if Dostiger speeds up his timeline he could have the weapon out of Afghanistan in a very short period of time. The next twenty-four hours are critical and you'll need to be prepared to adapt to any changes in the situation."

Bishop nodded. "Don't worry, my team's good to go. Hey, one last thing. I was wondering, has there been anything out of any of the government agencies? Anything to indicate that someone other than MOIS is tracking this?"

Vance shook his head. "Nothing; we haven't picked up anything in reporting. Even after the intelligence we leaked, MI6, Mossad, CIA, none of them seem to be doing anything."

"Typical. Anyway, that's not a bad thing. Right now the last thing we need is extra heat on Dostiger. Alright, before I go I just want to say the support you guys are giving us is really appreciated. Pass on my thanks to the rest of the team."

Vance smiled. "OK, stay safe, bud. Check in as soon as you can."

"No worries. Bishop out."

The connection with Kiev terminated, Vance leaned back in his chair and emitted a sigh. "I hope he's right."

Chua was already heading out the door. He stopped and turned to face Vance. "When is he ever not right?"

"Yeah, that's what I'm afraid of."

CHAPTER 22

CLUB KYIV, KIEV

"So to what do I owe the pleasure of your presence, Agent Ebadi?" Dostiger smiled graciously, pouring Saneh a glass of champagne.

"I'm here on behalf of the Iranian government, Mr. Dostiger," Saneh replied curtly. She was a little taken aback by the lavish surroundings and the chivalrous behavior of her host. Dostiger was not at all what she expected. His file had disclosed an arms dealer notorious for his ruthlessness and abrasive personality.

"Ahhh, I thought as much. But I did not think that Iranian intelligence employed movie stars." The Ukrainian leaned back in the antique armchair, running his eyes over the woman who sat opposite him.

She blushed and Dostiger smiled, unabashed.

"So what does the Ministry of Intelligence and Security want with a simple businessman like me?" he asked.

"Well, you have served us well in the past and we think you are now in an even better position to provide what we need." She watched the arms dealer's face closely.

"And what is it that Iran needs, Miss Ebadi?" Dostiger's face remained impassive. "Surface-to-air missiles, antitank rockets, sniper rifles? I know, you want antiship missiles for the Hormuz Strait."

"Actually, we are thinking of something a little more strategic."

"Hmmm, maybe a long-range ballistic missile such as the SS-4?" Dostiger took a sip from his glass of scotch. "I happen to know a Russian General who owes me a favor."

"Mr. Dostiger, I'm not talking about missiles or rockets. I think we both know what Iran really needs."

"Yes, Miss Ebadi, and I have made it perfectly clear in the

past that I am not in a position to provide that type of weapon."

Saneh placed her glass on the table. "That's not what my sources are telling me."

He placed his own glass down and looked at her icily. "Then they are either misinformed or lying."

Saneh met the man's eyes and they sent a chill down her spine. Before she could respond, Dostiger rose from his chair, clutching his cane for support. "Now if you don't mind, Miss Ebadi, I have another appointment that I need to prepare for. If there is anything else that I can help you with, you know how to contact me."

"We'll match any offer that the IRGC has made." She thought she saw the faintest gleam of greed in the man's eyes, but then it was gone.

"I have no idea what you are talking about. Our business here is done." He gestured for the door.

"They can't be trusted, Dostiger. This will end badly for all of us," she said as a burly security guard shepherded her through the doors of the office and back out into the club.

A manager greeted her at the bottom of the stairs. "Ma'am, Mr. Dostiger wanted you to know that the drinks are on the house."

"Thank you. Tell Mr. Dostiger he is most gracious." She took up a position at the bar and ordered a non-alcoholic cocktail, wondering if Fischer would show up.

***

According to Bishop's internet research, Club Kyiv was one of the Ukrainian capital's most exclusive nightspots. The club's vibrant web page boasted that it played host to elite clientele from all over Europe, with the hottest international DJs and capacity for over a thousand patrons.

Bishop wasn't big on nightclubs; jumping around on a dance floor with hundreds of people off their heads on drugs hardly seemed like fun. He preferred the intimacy of a cocktail bar or a good old-fashioned pub.

The club was certainly well located, built in the middle of Kiev's business district in what looked to be an old warehouse. Aleks and Bishop had already driven past, scoping the venue through the tinted windows of the BMW. In the early evening it hadn't looked exciting: just a pair of sturdy doors halfway down a narrow street. Hemmed in by tall buildings, only a small neon sign identified the entrance.

Now it was late in the evening and Bishop knew the club would be getting busy. He glanced at the digital clock on the BMW's dashboard; it was almost time for his meeting with Dostiger. Aleks stopped the car short of the venue, pulling into a parking space a couple of blocks up the road.

Leaning forward in the passenger seat, Bishop removed the compact Beretta pistol and holster from the back of his pants, placing them in the glove compartment. "Aleks, keep the car here. If I get into trouble, I'll call."

"*Da*, boss, I am ready if you need me." Aleks grinned. He had an MP7 submachine gun slung across his chest and was wearing his body armor under a heavy leather jacket.

"If it all goes to shit, you'll need to hit the front of the club hard. We're not going to want to hang around." They knew the narrow street in front of the building would be tight for a hot extraction and Dostiger's men would likely be armed.

"I know. 'Stick to the plan.' No problems." Aleks smiled.

"Yeah, no problems, Aleks." Bishop opened the door and stepped out into the crisp night air. He had thrown a long black cashmere coat over his pinstriped suit and was wearing a pair of Kevlar-lined leather gloves. His PRIMAL phone was back at the safe house and nothing he carried could be traced back to his parent organization. All he had was his local cell phone, a money clip of crisp US hundred-dollar bills, and a fake passport. He wasn't particularly happy about going in unarmed but there really wasn't a need. As he had pointed out to Chua, Dostiger had no reason to suspect him.

Bishop strode down the road, his face smarting in the nighttime chill. As he strolled toward the club, the thumping bass emanating from the large building hit him. He could feel it in his chest a good fifty yards from the entrance. Clearly there were no sound restrictions in this part of the city or Dostiger had enough council members in his pocket to do whatever he wanted. One of his black Range Rovers was parked on the sidewalk next to the entrance, the lack of license plates more evidence of Dostiger's influence.

A long line of patrons waited outside the entrance. Club Kyiv's 'exclusive' clientele appeared to consist of young rich kids intermingled with overweight businessmen in suits and gold-digging prostitutes. Bishop couldn't tell the difference between the working girls and the women there simply for a good time. To him they all looked the same, and he had never seen so many fake breasts, collagen-enhanced lips, hair extensions, and spray tans in one spot before.

These girls wore the shortest skirts he had ever seen. How the hell do they stay warm showing that much skin, he wondered. They looked ridiculous in their winter coats with skinny bare legs protruding beneath them. Like ostriches, he realized with a smile.

As Bishop walked past the line a number of the women were already eyeballing him. He walked straight to the front, where controlling the throng of scantily clad women, testosterone-fueled punters, and fat, balding suits, were two of the biggest bouncers he'd ever seen. These guys made Ice look small. Bishop wondered if they were grown in a lab and how the hell they found clothes to fit them. Their long black jackets were huge, easily covering their radios and whatever weapons they were carrying.

Perched between them was a petite hostess. Bishop instantly forgot the two bouncers. She was a stunning blonde with high cheekbones, pale gray eyes, and full red lips. A typical Russian beauty, she too appeared to have the ability to stay warm wearing just a short dress with only a tiny fur coat covering her shoulders. Bishop smiled back.

"I'm here to see Mr. Dostiger." He passed the hostess his card.

One of the bouncers glared at him like an angry, steroid-abusing Doberman and plucked the card from the blonde's delicate hand.

"Wait here," he muttered, turning his back, speaking into his radio.

The hostess returned her attention to the waiting line while the other security guard continued to eye Bishop warily. The doormen seemed to take great pleasure in wielding power over the club's clientele, in particular the rich tourists with their expensive clothes and arrogant attitudes. No doubt they thought Bishop was just another soft Western businessman here to ask favors from their boss.

They kept Bishop waiting for a full two minutes before the first bouncer addressed him.

"Mr. Fischer, it seems you're expected." The scowl on the huge man's face told a different story.

The surly guard escorted Bishop through the heavy front doors into a dimly lit foyer. Another gorgeous hostess took his coat while the thug ran a metal-detector wand over him. He raised his arms and smiled charmingly until the wand ran up the inside of his leg, smacking into his groin. Bishop flinched in pain. He knew Dostiger's men were just trying to intimidate him. The arms dealer wanted to set the rules before negotiations had even started.

The bouncer gave him a rough shove past the cloakroom toward another short corridor leading to the main room. As Bishop turned the corner, a wall of sound hit him and he was confronted with a seething mass of people on an enormous dance floor. The music was hard-core electronic, high tempo with a powerful bass, and the DJ occupying the central booth worked it like the leader of a strange cult. He manipulated the pulsing laser lights and smoke machines in concert with the crescendo of the bass line, playing the crowd into a drug-and-dance-induced trance.

He noticed the dance floor was packed with youths, no doubt the children of Kiev's elite. Dostiger must make a fortune selling drugs to these kids, he thought, noting the designer clothing and handbags. It wouldn't have surprised him if the arms dealer had ties to both Afghanistan and South America.

The older clientele, the soft businessmen with their escorts, lounged in private booths to the sides of the main stage. Sprawled on the low-lying leather couches, they watched the podiums where lithe bodies twisted seductively around brass poles. More scantily clad women served the drinks, premium vodka purchased by the bottle and French champagne flowing freely. The less wealthy men bought their drinks from the busy bars off to the side, mingling with less exclusive ladies or just ogling the multitude of gyrating bodies.

The whole place was a spectacle of hedonistic sex and escapism played to a pounding bassline in an expensive, flashy, overdesigned cavern. It was no wonder the club was popular with Kiev's social elite.

Bishop's minder, the massive security guard, guided him firmly to one of the two sweeping staircases that buttressed either side of the dance floor. Lounging on the stairs were more stunning women looking for prospective clients. It looked like a Victoria's Secret runway show.

As he padded up the marble staircase, he glanced down at the crowded space below, searching for Dostiger's guards, planning an escape route he hoped he wouldn't need.

His eyes lingered on the bare back of a dark-haired woman facing the bar; her glossy black hair was exotic in comparison to the blondes that filled the club. As she turned from the bar, he caught her eye. Bishop's chest tightened as Saneh flashed him an ever-so-slight smile. He continued up the stairs, following the menacing security guard onto the exclusive second level.

Upstairs was far more relaxed than the narcotics-fueled main room below. They walked along the balcony that overlooked the dance floor and he could hear laughter from the private booths, curtained off from view. The bouncer led him to the end of the walkway, where another ogre-like security guard stood in front of a heavy door.

"Mr. Fischer to see the boss," the man escorting him said in broken English, more for Bishop's benefit than for the other man. The guard looked their guest up and down before he opened the door, gesturing for him to enter.

"I hope we meet again soon, Mr. Fischer." The original bouncer gave a sadistic grin.

Bishop met the guard's icy stare. He knew that for all his bravado, the muscle-bound thug wouldn't last two seconds against the highly trained members of his team.

Dostiger's waiting room smelt like cigars. The furnishings were more evidence of expensive taste, with heavy, gilded, velvet-upholstered chairs and Impressionist paintings on the windowless walls. An antique silver drink stand in the corner of the room sported a number of bottles of very expensive liquor beside an assortment of glasses. Bishop picked up a bottle of thirty-year-old Talisker.

Holding the bottle, he looked across at the double doors that no doubt led to the arms dealer's office. He had no idea how long he would be waiting. He shrugged, uncorked the scotch, and poured some into a weighty crystal tumbler. There were so many things that could go wrong with the meet, he reflected. Saneh might have already sold him out, Kurtz and the rest of the team could screw up the break-in, or Dostiger could simply take a dislike to him. His Neanderthal bouncers certainly had.

Bishop sat in an antique chair and savored the fine whiskey. Just like Aleks said, he thought, everything's going to be fine. He pulled his cell phone from his pocket, expecting Kurtz to report in shortly. There were no new messages.

CHAPTER 23

DOSTIGER'S RESIDENCE

Even from a distance you could tell the man was drunk, the reek of alcohol overwhelming the foul stench of homelessness. He lurched down the dimly lit street, occasionally tripping and collapsing onto the sidewalk before hauling himself to his feet and continuing his stumbling journey. Once he stopped to vomit, steam rising from the bile as it made contact with the frozen concrete.

The drunkard was dressed in a heavy overcoat, patched in half a dozen places, with a thick woolen beanie pulled down low over his eyes. A piece of rope was tied loosely around his waist and battered boots protected his feet from the cold. For a homeless man he was well dressed, and although he stank, he would probably survive the cold spring night.

Less than a hundred yards down the road, inside his heated guard box, a uniformed security guard watched the bum's progress through a thermal camera, laughing as the drunkard toppled over. Using the high-resolution lens he zoomed in as the disheveled man wrestled with a trashcan in an attempt to get back on his feet. As humorous as the situation was, he hoped the bum wouldn't continue his journey past the gates of the residence. His boss was completely unforgiving when it came to the aesthetics of his suburb and it would be the guard's task to remove the man if Dostiger returned while the drunk was still around. He glanced at the time displayed on the video screen; the boss wasn't expected to return for at least another hour. If required he would hurry the nuisance along with his boot.

The guard panned the camera out and switched to another view, looking for his partner, who was patrolling the grounds. He spotted the other guard by the boat sheds at the back of the property. If Dostiger had been at home, no less than ten heavily armed men would be on duty. However, tonight the arms dealer had taken most of the men with him to the club. Only two guards remained to secure the house.

Methodically the guard continued flicking through the camera feeds. He paused on an image of one of the bedrooms shown from a hidden camera. The field of view didn't quite extend to the smaller bedroom next door that was currently occupied by a lovely Russian model. So far the guard had only caught a glimpse of her sultry curves but it didn't stop him from constantly checking the feed.

The guard switched back to the view covering the front of the gate, looking for the drunk. Panning the camera back and forth, he wondered if the wretch was in one of the blind spots.

Without warning there was a loud thump. The guard glanced up from the video screen and was startled to see the dirty face of the drunkard peering at him through the bulletproof glass. The bum smeared his face against the window, flailing at it with an empty bottle. Rising from his chair, the guard grabbed his jacket and a baton from the desk. On his way out he pressed the release button for the heavy iron gate, opening it a few feet.

His feet crunched on the gravel as he walked across to the gap in the gate, slapping the baton into the palm of his gloved hand. He cautiously squeezed through the opening and paused, looking around until he saw the man, passed out at the bottom of the guard box.

"Hey! Get up!" The guard strode over and gave the bum a swift kick. With a groan, he mumbled something incoherent and proceeded to vomit onto the sidewalk.

"Ah, fuck!" The guard leaped backward to avoid the splash of acidic green liquid. The stench was overpowering and he dry-heaved. He watched the homeless guy struggle to his feet and wipe the vomit from his mouth. As the man stumbled forward, the guard held out his baton in an effort to keep the vagrant at arm's length. It was one of the last things he would remember. The bum caught the stick under his arm, grabbing it firmly with his left hand. His right fist flashed around in a well-timed hook as he pulled Dostiger's man in close. The lead-packed Kevlar glove caught the guard on the temple, his eyes rolled back, and he crumpled in a heap.

"Very nice, Kurtz." Pavel appeared from the shadows wearing a copy of the unconscious guard's uniform. He knelt next to the man, pushing an auto-injector up against his neck, and a shot of compressed air pushed microscopic particles of a sedative through his skin. The guard would stay under for at least twenty minutes before awakening with a splitting headache. The two men grabbed his arms and legs and carried him through the open gate. Kurtz used the guard's keys to open the security door and they dumped the body on the floor.

Pavel sat at the guard's computer and inserted a USB key into the terminal. A custom program on the device immediately bypassed the surveillance system's security measures, giving the Russian unrestricted access. Now he could manipulate the video footage, removing any trace of their activities. He could also control the alarms, switch off the internal motion sensors, and keep tabs on the movement of Dostiger's second guard.

"Kurtz, can you hear me?" Pavel transmitted into the radio mike attached to his collar.

"*Ja*, loud and clear," the German responded. He had already left the guard box and was halfway to the house, using the shadows of the trees to avoid the floodlit lawns. Even though there was only one guard, he remained cautious.

Pavel flicked through the screens at the computer terminal until he found the master floor plan. "Kurtz, I've located Dostiger's office. It's on the second floor. You need to enter through the western-side door and use the staircase just inside on the right."

Kurtz hit the radio switch in his sleeve. "Acknowledged. Where is the other guard?"

"Still down by the river, comrade. We should have about ten minutes."

"*Gut*, I will be in and out in seven."

***

The former German counterterrorist officer paused at the edge of the perfectly manicured lawn. There were no flowers or hedges; it was all trees and perfectly trimmed grass. He would have preferred a little more cover, even with Pavel watching the cameras.

Kurtz identified the side door and sprinted across the lawn. He crouched next to the entrance and pulled out the keys he had taken from the guard. Taking a deep breath, he drew a suppressed pistol from inside his jacket and grasped the door handle firmly. It turned slightly, unlocked. He gently pushed the door open and slid inside.

The lighting in the stately manor was soft and the long wood-paneled hallway was decorated with artwork and antique furniture. He padded down the corridor until he reached the hardwood staircase. With trepidation he eased his weight onto the well-worn stairs. There was no creak; they were as solid as the day they were made. He crept up the stairs and onto the landing on the second floor. At the top he paused, looking up at the CCTV camera pointing down the corridor.

"Pavel, anyone on the top floor?" he whispered softly.

"*Nyet*, it's possible that someone is in the bedroom to your right, but the lights are off. I can't see anything. Dostiger's office is the second on the right."

He crept down the hall, past the bedroom, stopping in front of the heavy wooden door that protected the arms dealer's private study. The lock was complex, a Medeco Cam lock, all but impossible for the average thief to pick. Kurtz wasn't your average thief. He pulled a device from his pocket and inserted the tiny probe into the lock. A sensor scanned the inside of the tumbler and the universal key on the other end of the device used hundreds of tiny threads of titanium to replicate the key. It took him fifteen seconds to open it.

"Very slick, my German friend, but you still set off no less than three sensors: one motion, one heat, and one weight in floor." Pavel was shutting the alarms down as they occurred, removing the events from the security system's electronic log.

"Herr Dostiger takes this all very seriously, *ja*," Kurtz whispered. "Where's the other guard?"

"Still down by the boat sheds. He's smoking now; you have time."

Dostiger's study reflected a man obsessed with the instruments of war. The room's oak-paneled walls were lined with antique weaponry, everything from a samurai sword to a battered lever-action rifle. Not a book in sight. Clearly the arms dealer wasn't academic.

In the middle of the room was a sturdy old desk that looked like it would be more at home in the captain's cabin of an eighteenth-century warship. On the desk was a laptop plugged into the wall via a clean power filter. Kurtz already knew that the computer was not connected to the internet.

He placed his pistol on the desk and spun the computer around. He didn't want to sit in case he left some of his homeless odor on the chair. He opened the screen and it immediately requested a password. Taking a device that looked like a cell phone from his pocket, he plugged it into the computer's USB port. A red light on the device blinked for a few seconds, then turned green. Bishop had shown Kurtz how to use the sophisticated device, and right now, as he understood it, a technician at MI6 headquarters in London was sorting through Dostiger's files, removing anything of interest. Kurtz watched the device in earnest; he had been promised that it would only take a minute or two. Finally the light blinked, turned yellow, and he removed the device, putting it back in his pocket. He slid the laptop back into its original position and picked up his pistol.

"All clear, Pavel?" he whispered into his mike.

"You have a couple of minutes. The guard is moving back to the house."

He left the room and closed the door with a gentle click. As he moved toward the staircase, the bedroom door in front of him began to open. He brought his pistol up. With the other hand he fished in his jacket pocket for an auto-injector. The door opened fully. Standing before him was a gorgeous woman clad only in her satin slip, the soft fabric barely containing her full breasts. Her eyes grew wide at the sight of the suppressed handgun.

His radio interrupted. "Damn! I am sorry, comrade."

Kurtz wordlessly stepped forward, pushing the girl back into her room with the barrel of his pistol, flicking on the light as he entered. "English?" he asked.

"A little," she replied softly. Her sensual lips looked so inviting.

"I'm not going to hurt you. You need to get back into bed." He lowered the pistol.

"Yes, OK," she said drowsily, moving back to the bed.

Kurtz watched her climb under the silk sheets. She didn't seem too afraid. Kurtz assumed, as the mistress of an arms dealer, she was probably used to aggressive behavior. He dropped the auto-injector into the palm of his hand and tucked the pistol inside his jacket.

"Close your eyes."

She did as she was told.

He lingered a second, disarmed by her beauty.

"You need to hurry, Kurtz." Pavel's Russian accent interrupted his thoughts. He placed the auto-injector next to her neck. Her eyes flashed open at the feel of the plastic. With a soft pop he delivered enough sedative to knock her out for at least an hour.

She looked at him for a split second before her pretty gray eyes closed.

"I hope we meet again in better circumstances," Kurtz whispered as he turned off the light and slipped out of the room.

He hurried down the stairs and bolted out the side door, coming to a crouch in the shadow of a large tree, the pistol back in his hand. Seconds later the guard turned the corner of the mansion and walked toward the same door he had just exited. He caught his breath as the guard stopped, looking around. It seemed the man was staring into the shadows straight at him. A few seconds passed before the guard lit a cigarette and continued walking.

Kurtz raced back along the lawn to the guardhouse. He didn't look happy as he helped Pavel move the body of the other security guard. "She's going to wake up in an hour and then we're blown. We need to warn the boss."

"I've already messaged him. Did we get what we need?"

"I think so. The device worked like he said it would."

They dumped the unconscious guard back at the camera's blind spot in front of the guardhouse. When Dostiger's man awoke in a few minutes, Kurtz didn't think he would be quick to admit to anyone that a homeless wretch had knocked him out with one punch. If the guard went back to check the cameras, there would be nothing to make him think any differently. Apart from the initial approach, Pavel had removed all trace of their break-in on the CCTV system and spliced in older video footage to cover Kurtz's movement through the residence. The perfectly executed break-and-enter should have been completed without a trace, but the unexpected presence of Dostiger's woman had ruined that.

On cue, a white Mercedes van drove up and both men jumped in through the sliding door. Pavel glanced at his watch; he had timed the cameras to start recording new footage two minutes after they left. They still had thirty seconds.

Five minutes later the guard moaned, showing the first sign of life since he was knocked out. He sat up, rubbing the side of his head, still dazed, then lurched to his feet, checking the keys in his pocket. He ran straight to the back of the guard box, frantically looking around. Everything seemed the same. He logged into the security system and ran a quick check over the log, the alarms, and the surveillance camera footage. No one had come through the open gate during the twenty minutes he was absent. The guard sat back in his chair, his heart rate slowly returning to normal.

CHAPTER 24

CLUB KYIV

Bishop had just finished his whiskey when the double doors of Dostiger's office opened and another muscle-bound henchman gestured for him to enter. He wondered if somewhere in Kiev there was a factory turning out the big bastards. The room was empty except for the security guard, who positioned himself inside the doorway, leaving Bishop the opportunity to acquaint himself with the lavish space.

The office was remarkable. The most impressive feature was the silence. Despite huge one-way mirrors that overlooked the dance floor below, you couldn't hear the music. Bishop looked down through the floor-to-ceiling glass at the throng of bodies dancing among the flashing lights.

The furnishings in the office were similar to the waiting room, except on a grander scale, contrasting with the modern decor of the main nightclub area. Dostiger's desk was an impressive, engraved hardwood antique, giving a clear message to visitors that the man they were dealing with had serious influence and money. The rear wall opposite the glass window was covered in an eclectic display of weaponry. Medieval swords were affixed to the wall among modern implements of death including the venerable AK-47 assault rifle. Bishop's eyes were immediately drawn to the middle of this arsenal, where a long missile launcher was mounted.

He moved closer to inspect what looked like a SA-18; an advanced heat-seeking missile system more than capable of downing a civilian airliner. As he ran his hands down the empty fiberglass tube, his blood ran cold. He wondered if this could be the weapon that killed his parents. His hand started to tremble and he dropped it to his side, sliding it into his pocket.

"One of my best-selling products." The harsh Ukrainian accent startled Bishop. "In the past ten years they have made me more money than any other weapon."

Bishop glanced at the two men who had quietly entered the office through a concealed side door. One was yet another guard; the other had to be Dostiger. He was smaller but exuded a far more intimidating presence. Dressed in a well-fitting suit and leaning on a polished wooden cane, it was his battered and scarred face that drew attention. Bishop stared at the arms dealer, suppressing the urge to leap over and snap the man's neck. Dostiger gave him a questioning look. "Is something wrong, Mr. Fischer?"

"Ah no, I was just admiring your collection."

"Do you like weapons?"

He would have been a physically impressive man once: not tall, but well built. A hard life had obviously taken its toll and he walked stiffly, with a slight limp. Bishop guessed his age to be close to sixty.

"No, not really. Don't get me wrong, Mr....?" Bishop extended his hand, trying hard to hold it steady.

Dostiger ignored the gesture and the question. "A pity, Mr. Fischer, a man's choice of weapon tells much about him." He directed attention to a heavy broadsword fastened to the wall. "The man that owned this sword, a Frenchman, believed it the only weapon worthy of his hand. He died with a peasant's arrow in his chest."

"The Battle of Agincourt?" Bishop maintained his British accent. "By my recollection of history, and I apologize if I am wrong, but didn't the French knights die as a result of their own arrogance?"

"Correct, Mr. Fischer. There may be more to you than I first thought." Dostiger pointed toward a pair of sumptuous velvet chairs. "Please. Sit."

The concealed door opened again and one of Dostiger's scantily clad women deposited two tumblers of whiskey on the low table in front of them.

"I did notice you like whiskey, Mr. Fischer."

"Indeed, and let me say your own taste is exquisite." Bishop took a quick drink, hoping the alcohol would steady his hand.

"One of a few things that eases the pain in my leg." Dostiger picked up the other glass. "So Mr. Fischer, we cut to business, yes? My man tells me you want to buy attack helicopters."

"That's correct. The company I represent is looking to acquire four gunships and an extensive support package."

"And what company is that, Mr. Fischer?"

"They would prefer to remain anonymous at this stage. Once we've formalized a deal, then I will be able to disclose their identity."

"My business is one built on trust…" he paused, looking up from his glass, "and without it, you and I, we have no business." Dostiger's emotionless gaze was penetrating.

Bishop found it uncomfortable to maintain eye contact. He swirled the scotch and casually sipped from the glass. "This is true, but the fact is you know far more about me than I know about you."

Dostiger laughed, causing him to shiver. It sounded almost manic. "You're not stupid, Mr. Fischer. This I like." He lowered his voice, his look intensifying. "But in this game, often things are not as they first seem."

Before he could reply, a guard walked over and whispered into his master's ear. Dostiger frowned and placed his glass on the table.

"I am sorry, Mr. Fischer. Something has come up that I must deal with." He rose stiffly from his chair. "Please, make yourself at home. This should only take a few minutes."

He felt a cold chill come over him as Dostiger limped through his concealed door. The phone in his pocket vibrated. He discreetly checked the message. It was from Kurtz:

Can't make dinner, heading to the office.

It was the code for possible compromise. Bishop's heart rate shot up and his throat became dry.

He looked back up at the antique weapons on the wall and wondered if he could rip any of them from their mountings and use it to kill Dostiger. Bludgeon him to death with a mace, or perhaps run him through with the broadsword. He doubted he would get very far; the guards would gun him down before he got within arms reach. Instead he concentrated on an exit strategy.

***

Dostiger's chief of security was waiting for him in the command center at the rear of the nightclub. From here his most trusted men tracked shipments of weapons, drugs, and other contraband across the globe. In the basement he even had holding cells and an interrogation room. Sometimes information had to be extracted from uncooperative competitors or unreliable suppliers.

"Dostiger, I think someone has been in your house." The chief of security spoke in a deep monotone. Yuri was a serious man, a former Ukrainian counterintelligence officer.

"Go on."

"In the last hour. One of the guards claims he was attacked and knocked out by a drunk. He says no one got in but…"

"But what?"

"Tatyana has also been drugged. She's breathing but we haven't been able to wake her."

"Did you check my office?"

"Yes, we conducted a full security sweep. None of the alarms have been tripped and the CCTV footage shows nothing."

Dostiger shook his head. "Too much coincidence. Two of my people… Do you have any other leads?"

"Not at this stage. I have people checking at the Ministry of Internal Affairs. If it was a local job, we will know soon enough."

Dostiger's ugly features remained blank but he smashed his fist down on a desk. "Yuri, I want to know who is behind this and I want to know NOW!" He drew in a deep breath. "Get that Iranian bitch back in here and wring any information you can out of her. She has to know something about this." He looked up at the CCTV monitors on the wall. 'Mr. Fischer' was exactly where he had left him, calmly sipping from his tumbler of whiskey. There was something troubling about that man, something he couldn't put his finger on. "I think we also need to have a little chat with Mr. Fischer. Take him down to the cells."

Yuri thumbed the transmit button on his radio to give the orders. He had been with Dostiger for over a decade and knew better than to question his instincts.

***

Bishop knew something was awry when the guard left his post at the door and walked purposefully toward him.

"The boss would like to see you downstairs in his other office, Mr. Fischer." The big man stood over him.

"Oh. OK, no problem," he said, smiling at the bouncer, trying to relax his racing heartbeat. He glanced at the other guard, only a few feet from the one-way mirrors that looked down onto the dance floor.

"I'll just finish my drink if you don't mind, gentlemen." Bishop stood up with the heavy tumbler and downed the last of the whiskey. He remembered a tip Ice had once given him after a bar fight: "Hit hard, hit fast, and use an ashtray."

He stepped toward the first guard, driving his knee into the bigger man's groin. With a moan he doubled over and Bishop used a two-handed grip to drive the base of the glass tumbler into the side of his skull. The solid glass held but the Ukrainian's head didn't, his temple caving in with a dull thud. As the man fell in a heap, Bishop spun and ran at the second guard. The man fumbled with his pistol. As he wrenched it free of the shoulder holster, Bishop grabbed it, pushing back against the man's grip, at the same time driving his forehead into the guard's nose.

Stunned, the thug released his hold on the gun as Bishop ripped it from his grip and pumped the trigger. Three rounds shot through the guard's stomach and into the office window, sending a spiderweb of cracks across its surface. Bishop drove forward with his shoulder, pushing the guard back with all his strength, driving him into the fractured glass.

They exploded through in a shower of shards, plummeting toward the dance floor below. The silence of Dostiger's office was replaced with crashing glass, screams of the crowd, and pumping dance music. The solid guard hit the ground with a sickening crunch, smashing his head into the floor. Bishop was luckier, the densely packed crowd saving him from injury. He threw his arms up to protect his face and landed sideways on a pack of drugged-up teens. They collapsed like deck chairs as they broke his fall, the pulsing beat drowning out their screams.

The music was still cranking, the DJ focused on his decks. Most of the club's clientele remained oblivious to the shattered glass and the crumpled bodies sprawled in the middle of the dance floor. Bishop hauled himself off an unconscious woman and shoved his way toward the bar, stuffing the guard's pistol into his pants.

Escaping the dance floor, he glanced up at the staircase, catching a glimpse of three guards at the railing, pistols in hand, searching the crowd. There was no easy way out. Guards were everywhere.

He had no choice but to try to blend with the crowd and slip through. He edged his way toward a side exit, moving slowly through the gyrating mob, dropping his jacket and tie. As he passed the main bar, a hand grabbed his elbow. He spun around, fist cocked, ready to break the hold. It was Saneh.

"THIS WAY!" she screamed over the music.

Bishop didn't hesitate, following her past the stairs into a dimly lit corridor marked with a toilet sign. A hard left turn and she pushed on the crossbar of a fire exit, bursting out into the icy-cold air.

They found themselves in a dark alleyway. Bishop looked around, finding his bearings. The lane was a dead end. It led out to the narrow street in front of the club. He pulled out his cell phone and dialed Aleks.

"*Da?*"

"Hot pick up, just past the entrance. I have the Iranian girl with me."

"OK, moving now."

He was still catching his breath as he hung up the phone and turned to the MOIS operative who had helped him. "Thanks."

"We need to go now. My people are just up the road."

"OK. My car's on the way."

They casually strolled around the corner, arms interlocked like lovers. The doormen and line of patrons were about twenty yards behind them and although the bouncers looked alert, the crowd was oblivious to the drama inside. Heavy bass was still emanating from the club and Bishop's heartbeat raced in time with it.

As Bishop and Saneh walked away from the club, they heard the distant roar of a high-performance engine. He looked back to see Aleks's BMW swerve into the narrow street. The headlights were flashing, engine revving, as Aleks tried to force his way past the clientele milling about the club entrance and the cars lining the street.

The sedan was about to clear the crowd when one of Dostiger's black Range Rovers barreled out of a side street, slamming into the BMW with a sickening crunch. The four-wheel drive knocked the sedan sideways, rolling it over some bystanders and wedging it against another parked car.

"ALEKS!" Bishop screamed, running toward the crash, firing his pistol. He was lucky to hit the window but the rounds didn't even dent the glass. The luxury four-wheel drive was armored. The back door of the Range Rover swung open and a guard brought an assault rifle up to his shoulder. Bishop dove behind a parked car as the gunman opened fire. A cacophony of automatic fire and ricochets filled the alley.

He crawled around the car, took a deep breath, and leaped to his feet to return fire. Before he could pull the trigger, a volley of rounds peppered the Range Rover, forcing the gunman back behind the armored door. Bishop glanced over his shoulder; a familiar white Toyota sedan was reversing at high speed toward him. One of Saneh's men was firing out the side window, laying down a withering rate of fire from a submachine gun.

"Fischer, let's go!" Saneh was crouched next to him, a mini-Uzi in her hands. She stood, spraying the armored Range Rover with more 9mm rounds. The Uzis weren't damaging the vehicle but they suppressed the gunman inside.

"I can't leave Aleks!"

Guards were already streaming out of the club, pistols brandished, pushing the confused patrons aside. A few of them had taken cover behind the armored Range Rover and the upturned BMW. Aleks wasn't moving; his unconscious body slumped in the wrecked vehicle.

"If we stay, we die. Let's go!" Saneh screamed back at him, tugging at his arm as the Toyota reversed up to them.

Bishop had a pained look as he took a final glance at Aleks' body. He knew she was right.

The MOIS agent in the back of the Toyota continued to fire as they sprinted the short distance toward him. They were only a few steps from the compact sedan when a volley of gunfire from Dostiger's men raked it, shattering the windshields. Saneh's gunman grunted as he was hit, managing to squeeze off a final burst. In the front seat the driver collapsed forward, his face blown across the dashboard. Saneh fired back up the alley as she wrenched the rear door open and dove onto the seat.

Bishop hauled the driver from the car, dumping his lifeless body onto the road. He dove into the driver's seat and mashed the accelerator to the floor. The Toyota's four-cylinder engine revved hard and the front wheels squealed in protest as they fought for traction. Another burst of fire thudded into the vehicle as they lurched forward. They cleared the end of the street in seconds; Bishop flicked the steering wheel and jammed on the hand brake. They slid sideways around the corner before accelerating up the street.

"Are we being followed?" he yelled over the roar of the engine and the rush of air coming in through the shattered windshield. Automatic fire cracked past them, thumping into the back of a truck ahead, answering his question.

"One, two. Yes, two of them." Saneh turned in the backseat to count their pursuers as she reloaded her machine pistol. "No, make that three. Three Range Rovers." She had stripped magazines from the MOIS operative beside her. The man was unconscious; dark blood soaked his jacket.

Another burst of automatic fire lashed the road to one side of the car as a Range Rover came into view, and Saneh returned fire through the missing rear glass. Bishop jerked the car around a slow-moving truck, dancing the sedan in and out of the light traffic, looking for any opportunity to evade the high-powered four-wheel drives. At this rate we're going to be dead in minutes, he thought.

Spinning the wheel he sent the battered hire car careening around another corner into a narrow side street. He reached into his pocket, threw his phone behind him onto Saneh's lap, yelling, "Hold down number one. Tell them 'Plan Alpha, Location Green: white Camry followed by three black Range Rovers.'"

Saneh fumbled with the phone, lifted it to her mouth, and repeated the message.

"Five minutes, Tim," she reported back.

Bishop knew it was only a matter of time before the Range Rovers caught them. Their powerful engines and all-wheel drive far outmatched the little Toyota. If they closed the gap, their wildly spraying gunfire might be able to hit something vital: a tire, the fuel tank, the engine, or worse still, him. He thumped the steering wheel with frustration. "C'mon, girl, give me everything you've got."

He spun the wheel again, throwing the little sedan sideways, almost losing control as the vehicle skipped over the curb, ran up onto the sidewalk, and sheared off a parking meter.

The meter bounced off the hood and Saneh yelled, "Careful! I still have to return this when we're finished."

He laughed. Well, he decided, if you had to die at the hands of a ruthless arms dealer, it was better to go down with a smile on your face.

CHAPTER 25

LOCATION GREEN

The rest of the FIST were back in the safe house when Saneh placed the call. Kurtz acknowledged the message immediately and the team went into action. Location Green was only a mile away and the van was already packed with everything they needed. Within seconds they had pulled out of the garage, turning right onto the main road toward the recently completed Rybalskyi Bridge.

Bishop had designated the construction yard on the far side of the steel girder bridge as Location Green. The bridge was still closed but the team had removed the barriers denying access to the across the waters of the Dnieper.

Three-quarters of the way across the bridge, the van stopped and Kurtz placed a briefcase on the sidewalk, carefully angling it across the dual lanes. He pulled a short length of wire from a recess on the case and checked an electronic firing device as he hurried back into the van.

The area leading off the bridge was still littered with the debris of construction: piles of rubble, empty drums, and metal remnants. The van dodged through the obstacles, entering the construction yard's well-lit parking lot. The area was the size of a soccer field and was packed with shipping containers, more construction waste, and an assortment of bulldozers, excavators, and cranes. At the far end of the yard, tall concrete pillars had been driven into the ground to support a ramp that would one day link the bridge to the adjacent elevated highway.

The van skidded to a halt behind a large shipping container at the back of the yard. Kurtz and Miklos sprinted from the vehicle and took up firing positions on either side of the clearing, using heavy earth-moving equipment as cover. They extended the bipod legs on their MK48 machine guns and racked the cocking handles as they each loaded a hundred-round belt of armor-piercing ammunition. Kurtz placed the electronic firing device next to his gun. From his position he had a clear view along the bridge and could still see the briefcase device he had placed earlier.

Pavel positioned himself slightly to the rear, behind one of the concrete pylons. He wanted to be able to engage Dostiger's vehicles head-on. Loading a magazine containing armor-piercing grenades into his assault grenade launcher, he knelt, bracing the weapon against the pylon.

Kurtz's voice came over the radio. "Ambush set."

***

In the distance, bursts of gunfire punctuated the cold night air that had settled over the murky waters of the river. As the shots got closer, the scream of engines could be heard and the three men prepared themselves for action. Safety switches were set to fire, weapons pulled in tight, triggers partially depressed.

The howl of a highly revved engine and the screech of tires heralded the approach of the little Toyota as it raced across the bridge. Once it hit the down ramp, Kurtz pressed a button on his firing device, arming the remote mine. The Toyota hurtled across the parking lot, sliding through gravel and dust to halt near the white van.

The first of the armored Range Rovers was only seconds behind. It mounted the bridge with a roar, rapidly building momentum. Unknown to the four heavily armed occupants, an invisible beam now cut across the bridge.

As the front bumper of the lead vehicle broke the laser, explosive charges in the briefcase detonated. The explosively formed penetrators tore through the thin armor of the Range Rover like cardboard, shredding the men inside. The blast launched the shattered vehicle over the concrete barrier and into the black waters of the river below.

The rear two cars were traveling close together. They plowed through the smoke and debris, hitting the down ramp off the bridge without slowing. Pavel engaged the first one with three 20mm grenades fired in quick succession. Two slammed into the engine block, a third punching through the front bumper into the left wheel. The alloy rim shattered, digging into the loose gravel causing the Range Rover to slide sideways. With a crunch, the following vehicle T-boned its partner, flipping it onto its side, and they both slid across the gravel before coming to a halt.

Kurtz and Miklos swiveled their machine guns toward the upright vehicle and unleashed a hail of automatic fire. The armored Range Rover offered no protection to Dostiger's men as the armor-piercing bullets smashed through the ballistic glass, ripping up the inside of the vehicle killing the four occupants.

The two gunners turned their weapons on the immobilized vehicle lying on its side. The occupants posed minimal threat, unable to open the heavy armored doors. A long burst of fire from Miklos' machine gun smashed through the cabin, ripping into the injured passengers.

The ambush was over in thirty seconds, during which time Bishop had sprinted from the battered Toyota to the white van, slid open the side door, and grabbed his kit bag. As the ambush raged, he slipped into his lightweight nanotech armor and loaded his MP7 submachine gun. Saneh still had her mini-Uzi and Bishop pulled one of the team's spare vests from the van, throwing it to her.

"Put this on."

"Thanks." She managed a smile as they ran across the construction site toward the carnage.

Kurtz rose from his position and advanced on the overturned vehicle with the big machine gun at his shoulder, Miklos covering him from the flank. Through the dark-tinted window he caught a glimpse of movement. The young German hammered a ten-round burst into the Range Rover.

"Any alive?" Bishop yelled.

"One, maybe two. They're all shot to shit."

Saneh's eyebrows shot up, hearing the strong Bavarian accent.

Bishop continued, "They grabbed Aleks; I need to talk to one of them."

One of the casualties inside the four-wheel drive moaned loudly.

"Could be a contender, *ja.*"

With the MP7 at his shoulder, Bishop advanced to the bullet-ridden side window and used his weapon-mounted flashlight to penetrate the dark interior. The cabin was a mess. Blood and gore were splattered over the expensive leather trim and three of the occupants had been torn apart by the hail of bullets. He shone the light to the rear and caught a glimpse of movement. Moving around to the tailgate of the rolled vehicle, he opened the rear door. The copper-sweet smell of blood wafted out. The fourth occupant moaned. He had crawled into the trunk, barely conscious.

Bishop slung his MP7 and reached in, grasping the man's tactical vest with both hands. The Ukrainian thug screamed as he was torn from the vehicle and thrown roughly onto the gravel.

"Do you speak English?" Bishop knelt with his MP7 aimed at the man's face.

"Yes, little," he whimpered.

"I'm going to ask you a few questions. If you don't tell me the truth, I am going to shoot you in the fucking head."

One of the other occupants of the vehicle groaned softly and Bishop nodded toward Kurtz, who unholstered his pistol. Kurtz stooped to look through the vehicle's rear door, saw one of the men was still moving, and raised the handgun. A single shot ended the moaning.

The wounded Ukrainian's eyes grew wide. Saneh stood by, watching silently. Kurtz casually holstered his pistol, lighting a cigarette.

"You, you will kill me anyway."

"There are worse things than dying, my friend." Bishop pushed the muzzle of his suppressed MP7 into a gunshot wound in the man's thigh. The Ukrainian let out a blood-curdling scream. Saneh bit her lip and turned away; she had watched men die before, but it shocked her that a British agent could be so merciless.

Bishop leaned close, speaking directly into the wounded man's ear. "Your boss has one of my men. Where will he take him?"

"Fuck, fuck you."

The suppressor crunched as it pressed harder into the shattered bone. "No, fuck you. Tell me where he is or I am going to shoot your leg off!"

The Ukrainian screamed in pain. "The club! They take him to the club. That's where they take everyone."

Bishop pulled the MP7 away and wiped it on his pants. He nodded to Kurtz as he turned. The German reached for his handgun, standing over Dostiger's man, who lay in a spreading pool of blood.

"NO!" Saneh exclaimed, grabbing Bishop by the arm. "That's enough, no more killing."

He shoved her away and she fell, sprawling backward into the gravel. He turned toward the van, focusing on the recovery of Aleks.

"You're as bad as them, Fischer," she screamed at his back.

He stopped in his tracks, turning to face her. Ragged and dirty, she looked so vulnerable lying on the ground glaring up at him. He glanced at Kurtz, who was watching him intently. "Zip-tie and sedate him, Kurtz."

The German nodded.

"Pavel, see if we can get that Range Rover started," he said as he pointed at the upright four-wheel drive. "Then throw the bodies in the Toyota and torch it." Leaning over Saneh, he grabbed her arm, hauling her to her feet. "C'mon, we're going back to the club."

CHAPTER 26

KHOD VALLEY

Mirza shook his head in an attempt to clear the cobwebs of fatigue. He'd been moving with Ice nonstop for eighteen hours and needed to stay alert; the Taliban were still out there.

He sat with his back against a rock, watching the valley for any threats while Ice scouted ahead. For a moment he was lost in his own thoughts and lifted his night vision goggles away from his eyes, gazing at the stars above the horizon.

The distinctive sound of gravel crunching under combat boots snapped his thoughts back to the task at hand and he raised his sniper rifle to his shoulder, looking through the thermal imager.

"Easy, Tiger, it's just me." Ice crouched next to him, easing his pack to the ground. He took the map out from his chest rig, laid it on the dirt, and draped a thin camouflage blanket over it. They lay facedown with their heads under the blanket and Ice activated a tiny light.

"This is where we are," he said as he used a pencil to identify the ridgeline on the map, "and this is where I think the recovery operation is being conducted." He made a little circle on another spot on the map just over a mile away. "I think you were right about the missile site being further up the mountain here." Ice used the pencil to mark a crest high above the extraction site. "They probably have a number of missiles positioned up there. We need to find them all by dawn."

Mirza's head nodded forward till it hit the map, then jerked upright as he woke himself.

"Mirza, Mirza, here, take this." Ice held out a white pill.

"What is it?" he asked, cursing inwardly at his weakness.

"It'll keep you awake. We need you switched on."

Mirza nodded, tipped back his head, and swallowed the pill.

Ice brought his attention back to the map. "We need to

avoid the camp, edge our way around this side of the mountain, then climb up toward the missile site."

"It's a good plan."

"OK, I'll check in with Vance. Then we go."

He left Mirza to fold up the blanket, moving a few feet away to contact PRIMAL HQ. "Bunker, this is Ice. Is Vance there?"

One of the watchkeepers answered the call. "Negative, Ice, he's offline. Do you have a message for him?"

"Roger, we're proceeding with the clearance op. I'll have the anti-air threat neutralized by sunrise. Is the Train on schedule?" He knew Mitch would be working relentlessly to get the aircraft repaired.

"Affirmative. The parts were delivered. You'll have your air support by sunrise," the watchkeeper replied.

"OK, we're on the move. Ice out."

He returned to Mirza, who was already gathering up their equipment. The stimulant had kicked in and he was fully alert as they continued up the mountain.

Using their night vision equipment, they had little problem negotiating the rugged terrain. The advanced goggles and thermal weapon sights were more sophisticated than anything the Taliban would be using. As the night temperature dropped, the heat signature given off by a human body increased, which would make the enemy far easier to detect.

***

High up on the mountain, two of Khan's men were on air sentry duty. They huddled together, seeking refuge from the bitterly cold winds that roared down off the Hindu Kush Mountains. Despite their thick jackets and blankets, they shivered continuously as the barren ground gave up the heat it had absorbed during the day and the temperature of the thin night air plummeted. They were under strict orders not to light fires, not that there was anything on the windswept mountain to burn. Khan was worried the Americans would spot them with their satellites and spy planes.

The two sentries had pulled the first shift while their two comrades remained warm, wrapped in their arctic-rated sleeping bags. Despite the death of Khalid and his men, morale in the missile team was still high. They had successfully driven off the Russian bomber and the operation could still succeed. With most of Khan's men dead, the payment split between the survivors would be much higher. The promise of fortunes warmed even the coldest of nights.

One of the warriors shrugged off the blankets and picked up the team's night vision binoculars, scanning the horizon. Before his demise, Khalid had reported a tiny aircraft flying in the distance.

"Do you see anything?" the other Afghan asked, not bothering to move from under the blankets.

"No, there's nothing out there." He panned the binoculars down to the extraction site. The sensitive image-intensifier tube picked up a slither of light spilling from underneath the camouflage nets. Khan had the locals working through the night; the plan was to be finished by dawn. He sat back next to his partner and retrieved a battered packet of cigarettes from his jacket. Using his gloved fingers he pulled out two cigarettes, turned to the other man who was still wrapped in a blanket, and placed one of them in his mouth.

"There's enough light coming from down there. No one will see us."

"Thanks," the other grunted.

A lighter appeared from another pocket. He shielded the flame with both hands in an attempt to light his partner's cigarette. The wind whipped the tiny flame away.

"Damned wind," he cursed, trying again. The flame sparked for a split second, enough for the cigarette to catch. He let his partner puff on the smoke, establishing the ember, then he used it to light his own.

"You know Khan said no smoking and no light," the other sentry mumbled.

"Have you seen the amount of light coming out of the

camp? Khan will not notice."

His comrade laughed. "By this time tomorrow, my brother, we'll be back in the village and Khan will not care about matches."

Mirza was scanning the terrain through the thermal imager on his rifle when he spotted the faint glow of the cigarette. To the naked eye it would have been invisible, but to the heat-hungry sensors in his scope, it was as if someone had ignited a flare. He adjusted the optic's sensitivity settings. The cigarette glowed again as the target inhaled and Mirza smiled with satisfaction. He could make out the head and shoulders of two men sitting in a hollow between two boulders.

"Ice, two men near the peak. Looks like a sentry," he whispered. With the wind he could probably scream without being heard.

"Acknowledged. I've spotted two others sleeping to the rear," Ice replied.

He scanned back up the slope and identified the two other men in their sleeping bags. Through his night sight, the sleeping Afghans looked like giant glowing slugs. He swung his weapon back to the smokers and watched as one of them lifted a pair of binoculars, scanning the night sky. Instinctively Mirza dropped onto his stomach, in case the sentry chose to scan the approaches to his position. After a few seconds he carefully raised his head. The man had finished his sweep and was settling back into his blankets.

He sensed the presence of Ice moving in beside him. A hand on his shoulder reassured him all was well.

"OK, Mirza, we need to find the missiles and disable them, but we can't kill the sentries; they'll know we're here," Ice said. Crouched behind cover and downwind of the Afghan position, they could talk at a reasonable level.

Mirza nodded. He didn't want to kill the men as they slept. Sabotaging the weapons was a far more palatable idea. "Ice, with these Russian missiles, if you take the O-ring out of the canister, the gas will vent and the seeker won't work." Mirza had used similar missiles during his time in the Indian army.

"How long will it take?"

"Ten or twenty seconds per launcher."

"I've no idea how to do it."

"It's OK, I will go."

"Are you sure?"

"It will be fine. I can do it with my eyes closed." Mirza placed his sniper rifle beside his pack.

"Alright, I'll cover you from here."

He nodded, pulled his pistol from its holster, and screwed a suppressor on the barrel. He slipped out of his bulky chest rig and left it on the ground next to his pack.

***

Mirza hunched over, moving cautiously from one rocky outcrop to the next. The tiny sliver of moon cast long shadows behind the boulders and crags, and he used them, disappearing into the darkness. At times he paused while one of the Taliban sat up to scan the horizon. Then Ice gave him the all clear and he continued, confident the American was covering him.

Mirza's goggles struggled to pick up the heat of the two sentries. He was reliant on Ice observing them through the more powerful optics of the larger sniper scope, telling him when it was safe to move.

As he crept closer, the icy wind died down and every noise he made seemed magnified in the still air. The crunch of sand under his feet, the rustle of his jacket, even the heartbeat pounding in his ears sounded loud enough to wake the dead. He was nearly on top of the two Afghans and any mistake could prove fatal.

Lying in a depression only a stone's throw from the sentry post, Mirza paused, assessing the situation. He needed to find where they had hidden the missiles and their launchers. The munitions would be close by, but not where the men were sleeping.

"All clear," Ice's voice came over his radio earpiece. "I think our two friends might be asleep."

He snaked out of the shadows, slithering forward on his stomach. He was thankful for the Kevlar gloves and kneepads; without them the sharp rocks would rip his skin apart. As he slid into the inky black shadow of another rock formation, he raised his head, looking for the two sentries, waiting for any sign of movement. He could feel the frigid sand sucking heat from his body. The stimulant Ice had given him was wearing off and the dull weight of fatigue was returning.

There was no movement from the sentry position so he rose to a crouch, using his night vision to methodically scan the terrain around him. The sentries were slightly to his right between two boulders. Up the gentle slope to the left he could make out the two other men sleeping. Now that he was closer, he could see that it was a campsite. Backpacks and boxes were littered around the sleeping bags.

He scanned between the two positions. An unusual rock formation drew his attention. Adjusting his goggles, he noticed the edge of the boulder moved slightly, flapping in the wind. It was a camouflage net.

"Mirza! Shift change." Ice's voice came through urgently over the radio.

He dropped to the ground, his hand grasping the grip of his suppressed pistol. If the sentries were swapping, they would walk right past him.

He slowly turned his head, lifting it slightly so he could see the sentry position. One of the Afghans was standing, stretching his arms. Mirza dared not move and placed his head back on the ground, willing himself to disappear. The wind eased off and he swore his thumping heartbeat would betray him.

He heard the man cough slightly and start to move, the crunch of boots in the sand sounding close. He waited for the footfalls to pass and sat up slowly, scanning the area. The sentry was now in the administration area, waking his replacement. Mirza didn't hesitate. He only had a moment before the two men would return to the sentry position. It took him a few seconds to reach the camouflage net. He knelt next to it and glanced over his shoulder. The guard had woken one of his colleagues and they were walking back down to the sentry point. He watched as the offgoing sentry said something to his replacement before making his way to the sleeping area. Another sentry change was unlikely for at least an hour.

Mirza lifted a corner of the net and peered in. There was little ambient light but in the center of the shallow depression he could make out the missiles. He ducked under the net and ran his gloved hands over the tubes. They were definitely Russian; with the distinctive gas cylinder attached to the front of the launcher. To Mirza it felt like a SA-18, an advanced missile that he had only seen once before.

He scrabbled around in the tiny space, making sure he found all the weapons. There were five systems in total. One of the tubes was empty, the missile fired at the Pain Train. He unscrewed the gas cylinder on the first weapon and used the point of his knife to remove the rubber O-ring that sealed the canister to the tube. Without it the gas would simply vent, negating the seeker head. It took him fifteen seconds to remove the first piece of rubber and two minutes later he had rendered all of the missiles useless. There were no replacements in the cache and any spares would probably be with the weapon cases, back down at the main camp. By the time the Taliban realized their missiles were useless the Pain Train would have destroyed the extraction site.

Mirza activated his radio, whispering, "All weapons disarmed."

"Nice work, our two buddies are sleeping like babies."

"I'm moving back now." Mirza slipped out from under the camouflage net, back into the icy wind.

As he crept back between the two positions, he could hear one of the men in the sleeping bags snoring gently. On the other side the two sentries were sitting close together, one of them with his head slumped forward on his chest.

It took another half hour for Mirza to cover the distance back to where Ice was holding his silent vigil. He fought the urge to race, forcing himself to remain disciplined, moving slowly and sticking to the shadows. Twice he lay silent in a fold in the ground as one of the sentries woke to scan the night sky with the binoculars. Both times the PRIMAL operative started falling asleep, his eyelids getting heavy and his head nodding up and down like a puppet. He needed another of Ice's pills.

It seemed like an eternity but eventually Mirza returned to Ice's hiding spot. They gathered their equipment in silence and moved back a hundred yards, finding a place they could rest out of the freezing wind. Mirza ate a protein bar while Ice contacted the Bunker on his satellite radio.

"Bunker, this is Ice."

There was a short pause before someone in the Bunker responded.

"Ice, how's it all going, buddy?" Vance's deep drawl surprised him. The PRIMAL commander was pulling some long hours.

"Everything's going to plan. The missiles are cactus and we are ready to call in the Pain."

"Awesome, great work, guys. Bad news is that the Pain Train is still six hours out."

Ice knew the Taliban would be working double time to reach their goal and had no doubt that, come dawn, they would be almost done. "OK, we'll push forward and get eyes on the target."

"Negative, bud, you've done enough. Lay up and wait for us to hit it."

"Damn it, Vance, you know as well as I do that we need eyes on the target. We miss this, or those pricks sneak off while no one's looking, and the next time we see this shit is when it hits the streets in downtown Jerusalem."

There was a pause at the other end as Vance weighed up the options. He knew Ice was right. The UAV only had two hours of fuel left, and due to the missile threat, it had been unable to confirm the exact site location.

"OK, but don't take any unnecessary risks."

"I never do."

"Find a good spot, lay low, and stay the hell out of trouble.

You only have to hold out for six hours. Alright?"

"No problem, Vance. Mirza and I are all over it."

"No doubt about that, boys. Happy hunting, Bunker out."

Ice pulled out his map as Mirza unfurled the camouflage blanket. He checked his watch; the glowing hands told him he had five hours till dawn. A few moments examining the map now could save hours later. They needed to find a place where they could get a clear view onto the excavation site while making sure they avoided any risk of compromise.

CHAPTER 27

CLUB KYIV

"They've been gone a while, eh?" said Nico turning to his partner.

"Yeah," the other heavyset doorman grunted. "Thirty or forty minutes maybe?"

"Fucking amateurs, they should've killed them by now." Nico was pissed off. Nothing would have pleased him more than to be in one of the three Range Rovers sent to kill the Englishman and his girlfriend. He regretted taking cover when the shooting started, missing his opportunity to kill the cocky foreigner. Men like Fischer always annoyed him; soft men who wore their fancy suits with their beautiful women but hadn't done a hard day's work in their life.

He reached into his jacket, placing his hand on the pistol in its holster. Nico thought it was time he was elevated from door duty to something better paid and a little livelier. After a year working for Dostiger, tonight had been the most action he had seen. Usually Club Kyiv was problem-free. Everyone knew what happened to people who caused trouble in Dostiger's place.

"They smashed that Beemer up good." The other bouncer pointed at the wreckage of Aleks's car.

"Wouldn't want to be that poor fucker now." A couple of Dostiger's heavies had dragged Aleks's unconscious body from the BMW, taking him into the club. No doubt he was being worked over down in the cells. Nico shivered at the thought.

Eventually the two doormen turned their attention back to the long line waiting for entry. Despite the incident, the line was still growing. No amount of gunplay would keep people away from the club; men came for the women, and women came for the drugs and money. Over the speakers, the manager had announced free drinks in an attempt to appease any upset guests.

Everything about Dostiger's operation was slick. Minutes after the gunfight in front of the club, a van had removed the dead bodies, washing down the road with bottles of industrial cleaner. All that was left of the engagement were a few shot-up cars and the smashed BMW. The Kiev police hadn't responded; they didn't dare stick their noses in the arms dealer's business. Some of them were on his payroll.

"The boys are back." The other doorman pointed to the Range Rover turning into the street.

"What the fuck!" Nico exclaimed. The armored four-wheel drive was riddled with bullet holes; even the ballistic windshield had gouges through it, the laminate opaque and cracked. The front bumper was crumpled, one of the headlights shattered, the grill buckled and bent.

Nico ignored the stares of the clientele lining the street and wrenched open the passenger door of the Range Rover as it stopped, paying no attention to the white van that pulled in behind it. He froze, looking into the face of the passenger in confusion.

"Fucking hello, champ!" Bishop's Kevlar-gloved fist plowed into Nico's face, sending him sprawling backward onto the sidewalk. Before he could recover, Miklos had jumped out of the back and kicked him savagely in the side of the head, knocking him unconscious.

The crowd looked on as two more armed men spilled out of the white van. Kurtz had the MK48 machine gun shouldered, aiming the barrel into the face of the second bouncer. He swung the butt of the weapon in a tight arc, catching the muscle-bound guard under the chin. The big man dropped with a sickening thud.

Miklos moved fast, the lithe Czech securing the unconscious men's hands behind their backs. Pavel was at the rear, covering the assembled crowd with his submachine gun, alert for any threat.

The pretty blonde hostess looked shocked to see Bishop again; the pinstriped suit she had seen him wearing earlier was now covered with a black armored chest rig, and he had a submachine gun at his shoulder, scanning for targets. She stared dumbfounded at the two helpless guards trussed on the sidewalk, then up at the three other men, all armed to the teeth. She was even more surprised when Saneh jumped out of the Range Rover, Uzi in hand. The Iranian's film star looks and flowing hair looked out of place with her body armor and submachine gun.

Bishop grabbed Saneh by the arm, pushing her toward the van. "Stay here with Kurtz."

She shrugged him off. "No, I'm going with you."

"This isn't negotiable." He nodded in the direction of the German. "Kurtz, if she tries to follow us, bag her and throw her in the van." Kurtz had been relegated to securing the vehicles; there was no way Bishop was going to let him loose with a machine gun in the close confines of the club.

Saneh gave a withering look but didn't push the point. Kurtz just smiled at her, lifting an eyebrow.

Bishop barged past the blonde hostess. "I'm on point, lads. Take down all armed targets, minimal civilian casualties."

He positioned himself next to the front door, flipping his weapon over to check the safety. Miklos grabbed the handle and wrenched it open. Bishop entered the cloakroom swiftly, his MP7 gun at the shoulder. The pretty attendant screamed and promptly fainted behind the counter. Once all three men had entered the room, they repeated the procedure on the entrance to the club floor.

They punched into the main room in a tight formation, weapons at the ready. The first guard to spot them was on the staircase.

"Tango high." Bishop didn't slow as he spoke, triggering a short burst, drilling three rounds through the target's chest. The suppressed gunshots were completely masked by the throbbing music. He smiled as he recognized the thumping Prodigy track, *Invaders Must Die*. The high-intensity beats and flashing lights made the situation surreal, almost like they were part of a video game. A number of patrons noticed the armed men and paid them no attention.

He led the team around the dance floor. Moving in a tight arrowhead formation, they pushed through the crowd, mounting the stairs that led to the upper level. The dead bouncer was lying face down on the marble stairs, his blood pooling on each step before trickling down to the next. Pavel ducked as a round ricocheted off the banister in a shower of splinters.

"Tango at the bar," Bishop transmitted, trying to get a clear sight picture through the crowd.

The stocky Russian turned instinctively, firing a long burst at a security guard behind the main bar, dropping the hostile. A stray round clipped the barman and the rest of the bullets shattered the bottles of spirits arrayed on the mirrored shelf behind him. A few clubbers screamed in terror, diving to the floor, but most remained oblivious, still dancing to the incessant music.

"Tango down," Pavel reported.

As they crested the staircase, Bishop lined up the bouncer guarding the entrance to Dostiger's office. He took the shot through the crowded balcony as the red-dot sight aligned on the guard's forehead. The man fell back against the door with a grunt, blood oozing from his third eye. The clientele on the balcony moved away nervously, making way for the armed men.

Bishop kicked the dead guard away from the blood-splattered door. Pavel and Miklos lined up beside him, weapons ready. He checked the handle. It was locked. He drew his Beretta, aiming at the handle. Miklos waved him away.

"Allow me, boss." With a snap of his wrist, the Czech flicked out an extendable baton, the sliding segments clicking into place. With a vicious swing, he knocked off the door handle. Reversing the baton he punched out the lock. A swift kick gained them access.

"Nice one," said Bishop as he charged through the door. "First room clear."

The waiting room was empty, the double doors to

Dostiger's office wide open. Miklos led the team in, rapidly clearing all four corners.

"Second room clear. Looks abandoned, boss," reported Miklos over the music invading the once serene office space through the shattered windows.

Bishop pointed to the long bookcase. "There's a hidden door over there."

Pavel covered the rear while Miklos and Bishop searched the bookcase. They flung books and ornaments from the shelves, looking for the trigger. Bishop was positive he had seen Dostiger enter through this part of the wall.

"Miklos, they know we're here. Time to shake up the party. Blow it."

The Czech grinned, ripping open one of the pouches on his vest. He pulled out a prepped half slab of C4. Twisting the timed detonator to ten seconds, he wedged the bomb into the bookshelf before sprinting out of the room to the waiting area, where Bishop and Pavel were crouched.

The seconds ticked by slowly until a thundering blast rocked the entire building, blowing the remaining office windows out onto the dance floor. When the explosion cleared, the music had finally stopped.

Miklos smiled. "Maybe now my ears stop bleeding."

"Hey, I liked that track," Pavel said laughing.

They rushed back into the office, ignoring the screaming and commotion from the dancefloor below. The charge had demolished the bookcase, blowing the hidden door inward. Bishop thought he heard voices beyond the opening. He ripped a flashbang from his vest and lobbed it in. It exploded with a thump and the three men surged into a narrow, well-lit corridor. On the left-hand side a door was open and Bishop turned into it without hesitating.

"Room clear."

The wall of CCTV screens and numerous computer terminals was a dead giveaway. This was Dostiger's operations room. It was empty, but one of the TV screens drew Bishop's attention. The video feed showed a big man strapped to a chair with two other men standing over him. One was holding what looked like a cordless drill in one hand and a metal prong with cables coming out of it in the other. The bald head of the prisoner was unmistakable.

"Aleks!" exclaimed Bishop, pointing at the screen. He peered closer, eyebrows furrowing. "What the fuck are they doing?" Aleks was convulsing. "Motherfuckers are electrocuting him!"

Violent rage overwhelmed him. He raced back into the corridor, weapon at the ready. Pavel and Miklos fell in behind. They charged down the hallway, only slowing as they reached an elevator. The elevator pinged. The doors slid open, revealing two of Dostiger's men.

The guards opened fire with pistols. Bishop grunted as a round hit his armor, knocking the wind out of him. At the same time his finger depressed the trigger of the MP7. He hosed the elevator with an entire magazine. The high-velocity bullets ripped through Dostiger's men, spraying flesh and blood across the polished steel interior of the elevator. He let the empty weapon drop on its sling as he drew his pistol, stepped into the elevator, and fired a round into each of the corpses.

He looked up at Pavel and Miklos, blood splattered across his face, lungs heaving. Standing next to the crimson-streaked stainless-steel walls, he almost looked like a butcher in a slaughterhouse.

"Sorry about the mess," he said, deadpan, as he holstered the pistol and slammed another magazine into his submachine gun.

They all crammed into the blood-stained elevator. Bullet holes stitched the walls.

"What level?" Miklos asked, but Bishop didn't reply, staring at the blood pooling around the dead bodies.

"I'm guessing he's on the bottom floor," the Czech said, pressing the button for the basement.

The elevator began moving and Bishop noticed his two men staring at him. "Basement, yeah. Let's get Aleks," he said, readying his weapon.

The doors opened smoothly, the muzzles of the three submachine guns leading the team out into another well-lit concrete hallway. Screams emanated from down the corridor, echoing off the metal doors. Bishop sprinted toward the noise and peered in through the window of one of the cells.

It took him only a split second to assess the situation in the room. Aleks was tied to a chair with his back toward the door. One man was standing in front of him, staring at the convulsing Russian, a drill pointed at his face. Over by the wall a second man was manipulating what looked to be an electronic switchboard.

Bishop could barely contain himself; he slid back the door's bolt with one hand and kicked it open. The man in front of Aleks didn't get a chance to look up before a burst of fire spread the inside of his head across the concrete wall of the cell. The man at the switch threw his arms in the air and backed away from the controls.

"TURN IT OFF!" Bishop screamed. "TURN IT THE FUCK OFF!"

The man lunged forward, hitting a red switch. Aleks stopped twitching and slumped in the chair, moaning. The stench of scorched flesh and burnt hair was overwhelming. Miklos was there in a flash, using a knife to cut the plastic restraints. The big Russian fell forward. Bishop caught him, ripping off the blindfold.

"Aleks, it's me. It's Aden," he said, holding the shaking man's head to his chest.

"Give... give me a second," Aleks said quietly. He lifted his hands to his face, wiping the sweat and tears from his eyes. Then with an almighty roar, he rose up like a grizzly bear, grabbed the chair that had held him prisoner, and smashed it into Dostiger's remaining interrogator. The man doubled over, trying to shield his face. Aleks dropped the chair and grabbed him by his collar, hauling him across the room. He swept the man's legs from under him, catching him around the neck in a powerful chokehold.

The Russian's bicep bulged and the man's face turned a deathly gray as Aleks whispered something in his ear. The man's eyes grew wide and he scrabbled at the arm in a feeble attempt to escape the deathly grip, then with a shudder, he went limp and was dropped to the floor unconscious. Aleks turned and spat at the corpse of the other torturer. "This piece of shit was going to drill out my eyes. Let's get the fuck out of here."

Pavel was covering the corridor as they came out of the cell. "Boss, message from Kurtz." He tapped his earpiece.

Bishop turned up the volume of his own headset. "Kurtz, this is Aden. Go ahead."

"Boss, *polizei* have arrived. We've had to move the van."

"Roger, where are you now?"

"Behind the club. Must be another exit, *ja?*"

"Roger, we'll try and find one. Keep us posted on police activity."

"OK, will do."

Bishop turned to the other three members of the FIST. "Well, the front door is no longer an option. Any ideas?"

Aleks shrugged. "I didn't see the way in. Had a bag on my head."

"The second floor in the elevator should be street level. There should be another exit there," Miklos pointed out.

"Good point. We'll try level two," Bishop said.

The team crammed into the blood-splattered elevator and moved up to the second floor.

Methodically they cleared the area, moving toward the rear of the club looking for an exit. The entire level was deserted and they moved through the offices quickly into a warehouse and loading bay. Miklos opened the roller door. Their white van could be seen parked a block down the street. He waved the vehicle forward. It pulled in next to the dock as Saneh slid the side door open.

The team piled in and the van sped off, hurtling through the dark streets back toward the safe house. Sprawled on the floor in the back of the vehicle, the men were too exhausted to talk.

Saneh spoke anyway. "Did anyone see Dostiger?"

Bishop had his back against the inside of the van. He looked at her wearily. "I think he must have left after they grabbed Aleks."

The others were silent, their bodies drained of adrenaline.

"Did you find anything interesting?" Saneh queried again.

"Not exactly." Bishop rubbed his bloodshot eyes. He wasn't looking forward to reporting in to Vance and Chua. Everything that could go wrong pretty much had. They were lucky none of the team had been killed. He knew the PRIMAL hierarchy was not going to be happy about Saneh working with them. Bishop could almost hear Vance's voice in his head lecturing him about the pitfalls of thinking with your dick.

Saneh redirected her attention to the battered Aleks. He sported superficial burns on his forearms and a number minor cuts and bruises. The big Russian grinned, lapping up her attention. Bishop watched as she cleaned his wounds and taped them. So far she'd impressed him. Maybe there's potential for her after all, he pondered.

CHAPTER 28

PRIMAL SAFE HOUSE

The ride back to the safe house was swift on the empty roads. Kurtz parked the van in the double garage. They gathered in the living room.

"Good work, team," Bishop said. "You all handled yourselves pretty damn well."

Kurtz looked down at the ground, scuffing at the worn carpet with his boot. "I am sorry about the break-in. It was an amateur move to be compromised. I'm a *Dummkopf.*"

"You got the data, Kurtz, that's what counts. And that ambush? Well, you saved our asses there. Gave Dostiger a bloody nose."

The German looked up with an ever-so-slight smile. "*Ja*, we showed those blockheads what real firepower is."

"What's important now is that we're all back here in one piece and ready for the next move. I'm not sure what that's going to be yet, but I've a feeling we're done here in Kiev." He didn't want to reveal too much in front of Saneh. "Get some rest. I'll take the first watch."

The men filed out of the living room and Aleks gave him a big bear hug before he left. "Thanks for coming back for me, Aden. I know you didn't have to," he said.

Bishop extracted himself from the big Russian's grip. "You feeling OK?"

"*Da, da*, a beautiful angel looked after me," he replied with a wink, giving Saneh a grin before heading to bed.

The Iranian sat on the battered couch, watching the team file out. Once they had gone, Bishop turned to her.

"I didn't get a chance before, but thanks for getting me out of the club," he said.

She smiled. "We made quite an exit, didn't we?"

"If it wasn't for you and the sacrifice of your men, I

probably wouldn't be here. You saved my life today, Saneh. That's not something I'll forget."

Tears welled in her eyes. "My men died trying to get me out too," she whispered quietly. She hunched over, shoulders shuddering as she started to sob.

Bishop stood in front of her, unsure of what to do. She looked so vulnerable, feminine, out of her depth. Part of him wanted to wrap her in his arms, hold her tight against his chest, and console her. Another, albeit smaller, part of him was keenly aware of this woman's reputation as a ruthless assassin.

She looked up at him with eyes smudged by makeup. They stared at each other. Slowly she stood and he felt his pulse quicken as she placed her arms around his waist and lowered her head to his chest. He held her firm as she cried, released all of the emotion of the last twenty-four hours.

"I'm sorry, Tim, this isn't like me," she sobbed, still clinging to him.

"It's OK, I understand, I've lost people before. It's always hard." Bishop sounded calm but his mind was racing. She eventually let go of him, sitting back on the couch, wiping her tears. He dragged one of the plastic equipment trunks over and sat in front of her.

"Well, I'm alone now." She sniffled.

"What are you going to do?" he asked, trying to hide his feelings. His emotions were in turmoil and he knew Vance would not approve of where they were leading him.

The intimacy was interrupted by the shrill ringtone of Saneh's phone. She pulled it from her handbag and examined the screen. "I really need to take this."

"Sure, you can use the kitchen."

"Thank you." She left the living room, shutting the door to the kitchen behind her. Once alone, she answered the call.

The voice was harsh. "It's Rostam. I told you to report in at twenty-two hundred."

"Sorry, sir, I was delayed."

"Stopped to get your nails done?"

"No, sir. I helped the MI6 agent escape from Dostiger's

men. My team members were both killed."

"WHAT! Both of your men are dead? How the hell did that happen?"

"Sir I… the…"

"Pull yourself together, Agent Ebadi. Tell me what the hell happened."

"Sir, the meeting with Dostiger was uneventful. I gained nothing of real value. As I was leaving, Fischer arrived… ah… Dostiger's men threw him through a window and I helped him escape. My men were killed in the alley. Fischer and I escaped in my car after one of his men was captured…"

"Go on."

"Dostiger's men chased us and the rest of Fischer's team ambushed them. I'm sure they're not MI6; they killed everyone."

"Is that all?"

"No, sir. Fischer and his men went back to the club and rescued their man."

"What about Dostiger? Did they kill him?" Rostam sounded concerned.

"No, he wasn't there. I think he fled south to his Odessa facility. My source mentioned it when we last spoke."

"And where are you now?"

"In Fischer's safe house."

There was silence and Saneh waited with apprehension.

"Congratulations, a perfect mess. Our only hope now is that Fischer has a plan to recover the device from Odessa. At least we're positioned to take advantage of the circumstances, aren't we, Ebadi?"

"Yes, sir."

"There is potential for this to slip through our fingers, Afsaneh. Our success is now intimately tied to Fischer and his actions. Get even closer to him. Ensure that he's successful. I don't care what it takes. Is that clear?"

"I understand, sir," she replied quietly.

"Do not fail me again!" Rostam terminated the call.

She slumped against the kitchen counter, her hands shaking.

She grasped the hem of her torn dress, contemplating whether to rip it higher. Instead she left it, wiped the tears from her face, and turned toward the door.

Bishop was on the other side staring at the door, wondering if PRIMAL was monitoring Saneh's call. That reminded him, he was due to report in to Vance and Chua. He checked his watch: three in the morning, around midday on the island. The team would all be up and waiting but he couldn't face them. In the last few hours they had botched a break-in, stuffed up a meet with Dostiger, and shot up half of Kiev. Vance was going to flip out.

He glanced at his laptop sitting on the table and decided he would send a brief update by email. There was no need to talk face-to-face when there was nothing positive to discuss. Dostiger had no doubt disappeared, and he'd probably blown his only chance to kill him. He just hoped the team had been able to pull something useful off the arms dealer's computer.

The door from the kitchen creaked open as Bishop sat in front of his laptop. Saneh noticed the glum look on his face. "What's wrong?"

"Huh? No, nothing. Just thinking, wondering where Dostiger would have gone."

Saneh smiled. "Odessa."

"What?"

"That call, it was from my source."

"You have a source?" She had Bishop's complete attention now.

"I told you when we first met, in the car park. I said I had other means."

She's right, he thought. I was too busy staring at her ass. "Tell me more about Odessa," he asked.

"After we escaped the club, Dostiger's head of security went, with his men, south to Odessa."

That would explain the lack of guards at the club, surmised Bishop.

"My source thinks they're expecting a big delivery. In the past they've escorted large shipments of drugs from the airport to a lab nearby."

He nodded, realizing a drug-processing facility would have a lot of the equipment needed to safely handle a chemical agent.

"Tim, I've laid myself open. That's all I have." Saneh sat on the couch across from him. "I want to work with you. Our governments are aligned on this." She took a deep breath. "We need to stop the Revolutionary Guards, otherwise a lot of people are going to suffer."

"You've lost your entire team, haven't you?"

"Yes, but I'll share all my information. My source is still active."

"Yeah, alright," he said, flashing her a broad smile. "So far we've turned out to be a pretty good duo."

She smiled. "If, by duo, you mean me saving your butt?"

Bishop laughed. "Yeah, I guess I owe you one. By the way, my name's not Tim. It's Aden."

"I already know that; your Russian let it slip. Oh, and it's two, you owe me two: one for saving you and one for my car's mirror."

"OK, OK. Look, Saneh, the mirror aside, if we work together, you have to understand a few things."

"What?"

"My mission is to stop Dostiger from supplying a weapon to a third party, any third party. If you work with me, there is no way your mission can succeed."

"How can you assume my mission is to recover the weapon? What if my mission is just to stop Dostiger from supplying it to someone else?"

Bishop continued cautiously, "Then our missions would align and we can work together. Just don't try to cross me, Saneh. We need each other's help at the moment, but that can change."

She met his intense stare. "You can trust me, Aden, and you need me. I don't want that to change."

"Me neither." His features softened and he found himself lost in her eyes. "Anyway, we need to get a few hours sleep before we work out our next move." He looked back at

Saneh's ragged black cocktail dress, borrowed cold-weather jacket, and scuffed calf-high boots. "And we should probably find you some appropriate clothing."

"I guess I am a little overdressed."

"Just a little." Bishop chuckled. "We can tackle that problem tomorrow. Right now you need some rest. You can have the couch."

"Are you going to sleep?"

"Yeah. I'm going to shoot an email to my headquarters before turning in, though." He was hoping Saneh's new information about Odessa would help him avoid the wrath of Vance and Chua. PRIMAL's commander, in particular, wasn't going to be happy when he found out about the incident in the club.

Saneh rose from the couch as he turned his attention back to the laptop. She walked over, leaned down, and kissed him on the cheek. "Goodnight, Aden."

CHAPTER 29

KHOD VALLEY

The time displayed in the bottom right corner of Mirza's night vision told him it was 0350 hours. In a little over sixty minutes the first traces of dawn would appear on the horizon and he and Ice needed to be in position well before then. Vance was expecting them to coordinate the bombing of the extraction site; that is, if the Pain Train was operational.

The pair had patrolled around the western flank of the mountain, sticking to the high cliffs overlooking the assessed extraction site. Their progress had been slow, strong winds and freezing temperatures making it difficult to traverse the rugged terrain. Using the map, they had identified a potential hide location, an outcrop with observation onto the whole southern side of the mountain. Inspecting the contours on the map, they had planned to move to the position through a small depression carved into the mountain by heavy winter rains. If they crawled, they hoped they could get in and out unobserved, even in broad daylight.

Mirza wasn't enjoying crawling over sharp rocks again. Despite his thick clothing, they dug into his knees and elbows, and the hard ground felt like permafrost. He crawled steadily in front of Ice, his compact sniper rifle cradled in his arms. It felt like an eternity before they could see the outcrop, only a few hundred yards ahead. He paused as his gloved hand touched something metallic. He focused his night vision, revealing a pile of heavily corroded cartridges and machine gun link.

It looked as if somebody else had used the same spot in the past, perhaps the mujahideen attacking the Russians. A tap on his boot reminded Mirza to hurry up; they were running out of darkness. He pushed the old cartridges aside, then felt something tight against the palm of his hand. Too late, he realized what it was.

Trip wire!

The rocket streaked into the air with a whoosh, startling both men. They instinctively pressed themselves flat against the ground. The flare ignited under a small parachute, bathing them in bright light. Mirza's shivering was immediately dispelled as his heart thumped hard, sending adrenaline burning through his veins. He knew there was a good chance he had condemned them to death.

The flare spluttered out, plunging the mountain back into darkness, but the PRIMAL operatives remained perfectly still. From down below they could hear yelling echoing off the cliffs. Both men knew they had well and truly stirred up the hornet's nest. If the Pain Train were on-station, it wouldn't have been a problem. They would simply crawl forward, laze the targets, and blow them all to hell. Mirza tipped his head skyward in frustration.

"Everything'll be OK, buddy," Ice whispered, activating his satellite radio.

"Pain Train, this is Ice."

"Mitch here. Go ahead."

"Mitch, we've been compromised."

"Roger, can you evade?"

"We'll move to an alternate location. When will air support be on-station?"

"ETA is three hours."

They didn't have three hours. Dawn was forty minutes away and the Taliban would come looking once it was light.

"Ice, you there?" Mitch queried the silence.

"Mitch, if we get in the shit we're going to head north."

"Acknowledged. Are you able to send us coordinates for the excavation site?"

"Yes, will transmit within the hour."

"Hey, Ice," Mitch said, pausing. "Listen, my good man, if it gets real hairy, just get out. We can target the camp ourselves. Get clear and we'll have you picked up."

"OK, but we need to move now. I'll check in as soon as we get the coordinates."

"Roger, Mitch out."

Ice switched back to the internal frequency he shared with Mirza. "OK, bro, let's move."

***

In the camp not far below Ice and Mirza, Yanuk was awake. The Russian had fallen asleep in the early hours of the morning, slumped against an equipment case inside his tent. As the flare popped, his eyelids had snapped open and he'd rushed out of the camouflaged shelter.

Standing in the middle of the camp, he stared up at the cliffs through his night vision binoculars, wondering if it was a false alarm. The Taliban had placed trip flares on any likely observation points. After yesterday's activity, he figured the Americans had probably inserted a team of Navy SEALs. Their numbers would be small but they would be well equipped. He knew they would make short work of any Taliban in the darkness.

Yanuk couldn't afford to waste time thinking about SEALs or any other Americans; he needed to focus on the dig. Cursing under his breath, he returned to the shaft, throwing back the two layers of heavy blackout curtains before reaching the red-lit interior of the tunnel. He yelled out for the village elder he had left in charge. The man took half a minute to emerge from the depths, covered from head to toe in dust, his eyes bloodshot.

"How far?" Yanuk barked.

"Ten more feet, sir." The man leaned against his shovel, barely able to stand.

Yanuk looked back down the shaft, mentally calculating. The locals were working well; raw fear of the Taliban motivated them. At this rate, in another three to four hours, they would break through to the main chamber.

"Keep digging," he ordered. With a wave of his hand, he dismissed the man.

As he left the shaft, he caught a glimpse of white robes. Like a ghostly apparition, Khan appeared from the darkness.

"Who do you think it is, Yanuk?"

"More Americans."

"I think you may be right. I will send more men to kill them. Dawn is approaching and they won't be able to hide."

Yanuk nodded. It was true. No one knew the area like the Taliban. If anyone could chase the SEALs from the mountain, it would be them. "If you can keep them away, in three hours we'll be through."

Khan reached out and grasped the stocky Russian's shoulder. "No more mistakes." With that, Khan turned on his heel and disappeared back into the darkness.

Yanuk fumed. He didn't need Khan's threats. They were almost through, and despite all the problems, he was sure the operation would still succeed. He took a deep breath and smiled at the thought of the money Dostiger had promised. Soon he would be a very wealthy man.

***

Mirza and Ice had given up crawling and were moving fast across the mountain. Scrambling over the rocky ground, they needed to stay one step ahead of the Taliban and get to another observation point before dawn. Time was closing in, and if the Pain Train didn't get on-station soon, they would have to abort and start escape-and-evasion.

They agreed the most viable plan was to go north, back toward the Afghan air-defense missiles. It would still allow them a good view down onto the excavation site, but if they needed to withdraw, they could drop off the northern slope and head to the more hospitable lands of the Hazaran tribes, the mortal enemy of the Taliban.

As they approached the new position, they slowed, alert for any wires or booby traps. Ice was on point this time; the trip flare had rattled Mirza's confidence.

Ice was particularly wary of mines. Nothing says you're not welcome like having your legs blown off, he thought. Nearing the cliff's edge, he slid forward on his stomach, wedging himself between two rocks. In front the slope dropped away sharply, running down toward the area he'd assessed as the probable location of the excavation site.

Through his thermal scope he could see a number of small hot spots, not as many as he expected. He pressed the backlight on his iPRIMAL, double-checking the grid coordinates Chua had given them. It was definitely the right spot. He carefully peered through his night scope again, zooming closer before he realized the Taliban were using countersurveillance measures. The entire work site was shrouded in camouflage nets. He'd never seen nets like these. They blocked the thermal signatures. There was no way the Pain Train would have been able to precisely locate the mouth of the dig site.

As he scanned, a tiny flash of light at the edge of the camp caught his eye. He focused on the area. A few seconds later he saw a lone figure walking toward the cliff. There it was again. As the figure disappeared into the cliff, Ice glimpsed a slither of light. It looked as if someone had a lantern behind a curtain and every so often the curtain moved, allowing some light to escape.

Figuring the mouth of the shaft was shrouded with blackout curtains, he used the built-in laser rangefinder on the scope to get an accurate coordinate, then transmitted it to Mitch.

The Pain Train's weapons officer responded immediately. "Job well done, Ice. Now get the hell out of there."

"OK. We're going to push north. I'll report back in a couple of hours. Ice out."

He switched back to Mirza. "We need to go, buddy."

Mirza rolled onto his side and looked back up the hill through his sniper scope. The sky had started to glow and in the predawn light he could clearly make out a figure standing at the crest, blocking their exfiltration route. It had to be one of the Afghans from the missile site. "Steady, Ice, we've got company. Top of the ridge, one sentry."

There was a pause before Ice responded. "There's more of them. Below us."

Mirza shuffled around on his stomach and looked down at the Taliban camp. "It's a clearing patrol. We can't stay here, once the sun rises they'll spot us."

"Do you think you can make the shot?"

"Yes, I'll drop the guy on the ridgeline and we can withdraw over the crest."

"Solid plan. Do it."

He rose to a knee and aimed his sniper rifle up the hill. He squeezed the trigger, the weapon emitted a muted crack, and the target toppled forward. As the corpse hit the ground, it let off a single round. In the still morning air the shot echoed off the cliffs like a thunderclap.

Mirza dropped prone, realizing his target's finger must have jarred the trigger. Below, yells filled the air.

He knew that it would only take minutes for the Taliban clearing patrol to be on top of them. At this distance they needed to maintain the element of surprise. He crawled forward and took up a firing position beside Ice. As they waited for the approaching fighters he pulled out two white phosphorus grenades.

The line of Taliban climbed swiftly. There were almost thirty of them covering a frontage of a hundred yards. The left flank would hit the pair first and initially only a few of the Afghans would be able to engage.

Ice gave Mirza a nod and they fired simultaneously. The first two Taliban toppled like bowling pins. The others dove to the ground returning fire.

Rounds cracked above their heads. They waited until the Taliban were throwing distance and tossed their phosphorus grenades.

Five seconds later the grenades burst into a thick cloud of smoke, hurling smoldering phosphorus in a wide arc. Mirza led as they sprinted up the hill, away from the screams of the burning men. Rounds skipped off the rocks as the surviving fighters fired blindly through the billowing white smoke.

Mirza crested the hill and glanced back. Ice was hot on his heels. He pushed on, scrambling over the crest and down into a steep gully. He looked back again. Ice was falling behind.

"You OK?" he yelled.

"Yeah."

The Taliban were still pursuing, moving around the burning smoke screen, firing blindly. It wouldn't take long for them to get a visual on the withdrawing PRIMAL operatives.

Mirza knelt and took up a firing position. As Ice got closer, reality dawned on him. He caught Ice as the big man stumbled, pulling him behind a large rock. He spotted the hole in the back of Ice's assault vest. Lifting it slightly he slid his fingers under the clothing. The wound was bleeding profusely. A round had punched into the lower back just to the side of the spine. There was no exit wound.

"Lie still," he whispered. Pulling a trauma kit from his vest he plugged the bleeding hole with a wound sealant. He hoped it was enough. Ice didn't make a sound as Mirza worked frantically, wrapping his torso with a bandage.

He glanced back. The Taliban were moving cautiously over the crest just a couple hundred yards away. Scraping a hole in the dirt, he grabbed Ice's assault rifle and placed it down with a grenade underneath. Then he slung his own rifle, heaved Ice's six foot five frame over his shoulder, and shuffled off down the rocky gully.

"Mitch! Mitch!" he transmitted over the radio, lungs heaving.

"Mitch here. What's going on? Calm down. Talk to me."

"Ice… Ice's been hit."

"How bad?"

"Lower abdomen, it's bad. I'm carrying him."

"You in contact?"

Mirza didn't get a chance to reply. He slid on the loose ground, falling heavily and dropping Ice. He realized he wouldn't be able to outrun the Taliban like this. Lifting his rifle up he scanned through the optics. A plume of smoke billowed from where he'd booby-trapped Ice's weapon. He snapped off a shot at the magnified image of one of the fighters.

"Mirza," Ice croaked. "Mirza."

He fired another shot. "Don't talk. Conserve your energy."

"Mirza, you have to go."

He fired again before crouching next to the veteran PRIMAL operative. "No! No, I'm not leaving you here."

"Bro, you have to go." Ice coughed, blood dribbling from his lips, his chiseled features contorted in pain. "One of us can still get out of here," he said slowly, "and it's not going to be me. You know what I need you to do."

Mirza nodded grimly. He pulled a Claymore directional mine from his backpack. Tears welled in his eyes as he stripped the last few grenades from their vests, placing them in the Claymore satchel. He wrapped the bag's shoulder strap around the mine and connected the firing device. He handed the bundle and the trigger to Ice.

"I'll never forget this, my friend. You're the bravest man I know," Mirza choked out his words as he grasped the other man's shoulder.

"Just make sure you keep Bishop out of trouble." Blood bubbled from Ice's lips and he gestured urgently. "Go! Get the fuck out of here."

He hesitated.

"I said get the fuck out of here! Go!" Ice coughed and blood streamed down his chin.

Mirza turned and left Ice lying in the dirt, holding the Claymore mine and grenades. Running wildly down the slope, he didn't look back, sliding on the loose rocks, and smashing through the shrubs. Thorns ripped at his pants and bullets cracked through the air, but he ran on. He only slowed when an explosion detonated behind him. His chest tightened, despair almost overwhelmed him, and he knew he was alone.

CHAPTER 30

THE BUNKER

"Sentinel is down, people," the female voice announced as the image on the central screen pitched rapidly toward the ground and disappeared. The little unmanned aircraft had finally run out of fuel after an epic twelve hours on target.

"How long until the Pain Train's on-station?" Vance asked.

"Eighty minutes, sir," the blonde watchkeeper replied.

"Do we have comms with Ice and Mirza?"

"No, their radio has cut out."

"Goddamn it. You mean to tell me we have no situational awareness?"

"That's correct, sir."

"Shit!" Vance slammed his fist down on the arm of his chair.

From the moment Mirza had tripped the flare, Sentinel had been watching over the pair, giving PRIMAL headquarters a bird's eye view of their movements. Ice had already provided the exact coordinates of the tunnel entrance. The plan was to follow their withdrawal, provide close air support, using the Pain Train if required, and extract them.

Vance paced the room. Things were not going to plan. Ice and Mirza were compromised, they had lost communications, and repairs to the Pain Train were taking considerably longer than anticipated.

"Somebody get me a tech," Vance growled.

A long-haired technician was on the operations floor within seconds.

"What's up, sir?" he asked.

"We just lost Sentinel and I've got a team doing E and E. I need visual ASAP and the Pain Train is still down. What can you do?"

"Without commandeering a satellite, not much, sir." The

tech pushed his glasses up his nose, shrugging.

"How long will that take?" Vance asked from his command chair.

The man looked at him dumbfounded. "Shit, sir, you telling me you want me to hack a Genesis bird?"

"Listen, bud, the name means nothing to me. I want real-time visual over our guys and I want it yesterday. I don't give a flying fuck how you do it, just make it happen."

The scowl on Vance's face was all the confirmation the man needed.

"I'll see what I can do, boss," he replied, rushing back into the intel room.

Vance slumped back in the command chair; the boys on the ground were in real trouble and he felt helpless. What they needed was air support. He looked up at the Pain Train's icon on the status board. It was still red.

The door to the Bunker hissed open and Chen Chua burst into the room. "Vance! I've worked through the data Bishop sent through," Chua said, waving a manila folder around.

The operations director spun in his chair. "Goddamnit, Chua, I've got men in contact. I don't need any more bad news from James fucking Bond."

"You're going to want to see this," the intelligence officer said as he raced into one of the Bunker's conference rooms.

Vance rose out of his chair and followed him in.

Chua began talking at a rapid rate. "I just finished going over the information Bishop's team pulled off Dostiger's PC. They hit the jackpot, and I mean THE JACKPOT." He opened the folder, pulling out a pile of printed documents. "I don't want to bore you with the details but our original assessment was correct. I can confirm that Dostiger is in fact attempting to recover a nerve agent from the site in Afghanistan. It's an—"

Vance interrupted, "Slow down, man. A nerve agent? What, like VX or Sarin?"

Chua caught his breath. "Much, much worse. It's an experimental weapon called a 'Novichok agent.' This stuff is seriously nasty, eight to ten times more lethal than VX, and doesn't have any of its shortcomings. It's persistent, heat resistant, and it eats through protective equipment. In the hands of the Revolutionary Guards this weapon is a game changer." He held up a printed sheet. "This is a report from the Russian testing facility that's buried in that mountain. They killed every test subject, over a hundred of them, with one hundred percent lethality! If this gets out, Vance, it's going to kill more people than the plague."

Vance's brow furrowed as he ran his eye over one of the data sheets. "Chua, if they get this shit above ground and we hit them, ain't it gonna spread?"

"That's right. We need to smash the tunnel entrance and bury it deep. If it gets above ground, explosives are only going to disperse it. If even a tiny amount of this chemical gets into the waterways, you can kiss every village along the Helmand River goodbye. The question is, will the Pain Train get there in time?"

"We don't have visual on the site."

"So we have no idea what stage the excavation's at?"

"Nope, we fucking do not. We're working on a non-air-breathing solution but right now we're blinder than Stevie Wonder in a blackout."

"Bit of a predicament."

"Right, Chen. They move the package and we are indeed up shit creek." He paused. "If they get this Novochick crap out of the ground, where they gonna take it?"

"Novichok," Chua corrected.

"Whatever. Where on this goddamned planet are they going to take it? Iran?"

"No, first it's going to the Ukraine. That's the other thing we learned from Dostiger's files. The plan is to get the agent to Odessa, weaponize it, and then deliver it to the Guards."

"So the IRGC want a functional device."

"It sure looks that way. My assessment is Dostiger will deliver the agent in a missile warhead. The Guards can then use their proxies in Hezbollah to launch it at Israel."

"Well, if we don't bury this shit in the 'Ghan, then we need to get Bishop and his boys down to Odessa, ASAP. Our last chance is to grab it there, right?"

"I agree. I've already got Ivan moving south to Odessa."

"OK, good." Vance ran his hands over his bald head. "But now that Bishop's shot the shit out of the nightclub, how do we know Dostiger's not going to change his plans?"

"Bishop has a source that confirmed Dostiger has already gone south."

"A source? Where the hell from?"

"I'm not sure. I do know he has the MOIS agent with him."

"Not that Iranian wench! What, are they working together now?"

"He didn't make it clear in his email. We're long overdue for his next vidcon, so I'll clarify that when we speak."

"He's sending us emails now, is he?" Vance pointed at Chua. "Right, you and I are gonna have a talk with Bishop. Pull him up on the vidcon. Let's find out what the hell he's up to, see if he can recover from the debacle in Kiev."

Chua spoke as he used a remote to flick through the menus on the LCD screen. "You should take it easy on Bishop. He's had a rough run but his team have come through with the goods. You snap at him and he'll get his back up. So play nice, OK?"

"What, are you Mother fucking Teresa all of a sudden? You never stick up for him. You told him not to meet with Dostiger, remember?"

"I know, I know, but we need to keep him on our side. The situation is still recoverable and Bishop's all we have right now."

"Yeah, I guess it could be worse. I mean, at least he hasn't managed to nuke Kiev yet."

Chua activated the secure conference call system, entering Bishop's number. The phone rang twice before establishing a secure link.

"Fischer here, wait up." Bishop used his cover name, indicating he wasn't alone. There was a slight pause before he spoke again. "Bishop here, go ahead."

"Bish, it's Vance and Chua. What's happening?" Vance asked.

"Yeah, it's all good. Had a few hours sleep. I've been waiting for your call."

"All good?" Vance said. "I just read your report and it didn't look 'all good.' Before this mission I seem to remember saying something about keeping a low profile."

Bishop's image nodded on the big LCD screen. "But we're in the clear now. No casualties, and we got Dostiger's files." He had been expecting Vance to lose his shit and was surprised he was so calm.

"OK. Well, Chua has been working through the data your boys collected."

"Anything good?"

Chua chimed in, "Gold mine, Aden, absolute gold mine. It confirmed that Dostiger is after a nerve agent and that he's planning to move it from Afghanistan to Odessa."

"Yeah, Saneh's source said they were all heading down there."

"Saneh?" Vance questioned.

"The MOIS agent."

"We know who she is, buddy. She still with you?" Vance's deep voice was cold.

"She has a source with Dostiger. I need to keep her close so I can tap it."

Chua and Vance glanced at each other. Both men were aware of Bishop's track record with women. They were also aware of the background of this particular woman; she was linked to the compromise of no less than five Mossad agents. The Israelis called her 'the Mantis,' an insect known for eating its breeding partners.

"Do you think that's such a great idea, Bish? You know she's wanted by Mossad."

"It's fine. She thinks I'm getting attached to her."

Chua grimaced at Vance. "Is your cover intact?" he asked. "Does she still think you're MI6?"

"It's all solid, Chua. I'll keep a close eye on her. Trust me on this one. She saved my ass last night and wants Dostiger as badly as we do."

"OK." Vance nodded at Chua. "We trust your judgment. What we need to discuss is your move down to Odessa."

"Yeah, we're good to go. The team is packed and ready to roll. Is Jumper still on standby at the airport?"

"She'll be waiting for you on the tarmac. I need you to get your ass to the airport ASAP. While you're moving, Chua and I will work up a detailed plan for you to use in Odessa. Ivan's already sorted transport at the other end and he's found a safe house."

"Sounds good." Bishop realized that if Vance was so keen to get him to Odessa, that could only mean one thing for the Afghan mission. "I, ah, take it things aren't going so well in the 'Ghan."

Vance and Chua were aware of how close Bishop was with both Ice and Mirza; as far as they were concerned, he didn't need the additional stress of worrying about his friends.

"Ice is still confident he can pull it off at his end. We just need to cover all contingencies. I'm also pretty keen to take down that fucker, Dostiger," Vance said.

"Oh, I'm not going to let that bastard get away, and I'm sure my man Aleks would love a chance for a little heart-to-heart."

"Alright, we'll send you the full plan once we've worked through it. You got any final questions?"

"All good, Vance. Just one thing for Chua, though."

"Yes, Aden."

"You were right about the Dostiger meeting, I screwed that one good."

"It worked out in the end, Bish. You always come through. Just stay alert and keep an eye on that MOIS agent, alright?"

"Will do. Thanks, guys. Bishop out."

The call disconnected and the conference room went silent. Chua drummed his fingers on the table. "He might be right about Saneh."

"Yeah, a source in Dostiger's camp is a pretty useful asset. I just want the intel team all over her like white on rice. If that bitch goes near a phone, I want to know about it."

"Of course."

A knock on the door interrupted the conversation and one of the operations staff stuck his head in. "Sir, the techs have the Genesis feed up and the Pain Train is airborne."

Vance jumped out of his chair. "Excellent, let's get this show started." They returned to the operations room and the director took his place in the Bunker's command chair. He looked up at the status board: The Pain Train's symbol was green and the time-to-target indicator showed forty-five minutes. He moved his attention to the central screen, where a grainy black-and-white image showed a dozen heat signatures moving across rugged terrain. The long-haired technician was sitting at a computer terminal staring at it intently.

"What the hell is this grainy shit?" Vance asked. He was used to high-resolution video feeds from the Pain Train and Sentinel drones. In comparison, the resolution of the NGA Genesis satellite imagery was poor, more like an old black-and-white television in a storm.

"It's not Hollywood, sir. This is as good as you're going to get from a hundred miles above the earth. In fact, this is cutting-edge. If our friends in Maryland knew we were using it, they would freak." The tech used a laser pointer to mark one of the smudges of heat moving down a narrow gully. A few hundred yards back, a dozen heat signatures appeared to be following him. Every now and then one of them would flash.

"We think this is Mirza, sir. The other heat signatures are hostiles are in pursuit."

"Where the hell is Ice?" asked Vance. His stomach churned and he knew the PRIMAL operative must be down. One of the staff interrupted. "Sir, a few seconds ago we received a message from Mitch. He's lost contact with Mirza," the man took a deep breath, "and he's pretty sure Ice is KIA."

Silence filled the room; only the fans of the electronic equipment could be heard. This was not the first casualty that

PRIMAL had experienced but everyone knew Ice personally. He had been there when PRIMAL started and had successfully completed more missions than any other operative. For the staff in the Bunker, losing Ice had never seemed possible; the man was indestructible. Everyone in the room felt like they had failed him; it was their job to keep him alive.

"OK," Vance growled. "Listen in, team, we need to focus. We still have a man in the field and he needs us on the job. We can mourn our loss later, but right now we need to be on point for Mirza." He pointed up at the satellite feed. "What's going on now?"

Up on the screen, Mirza's heat smudge had stopped. Ahead was another group, a long line of heat signatures. Behind him, the dozen smudges continued to close in. "Zoom out one frame," Vance directed, wondering if Mirza had been captured. The image adjusted and they could make out the edges of the new group. There were about twenty figures in total and they looked to be lying down, totally still. "That's a motherfucking ambush!"

***

Mirza's pace had slowed to a fast walk, hindered by a graze to his calf from a Taliban bullet. He stopped to bandage the wound and noticed that another round had struck his radio. The compact device had probably saved his life but was completely destroyed. Now he only had the short-range emergency radio. He tried to raise Mitch but it returned only static. The UHF frequency wouldn't work unless the Pain Train was directly overhead.

His adrenaline had well and truly worn off as he reached the bottom of the long gully. Exhausted and thirsty, he hungrily scooped water from a flowing creek, resting for a moment. He drank quickly; he couldn't stop for long as the Taliban were still in pursuit.

A burst of gunfire confirmed their presence and he hobbled from the creek as rounds snapped overhead. At least half a dozen automatic weapons joined the first and he knew they must have run to catch him.

He looked tiredly at the sniper rifle in his hands. There was only half a magazine left and it wasn't going to slow down the horde following him. Angrily he fired off the last few rounds toward his pursuers, before stripping the weapon and throwing the parts away. His chances of running were better without the weight.

He forced his heavy legs to start moving again. For Ice, he told himself. Armed with only his pistol, he pushed on, ignoring the pain and fatigue. Rounds chased him down the valley, ricocheting off the rocks, whistling through the dry vegetation. He burst through a thick patch of bushes, stumbled, and fell into an open sandy clearing. Struggling to his feet, he spotted at least three Afghans lying behind cover twenty yards ahead. Their weapons were aimed directly at him.

He collapsed to his knees, lungs heaving, dropping his head as the pistol fell from his hand. A single thought ran through his mind: Ice, I've failed you.

The valley exploded in a cacophony of gunfire. The unmistakable sound of an ambush. For ten seconds the weapons blazed then the valley fell silent.

***

On the screen in the Bunker the ambushing group had stopped flashing. The flashing had lasted for a good ten seconds and now the shapes following Mirza stopped moving.

Vance knew exactly what he had just watched. A dozen men had died in a well-executed ambush. For the time being at least, it seemed Mirza was safe. He looked at the Pain Train's time-to-target counter. Forty minutes.

***

Mirza looked around in disbelief; not a single bullet had hit him. The men in front of him climbed out of cover, their smoking weapons cradled in their arms.

"*As-salaam alaykum*," one of them greeted Mirza with open arms.

"*Wa-alaykum as-salaam*," Mirza responded quietly.

The man came forward and crouched next to Mirza, speaking Pashto. "Who are you, my son, and why do the Taliban pigs hunt you so relentlessly?"

"My name is Mirza," he managed. "I came to this place with my friend to kill the Taliban on the mountain."

"Where is your friend now?"

Mirza looked up at the worn face of the elderly man. "My friend died on the mountain. He gave his life so I could live."

"You came with only one man to kill those who have stolen our families and taken them to the place of poison? You are either brave or very stupid."

"I did not come alone. I brought death from above."

The old man's eyes grew wide. "You came with bombers?"

He looked over his shoulder at his men. They nodded and talked nervously among themselves. The local tribe had been watching the Taliban closely. Their scouts had witnessed the Pain Train's bombing run, and they had seen the Taliban reinforcements get cut to pieces. The old man had waited anxiously for this opportunity to rescue his enslaved kinsmen from the excavation site but now the possibility of another air strike changed everything. "Where are these bombers now?"

Mirza checked his watch. It was still early morning. Last night seemed like an eternity ago. "We will have bombs within the hour."

"Can you talk to them with this?" He pointed to the radio on Mirza's vest.

"If I am close enough, then yes."

"You must come with us, Mirza of the mountain. Many of my people are slaves up there. We will free them. We will defeat the Taliban and stop them from taking the Russian poison from the earth." He pointed at Mirza with a gnarled finger. "You must stop your bombers from killing our people."

Mirza shook his head. "It is too late. We won't make it in

time."

"I am Syed of the Hazara, Mirza. I come with forty men and as many horses. I will free my people before your bombers come."

Syed raised his hand. Mirza sat speechless as the Hazarans gathered around him. Twenty of them assembled, fresh from ambushing the Taliban. Others to the rear brought forward their horses, tough, stocky animals that looked bred for the purpose of climbing mountains. A mount was handed over to Mirza and a Hazaran passed him a dead Taliban's AK-47.

Syed raised his rifle in the air. "My brothers, today we return to the mountain to stop the Russian evil from once again poisoning our lands and kill the Taliban dogs who enslave our people. IT IS GOD's WILL!"

Forty men held their weapons high and shouted the words of their chieftain. As one, they spurred their sure-footed ponies up the mountain.

CHAPTER 31

THE FACILITY, ODESSA, UKRAINE

The Facility, as Dostiger called it, was located sixty miles from Odessa in a former Soviet weapons storage base. Surrounded by dense forest and a high electric fence, it was a purpose-built drug laboratory.

Dostiger's men had stumbled across the abandoned base in the months after the fall of the Soviet Union, during a search for weaponry to sell on the black market. A few carefully placed bribes had secured the rights to the property and now it was part of Dostiger's empire.

The single-story, gray concrete buildings contained modern refining equipment that processed opium bricks arriving from Afghanistan. For over fifteen years the Facility had supplied Europe's heroin addiction with a constant stream of high-grade product.

Dostiger's latest project had nothing to do with the drug trade. Now he was focused on something far more dangerous and lucrative; weaponizing the Novichok nerve agent. It had taken Dostiger six months to find technicians with the ability to load the chemical agent into warheads that would fit the Iranian Fajr-3 rockets. He had spent millions of dollars on sensitive equipment to ensure the warheads would deliver their deadly payload with maximum lethality. Overall this project had cost him huge amounts of time and wealth, and now it had the potential to collapse around him.

The Audi four-wheel drive didn't slow as it was waved through the front gates by the armed guards. He had over thirty men stationed here, almost twice the number he had in Kiev. Most of his henchmen were experienced and aggressive Chechen mercenaries. The rest were his usual Ukrainian guard force, many with former military experience.

Although his men were reliable, Dostiger insisted on

personally monitoring this phase of the operation. He wasn't going to take any chances and was furious this Fischer character had killed ten of his best men and shot up his nightclub.

The big four-wheel drive stopped in front of the main building. Dostiger was about to exit the vehicle when his satellite phone rang. He looked at the screen; it was his Iranian client. He had tried to call the senior IRGC commander no less than five times already on the drive down from Kiev and now, eventually, the man had decided to call back.

"So now you have time to talk," Dostiger said once the encryption was enabled. His heavily accented English became even thicker when he was angry.

"I am a busy man, Dostiger. Some of us have armies to run," a sinister voice replied.

"Well, if you want your warheads, you must listen. Your arrogance has already cost us dearly."

"Stop speaking in riddles. What do you want?"

"I want to know who killed my men. I want you to find out which of your countrymen sold me out to the British, but most of all I want *you* to know… the price has doubled."

"How do you know it was an Iranian?"

Dostiger screamed into the phone, "Because I had a visit from a pretty MOIS agent. Then I watched her help a FUCKING ENGLISHMAN escape from me."

"Calm down, Dostiger. Think clearly. They are just fishing; they don't really know what we are doing."

"My men in Afghanistan are dead, my men in Kiev are dead. My house has been violated and my fucking nightclub is fucking shot to pieces! Are you stupid? Somebody knows exactly what we are doing! Your organization has a leak!"

"Perhaps the leak is at your end, Dostiger. The loyalty of criminals is cheaper than soldiers."

Dostiger ignored the taunt. "Even with the leak, we have almost extracted the chemical. I'll have your precious rockets on time, but now the price has doubled."

"The price stays the same. Remember who you are

threatening." The voice was deadly calm.

"The risk is too high and I have already lost too much. The price must increase."

"The price is set. You deliver the weapons and when I am running Iran, then you will have wealth beyond your imagination."

Dostiger paused. The buyer was a ruthless megalomaniac, not an enemy he wanted to make. The Iranian Revolutionary Guards general's influence had spread throughout the Middle East to include some of the arms dealer's best customers. If the commander's plans came to fruition, Dostiger would have a very powerful ally, a customer with deep pockets, and unparalleled access to weapons markets in the Middle East.

"Very well, but you need to find out who is onto us. They are making us look like fools."

"I will take care of that. You just have the missiles ready." The Iranian hung up.

Dostiger got out of the car, slamming the door behind him. His chief of security approached, hand outstretched, ready to greet him.

"Yuri!" Dostiger snarled, brushing the man's greeting aside. "I just spoke to the Iranian; he knows nothing. What do you know?"

"My man in MI6 just got back to me. He assures me that they're conducting no operations in the Ukraine."

"What about the CIA?"

"Perhaps, but it's unlikely. The Khod valley site would have been completely destroyed. There would have been no hesitation."

"You're right. Whoever this is, they do not have the assets of the US military behind them." Dostiger paused, scratching his pitted chin. "Perhaps our MOIS agent is no longer working for Iran."

"You think she might have been turned?"

"I'm not sure, but this sounds like Mossad's work."

Yuri nodded in agreement. "There's really no one else who would be so audacious, is there?"

Dostiger smiled. "That means they'll have very limited assets here in Odessa and in Afghanistan. Contact the Ministry of Internal Affairs. I want the Militsiya presence at the airport doubled. And I want at least a platoon of Alfa commandos on standby. I don't care what it costs."

"Yes, boss." The chief of security smirked. With the additional manpower he would have a hundred men at the airport and another fifty here at the Facility. The men were all well equipped, experienced, and ready to kill.

CHAPTER 32

KHOD VALLEY

Mirza's sure-footed pony never faltered as it followed the Hazaran chief's horse up the mountain. It was the first time the Indian had ever ridden and he clung to the animal's mane with one hand, the other clutching his AK. The pony's pace slowed slightly as they hit steeper terrain but the stocky animal wasn't even breathing hard.

He was thankful they followed a slightly different route to the steep gully he had escaped down earlier; he didn't need to see the remains of his partner. Ice would live on in his memory as the indestructible and ever-poised warrior, not a mangled corpse.

"How far now, Mirza of the mountain?" Syed asked, turning in his saddle.

"A little further." Mirza pointed ahead. "Across that ridge then down onto the Taliban."

"Good, good." The grizzled warrior grinned, spurring on his horse. Mirza's pony followed suit, breaking into a trot, the jarring action nearly dislodging him from its bare back. He clung desperately to the little animal, failing to register the approaching helicopter until it thundered overhead and disappeared beyond the crest.

"Hurry, Mirza," Syed yelled over his shoulder. "Now they know we are coming."

Mirza was more worried the Taliban would get away, not with the chemical weapon, but with their lives. He wanted to avenge Ice. He wanted to kill every last one of them. He finally understood the rage that had driven Bishop through the refugee camp so long ago.

***

"Wolf Troop, this is Eagle. I am approaching your position."

"Acknowledged, Eagle, we have you now. You're clear to land," answered one of the Afghans at the air-defense site. They were ready for the approaching helicopter; all three men spread out, facing different directions, with the SA-18 missiles on their shoulders. Now that the chemicals had been recovered from the Russian facility, they were at their most vulnerable, and Khan was taking no chances.

The Mi-17-1M high-altitude helicopter was designed for the thin air of the mountains. It powered up over the ridgeline surrounding the excavation site, and hovered above the camp. One of the Taliban waved it onto a makeshift landing zone. The helicopter followed his directions, slipping sideways before descending in a whirlwind of dust. The rotor wash wrenched one of the camouflage nets from its poles, sending it dancing into the sky before it was caught on a rock high up on the cliffs. The pilot throttled back the turbines, flattening out the blades to minimize the downwash. The side door swung open and the loadmaster jumped from the cabin.

Yanuk strode forward from where he was standing with Khan and his remaining entourage.

"Greetings, comrade," he addressed the loadmaster in Russian, shaking his hand.

"Greetings to you, my friend. I take it you are ready to load?"

"Nearly. We are preparing the cargo for movement now."

By working their slaves to the bone, they had finally broken through to the hidden Soviet facility. Two full canisters of the Novichok agent had been recovered, more than enough to complete their mission.

"I was told to expect a payload of two hundred kilos cargo and thirty persons."

"No, now we only have seven persons, and at most, one hundred kilos." Khan's few remaining men would leave all their heavy equipment for the local Taliban.

"Good, with less weight we will not have to refuel before

reaching the border. I'll prepare the hold for your cargo. We will leave when you're ready."

Yanuk nodded and walked back toward Khan.

"Oh, one other thing, comrade," the man yelled after him. Yanuk paused, turning back. "We spotted a large number of horsemen coming up the mountain from the other side. I wasn't sure if you were expecting them."

Yanuk's face went blank. Khan had not mentioned any more Taliban. He rushed over, blurting out in his halting English, "Khan, the helicopter spotted horsemen coming up the mountain."

Khan's face turned a livid shade of red. He screamed orders to the group, sending them sprinting away.

The warlord turned back to Yanuk. "Tell your peasants to load the canisters NOW. We have little time, we must—"

He was interrupted by the air-defense position cutting in over the radio. "Khan, we've spotted a Russian transport plane on the horizon. Are we free to engage?"

"Engage it. Shoot them down!"

***

Onboard the Pain Train, the atmosphere was tense. The entire crew had heard the desperate call from Mirza, and to a man they had worked relentlessly through the night to get airborne.

Although they knew it might be too late to save the two PRIMAL operatives, they were still focused on the chance they could salvage the mission. The pilots had redlined the Pain Train's turbines all the way from Kandahar. The hastily repaired engine was running hot and burning oil, but it was functioning.

Tucked in behind his weapons station, Mitch had tracked Khan's helicopter as it approached and landed at the excavation site. Flashing icons on the digital map showed the release point for the bombs that would seal the excavation site and destroy the Afghan missile position. The time-to-target counter indicated eight minutes to release. In a few minutes he would activate the aircraft's targeting pod and acquire live video of the actual dig site.

An icon appeared in the menu bar at the bottom of the screen, a flashing blue speech-bubble with a camera in it. Mitch hit the icon and a screen jumped up with the face of Vance.

"Mitch, how you doing, buddy?" Vance asked.

"Yeah, I'm OK, all things considered."

"Listen, we need you to hold fire on your attack run. We've established a weapons exclusion zone around the excavation site."

Mitch's jaw dropped in disbelief and he checked his digital targeting map. Sure enough a red circle had been overlayed around the extraction site and his target coordinates had been aborted. "What the hell, Vance?" He leaned in toward the camera. "Ice and Mirza are probably dead and you want us to just—"

"Shut up and listen! I know how close you and Ice were, but you have to ditch all thoughts of vengeance. That helo you're tracking wouldn't be there if they weren't ready to load it. We're too late."

"Vance, we're seven minutes out. We'll bomb the chopper, destroy the target. We're not too late!" Mitch responded angrily.

The calmer voice of Chua interjected. "We can't do that. I know you're upset but we have a damn good reason. Dostiger's men are attempting to recover a nerve agent called Novichok. If you hit the target and the canisters are in the open, you'll kill thousands of villagers downstream. The entire waterway down from the Khod Valley will be poisoned."

"You're kidding me? Nothing's that deadly."

"This shit is. It's ten times more deadly than VX. Blast and heat-resistant, and persistent enough to make it downstream in the next rains," explained Chua.

Mitch wasn't buying it. He wasn't prepared to accept they may have lost Ice and Mirza for nothing. "What if it gets away from us? What if it ends up in a city and kills millions, then what? I say we hit it now and take the chance. If it kills a few Afghans, so be it."

Vance's commanding voice interjected. "The decision has been made, Mitch. Follow your orders. Bishop is in place to interdict the weapon in the Ukraine. I'm making the call on this. We will not run the risk of killing civilians."

"So that's it then, is it, chaps? We're done?" Mitch sounded defeated.

"Negative. Our satellite imagery shows a large ground force posturing to assault the extraction site. We don't know who they are, but we think Mirza may be with them."

"You think he's still alive?"

"We can't be sure, but there's a good chance. I want you to abide by the exclusion zone and provide what air support you can."

"Acknowledged. If Mirza's down there, we'll support him, and we'll track the helo if it takes off."

Vance nodded. "OK, bud, good hunting. We'll leave you to it. Bunker out."

The video screen disappeared, replaced by the feed from the aircraft's targeting camera. Mitch could make out the flat area at the top of the valley, remnants of the old Russian facility. A red circle had been superimposed around the site, designating the no-fire zone. He toggled the joystick and the camera panned upward to the Afghan air-defense position near the top of the mountain, well outside the zone. He smiled.

The pilot's voice came over the headset. "Mitch, we're in SAM range. Standby."

Down on the mountainside, all three Taliban had the missile systems on their shoulders aimed at the rapidly approaching aircraft. As each man activated his weapon's seeker head, the argon cylinder in front of the handgrip vented, blowing a cloud of freezing gas onto the firer. Without the gas to cool the thermal seeker head, the missiles would never lock on to the Pain Train.

As the cargo jet thundered over, the Afghans scrambled to prepare additional missiles. They were too late.

The Pain Train's fragmentation bombs exploded among them. Blast and shrapnel tore them apart.

The Pain Train banked, moving into a holding pattern above the excavation site, allowing Mitch to zoom in the targeting pod.

He cursed to himself as the image of a helicopter came into view. The white-hot plume from its engines was clearly visible through the infrared camera. Mitch could see the rotors gradually turning faster. It was preparing to take off.

***

The wild band of horsemen crested the ridgeline and halted on a small plateau, a hundred yards from where it dropped down to the extraction site. This was ground Mirza had covered earlier. He glanced back down into the gully that was Ice's final resting place, then turned toward the Taliban position. Mirza handed his mount to one of the Hazarans as they pegged their horses. He looked around and noticed the body of the Afghan sentry he'd shot at dawn had been removed.

"Mirza, come now," Syed demanded. "The bomber, it's coming." The Hazaran leader pointed out to the horizon.

Mirza could barely make out the tiny dot in the sky.

"Spread out, my brothers," Syed ordered, dispersing his men across the ridgeline. "Radio the bomber, Mirza."

He took the compact emergency radio from his pouch and activated it. His headset filled with white noise as he adjusted the settings.

Without waiting, Syed initiated a blood-curdling scream that echoed off the cliffs, "AIIIIII!"

The Hazaran warriors charged down the slope and the chatter of automatic gunfire filled the air. Below them in the excavation site, Taliban guards rushed to find cover, blasting away at the charging warriors with their own weapons.

Mirza sprinted after the Hazarans, holding his AK-47 with one hand as he keyed the radio with the other.

"Pain Train, this is Mirza, over." Nothing.

"Pain Train, this is Mirza, over." Still nothing.

A burst of fire showered him with splinters of rock. He crouched behind a boulder, steadying his weapon. The Hazaran assault bogged down as the Taliban mounted heavy resistance. Khan's warriors had the advantage of better cover, fighting from behind sandbags and piles of excavated rock. The few enslaved workers outside the mineshaft cowered among them.

The firefight raged, Hazarans inching down the slope. Mirza could see the Afghan helicopter still on the ground, its rotors turning faster and faster as it prepared to take off. He looked up at the airplane circling high above.

A huge explosion answered his prayer. A few seconds of silence fell over the battlefield as everyone stopped to stare at the mountain peak that had disappeared in a cloud of dust. Expecting they would be next, he hunkered down behind the boulder and frantically ripped the radio from his harness, checking the frequencies. Rounds cracked through the air around him.

"Pain Train, this is Mirza, over. Pain Train, this is Mirza, over," he repeated, thumping the radio with the palm of his hand. The gunfight raged on. He spotted another group of Taliban appear from a gully, reinforcing Khan's men.

***

"Mitch! You hear that?" one of the pilots said over the radio.

"Wait, I've got it. We're picking up a signal," Mitch replied over the headset. His fingers danced at lightning speed across his keyboard. A frequency bandwidth indicator replaced the battle map. "It's one of our tactical radios. Patching through now."

The signal was weak. Mitch made some quick adjustments. The targeting pod slewed over to a new group of armed men near the ridge overlooking the site. Finally a clear voice came in over the carrier wave.

"Pain Train, this is Mirza, over. Pain Train, this is Mirza, over."

"Mirza, this is Mitch. Damn, are we glad to hear from you. We thought we'd lost you." He could hear intense gunfire in the background.

"I'm still here. Ice is gone. Mitch, you need to ceasefire. There are friendlies on the target."

"Acknowledge your last. We already have a weapons exclusion zone over the site. I repeat, we will not engage."

"OK, Mitch. We're assaulting from the northwestern side. Have you got visual?"

"Yes, I have you," he confirmed. He could see the flashes of gunfire on his screen.

"Resistance is heavy. They have us pinned on the slope. Can you engage the Taliban moving into the camp from the south?"

"Roger. We'll cover the approaches but we need you to push forward and stop the chopper."

"Negative. The helicopter is airborne. I repeat, the helicopter is airborne and we cannot move."

Mitch centered the targeting camera back on the excavation site. He could clearly see the Mi-17 had taken off and was flying away from the target area, heading south.

"Goddamn it!" Mitch said, smashing his fist down on the keyboard. "We missed them. Mirza, wait out, I'm going to engage hostiles." He scanned further to the south, identifying a group of armed men running to join the battle. Selecting the drop point, he allocated ordnance and fired. The aircraft shuddered as the last of the bombs were launched. Mitch watched dispassionately as the men on the screen were obliterated in a series of flashes.

"That one's for you, Ice, old man." Mitch activated his radio again. "That's it, Mirza. We're all out of bang. What's the situation on the deck?"

"Facing light resistance. The Taliban have started to withdraw." The Hazaran assault had reached the first line of camouflage nets. The hardened warriors pushed forward methodically, executing any wounded Taliban as they converged on the gaping shaft in the mountain wall. "The site will be secure within a few minutes," Mirza confirmed.

"Roger. Your job is done now. We have to pull you out."

"Can you wait five?"

"Negative, Mirza, we're finished at the site. The chemical's on that chopper and we have to follow it. If we can't get you out in the next five minutes, you'll have to wait for a pickup from the Yanks."

"Understood. I am ready to go now."

"OK, I'll drop the package. Be prepared to extract." Mitch selected the landing point for the Fulton extraction package and the pilot banked the plane, bringing it on course.

"Acknowledged."

"Good luck. I'll see you on board in a few minutes. Mitch out."

CHAPTER 33

KHAN'S MI-17

Yanuk, Khan, and a squad of the warlord's fighters sat in the canvas seats that lined the hold of the Mi-17 helicopter. The Russian combat engineer sat in silence staring at the two stainless-steel canisters strapped to the floor. They looked benign, each about the size of a small fire extinguisher.

Yanuk looked out the window at the rugged scenery flashing past, thinking instead of the money and the women. He had no idea what Dostiger wanted the canisters for. He didn't care; this was simply business. All he wanted to know was that he was being paid more money than he could ever spend to deliver the two canisters intact. As far as he was concerned, the job was as good as done. All he needed to do was babysit the package for a little longer.

Yanuk glanced across at Khan. For a man who had lost thirty of his best men and very nearly failed his mission, he seemed completely at ease. His thoughts were interrupted by the vibration of his satellite phone. He pulled it from his chest rig and answered in Russian.

"Hello."

"Yanuk, it's Yuri. I want to confirm you have the items," Dostiger's head of security asked.

"Yes, I have two canisters."

"Excellent, the helicopter will transport you as far as our staging base in Turkmenistan. My men will meet you there with transport. You will escort the canisters all the way through to Odessa."

"What about the Americans? I don't think you realize how close they came to stopping us."

"Turkmenistan is heavily guarded; the local military commander has an arrangement with us," Yuri reassured him.

"I don't think we should underestimate the Americans."

251

"You worry too much. Everything has been taken care of. I will see you at the airport in Odessa."

"I look forward to it, comrade." Yanuk ended the call. He was anything but reassured by the Ukrainian's confidence. From what he had seen, the men trying to stop Dostiger's operation were resourceful and tenacious. He just hoped Yuri was right and they were leaving the trouble behind in Afghanistan.

***

The Taliban's attempt to reinforce the defenses of the extraction site had been decimated by the Pain Train. The few remaining Taliban had only put up a brief fight before being overwhelmed by Mirza and the Hazarans.

"Mirza of the mountain," Syed called out from where his men were crowded around a group of the enslaved workers, now freed and reunited with their kin.

"Yes, Syed," Mirza answered wearily.

The veteran commander strode over to where the PRIMAL operative was sitting propped up against a rock.

"My people are safe, thanks to you, Mirza." Syed crouched next to him. "I know it will not go far in easing your pain, but you saved many lives today, my friend."

"You saved my life, Syed. Without you, the Taliban would have killed me."

"This is true, Mirza, but Allah wanted you to live, otherwise he wouldn't have sent me to the mountain."

"Allah's will, Syed," he murmured.

Syed gestured to the tunnel. "When I was a young man the Russians brought many of my people to this mountain. Only one ever returned and he told stories of the poison that killed everything it touched. I pray to Allah that this evil has not been released upon the world. If it has, our only hope is that there are more men like you and your friend to stop it."

"There are many more men braver than me that stand ready to face that evil, Syed. Just promise me that you and your

252

warriors will guard this site until the Americans come to bury it."

"This I can promise you."

The roar of a low-flying aircraft interrupted them. They looked up as the Pain Train screamed over a few hundred feet above. A bundle tumbled out of the aircraft. It jettisoned a parachute and the object continued its descent until it landed with a thump on the abandoned helicopter pad.

"I think that's my ticket home," Mirza said. Syed watched him unzip the duffel bag and pull the contents out onto the ground. It contained a full-body harness, a length of high-tensile cable, and a gas bottle connected to a large red sack. The Skyhook extraction system had been pioneered by the CIA during the Cold War. Although rarely used, it was perfect for this situation. Mirza was glad Ice had the foresight to show him how to use it.

"What is it?" the Hazaran chief asked.

"It's a balloon."

The old man looked on in disbelief as Mirza slipped into the full-body harness. "You are going to float away under a balloon?"

Mirza smiled as he tightened the harness straps. "In a way, yes." He hooked the braided wire cable to the front of the harness and turned the tap on the gas bottle. With a hiss, the red sack inflated into a miniature airship, complete with fins. It sailed into the air, dragging the cable with it.

"I think your balloon is a little small, my friend." Syed laughed as the balloon reached the end of its tether and Mirza remained firmly planted on the ground.

"Thank you for saving my life." Mirza pulled on a pair of goggles and placed both hands across his chest. "I will never forget it."

"You are a brave warrior, Mirza," Syed yelled over the roar of the aircraft as it flew directly over them.

Before he could respond, the Pain Train snatched the balloon from the sky and he was ripped off the ground. The rush of wind filled his ears and his stomach lurched as he accelerated to 300 kilometers an hour in under five seconds. All Mirza could do was focus on keeping his arms and legs pressed tightly to his body. His world consisted of the roar of the wind and the biting pain of the harness. All of a sudden he felt hands grab him and he was hauled into the hold of the Pain Train. The ramp closed with a thump and Mirza climbed unsteadily to his feet.

"Welcome back on board, Mirza." Mitch grabbed him in a crushing bear hug. "I'm so bloody glad you made it."

"I'm sorry about Ice. It was my fault, I tripped a flare," Mirza lamented, removing his goggles.

Mitch released his grip and looked Mirza in the eye. "You can't dwell on it now," he said sincerely. "We need to focus on finishing the job. That's what Ice would want."

He nodded. "I don't understand, Mitch. We had that helicopter on the ground cold. One bomb would have ended it."

"It wasn't that simple. This nerve agent they've got their mitts on is bloody deadly. If we'd shwacked that chopper, every Afghan from here to Helmand would be pushing up daisies."

"Is that why there was an exclusion zone?"

"Yeah. Vance made it pretty clear that spreading a nerve agent over half the sandpit wasn't an option," Mitch explained as he helped Mirza out of the harness. "Right now we're tracking the chopper. You need to get some rest."

Mirza was a mess: clothing torn and tattered, eyes bloodshot. "Good idea," he said. "Wake me when we catch that helicopter. I'm not letting those evil bastards get away. I owe Ice that much." He staggered down the aircraft and collapsed onto the web seating.

Mitch helped the loadmaster refurbish the extraction kit before returning to his terminal. He brought up the radar feed and confirmed the pilot was on course to intercept the helicopter. It was heading northwest toward the border with Turkmenistan, due to cross at least ten minutes before they caught it. Borders, though, meant nothing to the Pain Train.

CHAPTER 34

KALAI MOIR AIRFIELD, TURKMENISTAN

The airfield at the isolated township of Kalai Moir, forty miles west of the Afghan-Turkmenistan border, had once been a staging base for Russian fighter-bombers. During the war jets had screamed across the border to bomb mujahideen targets deep within Afghanistan. Over the two decades since the withdrawal of Soviet forces, the six thousand foot airstrip was abandoned and had fallen into a state of disrepair.

The local authorities turned a blind eye to Dostiger's use of the runway. His aircraft, an ancient and battered AN-12, landed on a regular basis. Every few months, the old prop-driven transport plane would bring in a shipment of weapons, transfer the cargo into one of his helicopters, and return to Odessa with a load of drugs. It was a simple, yet highly profitable venture in Dostiger's business portfolio.

It had taken only an hour and forty minutes for Dostiger's helicopter to travel from the extraction site. Yanuk ended up spending most of the time sitting in the cockpit, chatting with the two veteran Soviet pilots about their time in the Russian military. As the old airfield appeared in the distance, the senior pilot pointed it out. "You ever been here before, Yanuk?"

"*Nyet*, comrade, Afghanistan was just before my time."

The pilot laughed loudly. "Lucky for you. This place is a shithole."

Yanuk scanned the airfield as the helicopter did a loop. It certainly looked like a dump; rusting abandoned aircraft sat alongside derelict fuel tankers and the runway was cracked and pitted. The ramshackle town wasn't much better, reminding Yanuk of a ghost town from a western movie.

The pilot noticed his intense gaze. "No need to worry, my friend," he said, taking one hand off the stick to point out a vehicle moving along the edge of the runway. "Turkeman Army, nearly a whole brigade down there. Missiles, tanks, all looking after you and your precious cargo. No one can touch you here, comrade."

The helicopter banked and Yanuk could see the armored vehicles and men positioned at the edges of the airfield. The surface-to-air missile systems and the anti-aircraft guns made him feel a little more secure.

"Do you fly here often?"

"Once or twice a month. We fly in with drugs, meet with the plane, and return with guns."

Yanuk whistled. "Good business."

"Pays for the vodka and whores." The pilot laughed again. "Hold on, we're coming in to land."

The helicopter flared and started to descend. Yanuk moved back into the cargo hold and strapped himself into the canvas seat. He peered through the side window, checking that everything was in order. The AN-12 was on the runway with its four engines idling and ramp lowered. Heavily armed men were carrying plastic trunks out of the aircraft, stacking them on the tarmac. He finally started to relax.

The helicopter rotated slowly, and when the rear doors faced the ramp of the transport plane, it touched down with a gentle thud. The pilots shut down the engines and the high-pitched whine faded as the spinning blades slowed to a halt. Even Khan looked happy as they disembarked, followed by his entourage carrying the two canisters.

One of Dostiger's men greeted them in English. "Welcome to Kalai Moir." The Ukrainian looked like he was straight from the pages of *Soldier of Fortune* magazine, complete with modified AK-47, low-riding thigh holster and baseball cap.

Khan gave him a withering look. "Here is the chemical," he said, as his men placed the two canisters on the ground. "Do you have my payment?"

"Yes, comrade, the weapons and cash will be transferred now." He gestured to the four armed men carrying black plastic cases down the ramp of the transport plane.

Khan nodded to the Taliban accompanying him and they moved to help Dostiger's men load the cases into the helicopter.

The Ukrainian continued. "Dostiger wanted me to tell you there is more whenever you need it."

"Good, very good. Then we are done." Khan turned to Yanuk, offering his hand. The mercenary's eyes widened as the warlord addressed him in fluent Russian, "Well done, Yanuk. I will tell Dostiger how hard you worked to make sure he got his precious chemical. Although I am sure you will be duly rewarded." He had forced Yanuk to speak English throughout the whole excavation. The tall Afghan strode back toward the helicopter, his white robes dancing in the wind.

Dostiger's representative interrupted Yanuk's thoughts. "Comrade, once the cargo is loaded, we'll leave. I am under strict instructions to have this aircraft airborne within ten minutes of your arrival."

"No argument from me. I'm ready to go," Yanuk replied before walking to the battered Antonov. Inside the cargo hold he inspected the stainless-steel containers to ensure they were lashed firmly to the floor. Satisfied, he took a seat as the five-man security detail returned and the ramp shut.

Yanuk smiled again as he glanced at the two steel cylinders. He was another step closer to his millions. He daydreamed about retiring to a tropical island, then chuckled to himself, looking out the window at the desert that surrounded the airfield. No, too much fucking sand, he thought.

***

Six miles east of the airstrip, the Pain Train began another sweeping turn. The pilots were keeping the aircraft away from the target to avoid detection, cutting laps to maintain observation. In this case Mitch was using the targeting camera to watch the transfer of the chemical from the helicopter to the cargo plane.

"Bunker, this is Pain Train. I confirm that transfer of the

cargo has occurred and the aircraft is moving for takeoff," Mitch reported. Now that the Pain Train was out of munitions, they could only observe.

"Roger, Pain Train. Can you give us the tail number?"

"Negative, we're too far out. We could move closer but it would risk compromise."

"Acknowledged. Vance has asked if you can push the boundaries. We really need that tail number."

"OK, I'll see what we can do. I'll get back to you." Mitch switched to the internal channel with the pilots. "Hey, chaps, we need to bring it in a little closer on the next run. Let's set the back side of the next loop tighter in, but no closer than three and a half miles." Mitch hoped no one on the ground was paying close attention to the horizon. Although the Turkmenistan Air Force was unlikely to be a threat with their two working fighters, he was wary of the Army's surface-to-air weapons.

The Pain Train banked over to one side, commencing the turn that would bring it nearer to the target. Mitch began recording the feed. As the image became clearer, he captured a series of stills, emailing them to the Bunker.

"They've transferred the nerve agent?" asked Mirza, as he dropped into the spare seat next to Mitch.

"Hey, Mirza. Yes, they've made the transfer. Couple more minutes and they'll be chocks away."

On-screen the antiquated transporter turned onto the main runway, its four propellers spinning. As Mitch panned out, they could see the helicopter was already flying away from the airfield, back toward the Afghan border.

"So that's it, then. They get away?"

"Not much we can do about it, eh?"

Mirza didn't say anything; he just stared at the screen.

"I'm sorry, Mirza. I want to make the bastards pay just as much as you."

He rose out of the chair. "There might be a way. I want to check something."

"You'll have to make it fast. I've got a feeling Vance is

going to cut us away soon. That engine's playing up again."

Mirza left the alcove and Mitch turned his attention back to his screens. Now that the tarmac was clear, the AN-12 started rolling forward. Mitch could see the heat streaming out of the four turboprops as it lumbered down the runway. With a lurch, it was airborne and heading west.

The video-conference symbol popped up on the bottom of Mitch's screen. He closed the feed from the pod, retracting the device back into its recess under the nose of the aircraft, then hit Accept on the video conference and Chua's face appeared.

"Hey, Mitch, good job on the image capture. We've tracked the aircraft. Tail number 76772 is registered to a company based in Kiev, no doubt linked to Dostiger."

"No surprises there."

"The aircraft is logged to fly from Mary Airport in Turkmenistan to Odessa International in the Ukraine."

"I figured it would have to be registered. There's no way you can fly through that part of town without being noticed."

"Yes, that's part of the reason we're sending you back to Abu Dhabi. We can track the aircraft from this end using the civil and military radar nets. The team has access to most of them. Bishop is on the job at the other end."

"Righto. For your info, we just lost the number-three engine again." Pushing the repaired turbofan hard coming out of Kandahar had come at a cost. Fortunately, free from her weapons payload, the Pain Train had been able to tail the slower helicopter.

Chua nodded. "Yeah, we've been monitoring it at this end. Vance is pretty keen to get her fixed up and ready for the next mission."

Mitch tipped his head in agreement. "The old girl's certainly in no state to tangle with a MiG anytime soon." The Ukrainians had a formidable fleet of advanced fighter aircraft. "Look, I think Mirza wants a crack at that helo. He's got some crazy idea that he's working on."

"Where is he?"

"He's back in the hold, sorting through the kit Ice brought

on board."

"Any idea what he's cooked up?"

"I've got an inkling."

"Well, the Pain Train is your command. Vance wants you to head back to Abu Dhabi but if you get a little sidetracked, he's not going to ask any questions."

"Hear you loud and clear, Red Leader."

"Good hunting, Bunker out."

***

The Mi-17 was cruising at a 135 knots in a direct line for Herat when the giant Ilyushin transporter swept over it. The big jet flew so close it nearly clipped the rotor on its way past. The helicopter bucked wildly as the back blast of the jet's turbofans hit its spinning rotor blades. The pilot fought with the yoke, his feet dancing on the pedals, managing to keep control of the shuddering airframe.

"Fucking asshole, how did he not see us?" the pilot exclaimed.

"That prick has radar. He should have picked us up from miles out," the copilot said.

Behind them, Khan ripped open the cockpit door. "What was that!"

"Ah, a plane almost crashed into us," the pilot replied, pointing toward the transport aircraft pulling away from the helicopter, "but don't worry, we are clear now."

Khan positioned himself between the two pilots, staring intently through the canopy at the outline of the heavy transporter. A spark of recognition flared in his eyes. "Dive! Dive!" he screamed at the top of his lungs. The big aircraft loomed in front of them.

The warning came too late.

As the Pain Train swept over the helicopter, Mirza lay on the lowered cargo ramp behind a Barrett .50 cal sniper rifle. The loadmaster had lashed him firmly to the ramp. The straps cut into his body but they held as the gusts of the aircraft's slipstream tore at his clothing.

Mirza peered through his scope. The helicopter bounced in and out of view. "We're too far away. Can you slow us down?" he screamed into his radio mike.

The pilot's response came through Mirza's headphones, "Any slower and we're going to fall out of the sky."

"I need to get closer; they're dropping back."

"Fuck it, I'm going to flare out. Wait, wait, wait, NOW."

The aircraft shuddered, slowing to stalling speed. It felt to Mirza like his guts were trying to force their way up and out of his throat. The helicopter filled the scope and he didn't hesitate. He squeezed the trigger. The rifle butt slammed into his shoulder as it spat its.lethal projectile at the target.

The bullet smashed through the Lexan canopy of the Mi-17 at almost three thousand feet per second. The high-explosive projectile detonated inside the copilot's chest cavity, the tungsten slug continuing through his back, the seat, the cockpit wall, and out the floor of the helicopter. To his credit, the pilot reacted instinctively, wiping the blood from his face as he banked the helicopter hard, throwing it sideways. Khan was thrown backward into the hold and fell against the cases that held his cash and weapons.

Mirza struggled to reacquire the helicopter. He glanced over the top of the high-power scope and saw the tiny shape in the distance, lower than before. Aiming downward, he looked through the scope again, lining up a second shot. The helicopter had dropped and was peeling away. Mirza had only a second before it would evade him.

The big rifle bucked once more as the heavy .50-caliber bullet left the barrel. At the same time, the Pain Train dropped forward.

The helicopter shuddered as the second round slammed into the starboard turboshaft. The spinning titanium blades disintegrated and sliced though the engine cowling and into the other powerplant.

With both engines destroyed, the pilot disengaged the drive, trying desperately to bring some form of control to the rotor blades. The additional strain on the damaged rotor head caused it to shear and the spinning disc ripped off, blades and all. Without lift, the fuselage of the aircraft went into free fall, gathering speed as it dropped toward the earth.

Khan struggled to his feet. He felt the aircraft drop and caught a glimpse of the transport jet through the shattered windshield. He swore at it in defiance as his helicopter slammed into the side of a ravine and detonated in a huge fireball. Khan, his crates of weapons, ammunition, and two million dollars cash were no more.

"Diving now, diving now," the pilot screamed. He forced the nose of the immense transporter down, trying to build speed before it fell from the sky. For a moment the aircraft hung in the air, trying to decide whether to fly or plummet to the earth. With a shudder, it tipped forward, winning its battle with gravity. The three working engines screamed and it gathered speed. The loadmaster hit the ramp switch, the wind subsided, and the hydraulic pistons slammed it shut.

"Nice shooting, buddy," the loadmaster said, releasing the straps holding the sniper.

CHAPTER 35

UKRAINE

Jumper, PRIMAL's Antonov AN-72, was not as sophisticated as the Pain Train. However, it did have one significant advantage over the larger Ilyushin transporter; it could take off and land on the shortest of runways.

The nimble twin-engined aircraft could land using drogue parachutes and on takeoff it generated extra lift from its own exhaust gases. The unique design allowed it to conduct covert operations from a short stretch of road or an empty field, an impressive capability for an aircraft the size of a small jetliner.

Bishop, Saneh, and the rest of the team had boarded Jumper in Kiev and were flying on a direct bearing to Odessa. As soon as the jet was airborne, Bishop locked himself in the aircraft's secure communications cabin, leaving Saneh and the men to prepare their equipment. The close-knit team had taken a liking to the beautiful Iranian and Aleks had assumed responsibility for her. Bishop had to laugh; the big Russian was treating her like his little sister.

The communications cabin was tucked-in directly behind the cockpit, alongside the toilet and galley. It took a few seconds for the secure link between Jumper and the Bunker to connect, displaying an image of Chua and Vance.

"So, how's the team, Bish?" Vance asked.

"Good, guys. Ready and raring to nail Dostiger to the wall."

"That's good to hear, bud, because this ain't gonna be an easy one."

Bishop laughed. "Are they ever?"

"That Philippines gig wasn't too hard."

"Fuck you, Vance. I got shot."

It was Vance's turn to laugh. "Harden up, you pussy." He winked and smiled. "OK, buddy, I'm sending through the plans for the job in Odessa. You're gonna be working with

Ivan on this one. He worked up most of the intel in the pack."

"No problems." Bishop opened the file that came through on the computer terminal. He looked over the first slide of the presentation, an overview of Dostiger's security at Odessa airport. "Hey, Chua."

"Yes."

"Are you nuts? This airfield has over one hundred soldiers guarding it! Last time I checked, I've got four men, not forty."

Chua looked hurt. "Go to the next slide, look at the plan. I think you can pull it off."

Bishop's concern faded as he flicked through the concept of operations. "Mate, this is bold. I mean there are a few bits that are going to be hairy, but overall it's pretty damn good."

A broad smile spread across the intelligence officer's features. "Thanks, Aden. Oh, by the way, there's something I wanted to raise with you." Chua was keen to take advantage of Bishop's good mood.

"Hit me."

"I'm a bit worried about Saneh. I know we raised this before, but I think you need to cut her away first chance you get."

"Chua, it's alright, mate. I'm all over it. I need her source at the moment. When she stops being useful, we'll drop her."

Something in Bishop's voice and the look in his eye made Chua think there was more to it than that. "You know if she's exposed to too much, we'll only have one option."

"OK. So, Vance, how did Mirza go with Ice?" Bishop redirected the conversation.

"He did a damn fine job. Slick operator. I had a quick word with Mitch before this."

"Good to hear. I knew he wouldn't disappoint. What did Ice have to say?"

"Bish, you don't have much time before you hit the ground in Odessa. If you don't have any more questions, we'll have to leave you to brief the team."

"Yeah, good point. One last thing, can you send me through that data on the Novichok agent? It would be nice to know exactly what we're dealing with."

"Can do. We'll send it now."

"OK. If anything else comes up, I'll call you."

"Roger. Chua and I will be online. This is our last chance. The entire team back here is going to be behind you. We'll be monitoring all police and military networks in Odessa. We also have Dostiger's aircraft on air traffic control radar. It's still a good five hours out. Should hit the ground at around twenty-three hundred hours your time."

"Right on. We should have a kicking little reception ready for them by then."

"OK, good luck. Bunker out."

The link terminated and Bishop took a few minutes to familiarize himself with the finer details of the Odessa plan. It was daring, but he was confident they could handle it. He transferred the data file to the screen in the main cargo hold, locked the door behind him, and joined the rest of the team.

"Listen in." Everyone gave him their attention. The pilots at the front of the aircraft would observe via a camera and microphone built into the cabin.

"Team, I'm not going to lie to you. The plan for this is audacious. Saying that, I have the utmost faith that we can pull it off. The simple fact is, if we don't succeed, there's a good chance that thousands will die and Dostiger will once again slip through the cracks."

"Nothing like a little pressure, boss." Kurtz grinned.

Using the screen at the front of the cabin, it took Bishop twenty minutes to outline his orders and give everyone their tasks. The plan had a lot of moving parts and he wanted everyone to understand their individual responsibilities and how they fitted into the bigger picture. Once finished, he opened the floor to questions.

"This sounds insane, boss," said Kurtz, tapping the side of his head.

Bishop nodded, smiling. The German continued, "There are a lot of variables, *ja*. I mean we're counting on the vehicles being serviceable, the guards not setting off an alarm, and

Dostiger's men at the airport not having heavy-weapons. I think there are a lot of things to go wrong."

"You're right, a lot can go wrong. But between us we'll be able to handle it." Bishop locked eyes with the tall German, who nodded.

"*Ja*," Kurtz said smiling. "As long as I get to blow something up, it's a good plan!"

The entire team laughed, breaking the tension.

"Right, guys," Bishop concluded. "We have about twenty minutes till we hit the deck. Let's do our final checks. I'll confirm orders again after we're on the ground."

The team returned to preparing their equipment. Jumper had been preloaded with everything they would need: a flying arsenal. Full-faced combat helmets, assault vests, submachine guns, TASERS, and boxes of ammunition filled the overhead lockers.

Bishop rapidly reorganized his own equipment. He grabbed a fresh set of armor and an assault helmet. He reloaded his pistol and submachine gun, checking batteries, ensuring everything was fully functional.

Once Bishop was ready, he looked across at Saneh, who was sitting with Aleks. The big Russian had given her a spare combat helmet and was showing her how to use its functions. Bishop caught her eye and gestured for her to take the seat next to him.

"The British Secret Service is very well equipped," Saneh said with a slight smile. "I'm impressed!"

"Is your gear good to go?" he asked seriously.

"Yes. Aleks was just showing me how to use it."

"OK. Come with me." Bishop got up and led her to the front of the plane. "I want to show you something."

He opened up the communications cabin and they squeezed in, Bishop letting Saneh sit while he stood behind in the cramped space. Her brow furrowed as she read the document displayed on the screen.

"Have you seen this before?" he asked. The Russian data sheet on the Novichok agent was originally written in Cyrillic, but PRIMAL HQ had translated it into English.

"No," she said as she read.

"I want you to know what we are dealing with."

"I had no idea," she added quietly. "I thought this was just another chemical weapon. Something that would cause fear more than anything."

"Now you understand why we can't let anyone have this. What do you think would happen if your government got their hands on it?"

"We wouldn't use it!" she said adamantly, turning around to face him.

"At the end of the day, that means nothing. What do you think Israel would do if they knew that the Supreme Council could deploy a nerve agent this lethal?"

She looked away. They both knew the answer to that question.

"What will you do if you secure it?" she asked.

"What do you think we should do?"

She looked directly into his eyes. "It should be destroyed."

"Easy to say, but I think your masters have other intentions."

"I'm here to keep that weapon out of the hands of the Guards. That's all!" she snapped back, wondering about Rostam.

"I don't doubt you at all."

The aircraft pitched forward, beginning its descent to Odessa.

"You actually trust me?"

"I trust you. You wouldn't be on this plane unless I did."

"No, I'm on this plane because my source is your only link to Dostiger."

True, thought Bishop. You're the only link to that murderous fucking bastard.

Saneh held out her hand. "As they say, the enemy of your enemy is your friend, so I guess we're a team, yes?"

Bishop grasped her hand and pulled her to her feet. "I guess so. Now let's get strapped in. It's going to be a bumpy landing."

***

Jumper approached the rudimentary airstrip under the cover of darkness, the pilots using night vision goggles, flying with a blacked-out cockpit. The aircraft came in at a little over stall speed, flaps and air brakes extended, creating as much drag as possible. It cleared the tall pines at the southern end of the strip by a few feet, touching down heavily on the freshly mown grass. The wheels failed to grip and the aircraft started to slide sideways until a drogue chute billowed behind it and a roar of reverse thrust brought it under control. The parachute detached as Jumper taxied toward a group of dilapidated farm buildings.

The pilots clamped the brakes on the left-hand rear wheels, spinning the aircraft to face back up the strip as the ramp lowered. From beside the farm buildings a shadow detached itself, running toward the jet. The figure waved the passengers off the ramp, directing them toward a barn. As the last person left the aircraft, the ramp closed, the pilots engaged full thrust, and the empty plane lurched forward, bouncing down the rough airstrip. It gained speed rapidly and within four hundred yards was airborne, disappearing into the darkness.

The barn was large, used to house tractors and farm equipment as well as animals during the harsh winters. Kurtz screwed up his nose in disgust. "Just like back home in Russia, hey, Aleks."

"Never was a bother for your mother when she visited."

Kurtz laughed, dropping his heavy equipment bag onto the straw-covered concrete.

As the team unloaded their gear, the man who had met them pulled Bishop aside.

Clad in blue jeans and a dark leather jacket, there was nothing memorable about him. If Bishop didn't know his background, he would have assumed he was just some local off the street. He was actually one of Chua's deep-cover operatives, part of a network that usually worked independently from the other PRIMAL members.

"Aden, I'm your man here in Kiev. You can call me Ivan." The Russian's softly spoken English was impeccable. "There's a lot to be done so I'm going to keep this brief."

"Sure." Bishop had never worked with Ivan before, but knew him by reputation. The Russian was trained by the KGB in covert operations and fluent in no less than five languages.

"The GAZ here is yours," Ivan said, pointing at a battered green van.

Bishop raised his eyebrows as he inspected the Soviet utility vehicle. "With our budget, that thing is the best you could do?"

"I realize it may not be as stylish as you are used to, Aden, but I assure you it is reliable. Inside you will find the ammunition for the armored vehicles. I've recced the depot and the personnel carriers are in good condition. However, they won't have ammunition and may require refueling." Ivan walked Bishop over to the corner of the barn where he had constructed a rough model of the camp on the concrete.

"The guards are in this building here," he explained, using a long stick to point to a square of wood representing the hut at the main entrance to the base. "They have already started drinking and are likely to be drunk by the time you arrive."

"How do you know they'll be drunk?"

"Because I bought them five bottles of vodka. I told them my son wanted to ride in a tank and that I'd be there tomorrow with him. Trust me, they're soldiers, they'll be drunk." He focused attention back to the model. "The vehicles are in these sheds here. You'll need to cut the locks on the hatches and you can refuel them here at the diesel point. Once you've loaded the ammunition, you should be ready for action."

"Sounds workable. Are there any other soldiers on the base?"

"No. The base doesn't house troops, just the guard force. A team of civilian mechanics are employed to keep the vehicles serviceable, but they won't be there at night," Ivan pulled a small notebook from his pocket. He flicked through the pages to confirm his numbers. "There are five guards on duty tonight with two dogs in the compound."

"Are they guard dogs?" asked Kurtz who had been listening in on the conversation.

"No, little itty-bitty sausage dogs like you had as a boy," replied Ivan.

"Shut up, *Dummkopf*, I don't like dogs."

"Shoot them, TASER them, whatever." Ivan pointed at another part of the model where he had used colored wool to create a map of the wider Odessa area. "We're currently located here at the Farm; the military depot is ten miles away." He pointed with his stick. "Odessa Airport is another nine miles down this highway. There are two GPS units in the GAZ with all the waypoints preprogrammed. I'll lead you as far as the military base, but from there I'll have to drive on to the airport to deal with the power supply."

"We'll have you on the satellite comms?" Bishop asked.

"Of course. I'll give you regular situation updates on the airport."

"Sounds good. My people in the Bunker are also monitoring the aircraft's approach, but it'll be good to have eyes on. So once we have the vehicles, how long will it take us to reach the airport?"

"At forty miles an hour, it takes twenty minutes to drive from the military base to the airport."

"Sounds about right. Hmmm, timing's going to be tricky here. Can't get there early but we need to catch them on the ground before they can transfer the cargo. Who knows where they'll take it. What about Dostiger, where's he going to be when this is all going down?"

"At a guess, in whatever facility he bases his Odessa operations. Chua wanted me to focus on the weapon, not Dostiger."

"Yes, of course."

Ivan checked his watch. "Alright, there's really not much time. You need to move in fifteen minutes."

"OK, let me brief the lads and we'll roll."

The team gathered around the model of the military base and the rough map of Odessa. Bishop quickly briefed them on the overall plan, updating the orders he'd already delivered on the aircraft. The team listened intently, their faces serious, ready for battle. They were back in their armored vests, MP7s in hand and combat helmets at their feet. Bishop smiled as he saw Saneh looking like any other member of the FIST, clad in a spare set of body armor, holding a submachine gun in one hand and a bug-eyed combat helmet in the other.

Everyone looked calm and prepared, ready to undertake one of the most daring assaults since the Israelis at Entebbe Airport in 1976. Funnily enough, thought Bishop, this plan is similar; the odds are a little worse but it's the same basic concept. Punch in hard, kill the bad guys, grab the loot, and get the hell out. What could possibly go wrong?

CHAPTER 36

ODESSA INTERNATIONAL AIRPORT

Dostiger's chief of security, Yuri, felt confident. The airport was crawling with close to a hundred men dedicated to protecting the incoming cargo. Over fifty were Dostiger's henchmen, heavily armed contractors with military backgrounds. They were supported by airport security police and a platoon of the elite Alfa troops from the SBU, the Ukrainian Security Service. The Alfa operators were Yuri's quick reaction force, a heavily armed SWAT team prepared to react to any contingency.

From his vantage point in the airport control tower, Yuri had a commanding view of the entire airfield. The 1.5-mile runway ran north–south, with the terminal and tower located a third of the way down its length. A grass emergency runoff separated the tarmac from the razor-wire fence and antivehicle ditch surrounding the airfield. Bright security lighting illuminated every square inch of the perimeter, casting long shadows behind the men patrolling the boundary.

Yuri had thoroughly assessed the security and was certain there was nowhere a team of Mossad agents could infiltrate unobserved. He'd positioned men in armored four-wheel drives at both ends of the runway with additional teams roving the perimeter with dogs. The security teams had been patrolling since midday and reported no sign of surveillance or attempted entry.

Inside the terminal the regular airport police were supplemented by more of Dostiger's men in plain clothes, concealing submachine guns under their bulky jackets and alert for any suspicious activity. The Alfa assault team was parked outside in black vans, on standby should anything unexpected occur.

The Alfa commander never left Yuri's side, the loyalty of

his team paid for in cash. The security chief smiled as he looked across at the sniper team positioned on the walkway of the control tower. He could barely see them, their black jumpsuits and balaclavas blending into the night. It gave him confidence to know that the marksmen, lying behind their Blaser sniper rifles, could put a bullet through a man anywhere on the airfield.

"Excuse me, sir," an air traffic controller interrupted his thoughts. "The flight has entered Ukrainian airspace. We'll have them on the ground in sixty minutes."

"Excellent. Warn me when they're beginning their approach."

"Yes, sir."

Yuri pulled his phone from the pocket of his heavy jacket and placed a call. Dostiger picked up after two rings.

"Yuri, what is happening?"

"It's all going to plan; no sign of Mossad."

"Stay alert, Yuri. I'm sure they are watching. Do you have enough men?" Dostiger had been paranoid since the assault on his nightclub.

"Yes, I have nearly a hundred. The Alfa team has been fully briefed on their security and escort duties. Once the chemical is delivered, they'll assist in delivering it to the Facility."

"Good, good, but stay alert. I know they will come for the package."

"We're ready for them. Let them try."

"Call me when the cargo is on the ground."

"Yes, sir."

Dostiger ended the call and Yuri placed the phone back in his pocket. He pulled a black radio from his belt. "All call signs, this is Command, radio check, over."

Each of the team commanders radioed in with nothing to report. Everything was in place and within an hour the cargo would be secure at the Facility. There Yuri had camouflaged bunkers, motion sensors, and a small army of veteran Chechen mercenaries, not to mention a company of Ukrainian mechanized infantry on two hours notice to respond. All he could do now was wait.

***

17TH MECHANIZED BRIGADE MOTOR POOL

The vehicle compound was a block the size of two football fields, surrounded by a high metal fence topped with razor wire. A simple checkpoint controlled the entrance with a boom gate and guard box. The adjacent hut housed the security detail, the soldiers taking turns to rotate through the mundane gate duty.

Less than a hundred feet from the checkpoint, down an embankment by the side of the road, the PRIMAL team crouched in a mud-filled drain. Bishop crawled to the road's edge to observe the guard box. Through the night vision goggles built into his helmet, the soldier on gate duty appeared in glowing red and yellow, standing out clearly against the green-and-black background.

The guard paced back and forth, smoking a cigarette. He stubbed out the butt with his boot and walked back into the warmth of the guardhouse to join his comrades. Occasionally Bishop would catch a glimpse of the men as they passed by the windows inside the hut. It appeared as if there was a party going on; he could hear men singing at the top of their lungs.

"He's right, you know. They're all drunk. Every one of them," Bishop whispered over the radio to his team.

"Do you see the dogs?" asked Kurtz.

"Negative, we'll tackle them if they appear. Saneh, are you ready?"

"Ready," she replied from behind the wheel of the utility van.

"OK, no change to the plan. On my mark."

The team moved in behind him, crouched ready for action.

"Go, go, go!"

They moved swiftly, weapons up as they silently

approached the guard shack. Lining up beside the front door, Bishop opened it with a gentle push, and rushed in.

The singing died off immediately as the team fanned out into the room, submachine guns at the ready. All five guards were there, sitting around a large wooden table strewn with bottles of vodka, empty glasses, and standard-issue AK-74 rifles. The wide-eyed Ukrainian soldiers were young, inexperienced, and unprepared for the sight that faced them.

The bug-eyed reflective lenses of their full-faced helmets made the PRIMAL team look like aliens from a Hollywood movie. They made no sound except for the faint hissing as they breathed through the respirators built into either side of the helmets.

One of the guards lurched forward in his seat, reaching for his AK-74. Kurtz shot him in the chest with the TASER mounted to his MP7. The convulsing body slid off the table and onto the floor, twitching in a spreading pool of urine. It was enough to dissuade any further attempts at resistance.

Bishop identified the senior rank among the men, grabbed him by the throat, and dragged the terrified soldier into the corner. Aleks and Kurtz bound the other guards as Bishop questioned their leader, pinning him up against the wall. The presence of the faceless assailants was proving to be a very sobering experience for the young man.

"Where are the dogs?" Bishop's voice was harsh through the helmet's vents.

The man began babbling in Ukrainian.

"Where are the dogs? The woof-woofs." He used his gloved hand to make a shape like a dog barking.

The man looked at him blankly.

"Fuck it!" He threw the soldier to the side, sending him sprawling across the floor. "Put him with the rest."

Aleks grabbed the man by his collar, cuffed his hands behind his back, and pushed him into the next room with the other guards. Pavel and Miklos were clearing the remaining rooms and the outside of the building.

"We found the dogs, boss. They're in cages out back," one

of them transmitted.

"Good work. Keep clear of them. I don't want to shoot them." Bishop keyed another button on his radio, transmitting to Saneh in the van. "Entry point secure."

"I'm moving now," she responded.

The old Russian van drove out of the darkness and pulled up at the entrance as Kurtz lifted the boom gate. The team piled in and Saneh drove them through the depot toward the vehicle bays.

Near the rear of the compound, lined up under security lighting, were twelve BTR-94s: enough armored vehicles to move a hundred men. The BTR-94 was a Ukrainian variant of a Russian armored personnel carrier. A little longer than a minibus, the eight-wheeled BTR had a crew of three and could carry a squad of fully equipped soldiers inside its armored hull. Its armament included a remote weapons turret that housed twin 23mm cannons and a 7.62mm machine gun.

Aleks was first out of the van once Saneh parked alongside the line of BTRs. He had always thought the big vehicles looked like bugs. Bristling with weapons and antennae, they resembled giant, death-wielding cockroaches.

The former Eastern Bloc members of the FIST took charge preparing two of the vehicles, with both Aleks and Miklos having prior experience with them. They would drive the armored personnel carriers during the assault.

Aleks used a pair of bolt cutters to cut through the padlock on the side hatch of his vehicle. He swung the heavy door handle, unlocked the mechanism, and the bottom part of the hatch dropped down, forming a step, while the top half swung upward. He flicked the internal lighting switch filling the hull with a yellow glow.

The inside smelled like a mechanic's workshop, the air heavy with the stench of diesel and solvents. Aleks clambered past the gunner's cage onto the driver's seat. He inspected the buttons and switches. The layout was different from the BTR-70 he'd trained on.

He flicked a few switches and thumbed the ignition button.

The big engine clunked as it attempted to turn over, the starter motor straining. He thumbed it again and the same thing happened; the engine refused to catch. Cursing, he was about to try again when Saneh slipped into the command seat next to him. She leaned forward and examined the control panel, flicking some switches.

"Try it now," she said softly.

Aleks frowned, thumbing the starter. The diesel engine turned once and caught, roaring to life. He lifted his bushy eyebrows in surprise.

"You need to turn on the fuel pump and glow plugs," Saneh yelled over the roar of the engine. "We have BTRs in Iran as well, you know."

He grinned at her, pulling himself from the driver's chair. Kurtz was already in the back along with ammunition boxes from the van. Aleks helped him load the heavy belted rounds for the cannons and demonstrated how to use the remote weapon station. Kurtz learned quickly, rotating the electric turret, using the camera to zoom in and out.

Aleks left him to practice, and ducked out of the cabin to check on the other vehicle. Pavel and Miklos already had their BTR ready: engine idling and ammunition loaded. All they needed now was to top up with diesel.

"OK, let's go, guys," he said before hurrying back to drive his vehicle. They didn't have much time left and he knew it would take a few minutes to fill up.

As the two crews drove their BTRs across to the fuel point, Bishop was sitting in the back of the van waiting for a call from Ivan. He glanced at his watch. They only had a few minutes. A beep in his helmet interrupted his thoughts.

"Fischer, this is Ivan. I'm in position at the airfield."

"Roger. Anything to report?"

"Yes, there's lots of movement here: over eighty hostiles, possibly more."

"Any sign of heavy weapons?"

"Negative, you chaps ought to be fine."

Bishop smiled. He found it amusing that Ivan's voice

sounded more like a British politician than a Russian trained spy. "Roger, we'll be inbound soon."

"Acknowledged, Ivan out."

Bishop used his wrist-mounted iPRIMAL to contact the Bunker.

"Bunker, this is Bishop."

"Chua here, target aircraft is twenty-five minutes out."

"Roger, we'll be rolling in five."

"Jumper will be waiting for you once you've recovered the package. Good luck."

"Thanks, mate. Bishop out."

He jumped out and walked swiftly across to the fuel point, where the team was finishing refueling the two BTRs. "It's on, lads. Aircraft is inbound; eighty plus hostiles at the airport with no heavy weapons."

"I almost feel sorry for the poor bastards, *da*," Aleks responded before thumbing the starter on his vehicle.

Almost on cue the roar of both big diesels filled the air as Miklos started his own vehicle. He and Pavel were in first BTR with Bishop. The other crew consisted of Aleks, Kurtz, and Saneh.

The two armored personnel carriers turned out of the barracks and onto the main road, Pavel following the GPS provided by Ivan.

Bishop checked his watch. They had exactly twenty minutes. Timing would be critical. They needed to reach the airport immediately after the AN-12 touched down and not a moment earlier. Chua had confirmed Dostiger's aircraft was on time, they had two armored vehicles fully loaded with fuel and ammunition, and the extraction aircraft was standing by. In a little over half an hour we should have this all wrapped up, he thought.

CHAPTER 37

ODESSA INTERNATIONAL AIRPORT

The AN-12 landed heavily, hitting the end of the runway with a squeal as the tires slammed into the tarmac. Yanuk grinned at Dostiger's men as they unclipped their safety belts and checked their rifles. "I can almost taste the vodka, comrades," he yelled over the roar of the turboprop engines. They all laughed; everyone involved in this operation was expecting a significant bonus, although none would receive as much as the engineer.

They turned onto the taxiway and Yanuk unclipped his safety belt, standing up. He walked over to one of the fuselage windows and peered out at the floodlit airport. There were armed guards everywhere. He smiled to himself.

The transporter slowed to a halt with the nose pointed back toward the runway and the tail facing the terminal. A whine of hydraulics announced the lowering of the ramp and Dostiger's men inside the aircraft shivered as the cold night air whipped into the hold.

Looking out over the ramp, Yanuk could see a blue armored van approaching with half a dozen black four-wheel drives in convoy.

The van turned and reversed while the four-wheel drives parked in a semi-circle, facing outward. As the van came to a halt Yanuk's brow furrowed. Over the idling turboprops he thought he could hear what sounded like the distant roar of a very large diesel engine, a sound that brought back vivid memories from the Chechen war over a decade ago.

He stepped halfway down the ramp and peered beyond the floodlit perimeter fence into the darkness. The growl of engines grew louder. Yanuk's eyes narrowed, then widened suddenly as the thump of a distant explosion plunged the airfield into total darkness. All the security lights, runway beacons, passenger terminal, and tower lighting died at exactly the same moment. Yanuk finally recognized the engine noise that was once so familiar.

"GO, GO, GO!" he screamed, desperately gesturing at the loadmaster, who looked at him blankly. Yanuk took two quick strides and roughly grabbed the man, shaking him, yelling in his face, "TAKE OFF! TAKE OFF!" The aviator thumbed his radio and relayed the message to the pilots. They began rolling forward, the ramp scraping on the tarmac.

From the airport tower Yuri stood in the darkness, watching as the black shape of the Antonov started moving away from his armored van. He had known something was wrong when one of the police patrols was cut off over the radio, a crashing sound transmitting clearly through the speaker on his Motorola before it went quiet. Then the lights had died, plunging the tower into darkness. Now the unmistakable sound of armored vehicles could be heard approaching in the distance. A feeling of dread filled his stomach.

***

Two minutes earlier Ivan armed a remote-detonated explosive device and reported in to Bishop over the team's radio frequency.

"Fischer, this is Ivan. The aircraft has just landed. No change to the security situation; we're looking at eighty-plus hostiles."

"Roger, we're turning onto the access road. Prepare to kill the lights."

"OK, standing by." The generator that fed power to the airport was located outside the perimeter fence and it had been a simple matter for Ivan to rig explosives to the power cables.

The two BTRs roared as they sped around the final corner. In the lead vehicle, Miklos spotted a police car blocking the road, its blue lights turning lazily. He stomped the accelerator to the floor. "HOLD ON!"

Thirteen tons of steel impacted violently with the sedan at

fifty miles an hour, flipping it sideways. The two policemen sitting inside were smashed into the roof and windows, breaking limbs, knocking them unconscious.

"SORRY, OFFICER," yelled Miklos as they plowed through the roadblock. He could see the airport now, the outer fence lighting and colored beacons above the control tower clearly visible.

"OK, kill the lights now," Bishop transmitted.

A moment later the airport was plunged into darkness. Miklos's night vision goggles automatically adjusted and he aimed for the end of the runway. The BTR maintained momentum as he barreled off the road, smashing through dense bushes and flattening trees. The front two wheels flew over the antivehicle ditch, the rear pair following with a jolt. The ditch was designed to stop cars, not eight-wheeled military vehicles.

The security fence was hit next, knocked over without slowing the armored juggernaut, crushed beneath its wheels. Miklos braked slightly as he hit the runway, waiting for the second BTR to catch up. Once both were side by side, they accelerated across the tarmac.

Bishop's voice came across the radios. "OK, team, weapons free, engage all hostiles. It's time to ruin Dostiger's day."

Kurtz was in the second BTR, using the weapons turret to scan for targets as they raced toward the taxiing AN-12. He identified the men and vehicles to the rear of the aircraft, their flashes of gunfire obvious in his night vision sight. As rounds pinged off the BTR's armored skin, he depressed the trigger and the vehicle shuddered as the twin cannons roared, spitting out their cigar-size projectiles. Chunks of concrete were gouged from the tarmac in front of the target.

Kurtz adjusted his point of aim and the electric motors whined, inching the long barrels slightly higher. He triggered another burst. The explosive rounds slammed into a pair of four-wheel drives, detonating their fuel tanks. The weapon sight flared white as the explosion overwhelmed the infrared sensors.

"*Scheisse*! Soviet junk." Kurtz smacked the screen with the palm of his hand.

"Aircraft's on the runway!" yelled Aleks from the driver's seat.

Saneh was sitting next to the Russian and screamed at the top of her lungs, "Ram him, Aleks, before he takes off!"

Aleks pulled the BTR in behind the Antonov as the rear ramp begun to raise. Gunning the engine he rammed it, tipping the aircraft slightly, jamming the ramp. Gunmen fired from the open hold and he ducked instinctively. Kurtz swiveled the turret around, opening up with the machine gun that was mounted beside the cannons. A twenty-round burst hosed down the side of the aircraft, bullets ripping through its thin skin and silencing the gunfire.

"Take it easy, Kurtz, you'll hit the cargo," Aleks barked as he swerved to get around the aircraft's wing and the spinning propellers. Kurtz depressed the gun turret and blasted the rear tires. The nitrogen-filled rubber exploded and the aluminum rims cut into the tarmac with a screech. The aircraft fell behind and pitched sideways. Aleks yanked the steering wheel to the side to cut it off. With a crunch the heavy steel armor smashed into flimsy aluminum, the front landing strut collapsed, and the Antonov dropped onto the back of the BTR. Aleks slammed on the brakes and both the aircraft and the personnel carrier slowed together, sparks streaming off the Antonov's bare rims while the BTR's brakes screamed in protest.

While Aleks' vehicle stopped the plane, the second BTR, carrying Bishop, had moved to the rear. Pavel had been using the weapons turret to suppress the security forces, expertly firing short bursts from the dual 23mm cannon, scattering Dostiger's men and ripping apart the vehicles. He had targeted the control tower, lashing it with the high-explosive projectiles, denying anyone use of the vantage point.

As the Antonov ground to a halt, the second BTR pulled in behind it, the side hatch swinging open. Bishop was first out, sprinting toward the lowered aircraft ramp. Behind him, Miklos lobbed a flashbang over his head. It detonated in the plane with a thump.

Bishop kept moving, the full-face helmet shielding his eyes from the blinding flash and blocking out the deafening boom. He strode up the ramp into the dark cargo hold, firing short bursts from his submachine gun at the glowing shapes of Dostiger's security team. Some were already collapsed on the floor, slain by Kurtz's machine gun burst. Others staggered or crawled, ears shattered by the grenade.

"Check!" he screamed, as his weapon jammed and he dropped to one knee, ripping out his Beretta.

"Covering!" Miklos dispatched another gunman before Dostiger's remaining man managed to return fire. A pistol barked and the Czech was hit, stumbled backward, then fell off the ramp. Bishop fired a single shot and the final gunman slumped forward over the precious cargo, pistol dropping from his hand.

He rushed forward and hauled the limp body off the canisters. Unlike the paramilitary guards this man was dressed in dusty work clothes. As he lifted, the man flipped onto his side, grasping Bishop's pistol with one hand and helmet with the other. He dragged the PRIMAL operative over his own body, throwing him into the side of the aircraft.

Bishop grunted as he slammed into the wall and fell forward into the netting seats. His pistol snagged in the net.

Behind him, Yanuk ignored his wounds as scrabbled on the floor, frantically searching for his pistol. Unable to find it in the darkness, he drew a combat knife and focused his attention on the dark armored figure struggling to extract his weapon from the web seating.

With a roar, Yanuk leaped forward, driving the knife down with both hands. The point struck between the shoulder blades but failed to penetrate the armor. He grabbed the edge of the helmet, searching for a gap to drive the knife into.

Bishop dropped his pistol and rolled out from under the attacker, landing with his back on the floor. The other man was on top of him in an instant, jamming the tip of a knife under his helmet.

"Boss, are you alright? Report?" Pavel's voice screamed inside Bishop's helmet. He ignored it, focusing on the knife penetrating his neck guard.

As he reached up to fend off the blade, his hand brushed one of the concussion grenades attached to his armor. He ripped the pin out, slid the grenade into his hand, and slammed it into his assailant's nose. The man screamed and Bishop smashed it forward again, shoving the small device between the man's teeth.

The explosive was not designed to kill when it detonated in an open space, merely stun. In the confines of Yanuk's mouth, it was deadly. The blast tore his jaw off and blew through the roof of his mouth. The expanding gas vented into the brain cavity, pushing its contents out through his nose, eyes, and ears in a bloody spray.

Bishop wiped the gore from his visor, shoved the dead body aside, and struggled to his feet. He shook his head; even with his enclosed helmet, the stun grenade had left his ears ringing.

"Boss, report." Pavel sounded frantic. Waiting in their BTR, he hadn't heard from the team leader since Miklos fell from the ramp.

"Aden here, hostiles have been neutralized," Bishop transmitted as he struggled to get his bearings. He stepped over the twitching corpse at his feet and checked the two canisters. "We've got the cargo. Get ready to roll."

At the front of the plane, Aleks was struggling to extract his BTR out from under the collapsed aircraft. The nose of the big Antonov was sitting on the back of the armored vehicle and the weight had pushed the front wheels off the ground. Rounds ricocheted off the hull as Dostiger's remaining security teams blasted away from the other end of the runway. Kurtz couldn't hit them; he had the twin cannons fully depressed but they were still pointing uselessly in the air.

"Come on, you bitch!" Aleks engaged the lowest gear and revved the big engine hard. "Come on, come on." The BTR groaned as it inched forward, creeping out from under the twenty-eight-ton transporter. "Yes, come on, you beast."

With a lurch it was free, the front wheels slamming into the ground, the crumpled nose of the AN-12 crunching onto the tarmac. Aleks spun the big steering wheel, bringing the BTR round in a wide loop. Kurtz acquired targets firing the 23mm cannons as they circled to support Bishop's team.

***

The Alfa commander had yet to commit his reaction force as he watched the two BTRs attack the aircraft. He turned to his second-in-command. "If we assault now, they will tear us to pieces."

"Yes, sir, without the snipers we won't stand a chance," the black-clad man replied.

The commander looked up at the shattered control tower. He had only barely escaped with his life. "There is only one way out; the factories block them to the south."

"An ambush?"

"Exactly. We hit them with the RPGs and the grenade launchers. Once we immobilize their vehicles, they will have no options left. They can surrender or burn in their vehicles."

"Good plan."

"Pass the word. We move now."

"Yes, sir." The second-in-command turned and ran into the darkness. The commander watched the aircraft for a few more seconds then moved back to the assault team's waiting area. He knew exactly where they needed to go. They would ambush the enemy on the northeastern corner of the runway. The vegetation grew thick there and almost reached the tarmac. The two BTRs wouldn't see them until it was too late.

***

Back at the Antonov, Miklos was still dazed from the concussion of the bullet that had struck his head. The helmet had saved his life but he would need a bucket load of aspirin.

He tore off the damaged helmet and staggered back to the BTR while Bishop loaded the two canisters.

"Miklos." Bishop grabbed him by the arm. "Mount up. We've got to go. We need to be at the extraction point in ten minutes." He guided him toward the open side hatch of their BTR. "You right to drive?"

The Czech shrugged off his assistance. "Yeah, yeah, it's OK. I'm fine."

"Good, let's get the hell out of here," Bishop yelled over Pavel firing the 23mm cannons.

They took off, closely followed by Aleks's BTR, both accelerating side by side down the runway back toward the northern fence. Bishop sat alone in the passenger compartment, the canisters sitting on the floor between his legs. He glanced at his watch; it was seven minutes till extraction. They were on time. So much for eighty men, he thought. Half of Dostiger's guards must have turned tail at the first sign of the BTRs.

He felt the armored vehicle slow as it approached the end of the runway, preparing to punch through the hole in the fence.

A flash in the dense vegetation to their flank caught his attention. He didn't have time to yell as two rockets screamed toward them. Both warheads struck his vehicle. One hit the armor on the driver's compartment with an almighty clang and failed to detonate. The other hit the rear and detonated into the engine compartment, the warhead's molten jet blasting through vital components setting the engine on fire. The personnel carrier ground to a halt and the internal halon fire suppression system activated, filling the interior with gas.

"BAIL OUT, BAIL OUT!" screamed Pavel as he wrenched open the inside hatch on the protected side of the vehicle. Bishop moved quickly, pushing the heavy canisters out onto the tarmac. With their fully enclosed helmets, he and Pavel had no problems with the smoke and gas. Miklos, on the other hand, wasn't wearing his damaged helmet, and as rounds rang on the side of the vehicle, the others dragged him outside, choking and spluttering.

Bishop was last out, jumping through the door as another detonation rocked the armored vehicle. All three huddled behind the wheels while automatic gunfire lashed the opposite side. Pavel checked that Miklos and Bishop were OK before climbing back inside the smoking BTR to operate the turret.

Bishop fumbled with his radio. "Aleks! We've been hit. You need to get back here." The other BTR had already pushed ahead and crossed the outer fence.

Saneh answered the call. "We've turned around, heading back for you now."

"Roger, we're taking heavy fire." The roar of the crippled BTR's dual cannons blocked out the sound of the radio. Pavel was working the turret like a man possessed, raking the tree line with high-explosive rounds. The weight of enemy fire increased, focusing on the turret. Bullets smashed into the optics, rendering them useless, but Pavel continued to fire blindly into the ambush site.

With a roar, Aleks's BTR plowed back through the fence, the twin cannons thundering as they blasted the tree line. They pulled in next to the immobilized vehicle and Saneh opened the hatch, reaching out as Miklos passed the canisters over and jumped in.

Pavel fired one last blast before he followed Bishop into the undamaged BTR. They slammed the heavy door shut and the eight-wheeled vehicle roared around in a circle, smashed back through the fence, and accelerated up the highway.

CHAPTER 38

ODESSA

Dostiger stared at the phone on his desk, willing it to ring. At any moment he expected Yuri to call, confirming delivery of the chemical weapon. Sure enough, the phone's shrill ring sounded and he picked it up.

"Dostiger, the airport has been attacked!"

"What?"

"Tanks! Tanks attacked us."

"Attacked? By who, the Jews?"

"I don't know. They have tanks. They shot up everything."

"You don't know? YOU DON'T KNOW?"

"The lights all went off. They came out of nowhere, with tanks. Our men could do nothing."

"No excuses, Yuri. Have they got the Novichok?" Dostiger asked coldly.

"Yes, the canisters are gone."

"And the Alfa team?"

"I can't raise them. They had tanks, Dostiger. We didn't stand a—"

"Say tanks again Yuri and you're dead," he snarled. "I want those canisters. Where are they now?"

"They'll need to get them out of the country. They were heading north."

"They'll try to fly it out."

"Yes!" Yuri agreed. "Yes, of course. Dalmak Airport. It's the only airfield close enough. They'll try to fly it out of Dalmak."

"I hope you are right, Yuri, for your own sake. I'm taking the helicopter and the Chechens. I'll finish this myself."

Dostiger slammed the phone down. Taking a deep breath he raised the handset and hit one of the speed-dial buttons.

A clipped military voice answered. "Hello."

"Ogi, it's Dostiger."

"Ah, my friend, how are you?"

"I have been better. Listen, I need a favor."

"What sort of favor?"

"I need a fighter jet over Odessa."

"A jet? When? Why?"

"I need it now," Dostiger said urgently. "Someone is trying to steal something from me."

"Now is difficult," the Ukrainian Air Force general replied.

"Ogi, do I need to remind you who pays for your children's schooling in Paris?"

"I'm not ungrateful, Dostiger, but questions will be asked."

"Listen to me, questions will be asked if you do nothing. Terrorists have just attacked Odessa Airport; the terminal has been destroyed!"

"What? Terrorists at the airport? I've not—"

Dostiger cut in, "There is not time for questions. Just get me a fighter. I'm not going to ask twice!"

"I could scramble one of the MiGs. We have them ready at the Moldova border."

"How long will it take to get to Odessa?"

"Fifteen minutes, no more."

"Make it happen. Tell the pilot there are terrorists trying to escape. He is to interdict any traffic attempting to leave Odessa airspace. He is to force down any suspect aircraft that fail to comply. Do you understand me?"

"I will do this for you, Dostiger, but then we are even. The debts are cleared: no more favors."

"Watch yourself, Ogi. Your debt is cleared when I say it is, and not before." Dostiger slammed the phone down on his desk.

"Fucking Mossad," he screamed. Every aspect of his operation had been compromised. "It must be the Israelis; no one else would be so daring. Fischer and Saneh!" He fumed as he limped across to a tall steel locker in the corner of his office and spun the lock on the front, counting out the turns as he entered the combination. "It has to be them. Like hell they are

British and Iranian. Mossad with stolen identities!" The locker clicked and he jerked it open. Inside he kept the most precious of his weapons collection. He removed a sniper rifle and ran his hands over the well-oiled weapon. The Dragunov was battered and worn, the butt marked with dozens of notches. "They will die here in Odessa. I promise them that."

***

Yuri's assumption was correct: Jumper was waiting on the tarmac at Dalmak Airport, five miles north of Odessa International. Aleks smashed the BTR through the locked gate, driving directly onto the narrow taxiway where the aircraft was idling in the darkness. A wizened old security guard waved his fist at them as they raced past his guard post with a roar.

Jumper's copilot greeted them as they pulled up behind the lowered ramp of the AN-72 and disembarked from the battered personnel carrier. "We need to get airborne, ASAP; all frequencies are going nuts."

Bishop nodded. "Give us a minute to transfer the package."

"Roger," the man replied, heading back into the cargo hold.

Aleks supervised the transfer of the canisters, strapping them to the floor of the aircraft.

As Saneh moved to board, Bishop grasped her arm gently, pulling her aside.

"I'm sorry, Saneh, you're not coming with us."

She looked at him with complete surprise. "What?" She shook her head, a look of anger replacing the shock. "After everything, you're going to abandon me?"

"Ivan will pick you up in a few minutes. He'll get you out of the country." Bishop fished in his pocket for a piece of paper.

"No! I want to finish this with the team."

"You can't come any further. It's for your own good."

"For my own good? This was supposed to be a joint effort. What about the canisters?"

"I'll make sure they're destroyed," he said, glancing at the plane. Aleks was standing on the ramp and gave him a nod.

They were ready to go.

"So you won't even let me fly out with you? Why? Because you don't trust me? After everything I've done for you."

"It's for your own good, Saneh. You need to be able to go back to Iran. If you stay with us any longer, they're going to think you betrayed them. If you get out now, they still might believe MI6 used you."

"MI6! Come on, Aden, we both know you're as British as I am." Her voice was edged with rage. "For all I know, I've been helping Mossad!"

"I don't work for political masters and I'm doing this to protect you."

"That's for me to decide, Aden, not you or your government."

Bishop snorted. "I don't work for any government."

"Then who the hell do you work for? The UN?"

He smiled at the irony and passed her a slip of paper. "Stay in touch. Maybe our paths will cross again in the future." He leaned forward and kissed her on the cheek, turned, and disappeared into the waiting aircraft.

Saneh stood and watched as the ramp closed and the jet accelerated down the rough airstrip. It catapulted from the end of the runway and climbed into the dark sky. She opened the slip of paper Bishop had given her and used the headlights of the battle-damaged BTR to read the scribbled note. It was an email address:

susurro@gmail.com

"Who are you, Aden?" she murmured as she looked up at the skyline, trying to follow the plane as it disappeared into the darkness.

Her emotions were in turmoil and she stood there for a moment, watching the night sky. A deep sound rumbled from the west. She turned her head slowly, a look of curiosity turning into fright. She jumped as a dark shape screamed across the sky directly overhead, twin tongues of flame streaming out behind it.

***

The PRIMAL transporter had cleared the runway and begun a sweeping turn when the pilot's voice came in over the intercom speakers.

"Team, we've got company. Ukrainian Air Force."

"Shit!" Bishop threw a headset on. "How far?"

"We're being hailed by call sign Raven; he's two miles out and coming in fast. Has to be one of their MiG-29s."

"Can you put him on my headset?"

"Roger, I'll open up a channel."

A burst of static announced the Ukrainian fighter jet. "Unidentified aircraft, this is Air Force call sign Raven. Identify yourself."

Jumper's pilot replied after a pause. "Raven, this is civilian transport Victor Victor 374."

"Victor Victor, you are to return to Dalmak Airport immediately and await further direction."

"Raven, we are a civilian aeromedical transport on track for Budapest. We cannot return to Odessa."

Bishop listened intently.

"Victor Victor, you will comply or I will shoot you down."

That escalated fast, thought Bishop. No doubt about it. He's working for Dostiger. "Keep leading him on. We need to get across the border into Moldova."

"I'll try, but if he lights us up with his radar, we're going to take evasive action."

"Roger," Bishop responded before switching off his mike. "Strap in, team. This could get rough."

Aleks and Kurtz quickly checked the tie-downs on the team's equipment and the canisters before returning to their seats and tightening their harnesses.

The Ukrainian pilot's voice came through again. "Victor Victor, this is your final warning. Return to Odessa or I will open fire."

"Raven, we are an unarmed transport with critically injured on board. Do not fire. I repeat, do not fire."

Jumper continued on its heading toward Moldovan airspace. The Ukrainian MiG was tailing it a mile away.

"He just lit us up," the pilot announced. "Deploying countermeasures."

The pilot threw Jumper's nose up and extended the air brakes, causing it to rapidly shed airspeed. The MiG couldn't slow fast enough and was forced to peel off. At the same time its targeting radar was jammed by Jumper's electronic countermeasures pod.

"Jam his communications as well," Bishop ordered. "Keep him at bay and try to make the border. It's our only chance."

"Yep, I think our cover is well and truly blown," their pilot responded.

"Just jump on the brakes and let him fly on by," Bishop said quoting *Top Gun*.

"You can be my wingman anytime," responded the pilot.

As the MiG circled around, Jumper's pilot made a dash for the border. He dropped all the flaps and pushed the throttles up against their stops. The stubby transport shook as it reached its maximum speed.

The pilot watched his radar warning receiver closely, and as the MiG lined up on his tail, he flared hard again, dropping the throttles. The sleek fighter's stalling speed was over twice that of the PRIMAL transporter, giving it only a split second to fire its cannon. The stream of tracer went wide as the MiG shot over Jumper.

"Shit, that was close." The pilot threw the aircraft into another dive and sped for the border. "How you all doing back there?"

Bishop looked around at the team. Aleks looked a little green but despite the violent maneuvers, everyone was OK.

"We're good, mate. How far from the border are we?"

"Nearly there. I'm not sure that he's going to fall for that again."

"You're doing great. You can shake him."

The MiG pilot had learned from his first attempt. After overshooting his target, he circled around in a broader arc, letting his prey gain distance, giving more room to maneuver. As he pulled out of the turn, he lined up the Antonov and raised his air brakes, rapidly dropping speed. The pilot smiled as he pulled the trigger and the MiG's 30mm cannon fired, spitting a stream of high-explosive rounds at the fleeing target.

The PRIMAL operatives felt their aircraft shudder and the pilot yelled over the intercom, "Christ, we're hit, portside engine and hydraulics are gone."

The pilot kept up his commentary, "I've lost all engine power and hydraulics are failing fast." The aircraft started to shake violently.

"Get us as close as possible to the border," ordered Bishop as he checked his harness for the fourth time.

"Yeah, if this asshole doesn't blow us out of the sky."

"Open up a channel for me with the MiG," said Bishop.

"Roger, you're up."

Bishop took a deep breath. "Raven, this is Victor. My name is Dr. Andrew Thompson. You have violated international law in shooting an unarmed medical transport. Cease fire immediately."

"Dr. Thompson, your jet has been damaged. You are to crash-land within Ukrainian territory or I will shoot you down."

With only one engine and failing hydraulics, Jumper was rapidly losing altitude. The pilot was sweating profusely as he fought with his controls to hold the aircraft steady. "Aden, we're fucked either way. What do you want me to do?"

"How many arrestor chutes do we have?"

"Two. I'll need them both to crash-land."

"How about make do with one and we give the other to this dickhead."

"I'm picking up what you're putting down. It could work."

"Do it."

The pilot checked his instruments; the MiG was directly behind them and holding steady. He took a deep breath and looked across at the copilot, who nodded. "You heard the man."

The pilot slammed the throttles back, deploying the landing gear and flaps.

The copilot held his finger over the arrestor chute release. "Eat silk, ball bag!" he said as his finger pressed the button.

The MiG pilot responded with lightning reflexes as the transport aircraft slowed suddenly. He pulled up hard on the stick to avoid a collision, firing his cannon at the same time, sending rounds smashing into Jumper's tail. He didn't see the parachute as it was jettisoned directly into the MiG's powerful turbofans, ripping it from the stricken PRIMAL transport.

The engines immediately jammed, and with a complete loss of power, the fighter stalled. The pilot instinctively reached down and yanked the ejection handle, launching himself into the cold night sky.

Back aboard Jumper, the pilot's voice announced over the intercom, "Brace for impact. We're going in!"

"BRACE FOR IMPACT!" screamed Bishop.

The pilot had moments to identify a potential landing site as he fought for control of the doomed aircraft. He aimed the nose at the first open area he could find.

Jumper slammed into the ground, crushing its landing gear as it skipped across the field. The pilot deployed the remaining parachute, but it tore free and the aircraft continued to slide on its belly until it crashed into a low stone wall.

CHAPTER 39

UKRAINE

"BOSS… BOSS!"

Bishop shook his head and tried to focus his vision.

Aleks shook him again. "Boss, snap out of it."

"Huh? It's OK, I'm OK." He reached down and released his safety harness. Something had struck his head during the crash, but apart from a nasty bruise, he was uninjured. "Is everyone alright?"

"*Da*, the team is OK but…"

Bishop forced himself to focus. He looked up at the Russian's concerned expression. "But what?"

"The pilots are dead. The plane hit something, crushed the cockpit."

The door to the cockpit was closed and Bishop didn't want to know what it looked like on the other side. He glanced around the cargo hold, relieved that the rest of the team was mobile, gathering their equipment and checking weapons.

"Get the team ready to move. Take all the ammo you can."

"*Da*."

"And bag the canisters; we'll have to carry them. I'm going to take a look outside." Bishop grabbed his submachine gun and clipped his helmet to his equipment vest.

As he made his way to the back of the aircraft, everything seemed intact. The emergency lighting was active and the hydraulic ramp lowered to the ground. He stepped out of the jet and checked his iPRIMAL. It was searching for a signal.

In the gray shades of early dawn he could see that the Antonov had crash-landed in an open field surrounded on all four sides by low stone walls and trees. Ignoring the biting cold, he made his way around from the tail of the aircraft, under the one remaining wing and up to the front. The damage was devastating. The nose and cockpit were a crumpled mess of twisted metal. The pilots had brought them down intact but paid the price with their own lives when they hit the stone wall.

He checked his phone again. It had finally acquired a signal and he dialed into PRIMAL HQ.

"Bunker, this is Bishop."

Vance came through immediately. "Holy shit, buddy, Jumper's signal dropped off the scope and we thought you'd cashed your chips."

"The team's fine. We've got the package but the pilots are dead. We need Ivan to pick us up, ASAP."

"That's a problem. We've lost comms with Ivan. Right now you're on your own and you're about to have half the Ukrainian Army crawling up your ass. Military radio chatter's gone off the scale."

"Roger, we'll be on the move in five."

"We'll keep trying to raise Ivan. In the meantime try and find somewhere to lay low."

"Will do, Bishop out." He checked the phone's mapping function. "Fuck!" They were still well within Ukrainian territory and there was no chance of a quick dash across the border. He zoomed in to the immediate area, quickly identifying a cluster of structures at the corner of the field. In the distance he could see a squat stone building and a couple of adjacent sheds. That would be their first move.

As Bishop pocketed the phone, he thought he could hear something on the icy morning breeze. He turned his head and the noise increased with a steady beat. Recognizing the sound, he sprinted back into the aircraft where Aleks was organizing the team.

"Grab your gear! Chopper inbound. Dostiger's onto us."

The four men had already donned their battle rigs: full-face helmets, body armor with pouches, and heavy weapons. They'd packed the extra ammunition stored on board the aircraft into their backpacks.

"Aleks, how are the canisters?"

"Bagged up and ready to go, boss." Aleks pointed at two black backpacks.

Bishop slung one of the heavy bags over his shoulder. "Big man, you grab the other one."

He noticed Miklos was struggling with his machine gun. "Miklos, you hurt?"

"Dislocated my shoulder. Should be OK."

"Give me the MG, mate." Bishop swapped his compact submachine gun with the heavy-caliber machine gun. Kurtz had the other MK48 and Pavel was carrying a grenade launcher.

"Aleks, I want you to take the team and set up a defensive perimeter in one of the buildings to the north."

"*Da*, boss, right away." The big Russian started off down the ramp and out into the faint glow of early dawn with the rest of the team in tow.

Bishop waited for them to leave before he slid back a panel on the wall of the aircraft, revealing a digital touch pad. He punched in a code and held up his phone, activating a custom app. The screen displayed:

-INTRUDER ACTIVATION ARMED-

Closing the panel, Bishop grabbed the handle of his machine gun and jogged down the ramp after the rest of the team. The helicopter was louder now. It sounded like it was landing somewhere to the south, beyond a thick line of trees. He ran faster. The cold morning air stung his lungs as he struggled with the canister and the machine gun.

Low farm buildings appeared out of the gloom and he made for the largest of them. The old stone barn was filled with farming paraphernalia: bags of fertilizer, machinery parts, and drums of oil. The men were already at work moving equipment, building a barrier across the open front of the shed.

"Good work, team," gasped Bishop, fighting for breath as he dumped the canister and his machine gun behind the barrier.

"Boss, there's a truck parked over by the other sheds. Bit beat up but I think I could get it started," Aleks said.

The beat of the helicopter's blades could be heard clearly to the south of the farm.

"It's too late. If they catch us in the open with that helicopter, we're finished. We have to hide here."

"And if they find us?"

"If they find us, we fight. Surrender is not an option. These aren't going to be regular government troops. Dostiger will have the best mercs money can buy and they're not going to give us any quarter. Pavel, you and I will cover the field and the crash site; we'll get the most out of the grenade launcher and the MG in the open ground. Miklos, you and Kurtz cover the northern and western sides. Be prepared to back us up when we need it. Kurtz, come with me. We need your gun covering the most dangerous approach."

He quickly toured the building, satisfied that it was as good a place as any for a last stand. There were a couple of tin sheds nearby, along with the truck, but they offered little protection. The barn, with its stone walls, at least provided some cover. The open front of the building wasn't too much of an issue. It faced back across the field toward the crash site: a perfect killing ground, easy to defend.

The eastern side was another matter altogether. There was only one window covering the other buildings fifty yards away. With the first glow of sunrise appearing on the horizon, Bishop could just make out the two sheds and a large elevated fuel tank.

"They'll come from the sheds, Kurtz." He gestured out the window. "If we're going to get out of here alive, you're going to have to hold them off."

The German was already preparing his position, laying out the ammunition belts. "Too easy, boss. I'll chop the bastards down like corn."

Bishop slapped his shoulder and turned back to check on Miklos and Pavel. They were already set in their positions; all they could do now was wait.

The team was deep within hostile territory and up against an army of unknown size. Bishop checked his watch; sunrise was only minutes away. Already darkness had started its retreat, taking with it the advantage of night vision.

Thank god Saneh's not here, he thought. There's no other way of looking at it. We are royally fucked!

CHAPTER 40

Dostiger was determined not to underestimate his enemy again. He ordered the helicopter to drop his force well clear of the crash site, fearful it would be shot down if it ventured within weapons range.

Now his men were spread out in the tree line to the south of the crash site, weapons covering the downed aircraft, while two of them probed forward to investigate.

All thirty fighters were battle-hardened Chechen mercenaries equipped with the latest weaponry. Wearing woodland camouflage and black balaclavas, they were an intimidating sight. Like half-tamed animals, these were killers who could never exist in a normal society.

Dostiger felt confident surrounded by the mercenaries. He watched with satisfaction as the two scouts crept forward, weapons raised, ready to cut down any sign of resistance. Clad in his own fatigues and armed with his sniper rifle, he felt like a young man again. The mercenary commander stood next to him, listening to the radio clipped to his battle harness. He turned to Dostiger, explaining, "The scouts are at the aircraft; it looks empty. Do you want them to proceed inside?"

"Yes," Dostiger snapped. "I must know if the canisters are there."

"Very well." The commander relayed the order and they watched as the scouts walked up the rear ramp of the aircraft.

As the pair disappeared into the cargo hold, the Antonov exploded. A bright-orange ball of flame obliterated the airframe and the blast threw Dostiger onto his back, sucking the air from his lungs. Twisted pieces of wreckage sliced through the trees above him, sending branches crashing to the ground.

For a moment Dostiger was back in the hills of Afghanistan and his damaged leg started twitching as he rolled onto his side, coughing heavily. He wiped the spittle from his face and slowly regained his feet. The commander was still on the ground, dazed from the blast. Dostiger had a wild look in his eyes as he hauled the mercenary to his feet.

"Find them!" he snarled. "Find them and fucking kill them."

Despite the shock of the blast, the commander responded without hesitation, barking into his radio, giving his team leaders orders to search the immediate area.

The lead group of ten fighters, Alpha Team, moved through the dense vegetation, avoiding the open ground and burning wreckage. They worked their way around the field toward the farm buildings, barely visible in the gray shades of dawn.

Having lost two of their men to the booby-trapped aircraft, the mercenaries were even more cautious. They probed forward in pairs, leapfrogging past each other, never moving without someone providing cover. The lead scout crouched when he reached a low stone wall at the edge of the trees. The slightest movement had drawn his attention to the window of an old barn. He keyed his radio.

The commander was still at the rear with Dostiger, watching the movement of their men. "Sir, Alpha team have spotted movement in one of the buildings."

"Good. Which one?"

"The stone one, just past the sheds."

A thin smile came to Dostiger's lips as he brought the scope of the sniper rifle up to his eye and inspected the building.

Lowering the weapon, he gave his orders, "Tell them to maintain observation. Get Bravo to provide fire support from behind the wall over there," he said, pointing out the wall the aircraft had collided with. "They can use the machine guns to pin the bastards down. Once Charlie are in position with Alpha, then we'll assault from the flank." He looked up at the shades of color visible on the horizon. "In a few minutes we'll have more than enough light."

The mercenary gave his commands over the radio and within seconds the balaclava-clad fighters were moving into position. Charlie team moved silently along the tree line to Alpha. The other mercenaries moved at the same time, crawling behind the stone wall until they took up their support position, ready to fire on the stone building.

As the last few men moved into place, the sun peeked over the horizon, throwing soft light across the battlefield. With smoke from the burning aircraft drifting across the farm, the setting was surreal.

The commander turned to report to Dostiger. The Ukrainian was steadying the barrel of his sniper rifle against a tree.

"Sir, we are ready."

Dostiger replied without lifting his eye from the scope, "No survivors. Open fire!"

***

"We've got company, boss," Kurtz announced from where he was crouching beside the window on the eastern side. "I can see at least three armed men. They're hiding in the tree line."

"Roger," Bishop replied. "I've got observation on two more on the other side of the field. Anyone else got anything?"

"Negative, Aden, nothing at the back." Aleks was covering the rear of the barn with his submachine gun.

"All clear north," Miklos reported.

"The shit is about to go down, lads. Miklos, I want you to take over from Aleks. Big man, you need to back up Kurtz. The fuckers will hit us hard from that flank. Fire support will come from the south, Pavel and I will—"

Before Bishop could finish his orders, a hail of gunfire hit the barn. The team hugged the floor as bullets ripped into the fertilizer bags and sparked off the stone walls, sending shards of rock slicing through the air. The initial burst of fire lasted only a few seconds before the mercenary force waited for return fire.

"Steady, lads, they're probing," Bishop transmitted.

"SMOKE!" Kurtz yelled as gray clouds billowed from the treeline.

"Shit, here they come," Bishop murmured. "Aleks, get over there now."

The big Russian crawled low across the floor, sliding through the dirt and straw to where Kurtz was crouched beside the window.

The German lifted his head and peered out. His goggles picked up at least ten figures dashing through the smoke to the cover of the other sheds and the fuel dump. He lifted the MK48 and fired a long burst into the running figures. Return fire smashed into the building and he dropped back into cover. "Two Tangos down!"

Bishop opened up with his own machine gun, sending a stream of tracer across the open field, raking the stone wall where Dostiger's support team was taking cover. The return fire was instant and intense. Bullets hit the barn with a deafening roar. The team's fully enclosed helmets adjusted, cutting noise while amplifying the team's radio traffic.

"Stone wall, Pavel. Give them a couple of HE grenades," Bishop ordered.

The stocky Russian had rolled onto his back behind a heavy, cast-iron plow, the grenade launcher held against his chest.

"My pleasure, boss," he said as he adjusted the weapon's sight and rolled out from cover, launched three grenades, and rolled back.

The high-explosive projectiles detonated among the fire support team, jagged pieces of shrapnel wounding one of the gunners and sending his comrades scurrying for cover.

With the machine guns temporarily silenced, Kurtz and Aleks took the opportunity to send a fusillade of bullets into the assault force. Their rounds ripped through the tin sheds being used to conceal their approach. The assault ground to a halt as the mercenaries stopped to return fire.

"Chewing through ammo fast, Aden: last four hundred," Kurtz announced.

"*Da*, I've got three mags, boss," added Aleks. Hundreds of spent cartridges were scattered on the floor around them.

"I can spare a belt," Bishop said as he tossed a belt of ammunition across the room before firing another burst.

"It's all clear on my side," Miklos yelled out as he crawled along the dusty floor, wincing as he tried to ignore his dislocated shoulder. "I'll back up Kurtz and Aleks."

The fire support resumed and rounds lashed the building relentlessly. Shrapnel and bullets ricocheted off the stone walls, forcing the team even lower to the ground. As Bishop worked frantically to change the belt on his machine gun, Pavel rolled out to fire another grenade.

At three hundred yards it was an easy shot for Dostiger. The 7.62mm round had less than half a second of flight before impact.

"ARRRGH! I'm hit!" Pavel screamed as he rolled back under cover, clutching at his bloodied thigh. He ripped open a pouch on his vest and pulled out a combat tourniquet.

Bishop worked the trigger of his MK48, smashing the enemy position with red tracer. "You OK?"

Pavel snapped the tourniquet around the top of his leg and worked the handle, cutting off the blood supply to the wound. "It's clean. I'm OK, I'm OK. We've got a sniper out there."

Bishop ripped through another two hundred rounds in short bursts. The exchange of fire was unrelenting and their assailants continued to fire at a steady rate while the PRIMAL team's ammunition supplies dwindled.

On Kurtz's side the mercenaries had advanced closer, throwing another smoke screen. The German's voice cut over the airways. "Boss, we're getting worked over pretty hard here and we're almost out of ammunition." He and Aleks had been reduced to firing their weapons blindly through the window. Miklos was there with them, stubbornly firing his submachine gun, despite his shoulder.

"Hang in there, lads!" Bishop said between bursts, racking his brain for a way out. They were pinned by the heavy gunfire striking the building from two sides, forcing them behind cover where they couldn't shoot back.

"INCOMING!" yelled Pavel as a rocket screamed in through the open front of the barn and slammed into the rear wall. It detonated, peppering the men's armor with shrapnel and sending a shock wave through the building. The roof groaned as the explosion lifted it a few inches then dropped it. The entire room filled with a haze of dust and smoke.

"This dump's not going to take much more before it fucking collapses," said Pavel.

He's right, thought Bishop. Couple of grenades are going to bring this old place down on us. They needed to break out. The team was wounded and almost out of ammo.

"Let them get closer, lads. Save your bullets," he ordered. "Once they get in real close, the fire support will have to stop."

"Hey, boss." Aleks's voice came over the radio.

"Yeah, mate."

"If we don't get out of this one, I want you to know it's been fun."

"Fun? Fun? You're a goddamn psychopath, Aleks! What about you, Kurtz, you think it's been fun?"

The German laughed manically. "*Ja.* Prefer to go out in a blast fucking over some arms dealer than die in hospital shitting in a bag."

He smiled grimly. Despite the situation he felt calm. If this is it, at least I'm going out with a good bunch of lads, he thought. "Pavel, you still with us?"

"Still here, boss." The Russian was ready to fight, despite his injured leg.

"What about you, Miklos?"

"I'm OK."

"Alright then. Job's on, let's roll," he said with a determined grin.

Despite the rounds hitting the building, all five of them waited patiently for the final assault. They checked their pistols and grenades, aware that the final battle was going to be brutal, face-to-face combat.

CHAPTER 41

"We have them pinned, sir," the mercenary commander reported. "They stopped shooting back."

Dostiger nodded approvingly. "Excellent. I hit at least one of the bastards. Have Alpha and Charlie assault. This time we'll wipe the Mossad dogs from the face of the earth."

Alpha and Charlie squad were ready, despite having taken a few casualties. They had pulled back into the cover of the fuel storage and equipment sheds. It would be a simple matter to dash forward and finish the job.

On the other side, Bravo team was still positioned along the low wall, taking turns at peppering the building with gunfire.

The man on the far left of the support team lifted his head and listened. Over the intense noise of the gunfight he could hear a vehicle. He turned his attention from the target building to the copse of trees at the end of the wall wondering if Dostiger had called for more reinforcements.

With a roar, a metal beast exploded through the trees and bowled over the mercenary, pulverizing his body beneath its wheels. The juggernaut continued its assault, smashing into the line of gunmen, crushing them against the thick stone wall. A few scrambled to their feet, only to be struck down by the vehicle's steel hull, its eight wheels churning their bodies into a muddy pulp.

Two of them managed to turn their weapons on the roaring beast. One fired an RPG at it from point-blank. It was too close and the warhead failed to arm. The rocket bounced off and the two mercenaries died with their comrades, pulverized by the armored vehicle.

"*NNNYET!*" Dostiger screamed as the armored personnel carrier decimated his entire fire-support team. He brought his weapon to his shoulder and fired rapidly through the trees into the vehicle. The rounds ricocheted harmlessly off the armor.

The BTR ground to a halt as its wheels lost traction in the mud and it slid sideways into a ditch. It roared like a wounded animal, digging further into the soggy ground, belching a cloud of diesel fumes into the air. One of the surviving mercenaries sprinted up to it, a grenade ready in his gloved hand. He climbed on top of the BTR and grasped the handle of one of its access hatches.

That's as far as he got. His body exploded as a high-velocity grenade struck him in the side and detonated, blowing him apart. His legs and hips remained upright before toppling off the side of the BTR. The grenade dropped onto the roof of the vehicle and exploded in a shower of white-hot phosphorus. Within seconds the burning chemical had set the weapons turret ablaze.

Dostiger and the commander stared in complete disbelief at what was left of the squad. The path of the armored vehicle was a trail of gore, severed limbs, crushed bodies, and broken weapons ground into the mud.

***

"Nice shot, Pav," said Bishop as the grenade blew the mercenary off the top of the BTR. "I reckon Ivan might have saved our bacon." With the enemy's fire-support team wiped out, the gunfire hitting the barn had dropped off.

"We're not out of the fire yet!" Kurtz's voice came over the radio. "There's more of them massing on our flank. I need back up now!"

"On my way," Bishop said. He leaped to his feet, the machine gun in the crook of his arm. "Pavel, launcher."

"Only two rounds left, boss," said the injured Russian, throwing the PAW-20 to him.

He caught it with his free hand and sprinted out the building, down to a wall at the eastern corner. Taking up position beside a pile of firewood, he lay behind his machine gun, covering the open ground between the barn and the sheds.

***

Dostiger and the mercenary commander left their position at the rear and moved down the tree line toward their remaining troops.

"This is far enough," the commander said as he reached out and grasped his boss's shoulder. If they moved any closer, they would be putting themselves in the line of fire.

Dostiger turned on him, viciously slapping the hand away. "I want them dead. Do you understand me? Fucking dead!"

"I understand, sir, but if you get any closer, your weapon won't be as effective."

Dostiger looked down at his Dragunov before returning his gaze to the mercenary. "Order them to attack. I want this finished here and now. I want those canisters and I want that devil Fischer's head."

***

Bishop tucked his machine gun into his shoulder. A pair of smoke grenades bounced into the clearing in front of him. They hissed and spluttered, filling the space with a billowing cloud of thick gray smoke.

"Here they come, lads." Bishop activated the thermal imager built into his helmet. The mercenaries glowed red through the smoke, their presence betrayed in the cool morning air by the heat of their bodies and weapons.

He took aim and fired a long burst, sending tracer rounds lancing into the advancing mercenaries. Their assault rifles barked in response and rounds thudded into the building. From the window Kurtz opened up with his machine gun and the rate of fire hitting the building faltered as Bishop and Kurtz shot up the assaulting forces, hitting them from two sides.

"Run, *Schweinehund*!" screamed Kurtz as the assault line faltered and drew back.

"Ammo check," Bishop transmitted.

"Fifty rounds," reported Kurtz.

"Two mags," said Aleks.

"Mag and a half," cut in Miklos.

Pavel reported last. "Two mags."

Jesus, thought Bishop, we're not going to survive another attack.

The fresh morning breeze swept the smoke from between the buildings, revealing the bodies of three more dead mercenaries. The farm was bathed in sunlight as the sun crested the horizon. His goggles adjusted to the sun's rays reflecting off the five-thousand-liter steel fuel tank raised high off the ground on four legs. He smiled grimly.

As the mercenaries regrouped for another assault, Bishop aimed the grenade launcher at the fuel point. He pulled the trigger and a grenade slammed into one of tank's four legs. The tank groaned as the thick steel leg buckled, but it failed to collapse.

One round left. This better bloody work, he thought.

He fired the final grenade. It detonated on the buckled leg and collapsed the tank, releasing thousands of liters of diesel. Like a mini-tsunami, the fuel wave washed through the attackers.

Bishop pulled a thermite grenade from his vest and flung it into the fuel. The diesel burst into flame, trapping the attacking mercenaries in a blazing inferno. As the burning men fled the fire, he machine-gunned them down in an act of mercy.

Kurtz followed suit, firing at the men as they screamed in agony.

The remaining mercenaries, most already wounded from the gunfight, beat a hasty retreat as the flames spread, consuming one of the sheds.

***

"Where are they going?" yelled Dostiger. He watched the last of his men retreat away from the inferno.

"I can't raise anyone on the radio," the commander replied.

"WHERE ARE THEY GOING?"

The mercenary turned to his boss. "Our men are dead. We

need to go."

"NO! NO!" He shook his head in disbelief. "Turn them around. Make them fight. I must have the canisters!" He limped down the tree line toward the fire and smoke that marked the demise of Alpha and Charlie squads.

The commander followed, trying to talk sense into the manic arms dealer. "Sir, we need to go. Reinforcements will be here soon and we can attack then."

"No! I will finish this myself. I WILL KILL THEM!" He stopped at the crumpled body of one of the men, slung his Dragunov across his back, and picked up an assault rifle. His knuckles were white and his face twisted as he raged, "No one comes to my country and fucks with me. NOBODY!"

The commander reached forward and tore the weapon from Dostiger's grip. "The attack's failed! We must—"

He lashed out, striking with his fist. The mercenary blocked the punch and caught his boss in an arm lock, dragging him away. "Sir, we must go. We can return with more men."

Dostiger's face was livid as they retreated back into the trees, putting distance between them and the carnage. Shooting pain in his bad leg added fuel to his fury. "This isn't the end, Fischer. I will make you pay. If I have to kill a thousand Jews to do it, I will."

**

Bishop breathed a deep sigh of relief as the last of their assailants withdrew into the tree line, leaving the bodies of their comrades to burn. A beeping noise in his helmet drew his attention from the blaze. He checked his iPRIMAL. It was a message from the Bunker.

Ukrainian military communications traffic off the charts. Response forces have been activated. Expect first Army units in your area within thirty minutes.

"OK, team, we've got to hustle," Bishop transmitted. "We

may have fought off Dostiger's mercs but Ukrainian military's inbound. Aleks, get that truck started, otherwise we're walking." The vehicle hadn't yet caught fire and he hoped it wasn't too badly shot up.

"OK, boss."

"Miklos, see what you can do for Pavel's leg. Kurtz, you're with me. We're going to find Ivan."

Bishop and the tall German stalked cautiously down the tree line toward the remains of Jumper and the wrecked BTR.

"Keep your eyes peeled," he said as he scanned the forest, machine gun at his shoulder. "There could be more of those balaclava-wearing bastards around."

The BTR was burning fiercely, the engine compartment and tires fueling the fire. Through the smoke billowing from its hatches, a lone figure could be seen sprawled in the mud beside the vehicle. As Bishop got closer, he identified the body.

"It's Saneh!" He bolted forward, ignoring the heat, and grabbed the Iranian agent under her arms, dragging her clear. He felt for a pulse. It was strong. Ripping off his helmet, he lowered his ear to her mouth. She wasn't breathing. He cupped her jaw in his hand and breathed two deep breaths of fresh air into her lungs. "Come on, Saneh!" He filled her lungs again.

With a cough and a splutter, she started breathing. Her eyes flashed open, making immediate contact with Bishop's. His panic subsided as her body convulsed with giant waves of coughing, clearing her lungs.

"This doesn't make us even," she rasped.

He couldn't help but laugh. "Not at all. We were all as good as dead till you showed up." He carefully helped Saneh sit up.

She glanced around. The absence of gunfire told her she was safe. "Lucky you left me behind, Aden, otherwise I wouldn't have been able to save you."

Bishop gave her a grin. "Does that mean you forgive me?"

"Oh, it's going to take a bit more than that." She laughed, coughing again.

"If you two are done, Aleks has the truck started, *ja*," the lanky German interrupted.

Bishop looked back across the field. A rust-streaked farm truck with a canvas canopy was churning across the muddy field toward them, belching out clouds of black smoke.

He helped Saneh to her feet. "Ivan, have you seen him?"

She shook her head. "He never showed up."

Bishop nodded at Kurtz, who steadied her as they walked. Bishop dropped back and phoned the Bunker.

Vance picked up on the first ring. "Bish, how's the team?"

"Yeah, Vance, team's alive, and we've still got the canisters. Had a run-in with some of Dostiger's mercs. Pavel's been shot but he'll be OK."

"Alright, buddy, we need to get you out, ASAP." Bishop could hear Vance issuing commands to the team in the background. It took a few seconds for him to gather all the information he needed. "Bish, you still there?"

"Yep, shoot."

"First things first. You got wheels?"

Bishop looked across at the battered truck approaching. "Yeah, sort of."

"That's good. Plan is you get back to your infil point at the farm. You lay low till dark and then RV with the Gulfstream at another airfield close to the border."

"Sounds workable. What about Ivan? Is he meeting us there?"

"Haven't been able to contact him. Will keep trying, but right now you've got to get moving. The Ukrainian Army can't be far away."

"OK, mate. See you soon."

The old farm truck slowed to a halt and Aleks greeted them with a broad smile. He'd found a dirty farmer's jacket and a cap to wear. With the grime of combat smeared across his face, he looked the part of a peasant farmer.

"Canisters are in the back, boss. Pavel will live and Miklos is complaining like a little girl," Aleks announced.

"Right then," Bishop said as he helped Saneh clamber up into the back of the truck. "We need to get back to the farm with the airstrip. Head east. Try to stick to the back roads."

Once everyone was under the faded canvas canopy, Aleks took off with a crunch of gears, crossed the field, and turned onto a country lane.

CHAPTER 42

"So where to from here, Aden?" Saneh asked as the truck bounced down the country lane in Odessa's rural hinterland. They were sitting in the back side by side, the rest of the team sprawled around them.

"The canisters will be destroyed and then I'm going to kill Dostiger."

"Do you really need to kill him? You have the canisters; the mission is a success."

He simply raised an eyebrow.

"You despise him, don't you?"

Bishop didn't respond. His thoughts were far away from the truck. He was back in Dostiger's nightclub, the image of the missile launcher on the office wall searing into his brain.

"Do you trust me at all?" she asked quietly.

He sighed, "Trust is not the issue, Saneh."

It was the beautiful Iranian's turn to raise an eyebrow.

"OK," Bishop said with a laugh. "I lie. A little bit of an issue."

"Please, I'm Persian and I am a woman. Two things you clearly have no idea about." She elbowed him gently in the ribs.

"Oh, I know about Persians—" The sirens of a passing police car caused him to pause. The wailing faded. "The fact you're from Iran isn't an issue for me, Saneh. Your nation has a lot to be proud of. It's the extremists that bother me."

"Is that how you think of me? Do you think I am some fanatic willing to die for my religion?"

"No, not at all. I think you're a lot like me."

"And how is that, Mr. Fischer? Jaded and despondent?"

He smiled. "No, you're a bit of an idealist: someone looking to make a difference." He leaned over and whispered in her ear. "Now's not the time." His eyes flicked to the rest of the team sitting in the back of the truck with them. "But if we get out of here, I'll talk with my superiors. You don't belong in MOIS, you—"

"Hey, boss." Aleks pulled back the cracked glass divider that separated the cabin of the truck from the back. "We're at the farm and it looks like Ivan's already here."

Bishop leaned forward to peer through the windshield. Ivan's battered Russian jeep was parked next to the open doors of the barn.

Aleks nosed the truck into the barn and brought it to a smooth halt on the straw-covered concrete.

As the truck stopped, a voice yelled out from the shadows.

"GET OUT! LEAVE YOUR WEAPONS IN THE TRUCK!"

Bishop whipped out his pistol and peered through the front cabin. He caught a glimpse of a submachine gun aimed at them.

"This is Iranian intelligence, Mr. Fischer," the harsh accent yelled out. "We have your friend here. If you do not comply, we will kill him."

So MOIS has decided to join the party, thought Bishop, and he looked directly into the eyes of the beautiful woman beside him. "Your friends, Saneh?"

"I didn't know, I promise," she whispered.

He turned away in disgust. "OK, I'm coming out!" he announced. "I'm not armed." He dropped his pistol onto the floor of the truck and moved to the back. Kurtz grabbed his arm as he passed. "We can take them!" he hissed, raising his machine gun.

"No," whispered Bishop and he climbed down from the truck.

Aleks was already out of the cab, his hands in the air, facing a group of Uzi-wielding men.

As Bishop's eyes adjusted to the gloom, he could make out the features of the five men in front of him. They looked like a group of badly dressed thugs from an eighties action movie, complete with skivvies and poorly fitting polyester suits.

They had to be Iranian, he thought. Not even Eastern Europeans wore outfits that bad.

If it were not for the weapons, including the pistol one of

them held to Ivan's head, Bishop may have burst out laughing.

The oldest of the men, athletic-looking, with gray hair and cold blue eyes, spoke. "Where is Agent Ebadi, Mr. Fischer?"

"She's in the truck."

"And the weapon?"

"I don't know what you're talking about." Behind him he could hear the rest of the team disembarking.

"Come now, Mr. Fischer, there's no need to be like that, what with this being a joint operation and all."

"Like I said, Mr....?"

"You can call me Rostam."

"Like I said, Rostam, I have no idea what you're talking about."

"Is that right, Aden?" Saneh walked past Bishop carrying one of the black backpacks. She unzipped the bag and handed Rostam the silver cylinder.

"So this is the wonder weapon?" the MOIS officer asked as he scrutinized the container.

"So I am led to believe," she replied.

"My dear girl, you fail to fathom the power that this cylinder represents." He switched his intense gaze to Saneh. "This will meet our requirements nicely. I must say, Fischer, to use a British term, you've done a 'cracker' of a job. Successfully denied the Revolutionary Guards their wonder weapon and delivered it directly to me. Don't think that MOIS isn't grateful for your efforts."

"You're making a big mistake, Rostam. The Western world isn't going to stand by and let you waltz off with that."

"Do you really believe that, Mr. Fischer? Or are you trying to justify your own shortcomings?" Rostam smiled. "The truth is you simply failed and no one, not MI6, nor anyone else, will do anything to stop me. You need to accept that despite all your shiny toys and resources, you were foiled by a pretty smile." Rostam placed his hand on Saneh's shoulder. "You're all the same, my boy, young, hotheaded, and driven by your loins and not your brain. All passion and no planning!"

Bishop said nothing, his face searing a hot, bright shade of red.

"I bid you farewell, Mr. Fischer. Better luck next time." Rostam nodded to the man holding a pistol to Ivan's head. "Release him!"

Ivan stumbled forward and Bishop caught him.

"Sorry, old chap, they got the jump on me."

The Iranians filed out as the roar of a low-flying helicopter approached. Saneh paused as she left the barn, looking back. "I'm sorry," she mouthed then disappeared.

The helicopter's engine note changed as it touched down briefly, then took off, the clatter of blades disappearing into the distance.

"That treacherous bitch." Kurtz's broke the silence. "She played us like a bunch of fucking Boy Scouts."

"A bunch of Boy Scouts caught with our dicks in our hands," growled Aleks.

"I don't think so," Bishop said quietly.

"What do you mean? You saw her; she sold us out!" accused Kurtz.

Bishop turned to him. "I thought the same at first, but I think you'll find she was as surprised as we were. You should've seen her face when that Rostam asshole told us to get out of the truck."

"Then why did she hand over the canister?" Aleks asked.

"Because she didn't have any other choice. She had to play along."

"That doesn't change the facts. Now Iran has the weapon and we don't have shit!" said Kurtz.

"Don't we?" Bishop asked. "I think if you check the truck, we still have one canister. Not ideal, I know, but better than nothing."

"*Da*, you're right, boss." Aleks grinned as he pulled the remaining backpack from the truck. "Maybe she didn't sell us out after all."

"Yeah, like I said, she didn't get much of a choice. You were all there when she saved us in that BTR. She didn't have to do that. She put her neck on the line for us and I'll wager she'll do it again if she gets the chance."

"If you don't think she sold us out, how in god's name did they find us?" Ivan asked.

"It's probably my fault. I let Saneh send a message to her boss when we landed. I'm guessing her phone had a tracking device in it."

"That would make sense," said Ivan.

"I get the distinct feeling that our friend Rostam is not one for trusting people. Even his own agents."

Ivan nodded. "A formidable foe."

"You still think we're in the game, boss?" asked Aleks. "Is there any way for us to get the canister back?"

"Maybe. That chopper has a limited range and we've got her phone number."

"Don't count on the woman coming through. She betrayed us once and she will do it again," Kurtz said harshly.

Bishop looked at him. "You might be right. Only time will tell. Right now we need to focus on getting out of Odessa and getting Pavel and Miklos medical attention. I'll contact my headquarters. Let's plan on extracting at nightfall. Till then we need to rest up. I've got a feeling this isn't over yet."

"We're staying here?" Kurtz asked.

"Yes. Moving around the countryside is too dangerous. The Ukrainian Army's looking for us, remember."

"But this place has been compromised. Shouldn't we at least move?"

"If Rostam wanted to hand us over to Dostiger, it would have already happened. No, we'll be safe here until nightfall." He checked his watch. "I'll report in and take first watch. Get Pavel and Miklos as comfortable as you can, then get some shut-eye."

There were no further objections. Each man was absolutely exhausted, clothing torn and bloodied. They turned their attention to the wounded men and finding comfortable spots among the bales of straw.

Bishop climbed the ladder up to the barn's loft, a vantage point to keep watch. He was not looking forward to updating

Vance and Chua.

CHAPTER 43

THE FARM

"So let me get this straight, buddy. Saneh rescues you from the crash site and you swing back to the Farm?" questioned Vance.

"That's right," answered Bishop.

"Except when you get back there, MOIS is waiting?"

"Correct."

"And now they've got one of the canisters and the girl."

"Yeah, that about sums it up."

"And you seriously think that she played no role in this?"

"I do," Bishop replied. "I firmly believe she had no intention of handing over the agent. I think that MOIS tracked her without her knowledge. There's a chance she'll help us recover the second canister."

Chua's voice interrupted, "Aden, that's pretty unlikely. She's a trusted operative with an extensive dossier of successful missions to her credit. MOIS would have no reason to doubt her integrity, otherwise she would not have been selected for such an important mission."

"Then why did she leave us the single canister?"

"Maybe in the heat of the moment she forgot it," Vance said. "Or maybe she felt guilty for playing you like a banjo at a hoedown. The truth is, Bish, I don't give a shit! At the moment I just want to get you, your men, and that goddamn Novichok agent out of Kiev and out of Dostiger's grasp. We can worry about the other canister later."

"Vance is right," said Chua. "We need to get you safe. The team is already working up options to retrieve the second canister from within Iran."

"Iran? Are you kidding me? We've got Saneh's phone number. There may be an opportunity to recover the chemical now and you want to talk about running black ops into

Tehran?"

"You need to snap out of it, bud," Vance said. "You're not thinking straight. You've invested too much emotion into this mission. First Dostiger, then Saneh—"

"Look, that evil bastard will get what's coming to him, but all in good time. Right now I owe it to Saneh to have a little faith. She's saved my life three times in the last forty-eight hours."

"You can have all the faith you want. Hell, you can have a whole goddamn church full of it. The bottom line, we NEED to get you out of there and that's the priority. You've got an army of angry Ukrainians running around the countryside looking for you guys. Now we're monitoring their comms traffic and so far so good, but you need to lay low and trust us to get you out."

"Yeah, OK. So what's the plan?"

"There's an abandoned airfield; Chua will send you the coordinates after this. Pick up time is nineteen hundred. Mirza will meet you with the Gulfstream. Don't be late!"

"Is Ice going to be with Mirza?"

"No, buddy, he's not... he's..."

"He's what?"

"Look, bud, there ain't no easy way to tell you this. Mirza and Ice ran into some trouble and Ice didn't make it."

There was silence for a moment before Bishop responded, "How's Mirza?"

"He's doing OK. You'll need to keep an eye on him though. He's taken it pretty hard."

"Do you know what happened?"

"Not really. Details are a little sketchy at the moment. You need to stay focused though, alright? Get your team out and then we can deal with the loss."

"You're right, we're not out of the woods yet. We'll stay low here then head to the airfield at the last safe moment."

"Once you're on board, we'll route the jet back to the island via the Emirates. Our people there will take care of your wounded."

"What about Dostiger? I want to finish that bastard, Vance."

"I know, I know, but we'll have plenty of time to deal with him once we get you out of there."

"Yeah, OK. Chua, so is there any chance we can track Saneh's phone?"

"Sorry, Bish," Chua replied. "Right now it's not transmitting. Last known hit was when she updated her HQ from your current location. If it pops up again, I'll let you know."

"I'd appreciate that. Look, I'm going to get some rest. You guys got anything else for me?"

"No, that's it, Bish. Keep your head down and we'll see you soon," Vance concluded. Once the call had terminated, he turned to Chua. "How do you think he's handling it all?"

"Not as badly as I thought he would," Chua replied, downing a mouthful of energy drink. "After the Kiev debacle, being played by Saneh, and then finding out about Ice..." He looked at Vance and shook his head. "I'm surprised he's holding himself together. Maybe our boy is growing up."

***

The rain started at dusk, a light drizzle that made the narrow roads slick with mud and grime. With its bald tires, the battered farm truck maintained a precarious grip as Aleks slowly drove through the countryside. Bishop directed him, using the mapping on his phone to avoid any of the main roads and likely checkpoints. They were still armed, but only with pistols; all the heavy weapons were now buried under the floor of the barn. Ivan had left them at the farm, disappearing into the night in his rusted Soviet-era four-wheel drive.

The truck turned down a disused track, little more than two overgrown wheel ruts winding their way through a thick copse of trees. A minute later the wheels hit concrete. The hard surface was dotted with weeds, growing in the cracks and seams of the abandoned airfield.

"Stop here. Lights off," ordered Bishop.

Aleks killed the engine and they sat in silence. Bishop checked his phone again; still nothing from Saneh. He kept expecting to hear her voice or at least the rumble of a BTR as she came barreling out of the darkness.

Pull yourself together, he told himself. She's not coming back; Rostam's probably filled her head with lies and she's moved on.

Bishop was furious that he'd let the MOIS officer outsmart him. It was embarrassing, to say the least.

"Boss," Aleks interrupted. "Look. Lights."

At the other end of the runway a green light flashed twice.

"Flash the lights three times."

Aleks obliged and the distant green light responded with another two flashes.

"It's Mirza. Let's go."

As they drove down the edge of the runway, the sleek shape of the Gulfstream business jet appeared out of the darkness. Aleks pulled the truck in next to the open door of the swept-wing aircraft. Mirza was waiting at the bottom of the stairs in the drizzling rain, an assault rifle slung across his chest. The lightly built Indian looked gaunt, dark circles under his eyes visible in the truck's headlights.

Bishop greeted him with a firm handshake. "It's good to see you, mate."

"You too, Aden."

The two men stepped out of earshot as Aleks and Kurtz moved the wounded into the aircraft and loaded the canister.

"Vance told me about Ice," Bishop said. "We all know the risks when we sign up. Ice died doing something he believed in; that's all a soldier can ask for."

"You don't know what happened. I—"

Bishop cut him off. "Right now I don't need to know. Right now I need you to focus. We can mourn Ice later. What I need to know is can I count on you?"

"Aden, you—"

"Can I count on you, Mirza?"

"You know you can!"

"Good. Now let's get on board and introduce you to the lads. Just remember they're hired help, though. They still think I'm MI6 and naturally they will assume you are too."

"Righto, chocks away then, biff biff and all that," Mirza said putting on his best British accent.

Bishop laughed and punched him in the arm. "It sure is good to see you."

They climbed up the stairs of the luxury jet and into the cabin. Bishop briefly introduced Mirza before checking on the rest of the team and ensuring the canister was secure.

As the plane taxied for takeoff, Bishop lowered himself into one of the business jet's plush leather chairs. He buckled his seat belt as the jet trembled, the engines pushing the aircraft forward. Looking out the window into the darkness, doubts assailed his mind.

What if it was all an elaborate plan, he thought angrily. Was Saneh playing me the whole time?

His Ukrainian cell phone beeped and his pulse quickened as he checked the screen. It was from Saneh.

You should come to Istanbul accommodation is much nicer than Kiev 1/105 Makastar St Uskadar

Bishop made a call on his iPRIMAL, the device was already linked into the aircraft's satellite communications.

"Vance, it's Bishop. Sanch has made contact."

"Roger, it just popped up on our screens. Chua tells me it looks legit."

"Good, we need to reroute to Istanbul. Do we still have that safe house?"

"Affirm, buddy, we'll send you the address. Chua is going to try and buy you some extra time by tipping off the Guards. They'll shut down every point of arrival into Iran. Should keep Rostam and the chemical in Istanbul a little longer."

"Good work. We'll hit the ground running and take down the MOIS location within twenty-four hours."

"You're lucky to get one more bite at this cherry, Bish. Don't mess it up!"

***

THE FACILITY

Dostiger's head of security paced his office, racking his brain. Yuri had failed his master twice and both times he had been lucky to escape with his life. After the gunfight at the aircraft crash site, he still had no idea if they were Mossad, CIA, MI6, or MOIS. Dostiger had returned without saying a word and had locked himself in his office with a bottle of scotch. Yuri knew better than to ask more questions.

"FUCK! FUCK! FUCK!" he screamed. If he didn't come up with answers soon, Dostiger was going to kill him. The only thing keeping him alive was the vague chance that he could use his contacts to stop the hijackers before they made it across the border.

He picked his cell phone off the desk, looking at the screen in apprehension. Still no word from any of his people. Yuri started to panic. The phone dropped from his hand and he turned to walk out of the office before Dostiger came for him.

The phone's trill ringtone stopped him in his tracks. He walked back to the desk, hands shaking as he picked it up. The number was blocked. He answered the call.

"Hello, who is this?" he asked.

There was a pause, then a deep voice spoke in Russian, "Is this Yuri Vasyliovych Derkach?"

"Yes, who is this?"

"That's not important right now, Yuri. What is important is that we know exactly who you are and exactly who you work for, or should I say, used to work for." The tone was ice cold.

"Who the fuck are you?" Yuri demanded, his voice wavering.

"Yuri, Dostiger is finished. Do you want to go down with him?"

His hand began shaking.

The man's voice became a snarl as he continued, "Yuri Vasyliovych Derkach, former SBU agent number two-three-eight-seven-nine-zero K, only son of Galina Derkach, answer the question. Do you want to go down with Dostiger?"

"No… no, I don't."

The man's voice returned to its frigid tone. "You no longer work for Dostiger, Yuri. Now you work for me. My name is Ivan and you will find that I am a most generous employer. Once Dostiger is gone you will continue to run his empire. You will be provided with guidance, but ultimately it will be in your hands. If you let me down, justice will be swift."

Yuri was confused. "But isn't Dostiger still alive? How can I—"

The voice cut him off. "I'll be in touch."

The line went dead.

CHAPTER 44

ISTANBUL, TURKEY

The PRIMAL jet made a quick detour to Istanbul, dropping off Bishop, Mirza, Kurtz, and Aleks. It would continue to Abu Dhabi where Pavel's and Miklos' wounds would be treated, and the Novichok canister would be disposed of.

Bishop navigated as Aleks drove the hire car from the airport; it was the Russian's first time in Turkey.

As they turned off the highway toward the suburb of Iskenderpasa, Bishop noted with a wry smile that Aleks was wide-eyed in wonder. "Tables have turned since Kiev, eh, Aleks?" He had used Istanbul as a base of operations in the past and was familiar with the city and its culture.

"I thought it would be much, much older," Aleks replied as they approached the capital. "Where is the famous big mosque?" Driving down the main boulevard from the west, the skyline looked like any other major city, with high-rises intermingled among older structures.

"No time for sightseeing on this trip," Bishop said as he directed them off the main road. "Tight streets and narrow houses. Just like Kiev."

"But hotter," countered Aleks, wishing he'd removed his leather jacket. Istanbul was warm and colorful in comparison to the drab gray capital of Ukraine. The bone-white buildings contrasted against red roofs, and the occasional park added greenery to the picturesque cityscape.

Kurtz interjected from the backseat. "No complaints from me. Look at the *Frauen!*"

A pair of local girls dashed across the street in front of them. Their tight shorts and T-shirts left little to the imagination.

"Are they not Muslims?" Mirza asked in surprise.

Bishop smiled. "They must be very liberal in their

interpretation of the Koran." As they slowed at an intersection, he indicated a side street. "OK, slow down. We're nearly there." They turned into the lane and Bishop read the house numbers. "That's the one we're looking for." He pointed out a neat, two-story town house. They parked in front of the building and Bishop used his phone to deactivate the alarm system before leading them through the front door.

The team threw their bags on the living room floor and Bishop opened his laptop on the low coffee table.

"Nice place, boss, much nicer than Kiev," said Kurtz. The interior of the house was newly renovated, furnished with sleek modern settings.

"Moving up in the world," Bishop said as he accessed the encrypted PRIMAL wireless network connecting the laptop back to the Bunker.

"So what now, comrade?" asked Aleks.

"The plan is we meet with Saneh and get the info on the safe house. Then hit it and grab the canister. Nice and simple."

"You're actually going to meet up with that woman?" Kurtz asked.

"Yes, as far as I'm concerned she's still on our side. We're obliged to get her out of the Iranian safe house before we bang in."

"Aden, I know I've come into this late, but could this perhaps be a trap?" asked Mirza.

"To what end? If Rostam wanted to kill us, he would have shot us at the barn. And it's not about the canister. He'd know we would have already sent it to a safe location. No, it's pretty clear that this isn't a trap."

"I still don't trust her!" said Kurtz.

"Well, I do," said Aleks. "She saved all of our lives at least once and she got the boss out of the nightclub. So in my book she is alright."

"You're just a sucker for a pretty face, *Dummkopf*," said the German.

"That's rich coming from you, borscht brains," Aleks shot back. "Miklos told me about the woman in Dostiger's house.

He said you were practically drooling."

Kurtz blushed and the rest of the team laughed.

They're a top bunch, thought Bishop. It's good to see Mirza smiling.

He waited for the banter to die down before continuing. "Right, lads, we need to keep this slick. There's not much time and this is probably going to be our last crack at the prize. Aleks and I will meet with Saneh in an hour. Concurrently, Mirza and Kurtz, you're on a close-target recon of the MOIS safe house." He pressed a button on his laptop and the fifty-inch flat-screen TV bolted to the wall activated, displaying a satellite image. Chua's team had already worked up a basic target pack. It contained satellite imagery, street view photos, and a floor plan.

"Kurtz, you're on overwatch. I want you to have the rear entrance covered. Mirza, you'll be at the front. You need to be ready to breach."

Both men nodded, scrutinizing the TV screen. Mirza had a notebook out and was scribbling some points.

"OK, we don't have much time if we're going to catch Rostam with his pants down. We'll leave in twenty minutes. Aleks will drive and we'll drop you two off on our way to meet Saneh. As soon as we've got her, we'll bang in."

Mirza raised his hand. "And if you don't meet Saneh? Rostam sounds like the kind of man who won't let her out of his sight."

"Or out from under him," added Kurtz.

Bishop gave the German a sharp look. "Whatever happens, we're going to hit that safe house. Remember Saneh's one of us; she's not a target," Bishop said pointedly at Kurtz.

"Understood, boss," Kurtz nodded. "What about weapons?"

"Guns aren't a worry."

"Not a worry? We didn't bring anything through the airport and it's not like we can run down to the shop and buy an Uzi."

"Good point. Maybe you should check the kitchen; you might be able to find a spatula."

Aleks laughed. "*Da*, I want to see Kurtz paddling that bastard Iranian's ass with a spatula."

Mirza smirked and Kurtz went red again.

"I'm deadly serious. The answer is in the kitchen."

The team followed him into a modern well-appointed kitchen. In the center of the room stood a marble-topped island complete with a four-burner cooktop. Bishop pulled out his phone and activated a custom app. With a hum the entire kitchen island slid across the polished tiles, revealing a set of stairs that disappeared into the floor.

"What's this, the dungeon?" Kurtz laughed. "Or maybe the wine cellar!"

"How about you jump down there and see what's on the wine list," Bishop said.

Kurtz crouched to climb down the stairs, his mop of blond hair disappearing below floor level. A few seconds later he yelled out excitedly, "Holy shit! Aleks, you have to see this. It's like a candy store."

His head appeared at the top of the stairs, a huge grin plastered across his face. "They've got all my favorite cellars." He struggled to lift an armful of weapons up onto the kitchen floor. "HK, Beretta, Browning, Remington, even Sig Sauer." He lifted a pistol out of the pile. "A Colt .45. 1911, if I am correct. A fantastic year."

Bishop laughed and turned to the rest of the team. "Grab what you need, lads. Job's on. We roll in ten!"

***

In the suburb of Uskadar, only a few miles away, Rostam concluded a secure call with his Tehran office. He pocketed the phone and turned to one of his men.

"Where's Saneh?"

"Upstairs, sir."

"Bring her to me."

The man disappeared up a staircase. A moment later he reappeared with the female agent in tow.

"Sir?" Saneh asked. She sat at the table opposite Rostam. "I'm just about to go out and get us something to eat."

"You're not going anywhere, my dear. It seems that the Revolutionary Guards have become aware of our little operation. They've got men at all the entry points into Iran."

"They know we have the canister?" Behind Saneh's surprised look her mind was racing.

"It would seem that way."

"How would they have found out? Only Fischer and his men know we have it. They would never tell the Guards."

"Perhaps Dostiger told them. Or perhaps Dostiger has captured Fischer and his men?" Rostam watched Saneh's face closely.

She looked down, pulling her phone from her pocket. "I can find out. My source will know."

"No, it doesn't matter now. Fischer dead or alive is of no consequence to me. We have more pressing issues."

"Like how we're going to get back into Iran?" Saneh slid the phone back into her pocket.

"Exactly. Fortunately headquarters is working out a plan for us."

"How long will that take?"

"A few days, maybe more."

"We're going to need food then, I'll—"

"No, I need to debrief you. I want to know more about Fischer and his team." Rostam turned to the two men sitting on the couch across the room. "Navid, organize the security detail. I want one operative on the street and one here in the apartment at all times. Heydar, I don't anticipate us being here for longer than three days. Sort out the supplies."

The two men responded in unison, leaving them alone at the table.

Rostam opened a leather-bound notebook. "Let's start with how you met Mr. Fischer."

***

Bishop and Aleks dropped Mirza and Kurtz off a mile short of the Iranian safe house. They had taken precautions to minimize the chances someone would notice them. The hire car was a nondescript hatchback and all four were dressed in locally purchased attire. Despite this, Bishop was still worried about Kurtz. The tall, blond German stood out and there was no doubt Rostam's men would remember his face.

"You sure about this, boss?" Aleks asked as he pulled the car away from Mirza and Kurtz's drop-off point.

"Yeah, I've got a strong feeling about Saneh."

"You mean strong feelings?"

Bishop laughed. "Don't get me wrong, she's attractive, but this is something else." He kept an eye on the GPS map on his phone as they wound their way through the narrow streets.

"I understand. There's something about that woman."

He looked questioningly at Aleks.

"You can see it too, boss. She's no extremist, that's for sure. She's too smart to swallow that shit. She's more like you and me."

"What makes you say that?"

"Little things, boss. She could have left us to die, more than once."

"That's true, but then the canisters would be in Dostiger's hands and her mission would have failed. It made sense for her to help us then."

"But like you said, why did she leave the other canister?"

"That's the big question, Aleks, and hopefully we will have an answer soon."

Aleks brought the car to a stop at a pedestrian crossing and Bishop admired the beautiful mosque outside the window. It was a statuesque sandstone building with Aramaic script embossed in gold above its door. A stream of people was strolling out the entrance, and the streets were congested with locals trying to cross the road.

A look of annoyance crossed Bishop's features as he glanced back to the crowd still crossing the street. His eyes were drawn to one of the pedestrians, a man wearing a cheap suit, carrying a large paper bag filled with groceries. Something about him seemed familiar. The man turned his head and caught Bishop's gaze.

Recognition was instantaneous for both men!

The Iranian reacted quickly, hurling his bag of shopping at the windshield of the car. It tore open on impact, the groceries exploding from the bag, a carton of eggs splattering across the glass.

"WHAT THE HELL!" bellowed Aleks.

"He's MOIS, stop him!" yelled Bishop, pulling out his Beretta.

Aleks stomped on the accelerator. The hatchback's four-cylinder engine screamed and the front wheels spun. The car lurched forward and Aleks flicked on the windshield wipers, swearing as they cleared the groceries but smeared egg across the glass.

Bishop had his window down, pistol in hand. "Over there!" he yelled as the Iranian ducked down a side alley.

Aleks aimed for the gap, horn blaring. Another group of pedestrians scattered for cover as the vehicle shot into the alley. The narrow laneway was short and launched them out to another street.

Bishop spotted the MOIS agent struggling with the door of a car. He fired rapidly shattering the windows. The Iranian abandoned it, running onto the pavement. Using the cars for cover, he sprinted down the sidewalk.

Aleks accelerated, trying to parallel the running man as Bishop looked for a clear shot.

"Boss, we're running out of street!" A solid stone wall loomed where the road ended.

"If he gets away we're screwed!" Bishop spotted a staircase to the left. "THAT WAY!" he screamed over the revving engine, gesturing frantically.

The Iranian turned down the stairs as Aleks wrenched on the hand brake and spun the wheel. The hire car slid sideways, hitting the ancient stone wall with a crunch. With a screech of metal Aleks drove the car over the lip of the stairs.

"FUCK!" exclaimed Bishop. It was a long, steep, flight of stone stairs with a number of landings. The car bounced off the first landing and his head slammed into the roof. Ahead the Iranian was already halfway down, jumping six steps at a time. Aleks mashed the accelerator into the floor and the little car gathered momentum, hurtling down the steps.

"FASTER!" screamed Bishop.

They hit the next landing at top speed, bouncing off the flat stone before nosediving forward and back down the final flight of stairs.

The MOIS agent reached the bottom and looked back desperately, a phone pressed to his ear.

The car hit him. The bumper struck just below his knees, flicking the helpless victim over the hood. He slammed into the windshield. Aleks pumped the brakes and the tires squealed in protest. The MOIS operative's body continued forward, slamming into a van parked across the street.

Bishop was out and checking the crumpled body before the hire car had come to a halt. Aleks took a few more seconds to catch up with him.

"He's dead. Neck's snapped," said Bishop as he rifled through the man's pockets.

Aleks found a cell phone on the concrete. He handed it to Bishop. "This what you're looking for, boss?"

"Yeah." Bishop checked the phone. "Shit!" The MOIS agent had managed to make a call and it was still connected. He hung up.

"Get the car started, Aleks. We have to go."

Bishop activated his iPRIMAL, initiating a conference call with both Mirza and Kurtz. Both men picked up after a single ring. "Lads, we've been compromised. Prepare for crash action!"

***

Ten minutes earlier, at the drop-off point, Mirza and Kurtz had separated, moving to their surveillance locations.

The German had crossed the busy street and entered the foyer of a four-story apartment block. He was dressed in gray coveralls, baseball cap, and a black backpack. No one noticed when he entered the internal fire escape and made his way up onto the roof.

Beside a pair of air-conditioning units, Kurtz crouched and unzipped his bag. A minute later he had assembled a Vanquish sniper rifle. He sat the weapon on its bipod legs and pulled another plastic case from the bag. The two Wasp miniature drones inside were each the size of a matchbox. He removed one of the delicate machines from its protective foam and placed it on top of the air conditioner. Using the touch screen on the lid of the case, he activated the insect-like drone and the Wasp started beating its electric wings furiously. With a buzz it launched off the roof.

The built-in camera allowed Kurtz to guide the surveillance drone and he flew it across the street into an alley. He picked a spot on the building to the rear of the suspected MOIS safe house and landed the bug on the wall, its tiny claws latching onto the rough surface. From here the man-made insect would cover the exit with its miniature thermal sensor and follow anyone Kurtz identified.

The Wasp in place, Kurtz crawled forward with his sniper rifle until he could see down across the busy main street and into the alley that ran behind the target building.

He activated his radio, "Mirza, I'm in position."

The Indian responded immediately. "As am I. Nothing to report."

Across the busy street from the safe house, Mirza sat outside a café sipping a strong black coffee and reading the local paper. With his casual clothes, heavy beard, and dark features, he blended in with the older men who gathered each day at the café to drink coffee and swap stories. No one bothered him as he sat watching the target house over the top of his newspaper.

A man walking along the street caught his eye; the crumpled, double-breasted suit looked out of place. He continued to watch as the man walked down the street and paused at the front of the safe house, checking his watch. With one last scan of the street, he walked up to the front door. Mirza caught a glimpse of a second man as the door opened and the Iranian operative disappeared from sight.

The Iranian Mirza had been watching entered the living area of the MOIS safe house, dropping onto the couch next to another bored-looking operative.

"Nothing going on. Give it five minutes and you can do the next two hours."

"Yeah, OK."

The two men spoke in whispers, taking care not to disturb Saneh and Rostam, who sat at the living room table dissecting the details of her mission.

Rostam stroked his chin, looking up from his notes. "This Fischer certainly sounds like MI6."

"He said he was, but now I'm not so sure."

"Who do you think he works for?"

"Not sure, could be a contractor," she said, shrugging her shoulders.

"That's possible; the Americans are using mercenaries for everything these days." Rostam jotted a few notes in his pocket book. "Tell me, Saneh, do you think that Fischer found you by chance?"

"As I said in my report, sir, he compromised us during the surveillance of Dostiger's residence."

"Perhaps, my dear, that is what he wanted you to think."

Saneh studied the table in front of her. "You're right. He knew my name! He knew my name at Dostiger's residence. He knew I was going to be there."

"Well, Saneh, whoever Fischer's working for, they've got a file on you and you're compromised. You realize this will have ramifications for your future in MOIS, don't you?"

She nodded, still looking down. Her thoughts were interrupted by Rostam's phone.

He stared at Saneh as he answered the call. The look that came over his face chilled her to the core. After a few short seconds the MOIS officer slammed the phone down on the table.

"They're here!" Rostam rose from his chair and circled the table.

"Who's here, sir?"

"Fischer and his men!" he growled, flexing his fingers, making a fist. He stood over her with a look that left her in no doubt.

Deathly white, her face was all the confirmation he needed. Rostam's voice was low and cold. "You already knew they were coming, didn't you, my dear!"

"No, no. I—"

"How else would they know we are here, Saneh?"

"I don't know!" she said, eyes flicking from Rostam to the other two MOIS operatives, who had moved to stand beside him.

"There is only one person on my team I don't trust. Do you know who that is?"

"You're making a mistake!"

"You knew all along because you sold us out."

"No. I never—" Saneh tried to stand as Rostam's fist struck her in the jaw, knocking her to the floor.

"You sold out your own people, you filthy, fucking whore." Rostam kicked her savagely in the stomach and she cried out in pain, curling up into a ball. He grabbed her by the hair, pulling her up onto her knees. She felt another set of hands grab her from behind. A plastic zip-tie closed around her wrists, cutting circulation to her hands.

Rostam slapped her across the face with the back of his hand and lowered his face to her ear. "You have betrayed your people and your culture, Saneh, and for that you will die a horrid death. I'm going to cut your throat and leave your body for the dogs." She slumped to the ground with a whimper as he released her hair. "Massoud, get the other car and bring it round to the back. Navid, bring the bitch. We're leaving."

The third operative entered the living room from his position guarding the front door, an Uzi submachine gun in his hands. "What about Heydar?"

Rostam pulled his pistol from under his jacket and checked the magazine. "Heydar is dead, you fool, and we will be too, if we don't get out of here fast." He hefted a black backpack from the floor and opened it on the table, running his fingers over the symbol etched into the cold steel of the Novichok canister.

***

Mirza's iPRIMAL vibrated in his pocket. Inside his ear a tiny wireless speaker allowed him to covertly answer the call.

Bishop's voice came through urgently, "Lads, we've been compromised. Prepare for crash action!"

"Roger, I've got visual on the target," whispered Mirza. "At least two of the Iranians are in the building." One of the old men drinking coffee gave him a strange look.

"I've got nothing in the back alley," reported Kurtz.

"Aleks and I are three minutes out." Bishop sounded breathless and the revving of a car engine could be heard in the background. "Mirza, you handle the front door, we'll bang in. Kurtz, stay in overwatch."

Mirza unzipped the sports bag at his feet and checked the sights on the grenade launcher inside. Around him, old men continued to sip their tea, oblivious to the pending danger.

CHAPTER 45

The hire car hurtled around the corner and screeched to a halt in front of the MOIS safe house, smoke pouring from its tires and overheated brake pads.

From the streetside café across the road, Mirza reached down and pulled a HK69 grenade launcher from his bag. He extended the collapsible stock, aligned the holographic sight with the front door, and fired.

Aleks and Bishop were already crouched behind the car in their body armor and Nomex balaclavas, MP7 submachine guns at the ready. The 40mm breaching grenade flew through the air inches above their heads, smacked into the front door, and detonated.

The explosion tore the heavy slab of wood from its hinges, smashing it into an Iranian agent walking down the passage. Splinters shredded his body as the blast slammed him into the staircase at the end of the corridor, killing him instantly. The overpressure of the explosion swept into the living area, deafening the four occupants.

Rostam grabbed the bag with the canister as one of the others wrenched the table onto its side and crouched behind it, his Uzi aimed at the doorway. The remaining MOIS agent dragged Saneh to her feet by her hair, his pistol pressed to her head, and followed Rostam into the kitchen.

As the front door was blown from its hinges, Bishop sprinted out from behind the car and in through the smoking remains of the entrance. Aleks was hot on his heels as they stalked down the corridor, weapons held ready.

Bishop rushed into the living room and a burst of fire caught him in the chest. He fell to the ground with a grunt. Aleks stepped past and blasted the gunman behind the table, riddling him with bullets.

"Man down!" Aleks screamed into his headset as he moved toward the kitchen. "Get your hands up!" he bellowed as he aimed his weapon at the face of an Iranian who held Saneh.

The MOIS operative had his pistol pressed against her head, his other arm around her neck with a grenade clenched in his fist.

Behind them, closer to the back door, Rostam stood holding the bag containing the Novichok nerve agent. "Put your gun down and no one else dies," he said calmly.

Aleks stood firm, his submachine gun pointed directly at the hostage-taker's head.

Saneh's eyes were wide, her face bloodied and bruised. The gunman continued to inch rearward toward the back door, dragging her by the throat.

"Drop your weapon!" demanded Aleks, taking another step forward.

Bishop's shot surprised everyone. He fired from where he lay in the living room. The gunman's head exploded in a red mist. The pistol dropped from the Iranian's hand, along with the grenade. It bounced once, rolled in a circle, and came to rest in the middle of the floor.

Aleks dove forward, pushed Saneh aside, and grabbed the lifeless gunman. He dropped the dead body on top of the grenade and threw himself on top of it.

The explosion lifted both men from the ground, throwing Aleks against the cupboards. Blood and gore covered everything; smoke filled the apartment.

Bishop stood slowly, ignoring his ringing ears, and stumbled through the room. Rostam was gone, the back door wide open. "FUCK!" He turned back to where Aleks lay writhing on the floor. The Russian looked an absolute mess, covered from head to toe in the remains of the Iranian gunman.

"You alive, big man?"

"*Da*, I'm good." Aleks sat up, shaking his head, his ears ringing. "Thought you were dead, boss."

Bishop thumped his torn vest with the palm of his hand. "Bullet splashed on my chest plate." He rushed over to Saneh. She was sitting against a cupboard, dazed and confused. He tore off his balaclava, crouching beside her. "Saneh! You alright?"

Her face was turning purple and puffy, but she nodded and managed a slight smile.

"Friendly coming in!" yelled Mirza as he entered from the front passage.

"Mirza!" Bishop said. "Look after Saneh and Aleks, then get the hell out of here." He was back on his feet, heading out the back door. "Kurtz! What have you got?"

The German's guttural tone came in over the radio, "Rostam has left the alley. I clipped him but he's still mobile. He has the package, I repeat, he has the package. The Wasp has locked on and is tracking."

"Acknowledged, I'm going to follow on foot. Target building is secure." Bishop burst out of the safe house into a dingy back street, his submachine gun held ready.

Kurtz's continued, "Rostam went down the first alley on your left. The Wasp is tracking. I think I hit him in the leg but the bastard's still moving fast."

Bishop turned the corner at a sprint, dodging a beat-up delivery van as it exited the narrow lane.

"He's still on the move, but slowing. In the market directly ahead," Kurtz reported. He wasn't able to see Rostam through his sniper scope and was relying solely on the grainy video feed being relayed from the drone.

The marketplace was bustling, an easy place to lose a tail. As Bishop dashed down the alleyway, he removed his jacket and shrugged off the shot-up body armor, stuffing it into a Dumpster. He draped the jacket over his submachine gun and strode out into the crowd. He could hear sirens and knew the police would be at the MOIS safe house imminently.

"Mirza, are you clear of the target building?" he asked over the radio.

"We're clear. Aleks and Saneh have seen better days. I'm taking them back to our safe house."

Bishop spoke as he pushed his way through the crowds, "Roger, I'll meet you there. Kurtz, where's our target?"

"He crossed the market but the Wasp has lost him."

"Last seen?"

"Just to the east of your position. I think he left the market down the street near those fruit stalls."

Bishop jostled his way across, looked up, and caught a glimpse of the Wasp circling, hunting for the target. He scanned the street and something shiny on the cobbles caught his eye. He paced forward and crouched, touching the wet stones.

"Kurtz, head back to the safe house. I've picked up the trail."

"*Ja*, boss. Good hunting."

The blood trail led down the narrow street. Apart from trash cans and parked cars, it was empty.

He's going to be looking for somewhere to hide and bind his wound, Bishop thought. A side alley or an abandoned building would be perfect.

He pulled his phone from his pocket and checked the digital map. Less than a hundred yards ahead there was a narrow laneway running between two multi-story apartment blocks. It led to a dead end.

He moved forward cautiously, MP7 held at the ready as he inched his way around the corner into the alley. It reminded him of a gully carved deep into the jungle, tall trees and cliffs blocking out the sun. Dumpsters and a battered delivery truck cluttered the lane. It smelled of rotting garbage. More blood stained the cobblestone pavement. Bishop paced forward slowly, searching for his quarry, alert for an ambush.

"It's over, Rostam!" he yelled, his voice echoing off the walls of the concrete canyon. "You're alone and wounded. Come out!"

He caught a glimpse of movement. A gunshot punctuated the silence of the alley, ricocheting off the brick wall. He dived behind a Dumpster, landing on a pile of garbage.

A volley of rounds slammed into the Dumpster before the sound of someone reloading prompted Bishop to stand and peer over the top.

"Got you," he whispered as he spotted the man behind the delivery van. "Give it up, Rostam. You're done!" Bishop yelled, firing a burst into the van.

A manic laugh echoed down the alley and another half-dozen gunshots hit the bin.

Bishop crouched, waiting for the Iranian to finish. When the gunfire ceased, he raised his MP7, lining it up on the edge of the van. He snapped off a single shot.

The bullet punched through the Iranian's hand, sending his pistol spinning across the cobblestones. Rostam let out a bloodcurdling scream and slumped to the ground, his bleeding hand clutched to his chest.

Bishop rushed forward, picked up the pistol, and slid the bag containing the canister out of reach. With his submachine gun pointed at Rostam, he knelt and unzipped the bag, touching the cold steel.

"You win, Fischer, you win!" said Rostam.

"This isn't a game, dipshit."

"Yes it is and this time you win. You got the weapon and the bitch. You win!" The wounded man groaned as he sat up. The blood from his hand was mingling with the blood flowing from a gunshot to his thigh.

Bishop slung his submachine gun across his back and pulled his belt from his pants. "You don't get it, do you. This was never about winning."

"As if it isn't. You're a young man; you cannot bear the shame of defeat."

Bishop leaned forward and slid the belt over the injured leg. He pushed it past the bullet hole and drew it tight. The Iranian winced in pain.

"Rostam, this may be hard for you to believe, but this was never about winning. This is about saving lives."

"Whose lives, Fischer? The lives of the tens of thousands of Iranians who died fighting Iraq? Or what about the thousands of Iranians who will die when your people decide that we have become too great a threat? With this weapon we could have kept the wolves at bay."

"You're a fool if you believe that. Your country would have signed its own death warrant with this." He gestured at the canister. "Do you think Israel and her allies would sit by and let you wield a substance this lethal?" He leaned in close. "They would wipe your country from the face of the earth. This isn't a Bond movie; this is real life. This is about keeping deadly weapons out of the hands of zealots and madmen."

Rostam's eyes narrowed. "Who are you, Fischer?"

Bishop ignored the question, placed his submachine gun and the pistol in the bag with the canister, zipped it up, and slung it over his shoulder.

"You did me the courtesy of not killing me in Odessa, so I'll do you the same. But if our paths cross again, you're a dead man."

"I'll find you, Fischer, and if she's alive, I will find her too!"

Bishop turned and set off down the alley toward the street. In the distance he could hear sirens wailing. He raised his phone to his ear. "Vance, any chance you can get a jet to Istanbul? I've got something here you might want to take a look at."

CHAPTER 46

THE FACILITY

"Listen to me!" Dostiger screamed down the phone. "This operation was compromised from the start. MOIS has been working with those Mossad bastards."

"Be careful what you're implying, Dostiger," the Iranian general responded calmly.

"Implying? I don't have to imply; the evidence is proof enough. Your lack of control over MOIS has killed any chance we had of success."

"MOIS are toothless dogs, you fool. They don't have the ability to do this, nor do they work with the Jews. Someone else has compromised every aspect of your security and you have no idea who it is!"

"This is not my fault. I think—"

"Then whose fault is it?" the general interrupted. "You have one month to find me a weapon, Dostiger, one month. Fail and I'll send my men to find you. I don't care what it is, I don't care where you find it. Just make sure I can kill a million Jews with it." The call terminated.

"AAAAAARGH!" Dostiger screamed at the top of his lungs, throwing the phone across the room. He limped across to his office bar. Hands shaking, he tried to pour himself a whiskey. The amber liquid spilled over the polished wood but a small amount made it into the glass. He dumped a fistful of ice into the tumbler and lifted it to his mouth. "How the hell am I going to find a new weapon in a month?" He took a swig. "A nuclear warhead," he mused. "It would cost millions but the effect would be the same. And this time I'll take care of security personally, no leaks."

He didn't know exactly how his security was compromised but he was sure Mossad had played a part in it.

Dostiger savored the whiskey. "I'll make them pay," he

promised himself. I'll watch Israel burn, Mr. Fischer, even if it costs me everything."

***

VALENCIA, SPAIN, FOUR DAYS LATER

On the outskirts of Valencia the sun shone brightly as laborers toiled among the vines. Bishop stood watching as they harvested the grapes. He had a perfect view from the balcony of the private cottage, looking out over the rolling hills and the township of Montemayor. For a moment he was a boy again, exploring the hills with his parents. Then it was gone. He was back in the real world. He took his phone out and dialed.

"Vance, I just wanted to confirm whether the package arrived."

"Affirm. We deep-sixed those nasty little fuckers. They're seven miles down under two tons of concrete. No one's gonna get to them there."

"That ought to do it."

"So how's Valencia, buddy? You and Saneh enjoying a little downtime?"

"Yeah, we're doing OK," Bishop answered with a smile. "It's good to have a few days in one place. I think she was getting sick of being on the move."

"Listen, Bish, you earned this break. You did a great job in Istanbul and Odessa. You came through with flying colors."

A sad look replaced his smile. "I just wish we didn't have to lose Ice."

"He was a good man."

"That he was. How's Mirza doing?"

"He's still beating himself up pretty bad over it. I think he'll be alright though. He's a bit like Ice, you know, all calm and collected. Scares the crap out of me. He certainly came through with the goods."

"Promise me you'll look out for him, Vance."

"Like he's my brother from another mother."

Bishop laughed. "How about Miklos and Pavel, they OK?"

"Hell yeah, tough boys, both of 'em. They shipped home from Abu Dhabi yesterday. I've been thinking about putting together a regular team for shock-'n'-awe-type jobs. All firepower and muscle. Those two are good candidates."

"I think Aleks and Kurtz would be even more suitable. That bloody Kraut's a loose cannon."

"Bit like someone else I used to know."

"Tell me I was never that bad."

"You were never that bad." Vance chuckled. "It's OK, Bish, you came good and so will Kurtz. In fact Chua's already got him and Aleks ready to tie up some loose ends."

"Dostiger?"

"Yeah, the boys are ready to meet you in Moldova. Chua tells me the situation in Odessa has calmed down so you shouldn't have any problem crossing the border." Vance paused. "You know we don't need you to do this."

"I have to. I owe it to my parents, I owe it to Ice, and I owe it to everyone else. That evil fucker needs to die!"

"There's no doubt of that, Bish, but it won't bring them back, and that big Russian buddy of yours and that manic Kraut could take care of it."

"What's wrong, Vance? You think if I kill him and find peace, I'm going to lose my edge?"

"About as much hope of that as Chua giving up energy drinks. Alright, bud, I'll let Aleks know you'll meet him and have Chua send the details to you. Hey, that reminds me, the Iranians have reported Saneh KIA, unknown location and unknown circumstances."

"That's good news. Does that mean what I think it does?"

"Yeah, about time we had a female operative. Chua is pretty happy that you two have eluded any possible follow-up. You're good to bring her home to meet the family anytime from now."

"I'll send her on by herself, but don't worry. I won't be far behind."

"OK, good luck, Bunker out."

Bishop dropped his phone back in his pocket and crossed

the balcony to an outdoor setting. The table was laid with breakfast and he sat in one of the wicker chairs and poured himself a coffee.

"Everything alright?" Saneh asked as she stepped out onto the balcony in a yellow summer dress.

"Yeah, everything's good. Perfect in fact."

She sat down in the chair opposite Bishop and he poured her a coffee.

"So when are we leaving, Aden? We've been here for a whole two days now." Before arriving in Spain the pair had moved through no less than three international airports, changing their appearance and documentation each time.

"What, you don't like it here? I thought it was an improvement on the safe house in Kiev," Bishop joked.

Saneh smiled as she thought back to that night in Kiev when they had escaped the nightclub together. It seemed so long ago now. "It's beautiful here. I just get the feeling it's not where we're going to stay."

"You're right, but I wanted you to come here." Bishop gazed out over the rolling vineyards, settling on a distant cemetery atop a bare hill. "This is where it all started for me." He turned back to Saneh. "Not so long ago my life changed here. I lost something dear to me but found something else. Something I've now committed my life to."

She sensed the tension in his voice and slid her chair around next to him.

"It's a little sentimental, I guess, but I wanted your journey to start here as well."

"I think I meet the criteria. I mean, I've lost everything. I don't have a home. I don't have a job. I can never talk to my friends again." She paused as Bishop grasped her hand. "I guess I'm as ready as I ever will be. So where to from here, Mr. Aden Bishop?"

"Do you trust me?"

She arched one of her eyebrows. "After what we've been through, you could drag me to the ends of the earth."

He laughed. "You're not far off. How about a tropical

island in the Pacific?"

"Sounds terribly romantic."

"Well, I'm not sure that's how Vance would describe it, but hey, we can roll with that!" Bishop leaned forward and kissed Saneh on the lips.

"Pack your bags, girl, you're going on a holiday!"

"Just me?"

"I'll be joining you. There's just something I need to take care of first."

EPILOGUE

THE FACILITY

"You'll have your weapon by the end of the month." Dostiger's voice was edgy as he hunched over the phone at his desk. He hadn't left the office in four days, his scarred face was covered in stubble, and he was still wearing the same combat-stained fatigues.

"You still have the resources for this?" the Iranian general asked coldly. He knew the arms dealer had invested heavily in the failed recovery of the Novichok nerve agent.

"You will get your weapon. This time there will be no mistakes."

"I should hope not… Be very careful, Dostiger. Nuclear weapons come with a greater level of risk. There will be many more eyes watching."

"Leave that to me. You will have your weapon. Use it. I want Mossad to burn for what they did to me." Dostiger spat his words with pure hatred.

"That I can promise you. Deliver the weapon and I will turn one of their cities to ash. Fail me and my men will come."

"I will not fail."

"Excellent. Contact me when you are ready to deliver." The Iranian terminated the call.

Dostiger placed the phone down and reached for the glass on his desk with a shaking hand. It was empty. He snatched up a bottle and pulled the stopper from it, splashing the liquid into his glass. As he raised it to his lips, his eyes fixed in a distant stare and he smiled. It had all become so clear. He leaned forward and pressed the intercom.

"Get me Yuri." Despite the security chief's failures, Dostiger had spared him. Loyal men were a scarce commodity these days.

Five minutes later there was a soft knock on the office

door. Dostiger put down his second whiskey. "Yuri! About fucking time."

The door opened and a man entered the room. It wasn't Yuri; it was a broad-shouldered brute with a shaved head.

"Hello, comrade," the man said as he leveled a shotgun.

Bishop entered the room following Aleks. "We meet again, Dostiger."

The Ukrainian's ugly features contorted in rage. "You! Fischer!"

"Actually, the name's Bishop."

"I don't care what name you use, you piece of shit. Where is it? Where is my chemical!"

He smiled. "Long gone. You're not getting it back."

Dostiger glared as he spoke slowly. "Listen to me. I will give you millions. I will make you richer that you could imagine."

"Your money won't save you now, Dostiger. Your fate was sealed when your men shot down an Israeli passenger jet back in 2004."

"So you are Mossad then."

"No, I'm just a concerned citizen of the world." He nodded at Aleks, who raised his shotgun.

Dostiger's eyes narrowed, and for a second, fearlessness flashed across his weathered features. "Go fuck yourself."

The shotgun boomed in the confines of the office, the round slamming into Dostiger's chest. The XREP Taser projectile buried its probes into his skin and delivered a high-voltage shock, causing the arms dealer to spasm in his chair.

"How do you like it?" asked Aleks. "Does it burn? Do you like having no control?"

Bishop moved around the convulsing body and pulled a syringe from his pocket. He twisted off the protective cover and jammed the long needle against Dostiger's neck. It punched deep into his flesh, delivering its toxic load.

He whispered into the dying man's ear, "That's for my parents, my friends, and anyone else who's died at your hands, you evil son of a bitch! I've just given you a dose of something not unlike your Novichok. I hope you enjoy it."

Bishop left the needle sticking out of Dostiger's neck and followed Aleks out the door. They didn't wait to watch the last few minutes of the arms dealer's life. Nothing could save him now.

Yuri was waiting in the corridor and Bishop handed him an envelope as he passed. As the security chief made to open it a guttural moan emitted from the office. With trepidation, he pushed open the door and looked inside. Dostiger was still sitting in the chair, head tipped back in an endless, silent scream. He looked to be frozen in excruciating pain, as if every muscle in his body had convulsed until his heart exploded. Blood and mucus ran from his mouth and nose, mixing into a putrid mess on the front of his shirt.

Yuri turned away in disgust, and with shaking hands, carefully opened the envelope he'd been given. There was a card inside.

Kurtz was waiting in a sleek black Mercedes parked in front of the Facility. Bishop slid into the front seat and the German gave him an enquiring look.

"It's done," Bishop said as he strapped in.

The Mercedes roared as Kurtz sent the rear wheels spinning

in the gravel. They sped off down the tree-lined driveway.

As they turned onto the highway that would take them to Romania, Bishop's phone rang. It was Vance.

"The target's deceased," Bishop reported.

"Good job, bud. How you feeling?"

"Relieved. I'm glad that bastard's dead. Now I'm looking forward to getting back to the island for a bit of R and R."

"That might not be possible just yet."

"What? Something else has popped up already?"

"Don't you know it. We've got a situation unfolding in Abu Dhabi."

"Oh, come on, Vance. You know how I feel about politics. Surely the local authorities can sort this one out on their own?"

"This ain't political, it's survival. Our generous benefactor needs our help and we need his funding."

Shit, thought Bishop, if Tariq needs our help, then the situation must be serious. "I'm guessing that Qods Force is behind this."

"Tariq will brief you when you get into Abu Dhabi."

"OK. What about Aleks and Kurtz?"

"We've made arrangements to bring them on board."

"You know, if we're going up against Qods Force, there's someone else who might be handy to have on the team."

"All over it, buddy. Saneh is already on her way."

"I'd better hurry then. Tariq has a way with the ladies."

Vance chuckled. "You just get some rest on the flight. We'll talk again when you hit the ground."

Bishop dropped his phone back into his pocket. He turned to Kurtz and Aleks. "Hear that, boys, we're heading to Abu Dhabi. Welcome to PRIMAL, where there's no sleep for the wicked!"

AUTHOR'S FINAL WORDS

When I first started banging out this book on a dusty keyboard in Afghanistan, it was only going to be a stand-alone novel. I soon realized it had the potential to be much bigger, so it spawned the prequel PRIMAL Origin and the next story PRIMAL Vengeance. Since then I've written even more PRIMAL adventures for you to enjoy. You can keep turning the pages to check out the beginning of Vengeance.

As always, I'm keen to hear your thoughts, and reviews really help. Emails and messages from fans keep me going during the long grind of writing a book and I appreciate them.

JS, out.

EXCERPT FROM PRIMAL VENGEANCE

PROLOGUE

Extract From News Article: "South Sudan's Independence—A False Hope" Published: 13 June 2012

South Sudan's decades-long conflict was supposed to have ended when the region won independence in 2011. Free from the oppression of Khartoum's reign and with a peace agreement ratified by the UN, the future looked promising. With over half the Sudanese oil fields situated south of the border, dreams of prosperity and development were rekindled. Some of the world's poorest people could finally look toward the future with hope.

Now, a year later, harsh reality has set in. Conflict in the border region continues and refugee camps are overflowing. Khartoum still controls the vital oil infrastructure, pumping the liquid gold into the Chinese market. The idea that any of the billions of dollars of oil revenue would be shared with the south is fading rapidly, and the old fighters from the civil war are preparing for a new struggle.

"Again we must take up arms against Khartoum," said Garang Abango, a freedom fighter who had been educated in the United States. "We are not an army, we have no tanks, no fighter jets, no money. But we have our freedom and we will fight for what is rightfully ours."

CHAPTER 1

KHARTOUM, SUDAN, 2012

Garang's hands were sweating, despite the cool air that flowed from the air-conditioning vent behind his head. He was more at home in the African bush than here in the boardroom of a major petroleum corporation. Not to mention that the PETROCON building was situated in downtown Khartoum—the heart of enemy territory and a thousand miles from his adopted home in South Sudan. It had been years since the civil war between Sudan and South Sudan had officially ended, but deep wounds heal slowly.

Garang's job now was to keep his tribal chief safe, and surrounded by hostile Sudanese forces, it was no wonder his palms were sweating. He wiped them against his olive drab combat fatigues and returned his attention to the two men at the negotiating table.

"This is a good deal; we both know it. You would be a fool not to agree," the Sudanese oil minister addressed the chief sitting opposite him. Garang had noticed that every time the man finished a sentence he licked his lips, almost as if he could taste the crude oil he coveted so desperately.

The chief leaned forward and pushed a pile of legal documents back toward the fat politician. "You want my people to sign their lands across to your Chinese masters for only four percent? We are not simpletons who can be swayed with a handful of beads, Omar. We are a proud people. The Dinka lands belong to the Dinka and that is final."

Omar slapped his thick hands against the table, upsetting a glass of water and spilling its contents across the table's surface. "You either take this deal or we take the lands from you!"

"Your threats are idle," the chief replied calmly. "You couldn't take our lands in two decades of civil war and—"

The politician slammed his hands against the table again.

"Look around you, old man." He gestured toward the floor-to-ceiling glass windows that overlooked the bustling city. From thirty-six floors up people looked like ants. "You're a long way from your grass huts. Times have changed and your shitty little tribe has been left behind. Now I have the power. I have the money. This is a new era and your people will not survive unless they submit. Sign the papers and I promise, you will spend your final years a wealthy man."

He paused, squinting across at Garang. "What about you, boy? Do you want your people to live in squalor or do you want to be a part of this?"

Garang swallowed, wiping his hands against his pants as he rallied the courage to speak. Before he opened his mouth his chief spoke for him. "There is no Dinka who will sign your worthless papers, Omar." The elder was dressed like Garang, olive fatigues tucked into battered combat boots. He was lean, dark skin drawn and leathery, a veteran African warrior. "We will fight to the last man to keep our lands."

Omar remained seated. "Yes, you'll get your fight soon enough. Before too long I will have more tanks and artillery to pound your pathetic tribe into the dust." He pushed his own chair back and pried himself from its clutches. "Your women will spend their final days being stuffed with Janjaweed cocks."

At the mention of the fearsome Arab militias the doors at the end of the conference room opened and a fourth man entered. He crossed the room to stand behind the Sudanese politician.

"You probably already know of Sagrib," Omar said.

At the mention of his name the man's lips peeled back to reveal a mouth almost devoid of teeth. Then he laughed, a revolting cackling sound not unlike the bark of a hyena.

The Dinkas knew the man only by reputation. The leader of Omar's private Janjaweed army was renowned for his brutal acts of violence. He was dressed in desert combat fatigues and had cloth wrapped around his head, the tan material draped over his shoulder. A gold Rolex adorned his wrist, hacked from the arm of one of his countless victims.

The Dinka chief ignored Sagrib and looked the oil minister squarely in the eye. "Your Chinese masters can give you all the weapons they want, Omar. Your forces will never defeat the Dinka while you continue to send pigs to fight us."

Sagrib turned his head slightly, angling his mirrored Ray-Bans toward the chief. Garang kept his mouth shut. He was starting to regret volunteering to protect the old man.

It was Omar who broke the silence. "You and your people are all alone. No UN, no Americans, no helicopters, and no tanks. I will ask one last time, sign the papers and your people will have a chance to live." He waddled across to a side table, retrieved a manila envelope, and threw it on the table.

"What about you, boy? I hear you were born in America. I'm sure you understand the value of this contract." He leaned across the table. "Get the old man to sign it and I will make you rich."

Garang paused for a second, his eyes drawn to the envelope.

The elder Dinka pulled him back. "This meeting is over." The chief's voice had a slight tremor. "Garang, we are leaving."

"You're making a very big mistake, gentlemen," Omar said as the pair retreated to the boardroom doors and into the path of a heavily armed security detail.

Garang spun on his heel. "What is this?" he yelled, pointing his finger at Omar. "You promised us safe passage!"

Omar shook his head. "You are too trusting, but you will learn. This will be an important lesson for you." He turned to Sagrib. "Kill the old man and make an example out of the boy."

The Janjaweed mercenary nodded, snapping an order at the guards, "Take them to the basement!"

It took only minutes for the guards to cuff the two men and move them into the elevator to the lower levels of the building. There, among the PETROCON vans, they forced the Dinka tribal leader to his knees.

Garang struggled against the guards who held him. One of them drove a baton into his stomach, doubling him over. His legs turned to jelly as he gasped for air but he was held up, forced to watch.

Sagrib stood over the Dinka chief, a rusty saw in one hand. With the other he grabbed a fistful of hair, wrenching the man's head back.

The old man looked up at the mercenary with hate in his eyes. "You can kill me, but you cannot kill all of us. Mark my words. Dinka warriors will bury you in the carcass of a pig."

"No, they will die like you. Like fucking lambs to slaughter." Sagrib brought the saw up against the man's throat and hacked it back and forth. The rusty blade chewed deep into the flesh and the chief gasped involuntarily as the jagged teeth tore through his jugular and windpipe. Crimson blood spewed out of the horrific wound as Sagrib sawed through the spine, laughing like a mad man as the tribal elder gurgled.

Garang screamed and thrashed against the men holding him. The baton returned, smashing his legs out from under him. The guards beat him savagely while Sagrib continued to hack at the once-proud elder's head.

The old man died without so much as a whimper. The last thing Garang saw before he succumbed to unconsciousness was Sagrib holding the severed head aloft, his uniform drenched in blood, toothless mouth grinning.

***

They found Garang on the outskirts of Khartoum, badly beaten and dumped in a pile of trash. Next to him was the chief's head, the body missing. Garang screamed in pain as they loaded him into the truck. None of them wanted to touch the severed head of their chief. Eventually it was a young warrior named Jonjo who rallied the courage to take the head and wrap it in a sheet. Tears rolled down his cheeks as he placed it in the passenger seat of the truck.

They drove south, trying to avoid the potholes in the old highway, as every jolt caused Garang to moan in pain. Jonjo was not sure the American would survive the long journey. He was not sure if any of them would make it home. If Omar had rescinded their safe passage and the Sudanese army found them, they would all be dead.

CHAPTER 2

PIRATE ALLEY, GULF OF ADEN

The *Tian Hai* churned its way through the lukewarm waters of the Gulf of Aden, heading north, bound for Sudan. Sitting low in the water the heavily laden cargo ship made a steady fourteen knots, slowly working its way through the region known as Pirate Alley.

High above the water on the ship's bridge a cigarette glowed faintly in the darkness. A shower of ash disappeared in the wind as the butt was stubbed out on the handrail and tossed into the inky black water. The Chinese security contractor pulled night vision goggles down over his eyes, a copy of the US-designed PVS-7, and scanned the horizon.

He was on the lookout for pirates, Somali criminals intent on seizing the ship and her cargo. Already the *Tian Hai* security detail had fought off two attempts to board the freighter. The pirates hadn't fared well, but the sharks had.

The guard almost wished for pirates as he mechanically scanned his zone of responsibility. The ambient light from the new moon struggled to penetrate the low cloud base, and through his goggles he could barely see past the end of the ship, over two hundred meters to his front. He lifted the goggles and reached for the packet of cigarettes tucked into a pouch on his assault rig.

"The cigarette will give away your position. Do not smoke again!" a voice spoke in Mandarin.

The contractor snapped his head around to see Yang step out of the shadows and into the faint glow cast by the ship's navigation lights. He was a slim figure dressed in black combat fatigues and a baseball cap. His only weapon was a sidearm on his hip.

"Yes, sir." The guard's hands flashed back to the QBZ-97 assault rifle slung across his chest.

"Have you checked your sectors?"

"Yes, they are all clear."

"Are they?" Yang nodded into the darkness.

The guard flipped his goggles down and scanned the horizon. At the very edge of the sensor's range he could just make out the faint glow of a fishing boat. The vessel was heading away from them. He flipped the goggles up and turned back to Yang.

"Sir, how ...?"

The man had disappeared back into the shadows.

***

Ten nautical miles ahead of the *Tian Hai* an unusual-looking aircraft hovered above the ocean. In the darkness it resembled a giant dragonfly, loitering on the surface of a pond as it searched for prey.

The AW609 was a civilian evolution of the US armed forces V-22 Osprey. Like its military cousin, it relied on a pair of giant propellers for conventional flight that when swiveled skyward allowed it to hover like a helicopter. The tilt-rotor had the speed and range of a fixed-wing aircraft, yet unlike a seaplane it could support water operations in the heaviest of seas.

The gray tilt-rotor hovered a few meters above the swell, the downward wash of the twin blades whipping the surface into a frenzy of spray and froth. It rotated slowly until its nose faced into the wind. The door on the left side slid open revealing a faint green glow from the cabin.

A black-clad figure appeared, quickly scanned the surface, and pushed a large bundle out into the ocean below. A number of smaller bundles followed before the man dropped from the aircraft and disappeared into the water. He was followed by a second man, who splashed into the ocean beside him.

With a roar the tilt-rotor climbed away into the dark sky, leaving the two men alone in the Arabian Sea, nearly a hundred nautical miles from shore.

"Beautiful night for a swim, mate," the first man said

cheerfully as he treaded water, holding on to the side of the large bundle he had pushed from the aircraft.

"It is nice, Bish, but I think I'd prefer a boat ride," Mirza replied from the other side of the bundle.

"Probably need a boat then. Get clear, I'll inflate."

"Roger." The former Indian Special Forces soldier pushed off the bundle and bobbed in the black water.

Bishop tore open a Velcro panel on the side of the package. With one hand bracing against the rubber he pulled hard on a plastic handle. There was a pop and a hiss as it split open and unfolded slowly. The hissing continued until it took the form of a small inflatable boat.

Both men climbed into the compact rubber craft, dragging in the various dry bags behind them. They worked quickly, preparing their personal equipment. The pair pulled on body armor over their wet suits and donned lightweight helmets. Everything was black, from their gloves and ropes to the suppressed MP7 submachine guns that hung from slings attached to their armor. Mission success was dependant on stealth.

"Rubber Ducky, this is Dragonfly," the pilot of the tilt-rotor checked in, his English accent broadcasting through the men's earpieces.

"Ducky here, go ahead."

"How's the water, chaps?"

"Surprisingly cool for this time of year."

"Told you to go the five mil over the three mil. Rookie error, boys."

Bishop laughed. Their pilot was also the PRIMAL team's equipment specialist and resident technician. He had helped them set up for the mission and had recommended thicker wetsuits.

"This is Africa, Mitch, not some shitty beach off Scotland. We'll be fine."

Mirza interjected, "I hate to interrupt, gentlemen, but we have a ship to catch."

Bishop laughed again. "Yeah, Mitch, now where the hell is

she?"

"OK, I have the *Tian Hai* on scope. She's eight nautical miles from your location to the southeast and closing."

"Cheers, Mitch, we're ready to roll."

"Roger, chaps, I'll be in a loiter here, keeping an eye on things. Drop me a bell when you need exfil."

"Too easy. Bishop out."

Bishop activated the data link on his iPRIMAL, the combat interface on his forearm that communicated wirelessly through the satellite radio attached to his back. Through the touch-screen he could access information being beamed from Dragonfly, or from PRIMAL headquarters over eleven thousand kilometers away. Scrolling through the available feeds he found the one he was looking for and activated it with a tap. On the screen he could now see the radar image from the tilt-rotor. It showed their own location and that of their target, the cargo ship *Tian Hai*.

Mirza activated the electric drive motor and the two men lay low in the boat while it skimmed through the water at ten knots. The small vessel sat a mere two feet above the water and there was no chance the navigational radar suite on the *Tian Hai* could detect its approach.

The combat interface on Bishop's forearm vibrated, letting him know they were eight kilometers out from the target. He retrieved a long cylinder from one of the dry bags and propped it against the inflated wall of the boat. Flicking off a safety bail in the middle of the tube he pressed a rubber switch. There was a loud thud, followed by a snap as the modified Switchblade drone shot out of the tube, flying into the darkness with a whirr.

The visual feed from the Switchblade appeared on Bishop's iPRIMAL. His fingers danced over the flex-screen to plot the UAV a route to the target. The sensors on the miniature aircraft easily detected the thermal signature emitting from the merchant ship's exhaust. An automated flight program would keep the UAV in a holding pattern above it giving the PRIMAL operatives an all-seeing eye in the sky. Now all they needed to do was get on board.

The *Tian Hai* appeared in Mirza's night vision goggles as a grainy shape. At one mile he could not make out any of the ship's detail. He aimed the inflatable slightly to one side of the mass and glanced at his partner. Bishop had his night vision goggles flicked up and was inspecting his combat interface.

"Looks like at least three hostiles topside." He whispered despite the throb of the freighter's engines as it bore down on them. "One on each of the bridge wings and one roving on deck among the containers. The port side looks like the best approach."

Mirza gave a nod and corrected their course. When the ship was only a few hundred meters in front of them he throttled back.

"She's sitting low in the water, Aden, must be fully laden," Mirza said.

"Just thinking the same thing. Looks like Chua's intel is solid."

Both men gripped the sides of the boat as they hit the wall of water being pushed forward by the bow of the cargo ship. The little craft launched into the air as Mirza powered over the wash. Thumping back onto the water he whipped the little craft around in a tight circle, accelerated, and edged forward until they were bouncing in the white water just behind the bow.

Their boat came in against the metal skin of the ship and Bishop leaned out and slapped a pair of rubber-coated electromagnets against the hull. They thudded in place and he pulled the tether ropes tight, locking them to the hulking freighter that towered above them.

Even with the *Tian Hai* sitting low in the water the distance between the rubber boat and the deck was over twenty feet. Bishop checked the UAV feed. One of the guards was now walking directly above them. Bishop looked up and spotted a gloved hand resting on the rail.

"Tango above," he whispered over the radio, flicking down the night vision goggles and raising his MP7. Seconds ticked by and Bishop's shoulders started to ache from holding the submachine gun at a high angle.

A glowing object dropped from the sentry and arced toward the men in the boat. Through night vision goggles it looked like a blazing meteorite trailing a shower of sparks. Bishop ducked as the cigarette bounced off the side of the boat and was extinguished by the waves.

"Filthy fucking habit," he whispered and checked his iPRIMAL again. The guard was moving away.

"Aden, did you see the glow?" Mirza asked.

"Yeah, NVGs. Chua's intel is definitely spot on." The PRIMAL intelligence officer had briefed them that the Chinese army had arranged the guards for this vessel. "Guys like this aren't going to be protecting containers of pirated DVDs and Armani knock-offs. Let's roll."

Bishop let his weapon hang from its sling and secured it to his side with a strap. He opened one of the dry bags and pulled out a coiled rope complete with a black rubber-coated grappling hook and an auto-ascender. He lobbed the hook high; it sailed over the rail and landed on the deck of the ship with a thud. With a sharp tug it caught on the handrail.

Bishop hefted another dry bag onto his back and hooked into the auto-ascender. He thumbed the activator and the tubular device bit into the rope hauling him up the side of the ship. In a couple of seconds he reached the handrail and pulled himself over. With a deft hand he unsnapped the device and let it slide back down the rope.

"All clear." He raised the MP7 to his shoulder and slipped into the shadows between the containers.

"Coming up." Mirza picked up his own dry bag before being hauled up the rope. He pulled himself over the rail, unhooked the grappling iron, and let it drop into the boat below. Moments later he was crouched next to Bishop on board the *Tian Hai*.

They hid in the darkness cast by the containers stacked on the immense deck. Bishop checked the UAV feed again. It was all clear. They crept forward, weapons held at the ready.

Dressed in black, they blended into the shadows cast by the ship's dim lighting.

Mirza led them toward the rear of the ship, their sophisticated night vision goggles fusing ambient light with thermal signatures, turning the darkness into a hazy green world.

"Target door ahead."

They stopped at the entrance that led from the ship's external walkway to the internal cargo holds. Mirza spun the wheel and the steel door swung open. Inside was pitch black and he could feel the hot, thick air. Only the superstructure and crew quarters were air-conditioned.

Mirza stepped into the darkness, activated the infrared light on his helmet, and paused.

"Reed switch," he stated, inspecting the entrance. Invisible to the naked eye, his infrared light filled the stairwell with a green glow when viewed through their NVGs. The illumination clearly showed a magnetic switch attached to the door.

Bishop swore, pushed in after Mirza, and closed the hatch behind him. Switching on his own light, he inspected the device, adjusting the focus on his night vision. Someone had attached a magnetic alarm to the door.

Bishop ran his hand slowly along the cable that connected the switch to a radio transmitter. He was sweating in his wet suit, beads streaming down his face. The eighty-pound dry bag on his back weighed him down. He checked the UAV feed; the guards on deck seemed to still be in their normal routine. Go or no go? he asked himself.

"Aden." Mirza spoke with urgency. "We need to make a decision now!"

"OK, let's do this as quick as possible. Consider the mission compromised: shoot to kill."

"Roger. We need to take the stairs down three more levels to the cargo hold."

"Lead the way."

They moved cautiously, keenly aware that someone could be responding to the triggered alarm. At the bottom of the stairs they reached another door. Mirza opened it and Bishop moved through holding his MP7 low, using its infrared flashlight for extra illumination.

Within the cargo hold the air was even thicker and the throb of the ship's diesel engines incessant. They closed the door and pushed deep into the hold, squeezing past stacked crates.

Bishop froze and held up his hand. "Holy shit!"

"What is it?" Mirza asked, creeping forward.

"Look!"

Through his NVGs Mirza could make out the hulking shape of an armored vehicle. Turning his head he could see a whole row of tanks.

Bishop climbed onto the front of a tank. "There's got to be over a battalion's worth of armor in here." He let out a low whistle. "The ChiComs have gone all out on this one. Chua's source was right on the money."

Mirza jumped up beside him. They had a clear view of the cavernous hold. "Main battle tanks, APCs, BM-21s," he observed. In front of them was an army of military vehicles. More of the squat main battle tanks packed in with boxy armored personnel carriers. Beyond that was a row of trucks sporting multiple rocket launchers. Vehicles filled the entire hold as far as they could see. "Aden, the rebels wouldn't stand a chance against this."

"Yep, Khartoum would eat them for breakfast. We need to deep-six this lot ASAP."

The pair split, moving quickly to each side of the cargo hold. They identified the vital points that Chua had briefed them in the pre-mission package. From heavy dry bags they drew out lengths of cutting charge. The prepackaged explosives had been specifically designed to slice through the ship's thick steel hull. It took them fifteen minutes to lay the charges.

"Charges set?" asked Bishop once they met back at the first tank.

"Yes, just as we practiced."

"Excellent." Bishop keyed his iPRIMAL and activated the

two radio detonators, synching their initiation sequence. Numbers appeared on the screen, a countdown from ten minutes.

They ran back toward the door that separated the cargo hold from the stairwell, lighter on their feet, no longer burdened with explosives. As the exit came into view, the hold's lighting activated, dim globes appearing bright white through their NVGs. They froze, eyes drawn to the steel door. The locking wheel in the middle of the hatch started turning.

The two PRIMAL operatives dashed for cover, flipping up their NVGs as they slid under the closest tank. Seconds later the door opened and harsh Chinese accents echoed over the throb of the ship's engines.

Mirza counted the guards as they entered, assault rifles held at the ready. "Four tangos," he whispered. The men split into two pairs, starting to systematically search the shadows with flashlights attached to their rifles.

"Only four," Bishop replied into his mike. "If they find the charges, we're screwed." He paused to think. "We'll take them down in pairs. Closest two first. Silent kills, yeah."

Mirza had crawled out from under the tank and was focused on the armored personnel carrier alongside, his brow furrowed in thought. "We may not have to fight. I have an idea."

"Now's not the time, mate. Eight minutes left." Bishop flicked off the safety catch on his MP7.

Mirza pointed at the stubby smoke grenade launchers mounted on the APC and explained, "I'll set them off, we get out. They're not going to find the charges in the smoke."

Bishop gave a wry smile. He couldn't argue with the logic. "Well, hurry up then, MacGyver."

Mirza's knife was already stripping the wires and he pulled out a spare radio battery. "NVGs ready?"

Bishop flipped down his goggles. Mirza touched the battery to the bare wires. The smoke canister assembly spat four grenades into the air. With a clang they slammed into the roof and ricocheted onto the deck. Gray smoke billowed from the grenades and filled the hold.

Shouts in Chinese were soon replaced by coughing. The smoke pod had been designed to create a thick smokescreen to hide tanks in the open. In the confines of the cargo hold it rapidly filled the space. The PRIMAL operatives took a deep breath and made their way toward the exit door. The thermal sensors on their goggles saw through the smoke, detecting the body heat of the guards. Treading softly, they avoided the heavily armed contractors and headed straight through the exit.

They secured the metal hatch behind them and hurried up the stairwell. "Five minutes," said Bishop between breaths. As they hit the deck level an alarm commenced wailing and red lights flashed. Mirza approached the exterior door cautiously, hoping the other guards were slow to react. It was already open. He covered the hatch with his MP7 as Bishop checked the feed from the Switchblade drone.

"Bird's on the wrong side of the ship," Bishop whispered. "I'll bring it round but we can't wait for the feed. Four minutes left!"

Mirza hesitated. "It would be wiser to wait."

"No time, mate, gotta go." Bishop moved past Mirza and bobbed his head out of the open hatch. He snapped it back as a burst of automatic fire blasted inches from his face, ricocheting off the open metal door. "Fuck me!" he exclaimed.

A metallic clang resonated up the stairwell from below. The cargo hold door had been opened.

"Looks like company from below." Mirza pulled a stun grenade from his vest and flicked it down the stairs. The electronic hearing protection in their headsets canceled out the explosion as it detonated.

"Switchblade's coming round." Bishop checked his combat interface again. "I've got three tangos on the walkway with weapons."

"I don't think you'll get a second chance if you stick anything out that door."

The footsteps coming up the stairs were getting closer. Bishop was starting to wish he hadn't let Mirza convince him to let the guards live. He ripped off a fragmentation grenade, pulled the pin, and lobbed it down the stairs. Fuck them, he thought as the grenade detonated. The stairwell lighting went dark and the noises stopped.

"Here's the plan," he said. "I'll use the Switchblade to hit the ChiComs. You make a beeline for the boat."

"And you?" asked Mirza.

"I'll be right behind you. Now stand by."

Mirza braced himself next to the doorway, pulling a carabiner from one of his pouches.

At a thousand feet above the *Tian Hai* the Switchblade drone pitched forward, the nose camera feeding a picture to Bishop's iPRIMAL.

"Ten seconds, Mirza."

The little craft gathered speed as it dove.

"Five seconds."

The picture showed the three Chinese guards covering the walkway.

"Four, three, two, one, impact!"

The Switchblade detonated a meter above the guards, half a kilogram of high explosive shredding the men with tungsten pellets.

Mirza sidestepped through the doorway and fired a long burst into the bodies that littered the gangway. He needn't have bothered; the kamikaze UAV had done its job. He sprinted past the bodies, Bishop's footsteps close behind him. When he reached where their boat was moored, he snapped the carabiner onto the rail and leaped over the side of the ship. The lightweight line fed through a descender attached to his chest from a pouch on his thigh. He pulled the line tight as he raced downwards, slowing to a complete halt when his boots hit the rubber boat.

Bishop was checking over his shoulder when Mirza jumped the rail. The walkway was littered with debris from the airstrike. The alarm was still wailing, the ship bathed in red emergency lighting. He glanced at his wrist; only two minutes until the charges detonated. He grasped the rail with one hand and made ready to snap onto Mirza's line.

That was as far as he got. A shadow leaped from one of the containers above, slamming him into the safety barrier.

Bishop's body armor bore the brunt of the impact and he bounced off the rail, raising his MP7 at the attacker. A savage kick tore it from his hands, breaking the sling's clip and sending it over the side of the ship.

His assailant was Chinese, small and lightly built, dressed in a black uniform, with only a holster on his hip. The man seemed deathly calm despite the fact he was facing a well-equipped operative.

Bishop snatched his pistol from its holster as the steely-eyed fighter unleashed a savage volley of kicks, forcing him back along the walkway. Even in the tight confines the Chinese fighter was able to unleash a maelstrom of blows against the larger PRIMAL operative. Bishop's pistol was knocked from his hand, NVGs were smashed off his helmet, and the comms cables were ripped out. Desperate, he covered up, using his arms to protect his face.

His combat interface vibrated on his wrist, a reminder that the timer had hit the sixty seconds mark. Bishop dropped his shoulder and charged forward. He was counting on his mass and the weight of his equipment to overwhelm his lighter opponent. He was wrong.

Yang sidestepped at the last moment, landing a blow against Bishop's jaw as he careened past. Stunned, Bishop tripped and slammed into the deck, his helmet saving him from being knocked unconscious. Instinctively he rolled onto his back, ready to fend off any further attacks.

Yang laughed. "You Westerners are all the same. You fight like a bull: all brute force, no finesse." The man hissed the final letters of the word like a snake.

Bishop rose to his feet, taking a fighting stance. He wiped the blood and mucus from his face with a glove. His other hand drew a combat knife from his armor.

An evil smile appeared on Yang's face. "Oh, so you want to try again?"

Bishop shuffled forward, the knife held blade down in his leading hand. Yang lashed out with a kick. The blow landed on Bishop's fist, knocking the knife to the ground. The lean Asian darted forward, stepping inside Bishop's guard, throwing a strike at his throat.

Bishop managed to deflect it and Yang grunted in pain as his fist struck an ammunition pouch. The PRIMAL operative seized the smaller opponent and pulled him closer, head-butting him with his helmet. The broken NVG mount dug into Yang's face, the solid plastic shell shattering his nose.

Yang sprang backward, shocked by the blow. Bishop grabbed his knife off the ground and pressed home his advantage, slashing upwards. Again the Chinese operative sidestepped and drove a powerful kick into Bishop's thigh.

His leg spasmed in agony but he hobbled forward, slashing wildly. Yang moved in under the blade and unleashed a volley of punches. Bishop covered up, absorbing the blows, hoping for an opportunity to retaliate.

Sensing the PRIMAL operative was nearly finished Yang positioned his leg to deliver a finishing kick. As he swung his boot forward Bishop lifted the combat knife and drove it into the man's thigh.

Yang grunted in pain but continued to press forward with another hail of punches to the face, knocking his opponent against the bulkhead. The blows stopped and it took Bishop a few seconds to regain his feet. When he did so he was staring down the barrel of a pistol.

Yang did not look happy. He was standing a few meters away with the knife sticking out of his inner thigh. Blood streamed from his nose where it had been smashed in by the head butt. The pistol in his hand was aimed directly at Bishop's face and did not waver.

"Tell me why you are on my ship!"

Bishop nodded at the knife sticking out of the man's leg. "Should get that looked at, champ."

"Answer me now or you will die."

"That nose doesn't look so good either."

Yang smiled. He looked comical with his bloodied, smashed nose. "As you wish."

The Chinese operative squeezed the trigger. At the same instant there was a muffled explosion and the deck lurched beneath them. Yang staggered and the bullet went wide, ricocheting off the bulkhead. Bishop lost his footing and fell back against the safety railing. Yang fired again as Bishop rolled over the railing and disappeared overboard.

Mirza was climbing back up his rope when Bishop flashed past him. He slashed the line and hit the surface a split second behind his partner.

Weighed down by armor, equipment, and ammunition, Bishop sank like a stone. He yanked the tabs attached to his floatation pouches. One of them inflated, slowing his descent, but the other pouch failed, the punctured bladder spewing forth a torrent of bubbles.

Mirza was also sinking, searching for Bishop. There was zero visibility through the black water and the throb of the freighter's propellers filled his ears. He started running out of air when his fingers brushed Bishop's arm. The bigger man was paddling frantically, trying to swim upward. Mirza gripped the arm firmly and yanked his own floatation tabs. For a split second they hovered underwater before the buoyancy of Mirza's pouches overcame their weight and dragged them to the surface.

Both men fought for air, floating in the wake trailing the *Tian Hai*. Despite her mortal wounds, the ship was still plowing stubbornly forward.

"Fuck me, I thought I was cactus," Bishop said between breaths, still holding on to Mirza.

"You and me both, Aden. What happened?"

"Some prick jumped me at the rail. He got off a shot that must have punched through my gear. One of the bags didn't inflate." Bishop threw away his helmet and started to dump ammunition, stripping off unnecessary weight. "You're starting to make a habit of hauling my arse out of the fire, Mirza."

"Isn't that why you keep me around?"

"Yeah, something about strength in numbers. Now, what's the go with the ship?"

The two men were over a kilometer from the *Tian Hai*. They could barely see her lights in the distance.

"The charges definitely fired," said Mirza.

"Yeah, I can confirm that. It's the only reason I'm still alive. Can you raise Dragonfly? My comms are buggered."

Mirza checked his combat interface and keyed the communications tab. "Mitch, this is Mirza."

There was a short pause. "Mirza, my good man, how's the water?" The tilt-rotor was tracking their GPS transponders.

"Damp. Can you pick us up?"

"Roger, I'm inbound now, mate. Knock-up job on the *Tian Hai*. She's breaking up and the crew are abandoning ship."

Mirza relayed the information to Bishop, who gave a thumbs-up.

As the two PRIMAL operatives bobbed in the water, they could faintly hear the death throes from the sinking ship. The charges had cut through her central support structures and now the weight of her deadly cargo was tearing her in two.

"We've bought South Sudan at least six more months of freedom," Bishop said as they floated side by side. "Job well done!" The satisfaction of mission success was stronger than the numerous aching wounds inflicted by the Chinese assailant. "Now all we need to do is get the UN to approve an increase in peacekeepers. Too easy, really."

They listened as the moans and shrieks of tortured metal cut through the cool night air until the turboprops of the approaching aircraft blocked out the eerie sounds.

***

Buy PRIMAL Vengeance at www.amazon.com

BOOKS BY JACK SILKSTONE

PRIMAL Inception
PRIMAL Mirza
PRIMAL Origin
PRIMAL Unleashed
PRIMAL Vengeance
PRIMAL Fury
PRIMAL Reckoning
PRIMAL Nemesis
PRIMAL Redemption
PRIMAL Compendium
PRIMAL Renegade
SEAL of Approval

ABOUT THE AUTHOR

Jack Silkstone grew up on a steady diet of Tom Clancy, James Bond, Jason Bourne, Commando comics, and the original first-person shooters, Wolfenstein and Doom. His background includes a career in military intelligence and special operations, working alongside some of the world's most elite units. His love of action-adventure stories, his military background, and his real-world experiences combined to inspire the no-holds-barred PRIMAL series.

jacksilkstone@primalunleashed.com
www.primalunleashed.com
www.twitter.com/jsilkstone
www.facebook.com/primalunleashed

Manufactured by Amazon.ca
Bolton, ON

17153668R00208